# INSECT DREAMS

# INSECT DREAMS

## THE HALF LIFE of GREGOR SAMSA

## MARC ESTRIN

BLUEHEN BOOKS

*a member of*

Penguin Putnam Inc.

*New York*

*The Poetry of Robert Frost* © 1951 by Robert Frost. Copyright 1923, 1969 by Henry Holt and Company, LLC. Reprinted by permission of Henry Holt and Company, LLC.

*Duino Elegies* by Rainer Maria Rilke, translated by J. B. Leishman/ Stephen Spender. Copyright 1939 by W. W. Norton & Company, Inc., renewed © 1967 by Stephen Spender and J. B. Leishman. Used by permission of W. W. Norton & Company, Inc.

BlueHen Books
a member of
Penguin Putnam Inc.
375 Hudson Street
New York, NY 10014

Copyright © 2002 by Marc Estrin

Library of Congress Cataloging-in-Publication Data

Estrin, Marc.
Insect dreams : the half life of Gregor Samsa / Marc Estrin.
    p.    cm.
Includes bibliographical references (p. 465).
ISBN 0-399-14836-1
1. Cockroaches—Fiction.    2. Metamorphosis—Fiction.    I. Title.
PS3605.S77 I57        2002                    2001035941
                813'.6—dc21

Printed in the United States of America
1   3   5   7   9   10   8   6   4   2

This book is printed on acid-free paper. ♾

Book design by Marysarah Quinn

# CONTENTS

## LOſ ALAMOſ, ΠℰW MℰXIℂO

*As Gregor Samsa awoke one morning after disturbing dreams, he found himself transformed in his bed into an enormous cockroach.*

# VIENNA

Wunderkammer Hoffnung—Amadeus Hoffnung's Cabinet of Wonders—had begun as the hobby of a diminutive, shy adolescent: his childhood rock and insect collections, his autographs of singers from the Vienna State Opera, the paintings made by his oddly talented cat, and what was clearly the largest ball of string ever imagined by his otherwise mocking cohorts. The idea that his collection could become a business was far from the thoughts of this lonely child until one day in 1907 when his parents bought a Victrola, the very model pictured on "His Master's Voice."

"You can start saving for your own record collection," his father said.

Karl Maria Hoffnung was not miserly, he simply wanted his son to learn the virtues of discernment and self-sufficiency. "I'll add a crown a week to your allowance, and you can put it away for music. Maybe you could charge people to see your collections," he added, prescient.

Thus began young Amadeus's quest. He saved his weekly crowns and invested his meager capital in the thrift stores and flea markets of Vienna. He haunted antiquarian bookstores and roamed the alleys behind the mansions of the well-to-do. His collection grew: a cracked and fraying coconut, some Indian beads and an African necklace, a moth with an eight-inch wingspread, a turtle shell of splendiferous colors, the skull of what had probably been a cow, an ivory tusk, a miscellany of outlandish amulets and small objects for a "talisman" collection, a nail said to be from Noah's Ark (only three crowns), a hand mirror rimmed with portraits of its owner from birth to seventeen (the last two frames empty), a mandrake root in the shape of a woman, a music box that played the "Ode to Joy," a small Chinese vase painted with graceful characters and mysterious mountains.

Still, he was not prepared to open to a cash-paying public until he found the most staggering item of all: a fossil cockroach in an ironstone nodule from the upper carboniferous rocks of the Sosnowiec coalfields. Three hundred fifty million years old, he was told, and not by the person who sold him the Ark nail but by a professor at the Technische Hochschule. Three hundred fifty million years old! He could feel its age weigh heavily in his hand. He could sense the three-inch insect ready to crawl, even without the last segments of its abdomen. Amadeus had invested three years and three hundred odd crowns, and now, with the coming of the stone roach, he was ready to begin. In 1910 he hung out his shingle: WUNDERKAMMER HOFFNUNG, I. MARK EINTRITT. The next four years brought in enough one-mark coins to finance the purchase first of *Parsifal* and then of the entire *Ring*—right up to the fiery destruction of Valhalla.

June 28, 1914, was an important day. A Bosnian Serb, Gavrilo Princip, put a bullet in the heart of the Archduke Ferdinand in Sarajevo, and the Magyar leviathan, Anton Tomzak, walked into the Wunderkammer Hoffnung in Vienna. Or rather, waddled—Anton Tomzak weighed 614 pounds without his shoes.

He had an interesting proposition. What would Herr Hoffnung think about his exhibiting *himself* as part of the *Wunderkammer*? Tomzak proposed to construct, at his own expense, a curtained-off area in the space adjoining the main exhibition room and, at specific hours, make himself available for display. He would begin working for nothing more than meals on the days he was present (but oh, what meals!). If, after three probationary months, Herr Hoffnung's attendance were up, especially on the two days a week Tomzak proposed to exhibit, they would then arrive at some fair remuneration and a plan to further publicize his appearances.

A living soul in his Cabinet of Wonders? Life could be . . . entertaining, he supposed. Life. At twenty-one, Amadeus was grizzled and wrinkling. What had seemed mere shortness and hairlessness earlier on was now playing out more and more clearly as Werner's Syndrome, a rare disease of premature aging and hypogonadal function. Should Amadeus, a probable freak among men, become a proprietor of freaks? Anton Tomzak's appearance held a mirror up to his life, like the one in his collection, rimmed by his own successive portraits. But the portraits were few, and the changes swift, with far more empty spaces at the end. A wondrous freak show. So why not? And why not now?

After advertising for the first few weeks, Amadeus found Tuesdays and Thursdays packed for Tomzak's afternoon and evening shows. Each of Tomzak's many pounds cried out performer. He joked and jibed, he performed bizarre stripteases with tear-away garments specially constructed. Audience members were invited to estimate his waist and thighs, and then to measure. Strong-looking men were challenged to arm wrestle. Trios were summoned on stage to try to lift him. But where to grab?

Small children came again and again and brought their parents to see them riding, fifteen at a time, on his head and shoulders, strung out along his arms, clinging to the clothes on his back and front, or with toeholds in his belt.

An article appeared in the *Neue Freie Presse,* featuring Tomzak, of course, but also describing in great detail the other artifacts and oddities of Amadeus's collection. And the crowds grew so large that groups had to be scheduled at half-hour intervals, as in the busiest of restaurants.

By the end of the first year of the war, many Austro-Hungarians, especially the Viennese poor, were wandering the streets. Karl Kraus thought Vienna "a proving ground for world destruction," and the "differently-abled," once supported by their families or the social system, were sacrificed first. As houses and institutions were destroyed by acts of war, the streets and parks became homes for the unfortunate, and people not usually seen in public became the object of stares and whispers.

Eight months after Tomzak's appearance, Clarissa Leinsdorf and her daughter Inge showed up at the museum. The mother was thirty-eight years old and stood eighteen inches tall. Her daughter was seventeen, the spitting image of her mother, but two inches shorter. Who might have impregnated Clarissa, and how, was beyond imagining, yet there they were, standing in the rain, asking, in grating twitters, to be let in. Ten days later, Milena Silovec arrived, an armless girl who could type fifty words a minute with her toes—without mistakes—who later became secretary to the burgeoning Hoffnung operation.

Within the course of a few weeks, the ambience of Hoffnung Wunderkammer had radically changed, and with the closing of music halls and theaters, the crowds increased so much that Amadeus had to rethink his entire operation—a collection of wonders that would burst the seams of any cabinet.

In short order, Amadeus became manager to Katerina Eckhardt, a beautiful Swabian woman whose wide skirt covered a second lower body protruding from her abdomen. Her attractiveness was not so compromised as to prevent her from giving birth over the next decade to four girls and a son, the last from her secondary body. Such are the confusions of war and inflation. On February 9, 1915, a large cloth bag was found at the museum door with a note: "Plese give home to my poor babie." In the bag a jar, and in the jar, a thirty-pound fetus pickled in brine. No eyes, no nostrils, huge ears, and a tail. And who found this gift? Yet another applicant, while knocking at the door, one George Keiffer, eight feet, six inches, rejected by the Austrian army because of his size and dismissed from a French prison camp because he was too big to feed. He could pick up an entire horse or cannon—and he did—to the great delight of the ever-expanding crowds at Hoffnung's.

And so the Wunderkammer became a circus, the Zirkus Schwänze der Hoffnung, an assembly of walk-through wagons, each featuring human anomalies, pathetic, astonishing, and willing. Zirkus Schwänze der Hoffnung—the Tails of Hoffnung Circus. The name reflected the mind-boggling collection of freaks and oddities there assembled—the cast-off "tailings" of otherwise normal production, the butt-end protrusions, the devil flaunting an anal thumb at the world. Perhaps it was not a circus at all: there were no trained beasts, no clowns and acrobats, and most especially no death-defying trapeze artists to titillate and awe the spectating circle. On this issue, Amadeus Ernst Hoffnung was scornful and corrosive.

"No trapeze acts!" he would bluster, and in this emblem he would subsume all other parodies of human freedom. "A family of acrobats high in the roof, balancing, swinging, hanging by the hair from their children's teeth! What a betrayal of humanity, what a mockery of holy Mother Nature!" The image enraged him. Did he imagine his own exhibits might better depict her maternal labors?

Leo Kongee, the "Man with No Nerves," rammed hatpins through his tongue and pounded spikes into his nose. Godina and Apexia, the "Pinhead Sisters," joked with horrified viewers about the angels dancing inside their skulls. Gerda Schloß, "the Homeliest Woman in the World," flirted with men and teased their female companions about their sexual competence. There was Josef/Josefina, "Man or Woman, Who Is To Say?" and Serpentina, "The Girl with No Bones." Glotzaügiger Otto could pop both his eyes right out of his face. And Steinkopf Bill charged ten groschen for pieces of the rocks broken on his head.

. . .

December 17, 1915, brought Amadeus more to celebrate than Beethoven's birthday—which is what he was doing in the semidarkness of the four-o'clock hour when Anna Marie Schleßweg's crew pulled its wagon into the cluster of wagons now inhabiting a huge empty lot in Vienna's Meidling district. The trailer marked "Büro" was lit by lantern light. Anna Marie knocked resolutely.

"*Jah*. Come in."

"Herr Hoffnung?"

"*Jah. Und?*"

"Do you have a moment?" Four of them peeked through the door. "We'd like to show you something."

"I don't need it. I don't need any more. I have enough problems. *Basta. Genug.* But come in already nevertheless, and close the door. You're letting out the heat."

"What is that awful noise?" asked one of the men—from well behind.

"Herr Klofac!" scolded Anna Marie, their doughty leader.

"That, my impolitic but honest friend, is what a deaf man hears inside his fortress skull."

Amadeus removed the needle from side three of Beethoven's *Grosse Fuge*. "It's my little birthday celebration. I play it every year."

"Happy birthday!"

"To Beethoven, not to me. Did you sing 'Happy Birthday' to him?"

"No. We drove all the way from Prague. . . ." Anna Marie began to explain.

"Without singing 'Happy Birthday' to Beethoven? Did you sing 'Happy Birthday' to him yesterday?"

"I thought today was—"

"Today and yesterday. He has two birthdays. Extraordinary people do extraordinary things. That's what Zirkus Schwänze der Hoffnung is all about. What have you got to show me?"

"I thought you said you had enough," Klofac pointed out.

"I'll make an exception. I like honest, boorish people."

"My men will bring in the—crate."

And Kramar, Klofac, and Soukup clomped out the door, down three wooden steps into the darkness.

"How old are you, madame?"

"Sixty-three."

"Good. What's your name?"

"Anna Marie Schleßweg."

"And how old am I?"

"I don't know. Fifty?"

"Fifty is a good guess. I'm twenty-two."

Crashing and grumping as the three ex-borders chez Gregor grind the crate against the door frame.

"Easy does it, gentlemen. I just finished paying off this trailer."

"Sorry, Herr Hoffnung. Soukup, tip this way a little. Klofac, lift. Okay, now up . . . easy. Where shall we put it?"

"Here, I'll move these chairs."

"Watch your fingers."

"There it is. Soukup, open it," directed Frau Schleßweg.

"Not me. You open it."

Amadeus stepped in. "I'll open it. I'm used to surprises."

But not like this one. Herr Hoffnung was stunned. Three hundred fifty million years swirled up at him from the bottom of the crate. His roach. His Sosnowiec roach come to call. The Great, secret Joy of his recent, and long-departed youth. He had to grip hard on the edge of the crate.

"Are you all right?"

"Yes. What is he?"

"I dunno. A big roach, I think." Klofac, always to the point.

"Is he alive?"

"He was last time we looked. Hey, Gregor, Gregor, wake up. Say something."

"He talks? He has a name?"

"Good and proper. Gregor, say something to Herr Hoffnung."

"You named a roach?"

"I think he wasn't always a roach," ventured Kramar.

"He was a man. Young. Early twenties," Anna Marie elucidated. "A traveling salesman. He lived with his parents in the Zeltnergasse."

"How did he . . ."

Silence.

"This is not some kind of joke?"

"Here, lift him out." Klofac was anxious to prove Gregor's authenticity. "Kramar, grab his butt. Soukup, reach in and get him under his chest."

"Thorax, my friend. But it's okay. Just leave him in there."

"No, no, you have to see for yourself. He'll respond. He's just shy."

Four pairs of hands reached down into the crate.

"Careful of his antennae. They break." Anna Marie, ever solicitous.

"Up . . . up . . . swing him over this way. Now down. Can we put him on the couch?"

"Let me put something down first. There."

In a brown flash, Gregor scrambled instinctively under the couch.

"He likes to be under couches," said Anna Marie by way of explanation for Gregor's rudeness. "He was always under the couch when I came in to clean his room. He always hid under there."

"Thigmotaxis, my dear," Herr Hoffnung explained. "Roaches are thigmotactic. From the Greek *thigma*, touch, and *taxis*, a reflex movement toward one thing or another. Roaches love to be touched all around."

"That's disgusting."

"Disgusting but true, my good honest man."

It was ten o'clock before negotiations were completed and plans under way. Gregor, recently—and understandably—depressed, had lost several kilograms. And even an exoskeleton can appear strikingly dehydrated. With the accumulated dust, hair, and bits of old food stuck to his back and sides, he was a shocking sight indeed. But his mad escape, freeing his family from their burden, his larval sense of adventure had all lifted his spirits—and when he heard the talk of exhibiting him as "The Hunger Insect," he whispered hoarsely from under the couch.

"No."

Five homo sapiens at the table whirled around to the couch.

"He does talk! Astonishing."

"What do you expect? He was a traveling salesman. They have to talk."

"Gregor? Is that your name?" Herr Hoffnung asked. "I said, is that your name?"

Silence.

"He stopped talking."

"Maybe his name has changed."

"I don't want to be The Hunger Insect. I want to eat. And I want to think. Eat, read, and think."

"He always had a lot of books in his room," Anna Marie confided to Herr Hoffnung.

"People won't pay to see a cockroach read and think," Soukup objected.

"What if I tell them what I'm thinking?"

"I don't think people care what a cockroach thinks."

"Just how many times a day do you expect to eat?" Klofac queried.

"And what did you have in mind for food?" Kramar was anxious for details.

"Gentlemen! Quiet. Our friend Gregor may be old hat to you, but I assure you that whatever he does—if he just sits there and stares—he will be a sensation."

"If he doesn't do something, they'll think he's stuffed."

"Or a statue."

"Wax."

"I'll move around. I'll get books off the shelf."

"Now he wants a shelf," Soukup snorted.

"So how many books do you want and what kind?"

Klofac: "The shelf will come out of your salary."

Gregor's first book, chosen right from Amadeus Ernst Hoffnung's glass-enclosed bookcase, was Johann Gotthelf Fischer von Waldheim's *Zoognosia: Tabulis synopticis illustrata, in usum praelectionum Academiae Imperialis Medico-Chiurgicae Mosquensis,* an immense leather-bound volume, with tables and illustrations of every known species of animal. He wanted to make sure he had something unique to offer.

He was five feet, six inches from the top of his head to the tip of his tegmina, not counting his cerci, which, because of the need to wear clothing, were most often strapped to his abdomen underneath. That is, he was an average-sized person, if a little short for a male. He stood anywhere from twenty inches to six feet, depending. It never ceased to be an issue whether to stand on all sixes, or to try to ape human verticality. As a six-footer, he was a bit awkward, somewhat tentative in his gait, but vertically, he could function well at cocktail parties, or at meetings, seated in a chair. At home, however, or among close friends, he preferred the horizontal, more natural for his anatomy. On six legs, he could scamper over mesa or mountain.

His most striking features—the most upsetting, at least to strangers— were his eyes, two huge compound eyes, seven inches across, of two thousand lenses each. In faintest light they would glisten, iridescent, ever-changing. Vision for those with compound eyes is both less—and more—exact than for those of us with mammalian organs. While the overall image was somewhat blurry, a mosaic of soft focus like the surface of a Seurat, his perception of motion was vastly more acute. As an image traverses from lens to lens, it ticks a sensor at each border that registers precise direction and speed. And so his peripheral vision was immense.

His mouth was far more adept than our own, with hard, chitinous jaws for chewing from side to side, maxillae with both soft and stiff bristles for grooming his antennae and legs. Keeping antennae and limbs spotless was not just good breeding: his smell and vibrational senses would have been compromised otherwise. He would fastidiously draw his long antennae through his maxillae, like dental floss that came out clean instead of fetid. And even though he was capable of eating a wide range of food, from prime rib to rotting garbage, he was equipped with both maxillary and labial palps to ascertain edibility—before taking anything unclean or unhealthy into his body.

His ears, so to speak, were subgenual organs located in each knee joint, so sensitive when he wore shorts that he could detect the footfalls of other, normal-sized roaches, and distinguish earthquakes as small as 0.07 on the Richter scale.

And he was wounded.

Gregor's injury was an extremely sensitive subject. It was about two-thirds of the way down the middle of his back, just over his heart. He had tried aloe, Doktor Klopstock's Ointment, zinc oxide, Balm of Gilead, and parenchymal extract all in vain. The wound was unhealable. It required continuing care, was a source of chronic mid-level pain, and led to endless embarrassment.

But it was both his cross and his salvation. To Gregor, it was essential.

## 3. PERSONAE *not quite* GRATAE

It is curious what small effect world-shaking events can have on a large cockroach, well housed and fed in an Austrian circus. On battlefields, poison gas wafted to unsuspecting lungs. In the seas, torpedoes swam toward unsuspecting hulls. Machine-gun bursts riddled the trenches, and those inside them. And on the home front—starvation. Gregor's problem was different, smaller: it is hard for a cockroach to read.

It would be almost five years—1920—before the first radio station sent its signal springing into space from Pittsburgh. Until that time, Gregor had only hearsay, conversation—and books. But how to see the words?

Amadeus was nothing short of munificent in this regard—as he would be in all things touching Gregor. He succeeded in contacting Bertolt Lindhauer, a lens-maker for Karl Zeiss and Co., who, through the hardships of war, had been able to continue working after hours on the astounding "Zeiss Projector" that would debut at the Munich Planetarium in 1923. Using lenses discarded from the projector, Lindhauer was able to design a pair of glasses to enable Gregor's reading.

The first four months were a period of adjustment, Gregor plagued with headaches and neck pains, trying to determine the least fatiguing position and the most efficient means of page turning. Amadeus, of course, was a great help, bringing him books and journals, seeing to his material needs, and engaging him in relaxing, stimulating conversation.

They talked of mice and men, of history and destiny. They reviewed funny people in the audience, and chastised Amadeus's rogue tomcat for peeing in Gregor's cage. Both he and Amadeus had thought a cage might be best during visiting hours, to reduce spectator fear and keep little children from snapping his antennae. The fun they had constructing it can be imagined from the photos taken, with Gregor mugging "the poor prisoner in his twisted gyves," and the "soul in hell."

.   .   .

His "act" evolved over time. Originally billed as "A Visitor from the Early
Carboniferous Period" (perhaps *"Vomfruhesteinkohlzeitbesucher"* seems less
awkward in German), he gave short talks about the steaming interior
marshes of the then single landmass of North America, South America,
Africa, Australia, Asia, Eurasia, and Antarctica. But this soon seemed
canned and phony, and Amadeus wondered if some in the audience
might think he was some kind of lifelike automaton. So Gregor went on
to giving advice. "The Advisor from the Early Carboniferous." People
would ask questions about business or personal problems, or what books
to read or (while the cinemas were still open) what films to see. Once a
child asked, "Are there really Angels, and do they bring the Christmas
presents, or do parents bring them?" Gregor assured her that no one feels
really at home in an interpreted world—which must have given her something to think about. At least she didn't cry.

He spent much time inventing and reinventing his act, trying to discover a formula both to satisfy audience and to stimulate himself. He
went from advice to political commentary, and when that became too
controversial, to reviewing books. Gregor's self-assignment was then to
keep the light of literature alive, to publicize the hard-to-obtain work by
the great authors of the extraordinary decades around the turn of the
century.

From his own bookshelves, and those of his father, Amadeus kept
Gregor supplied with a stream of brilliance: Hugo von Hoffmansthal,
Arthur Schnitzler, Karl Kraus, Robert Musil, Hermann Broch, Thomas
Mann, Hermann Hesse, Frank Wedekind. The recipient was especially
pleased with gifts from his beloved Prague: Werfel, Brod, Meyerinck, and
his favorite—Rainer Maria Rilke. For several months, he did nothing but
recite the latest to appear of the *Duino Elegies:*

*With all its eyes the creature-world beholds the open . . .*

He wondered how Rilke—untaintedly human—could know these
things, things just beginning to articulate within his hybrid being.

*a free animal*
*has its decrease perpetually behind it*
*and God in front, and when it moves, it moves*
*into eternity, like running springs.*

How inspiring! Eternity, he thought, would provide a wide swath in which to work.

For the most part upright at the lectern, Gregor would occasionally drop to all sixes and begin to pace slowly, reciting from memory. In this position he became more frightening to the crowd, and though those in the rear strained on tiptoe to see, there was always a general movement away from the cage, and toward the back wall.

Nevertheless, he sang to them Rilke's song of pure, open space, of a world unlike theirs—or his—in which there was *niemals Nirgends ohne Nicht,* "never nowhere without No."

*A child sometimes gets quietly lost there, to be always*
*jogged back again.*

In his first readings, he would move up to the bars and reach out toward the nearest child, placed in front to be able to see. The first two times—extraordinary—both children reached back to touch him. And each was snatched back by a fearful parent, afraid of what such openness might attract. The third time, the child, a lovely, dark little girl, shied and cried, hand into mouth; her father grabbed her up and pushed his way out of the crowded room. Perfectly timed to Gregor's own reactive emotions:

*And yet, within the wakefully-warm animal*
*there lies the weight and care of a great sadness.*

Child or no child, Gregor often had difficulty holding back tears, and many times, his view was blurred, turning his gaze inward.

*For that which often overwhelms you clings*
*to me as well—a kind of memory . . .*

His face turned wistful—haunted even—as he and Rilke recalled a
time, a place that

*was once nearer and truer and attached to us*
*with infinite tenderness.*

Gregor studied the ragged, uncomprehending audience, bundled
against the cold.

*Here all is distance,*
*there it was breath.*
*Compared with that first home*
*the second appears ambiguous and drafty.*

He knew people might think of their bomb-damaged homes and
bullet-pocked walls. . . . Never mind. The great lessons to be learned
were not the obvious ones.

*But you, spectators always, everywhere,*
*looking at, never out of, everything!*
*It fills you. You arrange it.*
*It decays. You re-arrange it, and decay yourselves.*
*Who has turned you around like this, so that you always,*
*do what you will, retain the attitude*
*of someone departing, forever taking leave.*

Then Gregor would close the folder of poems—"Thank you"—drop
to the ground, and walk slowly off to the curtained part of the cage,
offstage.

It was a phenomenal performance. Though his voice was creaky, his
presence, the full fact of his Otherness created ten minutes of high un-
canniness—but deep, soul-shiveringly deep. Which might explain the lack
of public response. Amadeus waited in vain for a jump in attendance, but
his audiences leveled off, even fell slightly, and the critics, had any attended, were silent. However, Godina and Apexia, "The Pinhead Sisters,"
came to every performance they could, timing breaks from their own, and

clapping politely and too long at the end. "The Dog-Faced Boy," and "The Alligator-Skinned Man," and Jana, "The Monkey-Girl" all came and wept. Gregor saw them there repeatedly. But they never spoke to him about it.

Amadeus asked him to change the act, to find something new.

Well, Gregor thought, if people won't respond to the deepest voices of their own artists, what about the exotic? What about a "Voices of the Enemy" series, readings and interpretations of the American barbarians? That would be sensational—if he could get away with it. He would learn English. He would translate the texts, and develop in his audiences a deeper understanding of the American people, the likely winners of the Great War. Was this disloyal? Would the censors silence a cockroach?

Amadeus put the kibosh on the notion. Gregor could study English if he liked—Amadeus would even supply the grammars and dictionaries. But it was simply too risky to be perceived as aiding and abetting the financiers, and now the soldiers destroying our land and slaughtering our sons.

These were agonizing times for Amadeus. As a child, he had loved all change, family trips, new dwellings, even changes of scenery at the Opera. But now change was the enemy. At the beginning of the war, officers' swords were still being sharpened by the regimental armorer, and soldiers were making grenades from empty tins of jam. Now, only four years later, they were advancing behind a shield of tanks, protected by air cover directed by radio from the ground.

And Amadeus's disease was also advancing exponentially. Muscle weakness, joint pain, periods of incontinence, loss of memory. But the source of greatest pain was his responsibility for the growing number of beings crouching in his circle of wagons, huddling in an empty lot on the outskirts of Vienna.

In the early years of the war, there had been some small amount of money for an audience to spend on entertainment—and on the kind of spiritual challenge a museum and freak show might evoke. But now, spare marks were needed for food and clothing—if not for oneself, then for family or friends. Those knocking at his door for work were ever more needful and bizarre, and at the same time, Amadeus needed ever more lurid displays to attract a weary audience, leery of parting with any money at all. These two movements—odder attractions and a need for odder attractions—enabled him to continue, but at great cost to his ethical being, his image of humanity.

Thus, by the end of the war, on the eleventh hour of the eleventh day of the eleventh month of the year, Amadeus had taken on some decidedly questionable "acts," and the circle of wagons had grown significantly larger. In and among them were the dregs of homo sapiens' storehouse, the most uncomfortable inhabitants of the human condition, a gruesome crew that Amadeus called "my apology for the world." How else could one understand such offerings as Fu Hsi, a man of obscurely Oriental origins, evidently with some kind of neurophysiological disorder, who lay in a coffin "undead," with no perceptible breath or heartbeat, yet who discoursed, with staring eyes, in accented German, about his death while building the Great Wall twenty-three centuries ago? Or Emil, the Hunger Artist Gregor refused to be, gripping the bars of his cage, staring dumbly with his great, sunken eyes, blind to the sign that was changed daily—125th day, 126th day—the implied invitation: Be Present at This Man's Self-Inflicted Death.

Children, no doubt with the permission of their parents, would vie to tickle, hurt, torture these men with most ingenious childish means. If their parents could not hear Fu Hsi's heartbeats through the stethoscope, if they could not see the mirror fog, perhaps little Hans or Anneke could expose him with a straw up a nostril, or a fingernail in an eye. Or perhaps the Hunger Artist would eat some horse dung, freshly picked, if it were smeared on his face, over his mouth. The adults, too, had their ways, less crude perhaps, but therefore more cruel. Grown men and women would volunteer to leave their beds and the warmth of their partners to stay up all night, watching at Emil's cage, so that no well-meaning guard or street person might offer him food, and he, in the hiddenness of night, eat it.

Amadeus knew of these activities, and they weighed on his arrhythmic heart. But for him, they were no more blameworthy than the more hidden lust for death exhibited by "normal" circus audiences, come to see—maybe, if things go well—the dashing of a falling aerialist's brains. Less blameworthy, if anything, because more honest. But blameworthy nevertheless.

In Gregor's opinion, Amadeus's own shoes were muddy from the slippery slope. Why else would he choose to place a glass case of pythons right next to Emil's cage so that crowds might watch them eat while the other starved? Doubtful. Morally doubtful.

From such behavior, one might conclude that Amadeus was going mad, that the chaos of his crumbling biology, of Austria at war's end, the insanity of his personal space—his room full of squeaking and yowling and croaking and cheeping—was taking its toll. But when he would enter his room, Amadeus had only to strike the table with his fist and yell: "Quiet, you rapscallions!" and the monkeys climbed quickly atop the four-poster bed, the guinea pigs scurried under the stove, the raven fluttered onto the circular mirror. Only the black cat, the soiler of Gregor's cage, unperturbed by his master's entrance, would remain calmly as he was, and begin to groom. In this taut silence, Amadeus would sit, and smoke, and think. Sometimes he would repair to his shop to work on a new display. When he reentered the world of his humanoid colleagues and creatures, he was rational, affable, even charming. But out there in the world, there was little method—only madness.

## 4. METAMORPHOSIS II: *An* INSECT *with* QUALITIES

1919 was Spengler year in German-speaking lands. Everyone was reading him, debating his message, wondering who this prophet was, with his furrowed brow, his dark, fierce eyes, his great domed head. Oswald Spengler, man of mystery, an unknown, retiring schoolmaster, with no friends in normal academic or literary circles. How his weighty tome had exploded into public consciousness!

And it wasn't only philosophers and historians reading *The Decline of the West*. Never before had a huge philosophical work been such a bestseller, invading serious academic seminars and drunken beer-hall banter, concerned church groups and flippant cocktail parties, political meetings left and right. Within eight years of its publication, it had sold a hundred thousand copies—and this at a time when families were hurting for food and housing, when books were low in priority. The book appealed to Germans and Austrians, the "losers" of the late conflagration who were prepared to listen and hear. *All right,* they said, *we may have lost the war, but you so-called winners, you also have lost.* Yet it was not only the losers who snatched up the work. The "winners," with more ebullience, and more money to spend—and especially the Americans with their intact publishing houses and huge economic surpluses—were also enthusiastic readers. People, it seems, like to read bad news.

And so it was not outrageous that Gregor would mount, as his first postwar act, his sequel to the *Duino Elegies,* a public seminar on Spengler's *Decline of the West*. On the contrary, it was a brilliant tour de force. For the last half of 1919, and early into 1920, Gregor's Spengler seminars became the thing to do in Vienna. While some circus-goers simply stumbled upon them, a constant stream of seasoned debaters from all circles was always involved in the discussion: here were the students and their professors, the beer-bellied philosophers, the concerned clergy and the chosen of their flocks, the haute monde and the demimonde, the communists, socialists, and proto-fascists. It was quite a debate. And it was good for Amadeus's bottom line.

. . .

During Gregor's seminars, one Spenglerian notion seemed always to generate the most light and the most heat: his prognosis for Faustian Man in a Faustian Culture, ever restless, ever longing for the unattainable. What, the blattid asked, might characterize the "Faustian winter" the world was in?

"No standards of taste," yelled one man, by his look, a starving artist. "Anything goes."

"Not anything goes," a well-dressed woman called out. "It's always middle-class values—even among the ruling class."

Boos and hisses.

"On the contrary, madame," a military officer politely offered. "We suffer from mindless, insouciant individualism, some ruinous need for unrestricted freedom."

But at every seminar, no matter who attended, the government came under fire: "All our so-called democracy is just a hollow mask obscuring the basic political reality—the triumph of money." The speaker did not at all look like a bomb-throwing anarchist. "Everything yields to the power of the rich. Politicians have no choice but to become paid agents of financiers."

There was general approval among the proletarians, and silence higher up the feeding chain.

Here was the bomb-thrower type, a pacifist: "Blood and soil, blood and soil! Ridiculous. We're harnessed by the state and exploited by the rich, fodder for their quest to master the world." This was a bit much, and the atmosphere would tense. "Eventually one Caesar will win out and establish a universal imperium. Cities will become the only places that matter, obeying any leader who keeps people fed and amused with vulgar, brutal diversions and escapist superstitions. Look around you even now . . ." The officer made for the pacifist, but was held back by the crowd. A not atypical Spengler evening.


The success of Gregor's seminars was a surprise even to him, and certainly to Amadeus, who thought he had a realistic view of the illiteracy that stalked the wasteland. Their worry was unnecessary, their doubts misplaced. At the very first session half the adults were already reading it; several had finished the first volume. Their comments drew in the innocents—even the older children—and as the innocents were initiated, Gregor found his expository work mostly done. He had simply to move the discussion on when it was stuck, call on those who had trouble breaking in, and continually focus on people's own, local experience. A population of war-weary survivors was not prone to intellectualize, and the stories and feelings flowed easily and with great intensity. At the end of the show, he hastened over to Amadeus's office to dictate his impressions.

By his third "performance," word had spread even to the academic community, and the temperature rose accordingly. The historians came to defend their history, the economists, their economic theories. Normal classroom decor was decidedly absent in this small, cloth-covered wagon with its two lecterns and a cage full of straw at one end. Though people were crammed shoulder to shoulder, and all could hear perfectly from any corner of the room, there was commotion and shouting, and louder shouting to overcome it. Gregor could command silence only by expelling air forcefully through all his spiracles, emitting a spine-tingling hiss. Because of his clothing, it was not apparent where the noise was coming from, but the crowd quieted nonetheless.

On November 7, at the close of a Friday evening seminar, Gregor answered the door behind the curtained, off-stage area of his cage. He knew it was Amadeus from his signature knock, the first four notes of *Death and the Maiden*. But standing with the *Zirkusmeister* was a wiry man with a high, radiant forehead and razor-sharp nose, a cigarette between his lips.

"May we come in?"

"Certainly. Uh . . . would you mind putting out the cigarette? All this straw . . . and the spiracles . . ." He indicated his axillary line. The man descended the four wagon steps, muttering, stubbed out his smoke, and returned.

"Gregor Samsa, this is Robert Musil, the—"

"*The* Robert Musil, of *Young Törless*?"

"Yes. This came out what, a dozen years ago?"

"It was one of my crucial books," Gregor said. *The Other Condition*, the world beyond the bounds of normal, limited existence. . . . I read it when I was still . . . before I . . . well, before I *was* The Other Condition."

"Thank you. It's rare that one's work is appreciated."

"Doctor Musil was at your seminar tonight."

"I can't see into the crowd. Did you say anything?"

"Don't call me Doctor, Herr Hoffnung, please. One of my many pet peeves: respected professors and denigrated writers. Professors have achieved their highest public standing since the world began, while writers are now being called 'men of letters,' which, I suppose, means people prevented by some obscure infirmity from becoming journalists."

"No, Herr Musil," Amadeus objected. "What about Thomas Mann, the great Thomas Mann?"

"Oh, Mann." Musil waved disparagingly. "Mann is too tolerant a human being, too much in tune with his times to ever achieve true unpopularity. He likes the world as it is too much, and is loved by the world in return. Mann writes for people who are here; I write for people who are not. At least not yet. I'm autistic, negative, and fanatical. But I like you, Herr Samsa. I like what you're up to. You are also a . . . being . . . out of your time."

Gregor felt suddenly shy.

"Herr Musil and I came to invite you for dinner chez moi, and a postseminar seminar."

The wind had stilled, and Orion was blazing low in the November sky. The three crossed the freezing mud to the other end of the lot and climbed the steps to Amadeus's office wagon. It was the largest of the motley collection, almost a boxcar on huge wooden wheels. The door creaked open, and the black tom ran among the legs of the guests, out into the night. Musil stubbed out his cigarette and followed the others into a well-lit room. The monkeys stopped grooming and climbed quickly to the top of the large bookshelf, while the raven walked with determination behind Amadeus's great reading chair.

"Have a seat, gentlemen, and give me a few minutes to prepare a humble board." Amadeus went to the woodstove at the far end of the wagon, poured water from pitcher to pot, and set it to boil. From the ice chest, he pulled a string of blood sausage, placed them in the water, and began to sharpen a knife for the cutting of bread. Musil and Gregor settled into the remaining armchairs, whose substantial cushions had brought forth much previous conversation.

"I've been to three of your Spengler seminars."

"You never said anything?"

"The primary job of the writer is to observe."

"And what did you observe?"

"A crowd of suckers, bamboozled, as usual, by fame."

"Spengler's?"

"And yours. Genius on genius. They'll do anything you want."

"But I don't say anything. I just ask questions, get them to talk."

"You're not out there when they pour down the steps. I stand and listen, and take down their comments. 'Genius.' I haven't done a word analysis, but I can assure you genius is the winner."

"But I . . ."

"You don't have to do anything. 'Genius, genius.' Nothing but genius in the world. Just leaf through the newspapers—you'll be truly amazed at how many profoundly moving, prophetic, greatest, deepest, and very great masters appear over the course of a few months. A few weeks later hardly anyone can still remember them."

"You're saying Spengler is just a fad?"

"He certainly is a fashion," Amadeus called over from the kitchen. "And I worry how long your act will be able to hold."

"A current, war-weary fashion," Musil averred. "And fashions are marked by two characteristics: one, that in retrospect, they seem ridiculous, and two, that as long as they last, you can hardly imagine taking seriously anyone who is not as engulfed as you are." Musil got up from his chair and began to pace, negotiating the small space with military turns. "What joy grins back at us in the mirror when we connect with the fashionable norm, looking, talking, thinking exactly like everyone else, even though everyone looks, talks, and thinks differently than they did yesterday! It's as though our character would scatter like powder if we did not pack it into a publicly approved container."

Amadeus returned from the kitchen with plates of bread and sausage, and handed them to his guests. Gregor decided to proceed with his dinner. In general, he did not like eating in front of others. It was one thing with Amadeus, but Robert Musil was a stranger, and worse, a famous writer known for his merciless eye. Still, it had been a long day, and this was Gregor's first meal since noon.

"I find Spengler quite original," he replied, his buccal cavity still full of bread and sausage. "I've never before—"

"I can hardly expect you to take seriously what I say, Herr Insect," Musil broke in. "Nor can I expect you to operate by the norms of human table manners. But while chewing with an open mouth, perhaps you might reflect on the conclusions one might draw from the strange unpleasantness of looking at old fashions . . ."

Amadeus returned again with beer. "My *Wunderkammer* is full of old fashions."

". . . as long as they have not yet become 'wonders,' or costumes, or 'historical ideas.'"

Aside from Gregor's chewing, a pensive silence hung in the room. What was there to say? Neither Gregor nor Amadeus had ever encountered such knifelike opinions or dark force of expression. Amadeus, the skillful host, tried to break the silence:

"So I take it you did not enjoy Gregor's seminars?"

"On the contrary. I've said how much I like you, Herr Blattid, how much I enjoy what you are up to."

"What am I up to?"

"A very Spenglerian activity: playing out the Faustian man, or in this case, the Faustian Roach—you are a roach, are you not?"

Gregor nodded.

"The Faustian Roach on his infinite quest."

"And what is that quest?"

"Am I wrong about the quest?"

"No."

"Then you tell me. What is the quest?"

"I'm not sure," Gregor said. "It has to do with the war. And with my— privilege, I suppose—to stand outside humanity to see . . ."

"To see what?" Amadeus moved to the edge of his armchair. This was important information he had been unconsciously seeking for the last four years. Gregor sat silently.

After a long minute, Musil quietly offered, "Let me help. The war. A good place to start. You will agree the war demonstrates a profound failure of all experiments, both personal and collective, to find a right way of living. While everyone has been searching for the factor that would summarize and unify all aspects of life, the war has found and swallowed them all. There's little left for the individual or the nation but a final flight into sexuality and slaughter."

"You sound like Spengler."

"But for me, there is hope," Musil added.

"What is the hope?" asked Amadeus.

"Our six-legged friend here, with the unhealing wound in his back."

"How did you know about that?" Gregor asked, alarmed.

"It is the writer's job to listen and observe."

"I told him. I'm sorry."

Gregor looked at Amadeus, hurt, betrayed—and turned back to Musil. "How am I the hope?"

"You are uniquely equipped to discover and model a new man for a new society."

"How is that?"

"Ontogeny recapitulates phylogeny."

"Haeckel's Law," observed Amadeus.

"Exactly."

"He was a friend of my father's in Jena," Musil said. "He died this past August."

"Sorry to hear that."

"Eighty-five. An admirable painter."

"What about his law?" Gregor asked.

"You are the first known throwback in the phylogenetic chain. Somehow, God bless, your ontogeny took a step back toward a more larval state."

"I am not a larva."

"Cockroaches, you surely know, demonstrate incomplete metamorphosis. You are as larval as you can be, not wormlike, but comparatively larval nonetheless."

"And so?" Amadeus pushed on through Gregor's discomfort. He was not normally so insensitive.

"And so, unlike Western humanity, which both you and your friend Professor Spengler might agree is 'finished,' you, Herr Cockroach, are unfinished. . . ."

"Like the *Art of Fugue*," observed Amadeus. "B-A-C-," he sang, cutting off the final H.

"Like that crawling complexity, yes. But unlike the unfortunate author, consumed by churchmen and children, you are healthy and alive—albeit with a wound that keeps you going. *You* can finish the *fuga* and write the further movements. You, as one of the great larvae, are here to reveal ontogenic transitions as you claim your true identity."

"I'll never go back. This is it. I'm sure."

"We don't need you to go back. We need you to go forward. But forward from the larval state, from a unique place which carries the capacity for real change."

"Let's say I do. Let's say I do go forward." Gregor carried his dishes into the kitchen. "How will that affect others? They're already finished."

"Ah, but society is not finished," Musil objected. "Society, too, is in a larval state. What it needs is a larval model to lead it onward, upward, and out of the corral. With an inspiring model, even human pathology might be turned around—"

"I'll do the dishes," Amadeus interrupted. "Just leave them."

Gregor returned to his seat.

"I thought you said humans were already finished," he said.

"But there are interesting contours to their pathological surface. Have you noticed that human experiences have recently made themselves independent of human beings? Who today can say that his anger is really his own, with so many people butting in and knowing so much more about it? There has arisen a world of experiences without anyone to experience them. It almost looks as though we will no longer experience anything at all privately, and our personal responsibility will dissolve into a system of formulae for potential meanings . . ."

One monkey leaped to the back of Musil's chair.

"Don't feed him."

"Perhaps I should stop talking and eat."

"No. Go on. But watch he doesn't steal the bread."

"Not the sausage?"

"He's from the French Congo. Loves baguettes."

"Where was I?"

"Free-floating experience," Gregor reminded him. "The larval state."

"There are men without qualities, and qualities without men. But people are poised on the edge of becoming possibilitarians, our salvation as a race."

"What is a possibilitarian?" asked Gregor.

"A possibilitarian does not say, for instance: Here this or that has happened, will happen, must happen. He uses his imagination and says: Here such and such might, should, or ought to happen. And if he is told something is the way it is, he thinks: Well, it could probably just as easily be some other way."

"This is our salvation?"

"If no more importance is attached to what is than to what is not, the consequences might be remarkable, wouldn't you say?"

"I would imagine that possibilitarians would get on everyone's nerves, condemning things people admire, and allowing things others con— MAX!" Amadeus yelled peremptorily as the black cat lifted his tail to mark Musil's leg. The beast scampered off, ever innocent, wondering about large, featherless bipeds. Amadeus apologized to his guest.

"I am not a possibilitarian," Gregor murmured.

"Listen to me!" Both Amadeus and Gregor jumped with surprise at Musil's sudden ferocity.

"We can't go on like this. Agreed?" A rhetorical question. He continued without their assent. "You, Herr Larva, are in a position to lead us back to a larval state from which we may rechart our course. You are the larval man of possibility, the unfixed man in all your ambiguity and ambivalence. Your open wound will remind you always of the need to heal, of the necessity to steer us toward a conscious utopia. Your very otherness will allow you to see life as a laboratory, to contemplate the union of opposites we need if we are not to slug out war after war. You, you, my friend, are the answer to Spengler, the catalyst to cure the human world. Get it?"

Musil circled his sausage with his bread, and took his first bite. "Without you, they are all a bunch of sheep!" He chewed disconsolately.

"But God loved sheep," Amadeus observed, "and often compared us with them."

Musil answered with a glance of scorn.

"I admit," Amadeus added, "that their fine expression of exalted consciousness is not unlike the look of stupidity."

Musil kept chewing and took his first swallow of beer.

"Maybe Nature is not all healthy," Gregor mused. "Maybe she is downright mentally disturbed."

"Is that what you think of yourself?" asked Musil.

"I don't know what to think of myself."

A loud banging at the door made Amadeus jump.

"Yes?"

"Telegram."

Amadeus exchanged glances with the others, and opened the door. "Sign here, please. Thank you."

He put the yellow envelope in his jacket pocket.

"Aren't you going to open it?" Gregor asked.

"I'll read it in private."

"We're here to help," said Musil, in an unexpectedly relaxed tone.

"No, I'll . . ."

In a flash, the monkey leaped off Musil's chair, snatched the papers from his master's pocket, and climbed, whooping, to the top of the bookshelf to offer it to his companion. She pulled the message from the envelope and held it out in front of herself, looking as if she were about to do a public reading. Then she stuffed it in her mouth.

"No you don't, Esmerelda!" In a flash, Amadeus rushed up the stepladder and ripped the paper from the beast's mouth.

"Message still intact?" Musil inquired.

"Well salivated, but whole," came the verdict.

"Clearly this was meant for public consumption."

"Herr Musil, you are prying . . ." Amadeus remarked.

"The profession of the writer."

Amadeus perused the telegram, and looked up at his friends. "ACCU-SATIONS OF FRAUD CONCERNING ROACH STOP ROENTGEN ACCEPTS OFFER TO X-RAY NOVEMBER 22 STOP WILL YOU ACCEPT CHALLENGE STOP TAGES-BLATT WIEN"

"What's that all about?" Gregor raised his mouthparts from his beer stein.

"Oh, I didn't want to bother you with it. At your last Tuesday's show, some six-year-old came out saying you were just a man dressed up in an insect suit."

"An inverted Emperor's New Clothes. How hilarious," said Musil, deadpan.

"He was overheard by some reporter, who figured this angle might get him a byline. I told him he was being preposterous."

"The wonders of journalism!" exclaimed Musil. "So now he's convinced his editors to go along with it, and they've paid old man Roentgen to trek down from Munich, lugging his equipment. Anything for science. And profit and fame."

"No, he's not like that. He refused a patent . . . any profit."

"Except," Musil observed cynically, "for free publicity, a battle you know you will win, crowds cheering on their genius. It's a winning hand all around."

"Except for the poor child," Gregor noted.

"We'll honor him as a young scientist, skeptical, as well he should be, of inexplicable phenomena. We'll give him a year's free tickets to Zirkus Schwänze der Hoffnung. What do they call it in America, Gregor? A boo-boo prize?"

Gregor shrugged.

"He'll love it."

"Eleven-fifteen," Musil observed, checking his pocket watch. "Late tram into town stops when?"

"Midnight."

"Well then, gentlemen, it's been a pleasure. I hope I wasn't too abrasive. But I did intend to be forceful. Herr Larva, some have greatness thrust upon them. I'm afraid that you, Gregor—may I call you Gregor?—you've been chosen. You are the possibility of newness. I can write only about how *not* to live, about what I oppose. It's not enough. Goodnight, gentlemen."

"Goodnight."

"Goodnight."

"Oh, did you hear the news today?"

"What news?"

"Eddington announced the results of the eclipse expeditions last May. Einstein's predictions were correct."

And Musil walked out under the blazing sky, Orion now high above, club raised, sword dangling between his legs, the second sword-star a fuzzy haze of glowing, formative gas, pregnant with eons to come: the Great Nebula.

Amadeus pushed on the door. The latch clicked.

*"Ewig, ewig,"* the raven croaked.

## 5. X-RAY: *The* FAUSTIAN ROACH *is not a* HOLLOW MAN

November 22, 1919. At Zirkus Schwänze der Hoffnung, all was festivity and happy end, a demonstration of authenticity in an oft-fraudulent world. The Viennese sky sparkled with an early winter brightness. It was a Saturday morning, and the spirit of Science made the air electric with anticipation. By ten, it seemed as if half the city were at the Zirkus. Most were there because their neighbors were, because the kids demanded it, because it was distracting, inexpensive entertainment. But some were there to appraise the *Tagesblatt*'s charges.

For the Vienna *Tagesblatt*, the event was yet another extravaganza to increase its already considerable circulation: a sideshow created from a sideshow. Vienna could stomach only so much of peace negotiations, balance of payment deficits, and economic indices. Let *Neue Freie Presse* readers marinate themselves in economic and political theory, the *Tagesblatt* would snag the others with more pressing concerns—like whether they were being defrauded at a local circus by a man in a cockroach suit.

The possibility of exposing a successful fraud was just the meat the *Tagesblatt* loved to chew, and they pursued it vigorously, with pictures of Gregor on the front page, Inquiring Photographer interviews with People on the Street (evenly split in their opinions), a long, "scholarly" piece on the history of Roentgen and his X-ray, and an artist's conception of how Gregor might look on the screen, should he be operated by a hidden man. Amadeus could not have bought such publicity for any fee. It was, as they say now, a win-win situation, and, as he knew the result, Amadeus was not above exploiting it for his own ends. ZIRKUS ATTACKED! WITNESS THE TRUTH FOR YOURSELVES—22/10, 10h!—SUPPORT YOUR LOCAL ARTISTS—22/10, 10h! EXPOSE THE FALSE ACCUSERS!—22/10, 10h!—FOR TRUTHFULNESS IN JOURNALISM!—22/10, 10h!

Huge painted signs circled the lot on all sides during the preceding week. Gregor would have none of this, of course. He refused all interviews and patiently put up with occasional taunts from that week's audiences. Let Amadeus have his fun; for Gregor, this was just one more lens on the late Faustian world.

Early on Saturday, Amadeus gathered his crew for a briefing. Was it all right with them to have the day off—with pay, of course, and with an equal division of the box? Cheers. Would they mind sitting on stage as witnesses, or perhaps offering themselves as demonstrations of the wonders of Roentgen Rays? Apexia wanted to know if the rays were dangerous for pinheads. Great laughter and applause. She was assured otherwise. Serpentina had a serious concern about her career. She had billed herself as "The Girl Without Bones," and what if it turned out she had some? She didn't *feel* as if she had bones, and she twisted her arm as if to demonstrate. But what if there really were bones in there, peculiar bones, perhaps ("Funnybones!" yelled out Leo Kongee, "The Man with No Nerves"), but bones, nevertheless? Would she have to change her name or her act? The meeting agreed she would be wisest to avoid Roentgen's machine. In any case, Gregor was the main event. The crew returned excitedly to quarters to get dressed in their Sunday best—no circus silks and spangles, but in the serious street clothing of serious citizens, as if for jury duty on a crucial case.

Amadeus expected Roentgen at ten, and what with setup and introductory activity, imagined that the big event would occur somewhat before noon. He had been given to understand that a demonstration would require complete darkness and a fairly constant electrical source, so all the wagons were removed to the periphery of the lot to make room for the huge canvas touring tent. The seams were stuffed with straw wherever they leaked light, and the walls were staked all around. Outside the tent, two of the strongest and most faithful horses were harnessed to a generator via a twenty-foot pole. When they trotted in a circle, which they were trained to do, they would generate a 60- to 80-volt current at 5 amps. Wires from the generator led to the small stage at one end of the tent. It was not entirely clear how Roentgen would be coming, or what he would be bringing with him, but Amadeus felt he had held up his end of the admittedly sketchy plan. He had images of Roentgen pushing heavy pieces of delicate equipment through the streets, or arriving with a crew from the railroad, unloading shipping crates of gear.

How surprised he was when, at ten minutes to ten, a fine Mercedes van arrived at the lot, and an old man in a black frock coat and cylinder hat descended, with help from his driver, from the passenger side. On the truck was written SIEMENS GMBH, ELECTRICAL AND X-RAY EQUIPMENT. Yes, of course! Why hadn't Amadeus realized? A medical X-ray van from the military. A complete unit, generating its own electricity. Better than horses by far.

There were introductions all around: Roentgen had been driven over from Munich by Professor Willy Wien, his younger colleague at the Physical Science Institute, and winner, by the way, of the 1911 Nobel prize for his work on black body radiation. With them was Arnold Sommerfeld, Wien's graduate student, later, of course, world famous for his atomic model, the first to explain the fine structure of spectral lines, but here today because of his strong back and laughing spirit.

Amadeus introduced himself and his contingent: here to help carry were 650 pounds of Anton Tomzak, emcee for the event, and George Keiffer, the jolly pink giant, who announced that if he could lift a horse, he could certainly lift the X-ray equipment without hurting his back.

But not much lifting, shoving, or even intelligence was necessary. The Siemens engineers and Mercedes designers had thought of everything: a rolling unit of Coolidge tube, shielding, generator, and induction coil lowered pneumatically to the ground, as did an excellent wheeled unit with seat, baffle, and adjustable barium platinocyanide screen. A child could have rolled them from the truck, though George was useful in pushing them up the ramp to the stage. From an elaborate panel in the rear of the van ran wiring to the equipment. The setup, running off the engine, could deliver a steady 30 amps at 150 volts.

On a dark November afternoon twenty-four years earlier, a younger Wilhelm Conrad Roentgen had been playing in his laboratory at the Physical Institute of the University of Würzburg. Along with many others, he was exploring the properties of the newly discovered cathode rays—streams of energy that emanated from excited wires in semi-vacuum tubes. Bendable by magnetic fields, they seemed to be made up of electrons jumping off the metal, penetrating through glass and a few centimeters through the air.

On the afternoon of November 8, 1895, the slim, elegant, bearded professor had placed such a tube in a light-tight, black cardboard box, to contain its glow and better concentrate its energy and visual effects. When he activated the current, he noticed a faint purple-green glow in the pitch darkness of the room. Thinking there might be a leak, he turned on the lights and checked the integrity of the box. Satisfied it was light-proof, he darkened the room again and flipped the switch. Again the glow, on a paper screen covered with barium platinocyanide, a material that fluoresces when struck by various energy sources. What was exciting such fluorescence? Could it be the cathode rays? But the paper was several feet away from the tube, much farther than cathode rays were able to travel through air. He couldn't move the glow with a powerful magnet, so the rays were not made up of charged particles. What was going on? He didn't come home for supper.

The next weeks were spent exploring the properties of this odd radiation. He found the rays could create fluorescence up to six feet away. And most unsettling of all, he found they penetrated most opaque material. He knew they penetrated black cardboard. He tried to block them with a deck of cards. He placed a thousand-page physics text between the tube and the screen. It was as if the book were not there—merely a weak shadow. The rays went through a wooden plank, and various thicknesses of aluminum. He finally discovered something that would stop them: lead. They could not penetrate even a thin sheet.

Then came the moment that changed the history of the world. Roentgen was fairly sure that he was dealing with a particle stream: it seemed to travel in a straight line and cast a sharp, regular shadow around the lead sheet. To further examine the nature of the shadow, he held a small, lead disk carefully between his index finger and thumb, positioned between the Crooks tube and the fluorescent screen. To his amazement, he saw not only the sharp shadow of the disk, but also the distinct outline of the bones of his hand. He shut off the current.

Roentgen was—as we would say now—spooked. It was a horrifying sight to this somewhat straitlaced man, his own skeleton encased in living flesh, a sight never seen except under traumatic or surgical conditions. Accompanying his sense of awe were grave doubts about what it might mean for his career, should he tell the world. He could be snared in controversy, ostracized from the world of respectable physics, all of his previous work discredited.

But scientist that he was, he continued—in strictest privacy, keeping all his observations secret. He photographed a box of lead weights: the weights were visible right through the wood. He made studies of his wife's hand: the gold wedding ring hung eerily around the bone.

Finally, convinced that he had reproducible results, he submitted his researches to the *Physical-Medical Society Journal* for publication. The paper, "A New Kind of Ray, by Dr. W. Roentgen," was a model of clarity and humility. Buried in the text, almost as an aside, is the single sentence, "If one holds a hand between the discharge apparatus and the screen, one sees the darker shadow of the bones within the slightly fainter shadow image of the hand itself." Such is the stuff of discovery.

Within a few minutes, a state-of-the-art radiology unit had been set up on a wooden stage in a canvas tent on an empty lot in a northern Viennese suburb on a splendorous winter morning of November 1919. The *Zirkus* crew was assembled earlier than expected, with Gregor still backstage. Reporters and photographers from all the local papers and several from Germany were given privileged seating in the first row. Only Emil Kahn, the child who had started it all, was missing. A late arrival, unexpected, but warmly welcomed by Amadeus, was H. V. Kaltenborn, European correspondent for *The Brooklyn Eagle,* a future pioneer in radio news, whose broadcast commentaries would play so large a part in Gregor's destiny.

At eleven o'clock, Emil arrived with his parents and took his place at the center of the crowded stage. Gregor and Roentgen were still outside in back, Tomzak was out front, barking the crowd, and Amadeus was scurrying back and forth—ushering, helping to seat people, making accommodations for the old and disabled. Onstage, what an array was to be seen! Sitting properly, even formally, was a group that reflected Mother Nature's wildest, most radical fantasies. So great was the press of irregularity that the normal-looking trio of Emil, Greta, and Karl Kahn seemed almost deformed, odd in the extreme. Farthest stage right sat Katerina Eckhardt, looking elegant, her second body concealed under a long, dark skirt. Propped next to her, on high chairs, Clarissa and Inge Leinsdorf, staring stiffly out, not knowing exactly what to do, and next to them Gerda Schloß, "The Ugly Lady," straining at the leash of propriety, occasionally calling out lewdly to selected audience members. Lying on the floor in front of the high chairs, on a blue cushion, was the other Emil, "The Hunger Artist," now in his 204th day of fast, close to death. Toward the center of the stage were Josef/Josefina and Leo Kongee, "The Man with No Nerves," without his pins and spikes, looking, for all the world, like your next-door neighbor—if your next-door neighbor looked a little strange. Child Emil and his family were in the center, and to their left, Glotzaügiger Otto, popeyed, but not frighteningly so. To his left, symmetrical with the Hunger Artist, the rather more perky Serpentina, who had resolved not to be X-rayed. Filling out stage left were the often-together trio of Dog-Faced Boy, Alligator-Skinned Man, and Monkey Girl. Behind the seated row, Herr Rauchenrücken supported the upended coffin of Fu Hsi, the "undead" Chinaman, while George Keiffer, the giant, stood next to the case of "The Giant Moleperson," who peered out from a cleared space behind his glass wall. Owning no more formal clothing than his swimsuit, he had chosen, for this event, to show only his face. Seated on the floor, in front of the Kahns, were Godina and Apexia, "The Pinhead Sisters," holding the Blumenfeldlichten as best they could.

At 11:15, Anton Tomzak made a grand entrance down the center aisle, lifted his huge weight up the two steps to the stage, and addressed the crowd in his delightful stentorian voice.

"*Meine Damen und Herren, Mesdames et Messieurs, Signore e Signori, Pani i Pane,* Ladies and Gentlemen!"

He was emphasizing the purportedly world-shaking nature of the event, though there were likely no French or Italian speakers in the crowd, and only one English speaker, Kaltenborn, who also spoke German. Czech, perhaps. But Tomzak liked the feel of the foreign words on his tongue.

"I'm sure most of you know what this is all about. It's been in the papers, and on our end, we have leafleted the local community. But somehow the news has gotten farther than our little Viennese circle. I'm told we have journalists from as far away as Munich."

"Brooklyn, New York," shouted Kaltenborn in his soon-to-be-famous voice.

Spontaneous applause swept the audience, though why an "enemy" reporter should be cheered was not quite clear. Perhaps they felt they should applaud his coming so far.

"Because there may be some of you who merely wandered in, or were swept in by the crush of the crowd, I'd like to introduce the little man who started it all, Emil Kahn."

More applause.

"Emil will tell us exactly what happened. Emil?"

The little boy walked to the front of the stage. He'd not been warned he was to speak, but he was not shy, being raised by parents who thought his every word a treasure, and who applauded his every performance. He wore short pants and kneesocks, though it was November, and a blue blazer embroidered with the double-headed eagle of the former Austro-Hungarian Empire.

"Well, I was just looking at the big cockroach, and even though he was standing on his skinny legs, I thought maybe there was room for a little man inside who might pull levers or something and talk out the mouth—"

Tomzak jumped in.

"I'm sure you're not the only one who has thought that way, Emil. In fact"—here he was pandering wildly to building dramatic tension—"there are several of us right here in the circus, the cockroach's fellow artists, who have had similar thoughts. How many of you up on stage have had such suspicions?"

Only Gerda Schloß raised her hand.

"It's hard to say bad things in public about your friends," Tomzak confided in the audience, "but I can assure you, I have heard people among us say so. And you out there—how many of you have seen Gregor's shows at the Zirkus Schwänze der Hoffnung? Stand up." Fully two thirds of the seated audience rose from their folding chairs.

"Now . . . stay standing . . . of those who have seen Gregor, how many think he may be a man in a cockroach suit? You stay standing, the others sit down."

Most of the standees sank back into their chairs, leaving a dozen mostly professor-looking types on their feet. Tomzak was prepared for any survey result.

"See how many of you he may have taken in! If he is a fake, a fraud, as Emil suggests, how many of you have had the wool pulled over your eyes! What does this say for the future of our country? What does this say about the effects of our cultural inheritance, here in the city of Mozart, Beethoven, Schönberg?

"Well, *meine Damen und Herren*, this little child's suspicions—you may sit down, Emil—may shine some light on the critical problem of authenticity in our postwar world. But a strange light it is that will be needed to solve the question. And here to tell you about it, all the way from Munich, courtesy of the Vienna *Tagesblatt*, the Siemens Corporation, and Mercedes-Benz, is the inventor of this strange light, the very first recipient of the Nobel prize in physics, *meine Damen und Herren*, we are pleased and honored to have with us today, the very great professor of physical science at the University of Munich, the unique, the incredible, Herr Doktor Professor Wilhelm . . . Conrad . . . Roentgen! Give him a big hand, *meine Dam—*"

The audience was on its feet, cheering and stamping and whistling.

"Professor Roentgen, Professor, you can come out now . . ."

A tall, somewhat stooped, seventy-four-year-old man walked sprightly from the stage-right wings.

"Professor Roentgen, would you care to explain your apparatus to those in the audience who have never experienced Roentgen or X-rays?"

He pronounced the "X" as if it were a word of holy power. How surprising then, the humble voice of the Nobel laureate:

"*Meine Damen und Herren*, it is a great pl—"

"Louder," prompted several at the back of the tent.

"*Meine Damen und Herren*, it is a great pleasure for me to—"

"Louder," the voices urged, more loudly.

At this point, Amadeus walked onstage lugging a different box, a heavy one, trailing a wire to the Mercedes. It was an amplifier and loud-speaker, one of the first in Vienna. From his bulging jacket pocket, he pulled a large microphone, uncoiled the wire, plugged it into the black box, and handed Roentgen the microphone. Roentgen accepted it naturally, with a grateful bow. Again the crowd cheered, for the resilient professor, for Amadeus saving the show, for the wonders of technology.

Roentgen spoke with assurance into the microphone. "May we have the machine, please?"

Leaving his post at the Giant Moleperson's case, George Keiffer joined Anton Tomzak in wheeling the fluoroscope onstage. It came out from stage right in profile, and they turned it 90 degrees, up and down stage, to face the audience.

"Thank you so much. Before I continue, a word: I am not the inventor of Roentgen rays, as our master of ceremonies too generously announced. I did discover them—by accident, I may add, and it took me a while to even believe in my own discovery. God was the inventor."

There was no applause for God.

"The electricity generated by our marvelous truck outside comes in this wire here, and heats the filament on this end. The electrons shooting off the heated filament bombard this target here—tungsten—and the tungsten emits the radiation. By aiming the tube appropriately, we can direct a stream of X-rays at any target."

"Is everybody following?" Tomzak asked the crowd.

Reassuring nods and mumbles. Roentgen continued.

"We will direct these rays at this fluorescent plate over here." And he spun the chair assembly around so that the audience could see the twelve-by-eighteen-inch glass plates in a lead frame.

"Between these two pieces of glass"—he tapped either side—"there is barium platinocyanide, the same material that I found glowing in my laboratory twenty-four years ago. When hit by X-rays it will give off a greenish-purple light."

More murmurs. A little child started to cry and was shortly removed. Swinging the screen/chair assembly back around to profile, Roentgen continued.

"Now, if we place an object between the tube and the screen, the rays will either pass through the object, or they will not."

"What about the cockroach?" yelled out a child in the second row.

"Patience, patience," Tomzak cautioned.

"All right," the professor acquiesced, "you may turn out the lights."

The tent was pitch black. Flicking the switch in his right hand, Roentgen set the Coolidge tube firing, and the screen glowed with eerie phosphorescence.

"Now let me show you the same thing I saw years ago when I held a small piece of lead in front of the screen to test its shadow."

Roentgen pulled from his pocket a circular lead disc the size of a mark and held it with his left hand between source and screen. No murmurs now, but a definite collective gasp! A skeleton of a hand, a marriage band loosely circling its fourth finger, came close to holding a mark-sized black circle. The deathly apparition began to wiggle its fingers, and a second skeleton hand entered the shadow to make what many would swear was the head of a horned and bearded devil.

"Lights, please."

Roentgen turned off the rays. The audience's eyes adjusted.

"The image you saw was quite clearer than the one I saw twenty-four years ago. The exigencies of three wars have perfected our technology. You can imagine how much easier it is for a surgeon using this equipment to extract a bullet from a wound, or set a bone correctly. If you haven't already seen it, you may afterward inspect the marvelous portable X-ray wagon developed by Siemens and Mercedes-Benz. It is out behind the tent here on my right."

"And now"–Tomzak stepped forward–"before the main event, the decisive testing of the charge of fraudulence, let's just see what this machine can do with the human form. Who in the audience wants to be a subject?"

No one came forward.

"All right, then, how about our company onstage? Which of you would like to be a guinea pig?"

"Me! Me!" squealed Godina. "Look at my pin-skull, look at my pin-skull!"

Roentgen sat Godina sideways in the chair between the Coolidge tube and the screen.

"If she screams you'll stop immediately?" inquired Tomzak with exaggerated concern.

"She won't feel a thing. Lights, please."

In the darkness, Roentgen switched on the rays, and an image of a tiny skull with a largish jaw and tapering crown flashed on the screen.

"Move your mouth."

And the skull performed a grotesque biting motion, like a strange, carved puppet. The audience laughed. Then it was silent.

"Lights, please."

Tomzak once again took center stage. "Has everyone seen enough to believe that if Herr Samsa were in reality a man dressed up in an ingenious cockroach suit, Professor Roentgen's rays would see through his imposture?"

No response.

"Good. Then we're ready for the main event, the Trial by Radiation. *Meine Damen und Herren,* let me now introduce to you the center of the controversy, a being many of you are familiar with, a being whose being has raised some concern. You know who I'm talking about, our very own 'Visitor from the Early Carboniferous,' Herr Gregor Samsa!"

Was the crowd tired? Were they simply holding off approbation until the charges were proved or disproved? Was all this becoming too much for them? Whatever the reason, the applause was thin as Gregor walked onstage, on all sixes, dressed in a new bathing suit in a style made popular by Harry Houdini.

Tomzak inquired, "Herr Samsa, is there anything you'd like to say before we begin?"

He spoke to the professor. "This is a remarkable piece of apparatus. Science is very wonderful, don't you think?"

"I do, I do," said Roentgen. "As for the machine, I am hardly responsible for its technical excellence."

"May I ask a question?" H. V. Kaltenborn raised his hand from the front row.

Tomzak replied, "Our American friend steps in where angels fear to tread. Certainly. Go ahead."

"Where is Herr Hoffnung in all this? Surely he has something to say."

Amadeus stepped out from the wings.

"I can say only that I am looking forward to the results of the investigation. I have complete faith in my gifted colleague, Herr Samsa, and complete trust in Professor Roentgen to interpret the results. I hope, Herr Kaltenborn, you will report this event in your own country. And may the truth come to light."

"Professor, will you proceed?"

The chair of the previous demonstrations was replaced by a modular tilt-table, which was set perpendicular to the floor. Gregor crawled up against the table to his full height of five feet, ten inches, and Tomzak strapped him on the tabletop to take the weight off his hind legs. His moist wound stained the tank top.

"Are you ready?" asked Tomzak.

"Yes," said Gregor.

"And you, Professor?"

"Ready."

"Lights, please."

Roentgen allowed the tent to remain black until the audience's eyes attained maximum sensitivity. Then he threw the switch. The screen revealed a twelve-by-eighteen-inch section of Gregor's abdomen. Those who doubted stared with mere curiosity. But those who already knew had a more complex response. As even an innocent person will send polygraph needles flickering when asked a key question, so these individuals in the know—including Amadeus and Gregor himself—experienced an irrational moment of fear. What if it *was* a hoax? What if *I* am a hoax? Such doubts are of short duration, but great depth, rising up out of one's *ontos* itself. What if knowledge is unreal? What if existence itself is a sham, a universal illusion?

"Emil," asked Tomzak, "would you describe what you see?"

Emil crawled carefully around to the front of the stage.

"I see a bug. An empty bug. With some guts in there, and what's that? Is that your heart all the way down there in your back? It's beating. Is that your heart?"

Gregor was silent.

"Is there anyone else who wants to comment?"

A voice from the back: "Move the screen up and down, so we can see all of him."

Roentgen slid the screen along its track, while Tomzak adjusted the beam to follow. All of Gregor was examined.

"Are there further requests or questions?"

Dead silence in the purple-green blackness.

"Lights, please," called Roentgen. And he switched off the beam.

It took a few minutes before the spectators made their way outside, shielding their eyes against the blinding sunlight. On the way out, one little girl was heard to say, "Maybe he wrapped his bones in something so you couldn't see them."

But no reporter picked it up.

H. V. Kaltenborn went home. It is interesting to note that "home" would still not tolerate his name—Hans von Kaltenborn. Though born and raised in Minnesota, he was still a potential victim of the deep American hatred of all things German. At least he wasn't black. Or Oriental. Or Jewish.

He reported his experience at the *Zirkus* in a two-part article for the *Eagle,* the first dealing with the test event, the second with the phenomenon of Gregor himself. The articles drew a bit of attention, some from the newly emerging public relations industry, and some from professors, including a long query from Sir Julian Huxley concerning Gregor's behavior, a letter he would keep as one of his treasures. But it wasn't until Kaltenborn's Third of July broadcast in '22 that American interest in Gregor took off. And take off it did! We don't know who was listening, or who initiated the idea, but within a month of the program, "the Gregor" was beginning to give the Charleston competition as the hottest dance craze, with its attendant music, consumer spin-offs, and advertising tie-ins. It may have begun as just another dance, but it soon began to take on the social and political overtones of an early ecological, collectivist movement.

The Charleston was a dance of mad individualism, flappers flapping, each dancer dancing basically alone. In contrast, the Gregor developed as a team dance, attracting the left-wing communitarians who nevertheless wanted to have fun after Study Group. Upper-class flapping vs. the Salt of the Earth, men and women committed to proletarian purposes, dressing down, if necessary, to further contrast the choreographies, embracing and glorifying the lowest of the low—for what could be lower than a roach?

All of which led American Cyanamide, in a brilliant preemptive move, to sponsor a series of dance contests specifically focused on the Gregor, and for all the political sophistication of the young Old Left, many dancers bought into it—to the scorn and dismay of more savvy comrades.

By the fall of 1922, the National Association of Gregor Dancers and Coaches was in place, and local contests coalesced into regional ones, with winners demanding a national Gregor "Olympics," to be held at

Madison Square Garden. Because of the underlying leftist thrust, the grand prize was to be split—half for the winning team, and half for Gregor himself, in the form of a first-class round-trip on the *Mauretania,* to the good old USA. They would have their hero to behold.

He, of course, was not consulted, so great was the dancers' zeal. In fact, he knew nothing about it. While teams were competing on Thirty-ninth Street from noon to six, Gregor, seven hours ahead, was having a simple dinner alone in his wagon, reading *A Midsummer Night's Dream* (in English!), and when the winning group was crowned at nine, he was halfway through a night of peaceful sleep. His dreams did not predict the next day's telegram, informing him of the contest and its results, instructing him to apply for a travel visa and to pick up his ticket at Cook's Travel on the Ringstrasse. Enthusiastic American presumptuousness. It has its not-so-charming side.

The reader may be interested in the performance of the winning team. This, a clipping from the New York *Daily News.*

### LONE STAR STATE SHINES IN BUG EVENT

Associated Press—The Brownsville Blattae, three energetic dancers from southern Texas, squeezed out the Petaluma Periplanets 43–41 to take the gold at the First Annual Gregor Olympics last night, here at Madison Square Garden. The event, sponsored by American Cyanamide, and emceed by H. V. Kaltenborn, was host to the semi-finalist winners of five regions across the country, the winners from a field of 375 teams, each sponsored by local business. The magnificent Cyanamide prize was $10,000, to be split equally between the team and Gregor S., the human roach, to support his fan-club tour of the U.S.

Points were given for the most ingenious and technically accomplished dance steps imitating roach behavior. Basic locomotion, which all teams must master, is difficult enough. Cockroaches, as insects, have six legs. Three are always on the ground, providing the bug with a constantly stable triangle. With speed, coordination is almost unworkable. The initial event of the Olympics is a 100-yard sprint, with negative points awarded for gait infractions. After that, teams are on their own to evoke, as beautifully as possible, the spirit of their model.

Upon being awarded the Golden Roach, Carol Braun, thorax and team captain, said, "For Duane and Alan and me, this is the greatest moment of our lives." Alan Torney, abdomen, said, "I just want to say a big thank you to Gregor for making all this possible. We'll see ya soon." Duane Babbit, head, nursing a facial abrasion, declined to be interviewed.

The event's corporate sponsor, American Cyanamide, is the manufacturer of Raid, a popular roach killer.

Telegram in hand, Gregor was perplexed. America. He could become fluent in English. He could get to know a culture that imagined the Fourteen Points—open covenants, freedom of the seas, arms reduction, marvelous! But he had his niche here. He was accepted. Still, he didn't have a terrific act at the moment—people were getting tired of "Thinking Together About Einstein." If he stayed, he'd have to find something else. But here he had friends. It might be even more lonely in America. But then he wouldn't have to stay. He'd be treated like a king, probably, then maybe he'd do a little traveling. One thing he was sure of: he wouldn't do any ads for American Cyanamide.

But what about the quest?

Gregor looked at the telegram again and became so confused and frustrated, he did something very unusual: he ate it.

"Herr W., Herr W., here he is!"

"Herr W., Elli, Epi, c'mere!"

Four blond, blue-eyed urchins came charging up to Gregor's cage to join their friends as he was taking the sun on a warm April morning. Behind them strolled a thin, sandy-haired man in a green cardigan.

"And how do you know he is a he, Herr Schiferl?" the man asked.

The children studied Gregor for a moment, who turned his amused attention on the conundrum.

"Because he doesn't have long hair," said Alois Schiferl.

"Because he's supposed to be smart," said Fritz Heer, for which he received a smart knuckle on the side of his head.

"Hey! Why don't you ever hit the girls?"

"Their heads are too soft. I pull their hair."

"I think he's a he because he's wearing a man's jacket," Elli Rolf offered.

"Is he a man, then, a human?" Herr W. asked.

"Maybe he's a puppet like the other ones, but bigger." Epi Schlüsselberger always had strong opinions.

"Like what other ones?" Gregor asked.

"He talks!" Karl Gasser shouted.

"Of course I talk. What other puppets? We don't have a puppet show."

"Oh, yes you do."

"Right down there; over by the fat lady."

"And the lady without bones."

Herr W. interrupted. "Forgive me, Herr Gregor, is it? My name is Ludwig Wittgenstein. I teach at the elementary school at Puchberg-am-Schneeberg."

"Oh, I'm honored! I—"

Wittgenstein cut him off, signaling something about the children.

"Where is that—Puchberg-am . . . ?" asked Gregor, chastised but confused.

"About forty kilometers west."

"Ah."

"My class was reading about you in Current Events, and they wanted to see you in person."

"Yes," Eugenie chimed in, "and only six of us could go, three and three, and we drew lots out of Herr W.'s cap—"

"And *we* won."

"May I introduce these traveling scholars?"

"It would be a pleasure."

"Alois Schiferl, Fritz Heer, Karl Gasser."

The boys clicked their heels and nodded their close-cropped heads.

"And Eugenie Pippal, Elli Rolf, and Epi Schlüsselberger."

The girls curtsied. Epi pushed her braid back out of her face. "Can we ask you questions?" she inquired boldly.

"You can ask all you want—if I get to ask one first."

They all agreed.

"I already asked it. What was the puppet show? I didn't think we had one."

"Punch the *Jude*." Two or three answered together.

"You mean Punch and Judy?" asked Gregor.

"No. Punch the *Jude*. You give him a punch. Herr W. says that means *Stoß* in English."

"With your fist."

"Ah, I see. *Faust,* too. So who was the Jude?"

"He was a Jew, and he had a big nose, and he wore a black gown and a black little hat."

"And he wanted to kill a little baby."

"Was it his baby?"

"No, his wife brought it to him. She was taking care of it."

"Why did he want to kill it?"

"He wanted to grind it up into flour to make . . . to make . . ."

"Matzohs," Epi coached.

"Matzohs," Fritz acknowledged. "It's a kind of bread Jews eat."

"It wasn't for flour," Epi said, "it was for the blood to make the dough. Jews need the blood of Christian children to make special matzohs for their holidays."

"Oh, that's right. It was for the blood."

"So did he kill the baby?" Gregor asked.

"He tried and tried. But the man doing the show came out and said that if we would punch him really hard, and get him to drop the baby, we might be able to rescue it."

"And what happened?"

"Well, different people tried to punch him and get him to drop the baby, but he ran all over the stage, and he was hard to catch 'cause it was so high up."

"And then, he called for his friend the Devil, and the Devil came and tried to protect him, and he pushed away everybody's hands."

"And his wife helped, too. She was pushing away everybody's hands."

"But then a big, fat kid pushed them all aside, and he punched the Jude right in the face, and he dropped the baby, and the kid grabbed it, and everybody cheered, and the man came out again, and he said about how Jews were trying to hurt us—"

"How we needed to protect our country . . ."

The children quieted down. Gregor was astounded.

"I need to see this for myself." He began to open the door to his cage.

"Oh, he's not there anymore. He just let the stage down and left."

"What do you mean, 'let the stage down'?"

"It was like he was wearing a big skirt. He would lift his skirt up over his head, and that would be the stage, and the puppets would come up over the top of the skirt."

"Ingenious. And then he just ran away?"

"Somebody told him to stop."

"A tiny little man with a squeaky voice and a huge fat man."

"They were from the circus," said Herr W. "They asked who gave him permission to do the show."

"What did he say?"

"He actually threatened them. He didn't give his name, but he said they'd be hearing from him and his friends. And he walked off, holding his skirt up out of the mud. I trust you will hear more from him."

"Aren't you Jewish, Herr Wittgenstein?"

"My parents were, until they weren't. How do you know?"

"You're Jewish, Herr W.?" Epi Schlüsselberger of the sharp ears.

Wittgenstein shushed her and walked a few paces away from the kids. Gregor followed him behind his bars.

"I just finished your book," he said softly. "If you can ever be finished with such a book. And I asked Meister Hoffnung about you."

"But it hasn't appeared yet."

"*Annalen der Naturphilosophie*, 1922. 'The world is all that is the case.' Ludwig Wittgenstein."

"You've got it memorized?"

"A striking opening sentence."

"Where did you come up with the *Annalen?*"

"That little man with the squeaky voice subscribes. He gave me his. He thought I might be interested."

"And were you?"

"I study a little of it every night."

Epi Schlüsselberger wasn't about to let go: "Are you a Jew? Herr W., are you a Jew? You didn't tell us you were a Jew."

"*Kleine Damen und Herren,* we are here today to discuss a tremendously difficult problem, one that more than ever engages—and eludes—the greatest minds of our time."

"What is it?" Elli Rolf was all ears.

"What does it mean to say something—or someone—is human?"

Ten minutes ago, the children would have laughed at the stupidity of such a question. But here, in Gregor's presence, laughter was not so easy.

"A human looks like a human," offered Alois.

"Remember those two who kicked out the puppeteer? Did they look alike? The tiny guy and the big fat man?"

"But they sort of do. They both have two arms and two legs. And a head."

"What about the woman with no arms and no legs? Is she human?"

"Yes," the children admitted.

"How do you know?"

"'Cause she talks."

"What if she didn't talk?"

Gregor joined the discussion. "I talk. And I read books, and I walk around, and I eat lunch. Am I human?"

"No." The children all agreed.

"Why not?" asked Herr W.

"'Cause you have bug eyes and six legs."

"So?" asked Gregor. "Did you see Katerina Eckhardt? No? Go see her. She has six legs. And Otto can pop his eyes right out of his head. Can you?"

The children were getting uneasy. What could be so hard about this question? Wittgenstein was reveling in his Socratic element. "How do you know Herr Samsa isn't a puppet?"

"'Cause nobody is working him. And the newspaper said there was no one inside."

"The X-rays." Karl Gasser was a good student. "Don't you remember?"

"Indeed I do," said Herr W. "And how do you know he's not some kind of marvelous machine that can move around and talk like a radio?"

"But there are people talking that make the radio talk."

"How can you tell that isn't the case with Herr Samsa?"

Gregor was charmed by the intensity of the children's struggle.

"Maybe," said Elli, "it has to do with how people—well, you know, be-ings, I mean people-like beings—act. Maybe it isn't what you look like or how you are made, maybe it's how you act."

"How do humans act?" asked Herr W., gently pursuing his checkmate.

"They say hello, they're nice . . ."

"We are made in God's image." Alois at catechism.

"My father isn't nice—especially when he's drunk. He hits me with his belt." Thus Fritz.

"Jews kill babies and grind them up for blood," Epi reminded them. "And they drop bombs on us."

"Do *you* do that?" asked Gregor.

"We don't have bombs," Alois admitted.

"But are you mean and cruel?"

"Sometimes," admitted Eugenie.

"I am. Especially to my little brother." Alois at confession.

"So," said Herr W. "You think the essence of human is to be mean and cruel?"

No one agreed. On the other hand, no one disagreed.

"Is Herr Samsa mean?"

"No."

"Does that mean he's not human?"

"No."

"If he's not not-human, is he human?"

Silence.

"Why don't we ask him what he thinks?" Fritz Heer, the social scientist.

"Yeah, he ought to know."

"Are you human?" asked Epi.

"I'm Jewish," said Gregor.

The children, all but one, burst out laughing. "A cockroach can't be Jewish!"

Epi: "Why not? Jews are vermin, right, and isn't a cockroach vermin?" Her formal logic was impeccable.

Gregor and Wittgenstein exchanged complex glances.

Herr W. took control. "Excuse us, Herr Samsa. The syllogisms seem to be getting a little out of hand. I think we need a bit more induction. I'll be back in a minute." To the children: "Let's go see more of the circus. Let's see the lady with six legs, and we can talk more about this question. Come, *Kinder.* Let's let Herr Samsa relax before his first show."

And off they went.

The lot was filling up with rowdiness. From where he stood, Gregor thought he *could* see a puppeteer just off the circus grounds, gathering a crowd.

Relaxation was out of the question. In the course of ten minutes, Gregor had gone from easy amusement to near despair. He knew Wittgenstein was just trying to get the children to think and reason, perhaps even, as in his book, to get them to understand there are some things that resist thinking, reasoning, and discussion. The notion that there was a fixed, definable, human nature had gone out with the Renaissance, when radicals, Gregor recalled, proclaimed the essence of man's nature to be *no* nature, no fixed human nature.

But if human character is infinitely plastic, he worried, what is to stop these children from being entirely formed by the resentments of their elders? He carried one such wound in his own back, unhealing, a permanent crater in his soul. If Jews killed Christ, why not babies, and won't revenge be sweet? *Teufellogik.* Building history from venomous scares and the scars of the woodshed.

Ten minutes until the first show. Einstein. Not for today, that ebullient, funny, optimistic man. What was pounding in his ganglia was the verse he'd studied yesterday for English, a new poem by Robert Frost, just published, and newly presented to him by Amadeus, the seductive schoolmarm.

> *Some say the world will end in fire,*
> *Some say in ice.*
> *From what I've tasted of desire*
> *I hold with those who favor fire.*
> *But if it had to perish twice,*
> *I think I know enough of hate*
> *To say that for destruction ice*
> *Is also great*
> *And would suffice.*

If it *had* to perish? Twice? Why this inexorable need for destruction, for self-destruction? Why . . . ?

"Herr Samsa . . ." A stage whisper.

Gregor spun around to the back left corner of his cage to see Wittgenstein clinging to the bars like some prisoner of the world outside.

"The children are safely climbing the fat man. There's just one quick thing I want to suggest—that answers usually show up as questions."

"You think I am looking for answers?"

"Yes. What are your questions?"

Gregor pondered while the crowd gathered behind him, and his upstage interlocutor explored the iridescence of his eyes.

"I have only one question," said Gregor. "Why are humans more bestial than beasts?" Wittgenstein waited. "Rilke says it's because they're always outside, looking in."

"And you, Herr *Unhumanisch?*"

"Jew human. Gregor Jew. Therefore, Gregor human."

"I believe the predicate object was 'vermin.'"

"Vermin. Human. What's the difference?"

"That is the question, isn't it?"

The audience was gathering. From the floor of the cage he watched them assemble, glaring at chest level, trying to see into the hearts of the adults, into the skulls of the children. He saw them as Roentgen might have seen them, a greatsmall shuffling of pulsing, shadowy interiors. He glared and he stared. His many eyes roamed the crowd, trying to recognize something, somebody. Nothing. Nobody.

"Perhaps we talk later? After the children are to bed?"

Wittgenstein saluted, and backed away into the gathering crowd.

Gregor looked at the clock, walked slowly over to the lectern, raised himself up, and gripped the top with his front claws. He looked for a long time out into the audience—and said nothing. The crowd waited. A child said, "Mommy, when is it going to talk?" and everyone laughed. And they waited again. Gregor scanned the room. Is he sick? What is this? A few people at the back began to leave. Then—very slowly—he said his poem, lowered himself to the ground, and crawled back into his private space.

> *He dreamed Epi was all alone*
> *Her parents were away from home*
> *And so she danced throughout the room*
> *A polonaise with ihrem broom*
> *When suddenly she saw before her*
> *A box of matches to make Feuer.*
> *"Oh marvelous, oh boy, oh boy,*
> *A match will make a schönes toy*
> *I'll light it right upon my shoe*
> *As oft I've seen my mother do."*

*And Fritz und Franz, the insects,*
*They waved at her their six legs*
*And both of them emotin'*
*"Your Vater hat's verboten*
*Oh no, no, no, oh can't you see,*
*Don't touch—you'll burn up terribly."*

*But Epi heard the roaches not*
*And so the Feuer twisted hot*
*It sprung up hearty, cracked with glee*
*Just like you in movies see.*
*And little Epi got quite wild,*
*A jumping-round-the-Zimmer child.*

*So Fritz und Franz made noisies,*
*And waved their little clawsies,*
*For they had taken Noten:*
*"Your mother hat's verboten!*
*Oh me, oh my, oh me, oh my,*
*Take care, you'll burn up in the sky."*

*The Feuer, whooping, was not fair,*
*It burned her skin, her bones, her hair*
*A pile of ash, two shoes that gleam—*
*That's all that's left in Gregor's dream.*

*And Fritz und Franz, the little ones*
*Are sitting there, their hearts undone.*
*He saw their clawlets flap in air*
*"Where are the stupid parents, where?"*
*Their tears make one big puddle,*
*And all is in a muddle—*

The knocking woke him. Thick darkness over all the land. Even darkness that might be felt.

"Come in?"

The cage door creaked. Dark.

"Herr Gregor, are you all right?"

Lantern light. Deserted lot. *What was I dreaming? I've forgotten.*

"Who is it?"

"Wittgenstein. Remember? From this morning?"

"Yes. The children. I fell asleep."

Gregor pushed himself up and put on his robe.

"There was a sign outside, NO SHOW TODAY DUE TO ILLNESS."

"Who put that up?"

"I don't know. I thought you did."

"Maybe I did. I don't remember. Come in."

"I can't see in the dark."

"So frail a thing is human. Here, I'll light the lamp."

Gregor crept over to the table, found the matches, and lit the kerosene lantern. Wittgenstein made his way through straw over to the single chair in the room, a wicker rocker, the Guest's Chair.

"May I sit down?"

"Please. Coffee?"

"I'd prefer tea if you have it. Cambridge, you know."

"I'll put up the water. I can't believe it. *Struwwelpeter.*"

"What about him? Is my hair that messed? Look, I just clipped my nails."

"No, no. I was dreaming . . . fire . . ."

Gregor shook himself half-awake. His guest came into focus.

"Herr Wittgenstein. What brings you?"

"You invited me. And I couldn't really talk in front of the children. They already think I'm odd. And there was a lot unsaid after Fräulein Schlüsselberger's satanic syllogism."

"Ah, yes." Awareness returning. "Jew human. Gregor Jew. Therefore, Gregor human." He took a glass from the cupboard and cut a slice of lemon. "What did all of you come up with?"

"We came up with an appropriate amount of confusion." Wittgenstein struggled out of his brown leather jacket and hung it neatly on the back of the chair.

"Are you enjoying yourself up there in the mountains?"

"No." He sat down and crossed his legs. "It is entirely disagreeable."

"How is that?" Gregor brought the tea.

"May I have some milk, please? The other teachers, the parish priest, almost everyone is completely hateful. Virulent, bogus intellectualism stuffed into shirts. The worst are the parents. They love it when we're strict, and they don't complain about corporal punishment—except when I do it."

"You must strike them as more odd than most. Odd People hitting children *verboten.*"

"They don't give a damn about their children. Want them to be farmhands period." Wittgenstein placed his tea precariously on the arm of the rocker.

"Do you mind if I smoke?"

"Yes. The straw. My spiracles . . ." Wittgenstein put his pipe back in his jacket pocket. "It sounds frustrating."

"These people are loathsome worms, not human at all, half animal, half human."

"You are angry."

"Odious and base."

"Why do you continue?"

"You'll laugh. To help the peasants improve themselves, to prepare them to cope with the disaster. To get them out of the muck."

"Tolstoy and his serfs."

"They're not my serfs, but Tolstoy, yes, definitely. Look, here." The visitor pulled a small, ragged volume from his jacket.

"Tolstoy's *Tales for Children*? You carry them around in your pocket?"

"Bedtime stories. We read and discuss them. They protect me."

"From what?"

"From stupidity, callousness, impetuosity, elegance." He handed the book to his host. Gregor leafed slowly through the pages.

"What's this one about: 'How Much Land Does a Man Need'?"

"What are all great stories about? Overreach. Greed. The idiot hero is offered as much land as he can walk round in a day."

"Say no more. But why elegance?" Gregor pursued. "You said Tolstoy protected you from elegance."

Wittgenstein took a sip from his cooling tea. "My family is still one of the richest in Europe."

"I had heard that."

"From?"

"Amadeus."

"Who is he?"

"The owner of the circus."

"Ah, Hoffnung, he of the great hope."

"I find him less and less hopeful. He's dying, you know."

"So are we all. What is *he* dying from?"

"Something called Werner's Syndrome, a type of premature aging. Not understood. No cure."

"I suffer from something similar."

"You? You look fine."

"You can't see my brain. Or my soul. I'm stupid and I'm rotten. May God help me! I'm barely awake enough to know I'm dreaming, and I can't wake up anymore."

"Why don't you go back to philosophy? Why is someone like you teaching grade school in a provincial village?"

"I've said everything I have to say. I'm bored. My mind is no longer flexible. I can't write anymore. And I hate philosophers and philosophy books. I know it sounds queer, but my spring has run dry. Werner's syndrome of the soul, I suppose—it's all beyond my strength."

Wittgenstein got up to pace, knocking the glass of tea to the floor, one more brown stain, spreading.

"Forgive me. I'm sorry."

"Straw on the floor. A marvelous, primitive invention. It will dry."

"Look," said the reluctant philosopher, "you're clever enough to see the pattern. 'In much wisdom is much grief: he that increaseth knowledge increaseth sorrow.' It's been that way since Eve and the apple. This unrestricted questing, this unlimited investigation with inadequate language, incomplete tools, scant preparation . . ."

"The Sorcerer's Apprentice."

"Exactly. The myth of our time. The magic word. What is the magic word, Herr Samsa, the spell that will turn things off once we've turned them on?" He was moving excitedly now, kicking the straw in front of him. "This war. Not just the *technos* of it—the so-called thinking behind it. It must be better thought out, more consistent with the little we know, and not get in the way of Justice."

"I see."

"You don't see. You and your quest! Curiosity will kill the roach—and perhaps a lot of others."

He sat down hard, as if in the hyper-field of his own gravity. High mass, low social skills: Gregor was embarrassed for his guest.

"May I get you some more tea?"

"Yes, please. No. Forget it. I'm already too excited."

"As you will."

"I'll predict for you how it will go, this cultural death wish we are enacting in our attraction to apocalypse. We seek to know. We seek some kind of absolute liberation, even suspecting it will lead to absolute destruction. It out-Spenglers Spengler!" He jumped up again and followed Gregor to the stove. "This cycle will have no successors. This is the final decline—of the west *and* the east and the north and the south, the physical, moral, spiritual torture and death of the totality of beings. Why aren't you laughing? Don't you see that our only real, predictable tool—reason— is simply inadequate? Simply and totally inadequate? And our Faustian search for transcendence will send us beyond the delusion of reason—directly into the sphere of total violence."

"It's possible."

"It's certain. And the most reasonable will produce the most violence. Mark my word. There will be scientists who, in the calm and cool of seminar rooms, will hatch the egg of world destruction. And you, dear Chitinous Apprentice, will see it come to pass."

Gregor handed Wittgenstein his tea and walked behind the curtain. He returned with a yellow envelope, delivering it to his guest as comment on his diatribe.

"I seem to have won tickets for a trip to the United States."

"Maybe you should go. Large cockroaches are suspicious enough here, but large Jewish cockroaches . . ."

"And if I like it, should I stay? Leave Europe?"

"Look, Herr Samsa—"

"Call me Gregor, please."

"I'm not comfortable doing that."

"Herr Samsa, then."

"If you think the naked rule of power will soon transform to Justice under Law—if you believe that story in the face of the last ten years, then stay here. On the other hand, if you subscribe to the Darwinian, to Life emerging out of primal slime and fighting its way upward—fittest dog eats fitless dog, then perhaps you should make yourself scarce—for you will be crushed and devoured."

"I don't know what I believe."

"I don't know what I believe either. But for me, it doesn't matter; I'm finished either way. On the other hand, you—perhaps you should decide. Is going to America part of your quest?"

"Everything is part of my quest."

"Incurable. 'Love has pitched his mansion in the place of excrement.'"

"What's that?"

"Yeats. The next line is 'For nothing can be sole or whole that has not been rent.' That's you, 'rent.'"

"Like rent a house?"

"No. Like ripped apart, wounded."

Wittgenstein deposited his half-full glass on the stove and put on his leather jacket.

"You're going?" Gregor asked.

"Shepherding nine-year-olds is a taxing affair for this vessel of iniquity. They'll be swarming in five hours. Thanks for your advice, Apprentice Gregor. Give my regards to Broadway, and good luck. But remember one thing while questing."

"What is that?"

"*Ignoramibus.* Pray for ignorance."

Ludwig Wittgenstein walked down the steps and out into the night, trailing straw from his immaculate cuffs.

Sleep was a problem for Gregor. It had been a problem when he was a fabric salesman in Prague, and it continued to be a problem in his new career. The electric street lamps, recently installed by the City of Vienna, made things worse, shining their bright modernity into his cage.

In insects as in humans, light has a kinetic effect, stimulating movement and heightened consciousness. Gregor's five-million-year-old nervous system had not evolved to deal with the output of incandescent tungsten. The light made him nervous, and nervous roaches have a hard time sleeping.

Cockroaches, of course, are most often nocturnal, and urban species especially so in their adaptation to the living patterns of their human hosts. In a natural sequence of light and dark, *Periplaneta americanus* undergoes a marked increase of activity around dusk, five or six hours of intense foraging, and then gradual quiescence until the next nightfall. The extended light of modern urban life shifts the biological clock until "lights out," at which time the same rhythm begins, but with a shorter recovery period. Such a shift is difficult enough, inducing a kind of permanent jet lag and fatigue. But how much more difficult was Gregor's task of actually reversing normal rhythm: eighteen hours of activity and six dormant, instead of the other way around. That way lies psychosis. Gregor performed heroically in his new role, but he did need deep sleep when he could get it.

The dream occurred on the night of May 1, 1923, twelve days after his encounter with Wittgenstein. Gregor remembered this date clearly, because every May first since childhood, he had read (or had read to him) Andersen's marvelous story "The Old Oak Tree's Last Dream." He read it yearly in commemoration of the May fly in the story, whose entire life encompassed only one day, who was intimately familiar with death, but happy, almost joyous, nevertheless. Even as a child, that attitude had struck him as a heroic achievement, something to be memorized deep within, and practiced when his own time would—inevitably—come.

Throughout the ages, dreams have been understood as divine message, as predictive announcement, as cure for disease, as fantastic extension of the waking state, and as "the royal road to the unconscious"—as the good doctor from Berggasse 19 so often insisted. But Gregor's May Day dream may have added another category to the understanding of the dream state.

It was eleven o'clock on a Tuesday night. He had fallen asleep reading Russell on Einstein, hoping to find a new pedagogical angle to liven up his deteriorating act. The Oak Tree's flying dream lay open next to his pallet. It took him a while to fall asleep, if sleep it was. Perhaps he simply went out, as he often did, to walk the dark, quiet streets of the Meidling district. As he turned the corner of Niederhoffstrasse, he experienced a sensation difficult to describe. He, of course, did not have the comparison, but it was just how those of us who frequent modern airports feel when we walk along at normal pace on a moving beltway, and the world whizzes by us, as if we were wearing seven-league boots. When we step from the rolling rubber to the marble floor, we experience a jolt in time, a radical, always unanticipatable deceleration, spacetime dragged in friction. It takes some steps before our world resynchronizes with the world around.

The first time it happened, Gregor thought he might have had too much to drink. But a bottle of Zipfer Dunkle had never affected him before. Perhaps it was an ear infection. But he had no ears. The second time it happened, he became afraid: what if this were the first sign of some degenerative disease—a subject he had thought much about since meeting Amadeus. Though he did not know the physiology, these were thoughts well taken. Hyperreactivity of the abdominal ganglia, hypersecretion of acetylcholine by the corpora cardiaca, or of serotonin from the CNS—recent work on *Periplaneta* has shown the power of minute neurohormone concentrations to create profound physiological effects.

By the fourth episode, he began to play with the sensation. It seemed to come and go, but he found he could bring on the phenomenon at will by performing a kind of Valsalva maneuver, contracting his abdomen as he did to hiss an audience to silence, while at the same time shutting down his spiracles to prevent the egress of air. Within a few seconds, the world began to speed by, and his own spacetime seemed expanded and slow.

Expansion. Easy speed. The feeling of flying. Why *not* flight? He had wings . . . why not use them? But he never had done so. They were folded under his hard external wings, the chitinous tegmentum that ran the length of his back. He loosed the cape from around his neck, extracted his front legs from his jacket, and wiggled out of the diaperlike affair he wore so as not to embarrass his human public. Naked in the Viennese night. A warm, late spring breeze. The pleasure was overwhelming. He took a huge breath of the daphne-scented air and Valsalva'd himself into a state of electrifying dizziness. As long as he did not move, neither did the world.

His abdominal exertion opened a sagittal split along his back, loosing the apex fold and anal lobe of his virginal hindwings. The wind had picked up from the west, blowing over the gardens of the Schönbrunn Palace, drying the delicate lace of his newly unfolded parts. He crossed the Ruckergasse intersection and stood, facing the broad western view. Could he fly? He would try a run down toward the palace. If, once aloft, he had to make a crash landing, it would be better to come down in the softness of the gardens than in the potentially lethal traffic of Wienzeile Linke. Taking another in-breath, he bore down hard against the closed sphincters of all twenty-four spiracles, began to trot, then to canter; his wings began to hum. The world roared by in fierce, thrilling distortion. Liftoff! It was easy!

With a two-foot-wide body, and four foot wings, his wingspread was a full ten feet, as wide as that of the largest condor, but carrying only half the body weight. The superior leverage of internally attached muscles lifted him easily, farther than he had intended. By using his lower ab-domen as an aileron, he was able to lower himself to an altitude of a hun-dred feet or so, cruising over the park, its statues, its fountains and zoo. "West," he thought, "I'm headed west, the land of evening, the direction of decline. West. Quest."

Although they are strong flyers, roaches are not particularly good navigators. Actually, Gregor was heading north. And a good thing, too, for after some minutes of confusion, he saw the Danube below, a silver streak in the moonlight, beginning its great, unmistakable curve to the west at Klosterneuburg. At Tulln, the broad and placid river narrowed into a restless twist of currents, and between Krems and Melk lay the legend-haunted valley of the Wachau, with its castles and fortresses, monasteries and abbeys at every bend of the river, its wine-growing villages and forested slopes spread out left and right below as Gregor flew, now southwesterly, upriver toward Linz.

The struggle between water and rock had begun early in creation. In the Wachau, the contest continued mightily, with hidden granite hurdles bringing forth great liquid leaps, and bays and inlets colonizing would-be land. The Wachau by moonlight. Had life ever been more beautiful?

Gregor was without fatigue or fear. Why turn back? Why not go all the way? But where was all the way? America. To the west. He looked around and saw Polaris behind him, to his right. He banked, lifted his tail, and began to climb with greater velocity, ever upward, into Minkowskian space. Geodesics. Great circles. Gravitational bending of spacetime. Einstein had imagined it; Eddington had proved it; Gregor would harness it. He was free, victim no more of the profound, once-absolute embrace of gravity's prison. With no force "pulling" him, but only free trajectory in the mass-induced curvature of space, he would use his wings against it, he would hook his claws into spacetime, as climbers hook crampons and picks into vertical walls of ice, he would navigate his own terrain. Free will! If humanity was too confused to understand, let a blattid lead the way! Newton's determined universe was no more, "objective" states were unmasked as the illusions they were. Reality was determined by the observer, by him, by Gregor, and Gregor alone. Above the atmosphere, he peered out at red-shifting galaxies, beckoning him on. Machian stars structuring spacetime solely by existing. The dark backward and abysm of time, Shakespeare called it. Back to the primordial ylem.

Across the Arctic Circle he flew, elliptical, tireless, inspired, rolling along non-Euclidian structures, past and future simultaneously present, equivalent, indeterminable. Greenland, then Baffin Island below, slightly off-course, as is usual for a roach, but crashing into nothing other than his own sense of awe. The moon was no more, northern Quebec an unbroken darkness. He drew his head upward, shielded many of his eyes under his pronotum, and hurtled, almost blind, into the Riemannian space of the earth's atmosphere. The lights of Quebec City called him back. The fading glimmer of Montreal, the Adirondacks and the Greens framing daybreak over Lake Champlain. Was that Albany to his right? He was weak on smaller American cities. But there, ahead, what did he see by the dawn's early light? Manhattan Island. The Long Island. He had studied the maps. It was New York!

Cautious with his new skills, he maneuvered himself over the broadness of the Hudson, between Nyack and Tarrytown. He spread his wings, lowered his tail against the wind, and as he stalled, his velocity cut to seventy-five miles per hour, he swooped down into active flight over Yonkers and the West Bronx. The clock on the Times Tower said 5:30 A.M. Gregor needed a place to land, but was wary of the streets with their early morning traffic and unpredictable culture. Even though New York had hosted the Gregor Olympics, they had never actually seen a five-foot-six-inch cockroach. And he had heard that in New York, roaches were considered "a problem," the same as Jews at home.

He looked around for the tallest building he could see, and there it was, on Twenty-third Street and Madison Avenue. He didn't know it was Twenty-third and Madison, but he saw it clearly all the same, a tall skyscraper, the recently completed fifty floors of the Metropolitan Life Insurance Building, the tallest building in the world, modeled after the Campanile of San Marco in Venice. He had seen pictures of it. Or were they pictures of the Campanile of San Marco in Venice?

Gregor eased down on the diagonal green brass roofing, taking the impact smartly and evenly on all six of his powerful legs. Was he here? In New York? Or was this a dream? He looked east toward the sun and saw the Long Island stretching away into the distance. He looked west and saw the mighty Hudson, and north and saw the great Central Park, just a few miles away. Being on the north side of the building, he couldn't see south. He sat for a few minutes, crouched on the roofing, and thought. A biplane circled in for a closer look.

What did he think? He couldn't remember. He was not thinking in words. He was not thinking in images. He heard no music in his head. It was as if he had left a mass of intellectual energy behind in the heavens, energy that was only now reloading in his brain in no discernible sequence, soaking his nervous system all at once, the way a spill might fill a sponge. And all of a sudden he felt tired, exhausted, hollow. He hooked his fore-claws into a seam in the brass and passed out.

Gregor called it a dream—accepted it as such. But left behind in his circus wagon was an envelope of train tickets, Vienna–London–Vienna, and a first-class ticket on the *Mauretania*, London–New York–London— all unused.

# NEW YORK

# 9. METAMORPHOSIS III: *The* ROACH AMERICAN

Some four centuries before the birth of Christ, the Taoist sage Chuang Tzu wrote of his own famous dream

> Once Chuang Tzu dreamt he was a butterfly, a butterfly flitting and fluttering around, happy with himself and doing as he pleased. He didn't know he was Chuang Tzu. Suddenly he woke up and there he was, solid and unmistakable Chuang Tzu. But he didn't know if he was Chuang Tzu who had dreamt he was a butterfly, or a butterfly dreaming he was Chuang Tzu.

How charmingly malicious. Even its author objects: "Between Chuang Tzu and a butterfly there must be some distinction!" But no, he concludes, there *is* no distinction: the dream is told in the classic that bears his name, in a chapter entitled "On Making All Things Equal."

Gregor felt himself in precisely Chuang Tzu's situation. Was he Gregor the cockroach, or Gregor the fabric salesman dreaming he was Gregor the cockroach?

Gregor was—at best—the sum of his confusions. His reality, at least early on, seemed to shift arbitrarily back and forth like one of those optically illusive drawings in which the beautiful maiden transforms visually into the deathlike hag. Which reality did he live in? Which reality was home?

But Gregor had not picked up Chuang Tzu to understand the interhovering of Realities. The dream section was a surprise to him, provocative, bittersweet. He came to the rascal philosopher for larger reasons: to try to clarify his quest. The principal theme of Chuang Tzu's book, Amadeus had informed him, was, simply put, freedom. How, he asks, can one live freely in a world dominated by suffering, chaos, and absurdity? Gregor's question exactly. Many Chinese sages proposed social reforms, political changes, new ethical norms to cure humanity of its ills, to free its inhabitants for creative, mutually beneficial lives. Such was Gregor's nebulous plan, made compelling by his general condition, and urgent by his wound. Chuang Tzu, he found, would have shaken his head and chuckled. But Gregor was left with only the conundrum of home.

THE OCCIDENTAL HOTEL
243 W. 43RD ST.
NEW YORK 36, N.Y.

10 May 1923

Dear Amadeus, Anna Marie, and Herr Kramar, Herr Klofac, and Herr Soukup:
    Now is pass one week since I am disappeared, and I am expecting your confusion and maybe disinpointment Very heavy, even sad. So in this one week education of me in sad America, of Mr. President Harding unexpectd sick. I will to . . .

The loss of a language can be greatly debilitating, and the change from German to English all the more so for their similarities. If one relocates, in China, say, or Japan, one abandons all attachment to a mother tongue, and languishes—or flourishes—in total otherness. But to hear speech you think you understand but don't, to use words and utter sentences that seem right but sound wrong—this is truly unnerving. Furthermore, what loss is here! German seems to speak another, more complex, order of reality. German case inflections and end-of-sentence verbs allow for truly complex constructions, with subtle, mischievous, multilayered relationships between words. A final verb can undercut or sabotage the entire thought structure that has preceded it, and layer irony upon irony, in a delicious confection.

Not so in English, especially American English, and especially in the 2,500 basic words of the beginner. The expansive openness of the German sentence is replaced by a short, clipped, subject-verb-predicateness, and the unbridled connectivity of compound German nouns is exchanged for a hash of words less than three syllables long. An eternal language-Present clouds any sense of embedded language history. Clichés of certainty replace Talmudic complexity. Such was the price of Gregor's trade-off. And with the postwar hatred of all things German, there was little sympathy for his accent or his mistakes, and certainly none for his thought patterns. But Gregor vowed to push on into a hostile unknown.

```
10 May 1923 excelent machine not hard to operateing.
Long time taking to find letters, but I get better al-
readily. I write Amadeus, Anna Marie when I am easier to
can write a good and information letter.

3 June Frank S. called to offer of job on chicken farm
in New Jersey—I would like more outdoors and hard work.
I tell no because I am meet interesting people in citty.
I probably take job in Ulla s hotel she offer me.
```

Ulla's hotel was the Occidental, on Forty-third Street, just west of Broadway. A robust, thirty-year-old Swede, fifteen years in America, Ulla Ekelund was now the manager of this middle-sized, upscale hotel in the heart of downtown, and the likely source of Gregor's typing paper. As secretary-treasurer of the Go-Gotham Gregors, she was there at the phone early on May Day when a good Samaritan dialed the number on the slip of paper in his pocket. She commandeered a sleepy cabbie, picked up the disoriented stranger on Twenty-third Street, and took him back to her rooms at the hotel.

On a theater poster in the hotel lobby: BRILLIANT MEN, BEAUTIFUL JAZZ BABIES, CHAMPAGNE BATHS, MIDNIGHT REVELS, PETTING PARTIES IN THE PURPLE DAWN, ALL ENDING IN ONE TERRIFIC SMASHING CLIMAX THAT MAKES YOU GASP. It wasn't Old Vienna.

```
5 June 23 I decide to take Ulla s job of elevator opera-
tor. She says I will meet many important people that can
do things for me. She lets me stay in her spare room. I
hope I will not be a bother her.
```

Ulla's offer of a room seemed entirely altruistic, if slightly tinged with hero worship. But lying in bed, at night, with only a thin, unlocked door between them, Gregor, lonely and confused, imagined he could hear her breathing. He certainly could hear her occasional moans. And the soft perfume of her abundant flesh made his antennae tingle.

The suggestive vibrations began on the very first night when they sat in what was now his room, talking late in the semidarkness. Tomorrow was his first day of work, and he wanted to be as sharp as possible. But despite his stretching and yawning (granted, more difficult to interpret in an insect), she refused to leave.

What is she thinking?

When the Swedish clock on the mantel piece rang out its twelve lovely chimes, rather than leaving, Ulla launched into a long story, full of sensual detail, about the clock, the one object salvaged from her relationship with Bjorn, her most recent lover.

Why is she telling me all this? Why doesn't she go to sleep? Is she waiting for something?

Because it was her apartment, Gregor didn't feel he could ask her to leave.

*Am I supposed to repay her generosity with . . . ?*

No, he would trade a tale with her, the story of the most important clock in *his* life, the amazing clock in the Old Town Square in Prague.

To this day, each quarter to the hour, tourists gather to gawk at the magnificent fifteenth-century creation of Master Hanus—a clock so marvelous that in the whole world there is none to compare. As a child, Gregor was drawn over and over to its huge double works, the upper, a twenty-four-hour clock face in gorgeous blue, crisscrossed with golden arcs, and the lower, an astronomical calendar advancing at the stroke of midnight one day at a time across seasons depicted in twelve rural scenes. More fascinating still was the hourly dumb show by Master Hanus's uncanny figures. Standing on pedestals at the upper face—the four great threats to Prague: a turbaned Turk, shaking his head with a slow "No" to the Christian city; clutching his money bags, a bearded Jew, perhaps Judas; Vanity, admiring her own reflection in a mirror; and finally, grasping his hourglass, Death, who reaches out to pull the cord that chimes the hour. Above these worthies, over the clock face, behind two small windows, the Apostles shuffle past, and finally the figure of Jesus appears, hands raised in benediction. At the sides of the lower face stand four still figures of virtue, including a beautiful angel hoisting a fearful sword. Anticlimactic and almost comedic: a cock that pops out, crowing, flapping its wings to signal the end of the show. Quite enough to fascinate a young Prague Jew-child who passed the clock twice each day. But more riveting still was the legend of its builder, Master Hanus, a story the five-year-old was told by his all-too-frightening father:

At the dedication ceremony, the learned university men had great praise for the clockmaker's pedagogy. For when studied carefully the huge upper face revealed the way the sun revolved around the earth, the positions and shape of the moon waxing and waning, the signs of the zodiac—six over, and six under the earth, and under what sign they were at any given time. It showed when the sun would rise and set on any particular day, where in the horizon the sun stood at any particular time, northerly in winter and southerly in summer. The lower face charted the days of the week, the months and the seasons, and labeled the holidays and saints' days for every day in the year. But with such information available, some professors grumbled, the populace might be distracted by the mechanical tricks of the Apostles and the bell-pulling Death. Some pronounced them "foolish embellishments." But they were few.

Those who were granted the privilege of inspecting the innards of the clock could only marvel that a single human mind had imagined and perfected the intricate interlocking works, the absolute precision of all the weights, cogs, and wheels, including the huge wheel of 365 cogs that required an entire year to rotate. Only one man understood the whole system, and that was Master Hanus.

At the opening event, one Janek Hrod, a competing clockmaker, asserted that the master's clock was divinely inspired, and that if he, Janek, had to care for or repair this machine, he would surely go mad. "I do not believe," he said, "that a more magnificent creation could be found anywhere in the world unless Master Hanus himself should build it."

Upon hearing this opinion, the mayor of Prague and all his councillors shared one frightening thought: Hanus could be hired by Budapest, or Vienna, or even Brno to build a still more inspired clock, refining ideas and techniques gained in building this one. Perhaps he was already at work on plans. So they set loose an odious plot, inspired by vanity, perhaps, but equally by greed for the tourists they might lose.

One moonless night, as Hanus sat at his bench, three masked figures entered his workshop and put out his eyes. The next morning his apprentices found their master bound, gagged—and blind. Though Prague was up in arms, Hanus had only simple advice for his avengers: "Stop looking. Though the culprits are near, they will not be found." He could have said more. But he simply sat in the corner of his workshop, sad, motionless, growing ever smaller, as dust gathered on his tools. This was the reward for his accomplishment.

Daily he grew weaker, more sunken and gray; the end, he knew, was near. Late one Tuesday morning, he called on Joachim, his boy, to lead him to the clock. There were no friendly greetings as the once honored master requested entry to the works. "I have a new idea on how to make the weights slide more smoothly," he told the guard, and Joachim slipped five crowns into his burly hand, as instructed. He led his master to the complex center of the works, and they waited—Joachim in the dusty shafts of light, Hanus in the sunless dark. In several minutes, the first whirring began, then another and another. The first of twelve bells chimed out as Death worked his rope. The windows opened above, the Apostles began their greetings. But before the benediction of the Lord, Master Hanus thrust his bony fingers into the core of the works, groped around, and pulled out two small pins. The wheels began to rotate madly, roaring and squeaking—and came to a halt. The Apostles froze. The cock never crowed. The great machine stood motionless as Hanus slumped to the floor. Clutched in his hand was the second of the pins, but what it was no one knew. It went with him to his hole in the ground—outside the town walls, the dumping place for criminals. It was eighty years before the damage was successfully repaired.

Child Gregor did not really understand the story, but the glorious clock, with its magical figures, was mysteriously tinged with an impenetrable, barely understood darkness. Yes, there was the image of the blinded clockmaker dead among his works. Yes, there was a childish, primitive notion of revenge. But those were not the operative opacities. There was something else, perhaps some "undiscovered country" that aged him spiritually, and prematurely.

. . .

As important to Gregor as the Prague clock may have been, it was not why he told its story late that night in Ulla's apartment. He told it to end the conversation, for what could follow such a tale? He told it to express his sense of vague discomfort, his pre-fear that goodness might transform itself into its opposite. He told it to affirm his own center before retiring to a strange bed.

Ulla responded as he had hoped. Without comment, she got up from her chair, silently walked over to Gregor, gave his left antenna a long, soft stroke, and walked silently into her own room, closing the door behind her.

Gregor undressed, hung his clothing on a chair, and slipped between the cool sheets. He did his nightly yoga breathing, then lay there in the darkness, still feeling the touchsmell of her hand as a tingling in his body. In the eight years since his transformation, he had not thought seriously of a woman, had not felt a need, an urge, to couple at any level, for his changes had taken much adjustment. And then there was that awful wound in his back. Oh! He had forgotten to tell Ulla about it, and surely there would be brown stains on her sheet, even through the dressing.

As he lay in the dark thinking of Ulla, of her blond hair and shapely, muscular presence, he felt a wave of nausea rise from abdomen to thorax. What was this? Why this sense of vague disgust at external muscles, fat, and flesh? How much neater he was, his soft parts packaged in hard glossiness. What a stupid idea, the endoskeleton. Why put softness on the outside, hanging there, vulnerable, indecent? What kind of inane design was that? His sister Grete owned a good, eighteenth-century Hungarian violin. She put it in a hard case to protect it. Grete. He hadn't thought of her that way before. A bag of flesh hanging on bones. Flesh pads on bone touching strings. Inside bones. Bones reaching for the cord that rang the bell . . .

Exhausted, he fell asleep. But the bed in Ulla's room—now his—was not ever to be a restful place. The moment the hardness of his back pressed into its sensuous softness, he began to think, to dream of women, of his hardness engulfed in their softness, enveloped in a warmth that only a cold-blooded creature can fully appreciate. Much pain would come in that bed.

. . .

Gregor's job was to align the car with the exit for the safety of his passengers and to open and close the gate. He enjoyed being in command of his machine, precisely lining up door and floor, and working the gate with its shiny brass handle and curiously pleasing sound.

The Occidental Hotel dressed its elevator operators to fit the image of technical expertise and service. The boys wore red gabardine double-breasted jackets, with epaulets, four rows of brass buttons, and flat braid at the wrists. Below, dark twill trousers with a red satin stripe along the outer seam. Topping the uniform off, a red pillbox hat emblazoned with the Occidental setting sun.

Gregor's case was a bit different. Though management was sympathetic to his peculiarities, giving him a modified stool to rest his tegmen on, and even pleased by his quasi-celebrity, no one was really sure the guests would react the same way. In consultation with the hotel tailor, a decision was made to dress him so as to hide, as far as possible, his true condition. His hind legs were thrust into regular men's shoes and stuffed white socks, which were held in place by a garterlike device fastened under his pants to his abdomen. His middle legs were contained by a cummerbund, thus making him appear to be captain of the operators, rather than the lowest in the hierarchy. His front legs were fitted into a stiff jacket with white gloves sewed on the sleeve ends, stuffed with batting, except for the third and fourth fingers, into which Gregor inserted his claws. His breathing needs were nicely met by the red gauze stripe along his spiracle line. He wore dark glasses and a high ascot that concealed his mouthparts. His antennae were carefully curled into the pillbox hat. Whether it was simply tactfulness on the part of his patrons, or their habitual silent staring straight ahead, as is common in elevators, he was never once confronted about his lack of a nose. Such is the delicacy—or estrangement—of midtown New York.

```
1 July 23 letter from Einstein in my post box!! I can't
believe. How he could have hear of me and my teaching?
Invitation I meet him tomorrow night.
```

And meet they did—Gregor and Einstein. Only it wasn't Albert. It was Isadore Einstein, the most famous and creative Prohibition agent in the entire United States. Izzy Einstein, agent extraordinaire, master of the comic-opera disguise and capricious capture. Izzy Einstein, a Roman candle illuminating dark, pervasive crimes. Jewish Roman. His nutty, comical schemes netted thousands of unsuspecting suckers—hard, sophisticated, cynical, daring outlaws—but suckers all the same. With all his ploys and disguises, this fat little man with the big cigar, the "incomparable Izzy," had made the grim game of Cops and Robbers into rollicking fun.

Gregor was lying in his room on a warm July evening waiting for his call, rereading Einstein's own *Relativity: The Special and General Theory: A Popular Exposition* so that he might not appear stupid for his honored guest, when the phone rang in Ulla's room.

"Gregor, it's for you."

"Ah."

He sprang up and headed for the connecting door. An image of his first struggle to rise from his bed in Prague flashed through his mind, and he laughed to himself at the disappearance of what had once seemed insuperable difficulties.

"Einstein on the phone," he said to Ulla. "For me."

"Really?" Ulla sat back down on the edge of her chair. "He has a Brooklyn accent."

"Hello. Gregor Samsa here. Yes. Mr. Einstein? We could talk up here? Ulla, would that be all right? Yes, seventeen-B. Fine. I see you soon."

They waited, each astonished in different ways.

A loud rapping at the door, the kind of knock that some in our time have dreaded. Ulla Ekelund, manager, hostess, and fan club chief, leaped up to get the door. Two men in tan suits and fedoras stood puffing cigars in the hallway.

"Mr. Samsa, please," said the short, fat one.

"Come in."

Ulla was already blushing at the thought of meeting the great man. But where was he? Gregor rose from his chair and extended a claw to each of the men, who took it, and shook it, with kind of rough ease.

"Izzy Einstein. This is Moe Smith, my partner."

"Welcome," said Gregor, and began to shut the door.

"Might as well leave it open," said Moe. "Fred will be joining us in a minute."

"Who is Fred?" Gregor asked, stepping back into the room.

"One of our musketeers," said Izzy. "But a *schvartza*, so he can't use the elevator. He'll be up as soon as he makes the seventeen flights."

"*Schvartza* is a black person," Gregor told Ulla, translating from German. "You mean colored can't use the elevator?"

"What kind of an elevator operator are you?" boomed Izzy. "You can't read? A big sign over the call button."

"Forgive, please. I am here only three weeks. I haven't notice." Ulla, like Gregor, was still confused over their visitors.

"Don't worry about Fred," said Moe. "It's good for him."

Fred arrived in the hall, quite out of breath, a tall, heavy black man in a brown suit.

"Fred Johnson, this is Gregor Samsa, and, uh, I didn't get your name, miss."

Ulla held out her hand to each man, and actually curtsied, an Old World nicety, completely out of place with proletarian servants of the law.

"Ulla Ekelund. I'm Gregor's roommate."

Eyes rolled in heads, as three Prohibition agents looked at one another in masculine disbelief. There would be plenty of locker room banter on this one. They checked out the bed for single or double.

"Very pleased to meetcha," said Izzy. "Miss Ekelund, would you mind if we had a word with Mr. Samsa alone? Government business."

"Oh, certainly," said Ulla. "Gregor, I'll meet you in the lobby when you're finished. You can come down with the gentlemen."

Gregor nodded, and she swished out of the room, aware of the seductiveness of her turn. Fred locked the door behind her.

"Shall we all sit down?" asked Izzy, and motioned each man and Gregor to their assigned places, as if it were headquarters.

"Excuse me," said Gregor, "but where is Professor Einstein?"

"I'm Professor Einstein! Isadore Einstein, Professor of Tricknology. You've heard of me?"

"In truth, no." Gregor squirmed. "But I'm very new, and all goes so quickly."

"It don't matter," said Moe. "We've heard of you."

"And we got a little business to discuss," said Izzy, chomping on his cigar. "We represent the Federal Government, the United States Government, and as a person of foreign origin, you would do good to cooperate with us. Understand me?"

"Oh, yes, yes," said Gregor, enthusiastically. "I'm honored to be here—"

"And if you want to stay," said Fred, "you'll help us with our little problem."

Izzy took charge.

"In two days you are scheduled to appear at the Gotham Gregor Dance Festival at the Hippodrome."

"Yes. July Fourth. America's anniversary."

"Afterwards, there'll be a party thrown by the Gotham Gregors for the winning team. Correct?"

"Yes. I think correct."

"The party is at Reisenweber's, Eighth Avenue and Fifty-eighth, a place so big and famous," Izzy interrupted, "no one thinks it can be touched. Well, we're gonna touch it."

"What kind of touching?" asked the insect.

"Pinching touching," said Moe.

"I don't know this word."

"It means when you catch someone and arrest them," Fred explained.

"Like Milizia? Arrest for what?"

"Mr. Samsa," Izzy began, "you are aware that we have Prohibition in this country. You are not allowed to sell or transport alcohol."

"I know," said Gregor. "I don't drink much, but it seems—you say featherbrainlike?—to me."

"It may be featherbrainlike, but it's the law," Moe observed. "And we enforce it. Reisenweber's is serving all the liquor it served before the law, but no one has been able to catch them. You got to have the liquor to show as evidence. You can't just drink it—you got to show it."

"The waiters and the barmen at Reisenweber's are too damn careful, too damn smart," Izzy said. "They won't sell unless they really know you. But you are going to help us get them."

"How? I can't—"

"You don't even have to be there, if you don't want," said Izzy. "We're going to put on cockroach suits, dress up as you for the big bash. Not a chance they wouldn't serve us in that kind of a scene. Actually, it'd be better if you came. We can't get our hands to look like yours. We'd look like goofballs in roach suits. So you be the real Gregor, and we'll just be fans, mascots at the party."

"I have to order a drink and trick them into being arrested?"

"It's called a sting."

"Cockroaches don't sting."

"Cockroaches who want to be American do," observed Fred.

"Then I will not go to the dancing festival, and then there will be no party."

There was a long silence while Izzy Einstein pondered his own version of special relativity. He decided to proceed with Plan A—the no-Gregor version—which turned out to be quite successful. Sixteen arrests' worth.

The agents spent the next half hour explaining the facts of American life to their host—in Colored and White.

## 10. LOVE, O LOVE, O CAREFUL LOVE

In purple dress and short-sleeved blouse, the frail-looking young woman, delicately colored and delicately made, stepped gracefully into the elevator at the sixteenth floor. Her head, her neck, her long slim arms, her little hands seemed cut from alabaster. Where had Gregor seen those hands before? The bones, the bones, ah yes, the bones in Roentgen's machine. Grete's bones. An endo-exo-skeleton! She hugged the wall to Gregor's left and made way for each of the passengers as they arrived, maintaining her place at the front, as if she were afraid to be suffocated. At the fourth floor, she smiled. Her huge eyes lit up like agates, and it was only then that Gregor realized he'd been staring. He whipped his head around, gave a little cough, and focused on the rising wall for the rest of the trip to the lobby.

The passengers pushed out of the ornate cage, and though she was in front, the woman in purple and white allowed them to pass in front of her, pressing her thin frame against the wall. When the car was empty, she walked slowly out and stood a few feet away, her back to Gregor, a lovely sculpture on the ornate carpet. The two were frozen in silence amidst the morning bustle.

Then the woman snapped her fingers, said out loud, "I knew I'd left something!" and spun around to get back on the elevator. For Gregor, it was a moment beyond calculation, courage, or foolishness. He simply asked, with European politeness, "I can get something for you, madame?" This was a woman used to delegating tasks, but it was not that which brought forth "Why, yes. Thank you, sir." She was deeply struck by the authentic gentility of the question, and had answered without thinking.

"Certainly, madam. I get if you give me key. What is it?"

"On the table near the bed you'll see three journals called *Equal Rights*. Could you bring them down to the lobby while I make a phone call? I'll meet you back here at the elevator." She looked him in the eye with a luminous glow. Her tiny hands fetched the key from her purse.

Gregor's calm had evaporated in her intensity. His palms would be sweaty if cockroaches had palms; his trembling white-gloved claw received the key. Remembering to bow, he turned to the elevator, got in, and closed the gate. Up he went, as fast as possible, ignoring the calls at 7 and 10, and whipping the gate open, he made his way along the carpeted hall to 1600. It was a small room, with a window facing Broadway. From it, he could see out over the East River, and there to the right was the clock tower of Metropolitan Life, his first berth in the New World. What was it she wanted? Three magazines in a pile. Table next to the bed. The bed. Her bed, still unmade. Her body in there, her lovely bones, minimally endoskeletal, caressed by the smoothness of white sheets. On the bed, a nightgown, neatly folded, but still a nightgown, a nightgown that had touched her nakedness. He could feel his tegmina starting to rise, involuntarily, his wings quivering underneath. His dorsal gland became slightly wet. No, no! Silly. Insane. Stop it. Journals. Bed table. *Equal Rights.* "Alice Paul, Editor." Is she Alice Paul? He checked the reservation envelope on the dresser. Yes, Alice Paul. Her name is Alice Paul. What a lovely name! Alice. Alice. And she is editor, an important person.

Gregor tucked the journals under his arm and stepped out of the room. Needing two hands to steady the key, he put the magazines down on the carpet. After locking the door, he dropped down on all sixes in the thankfully empty hallway, opened a cover with his mouth, and began to read the Declaration of Principles "1. That women shall no longer be regarded as inferior to . . ."

*Mein Gott, was tue ich?* he thought to himself, and scrambled his front legs up the wall until he was once again upright, leaving the journals on the rug. "Here need I a better-more-easily-bending-body," he thought, still translating from the German. Flexing his lower legs (a task made more difficult because of the supports in his pants), his front legs on the wall, he succeeded in lowering himself enough for his middle legs to be able to reach the journals. But *Scheisse!* they were all bound up under the cummerbund, which he could not loosen without losing his grip on the wall and tumbling floorward again. A well-dressed young man came out of 1610 and stopped in his path.

"Need a hand, bud?"

"No, I . . . yes . . ."

"Here, let me . . ."

"Thank you. I just . . . If you could . . . those magazines on floor . . ."

The good Samaritan retrieved the journals and placed them in Gregor's hands.

"One million thanks. I will take you down in elevator. You are going to the lobby?"

"Yeah, sure. Sure you can make it? Maybe you should ask for time off."

"No, I am fine. It was only bending to get the journals that was problem. My back."

Gregor gestured the guest into the elevator, closed the gate, and pushed the lever to the left. "How long have I been? *Mein Gott,* I've been keeping her waiting so long." He ran the elevator past callers on 11, 9, and 8, and at each of these floors there were shouts as he shot by. He opened the gate in the lobby and thanked his savior yet again.

"Yeah, sure, anytime. See ya. Don't take any wooden nickels. Oh, hey, want some tickets to a ball game? Here you go. Got another date. Use 'em or give 'em away."

"Wooden nickels," Gregor thought. "What is that, wooden nickels?" But he had no time to go through his idiom list, for there, coming directly toward him from the bank of phones, was Alice Paul, his love.

"Thank you so much, kind sir."

She smiled, and reached for some change in her purse.

"Miss Paul?"

"How did you know my name?"

"Oh, I, uh, I, I am looking at the journals, and your name is on it. I just assume you are the editor. I'm sorry—forgive me if I am mistaken—"

"No, no. You're absolutely correct. I am Alice Paul, and I am the editor of the journal, and I'm flattered you took the trouble to look at them. It's very nice to meet you." Gregor's heart skipped a beat.

"Miss Paul?"

"Yes?"

"You probably tell from my speech, I am new in America."

"I did think so, yes."

"And just now, a nice man give me these two tickets to—I don't know what . . ."

"Here, let me see." Gregor extended his hand. "Two tickets—and they look like good seats—to the Princeton–Yale championship baseball game this afternoon at Yankee Stadium." She handed them back.

"Miss Paul, would you, do you think could you . . . go with me to this baseball game, and explain it me? I know it is the national sport, and I feel I must know how it works, a baseball game. I am lucky to be give such tickets, true?"

"Yes, you are lucky. And it's nice of you to ask me to come with you. But I don't know anything more about baseball than you do. It's a man's game—"

"They don't let women?"

"No, I think they do. In fact, they advertise 'ladies' days' with free admission. But it's just to attract more men."

"So you won't to go with me?"

"What time does it start?"

"Two P.M., it says. Fourteen hundred hours."

"It might be fun. Interesting, anyway. I have a meeting now, which probably includes lunch. But I can be back by one. We can make it. I'll find out how to get there, and I'll meet you here in the lobby at one-fifteen. Is that all right?"

"Oh, it's wonderful! Thank you so many times! I am finish at ten o'clock. I have work all night."

"Then you'd best take a little nap. I'll see you at one-fifteen."

"Oh yes, a nap, a siesta—you say that here?—I take a nap and I see you at one-fifteen. Thank you so much."

Needless to say, Gregor's attempt at napping was only moderately successful. He plopped down on his bed, took off his hat, lay there for five minutes, then sprang up and turned on the radio, and lay down again. After a minute he jumped up, turned it off, and paced the room, taking off his wig, allowing his antennae to uncurl to their full, glorious length. He shut the door to Ulla's room, took off the many layers of his uniform, and lay naked on his bed, kicking his legs above him, remembering Prague, and the picture of the woman in furs on his wall. Alice was far more beautiful, far more. She had a long neck, many, many neck bones. And long, long hair if she would let it . . . The vision broke, and he fell asleep.

"Whoever wants to know the heart and mind of America, had better learn baseball," wrote Jacques Barzun. The insight was exact. Recent changes in our decades of greed have been accurately reflected in our "national pastime": the wealth and avarice of owners and players, the angry factions, the language of "rights." In 1923, however, the game had a cultural freshness all the more sparkling for the recent scandal of the century, the "Black Sox" throwing a World Series for payoff. The country was quick to react, to wash its dirty laundry clean, and today the sun shone brightly on a newly built and two-months-opened Yankee Stadium gleaming on the upper Harlem River, directly across from the Polo Grounds.

On June 26, the Yankees were away at Chicago, and the stadium had been rented to Princeton and Yale for their end-of-season play-off. Gregor and Alice made their way from the Woodlawn Avenue Elevated (an exciting trip!) to the north entrance, and through the tunnel on the third-base side. Gregor was unprepared for the explosion of green that greeted him. The cockroach eye is extremely sensitive in the green and yellow range, and after his morning of muted interiors, and his afternoon of gray sidewalk and steel, the young Blattarian was overwhelmed by the intensity and hue. Green-how-I-love-you-green charged through his giant neurons, the American frontier, the myth of innocence, the "fresh, green breast of the New World." This was the perfect American day, in the perfect American place, the *mens sana* of universities in the *corpore sano* of sport, and here he was with his newly beloved leading the way, *das Ewig-Weibliche*, Democracy in America!

They wended their way down the concrete steps to their box seats on the third-base line. Gregor was almost speechless with the beauty, excitement, and joy of it all. A billboard for Ajax flypaper over the left center bleachers: LAST YEAR WHITEY WITT CAUGHT 167 FLIES, BUT AJAX CAUGHT 19 BILLION, 856 MILLION, 437 THOUSAND, 665. So excited was he by this paradise of green and brown—dropped in the middle of a city, surrounded by apartments, served by the El—that he laughed at the message, and did not shudder. Surely there was nothing in weary old Vienna to equal The Yankee Stadium in The Bronx, America.

"Why is there a pile of earth in the middle of the field? Will not the baseball players run into it?" The only game he knew was soccer.

"I believe it's called the pitching mound," said Alice. "The players don't run across the field, they run around the bases. See them, the three bags? There's one right here in front of us. "

"Ah, yes. On the land without the grass. Do they go around and around as long as they can?"

A vendor descended the steps toward them. "Hot dogs! Get your red hots! Hot dogs!"

"*Mein Gott, Wienerschnitzel!* Oh, we must have. You would like? Yes? Two plates, please, with brown mustard."

"We don't got plates, bud. Just buns. Mustard we got."

"How much do they cost?"

"Ten cents. For you, two for a quarter."

"Gregor," Alice said, "thank you, but I'll pay for my own."

"Please, Miss Paul, let me pay. It is I have dragged you here . . . Two, please, sir."

"You want sauerkraut? No extra charge."

"You speak German!" Gregor was pleased and excited.

"German? I wouldn't even talk to a Kraut. Here's your dogs."

"I'll have one, too, friend," said an older man in the next box. "My grandfather was German, and my grandmother was Austro-Hungarian. Will you still sell me a frankfurter?"

"Don't gimme a hard time, Charlie, I'm just tryin' to make a livin' like everybody else. Here's your dog. Mustard and sauerkraut."

"*Vielen Dank.*" The man tipped his gray fedora.

Gregor leaned over. *"Sie sind deutsch?"*

"No."

"But you have a German grandfather and Austrian grandmother . . . Oh, excuse me, this is Miss Alice Paul . . . and I am called Gregor Samsa."

"Charlie Ives. Glad to meet you. No, my grandfather and grandmother were American—both sides—and their grandfathers and grandmothers were American, all the way back. We came over on the *Mayflower*, as they say. Practically founded the country. We did found Danbury, Connecticut."

"Why then you told the frankfurt man you were . . . ?"

"He was being a jerk about not talking to Germans, standing there selling German food. Hell, Beethoven was German. Excuse me, ma'am. And Mozart was Austrian."

"You are a music person."

"Some might say so. Some would laugh."

On June 26, 1923, Charles Edward Ives was forty-eight years old, partner and CEO of Ives & Myrick, the most innovative and successful insurance firm in America. He was also a composer whose technical inventions and fearless imagination anticipated and inspired much avant-garde twentieth-century music. But he had stopped composing.

"Sounds like you might need a little orientation to the national pastime, son. Where you from?"

"I'm from Prague, a big city in what is now Czecho-Slovakia, and Miss Paul is from . . . ?"

"Moorestown, New Jersey."

"Did you say she was Alice Paul? *The* Alice Paul? From the Nineteenth Amendment?" Alice nodded. "Miss Paul," said Ives, "I'm honored to meet you!" He tipped his hat. Gregor beamed with pride, though he didn't know the Nineteenth Amendment from the Thirteenth. "I'm planning to organize for an amendment myself."

"What is that?" asked Alice.

"The Twentieth Amendment. We need to get politics out of governing, and give power to the real people. We don't need any more of these skins-thick, hands-slick, wits-quick, so-called leaders with their under-values. My amendment proposes a direct referendum beginning nine months before the election . . ."

Just then, the Princeton team burst onto the field.

"We need to talk more about this. Here's my card. Will you come see me?"

"I live in Washington."

"Well, I'll come see you in Washington. Is that all right? Do you have a card?"

"Just call the National Woman's Party."

Gregor chewed his hot dog and listened in amazement. Who were these people? Who was this woman who lived in the Nation's Capitol? Oh, no, Washington. Is far away. How far away is Washington? Is there a train from New York to Washington? The Yale and Princeton megaphone men yelled, "Please rise and join in singing 'The Star-Spangled Banner!'"

It would be eight years before the old song became the obligatory national anthem, but the college boys were early on to something big.

"Do you know this?" asked Alice.

"I don't know all the words."

"Just move your mouth," said Ives, "and hold your hand over your heart." Gregor put his claw on his left chest and not over the wound in his central lower back.

During the singing, Ives, with hat in hand, and stars in his eyes, sang a most remarkable obbligato to the awkward tune in his high, cracking tenor, and ending fortissimo, brayed out "home of the brave" a convinced semitone above the tonic, and bowed, humbly, to the cheering crowd.

"Mr. Samsa, switch seats with Miss Paul so I can explain what's going on."

"No. I want her to hear, too, so she can later explain me again."


Exhilarated talk went on throughout the game, often yelled over the roaring throng: the history of Ivy League rivalries, baseball as American myth, man love vs. fairy love, Abner Doubleday and the fraudulent American origin of the game, hitting tricks, coaching strategy, fielding technique, pitching philosophy, advertising in the ballpark, comparison with the pros, baseball and the pursuit of innocence, the physics of curve balls, male bonding and its dangers, the new harder ball, why the bullpen is called the bullpen, likely trends of the coming post-Ruth era, the Common Law origins of the infield fly rule, the oppressive labor conditions brought about by the reserve clause, the Taftian origins of the seventh-inning stretch, American transcendentalism, the segregation of colored players to the Negro leagues, and of colored fans to the bleachers, to bleach themselves, perhaps, in the unremitting sun, baseball idioms that have become part of everyday language: out in left field, three strikes, you're out, off-base, switch hitter, wild pitch, in the ballpark, to throw someone a curve ball, unable to get to first base—with Gregor furiously taking notes.

He asked amazing things like, "Why do the men just sit in the club-house?" (He meant dugout.) "Why don't they run out and try to stop them from catching the baseball?" A not unreasonable question. Or, "What would happen if the batter would run or to first base or to third base—whichever he wanted, and just make the same direction till he makes a home run?" (He meant a runner could advance clockwise, according to the same rules, until he scored.) What an addition that would be. What complex fielding it would cause!

Alice made anthropological remarks about the anthropoids on the field, their sexuality, their gestures, their politics, and about the anthropoids in the stands, their reactions, their sense of good and evil, their piggish eating behavior and slovenly treatment of the seating area, and their "baseball Sadies," mindlessly along for the ride.

Ives contributed detailed information on technique (he was a pitcher himself), baseball history, anecdote and myth, insurance problems concerning large crowds and fast-moving hard objects, balls and bottles, and also some speculation on crowd noise as a model of complex sound for symphonic composition.

Even twenty years later, Gregor remembered one thread of the discussion, a theme he would encounter, significantly, to the end of his days. It began in the fourth inning when the plate umpire was hit and slightly injured by a ball fouled back. The crowd went wild with cheering. He was puzzled as to why they should enjoy seeing someone hurt.

"It's not just 'someone,'" corrected Ives, "it's the umpire."

Gregor didn't understand the distinction.

"The American psyche," Ives continued, "is stretched between its love of law, and its love affair with lawlessness."

"Ah, the outlaw-hero," Gregor observed. "Jesse James, Billy the Kid."

"The batterer and rapist," added Alice.

"Ty Cobb, the base-stealer. Precisely. Americans are a legalistic people, and baseball has a far more elaborate set of rules than any other sport. We like it that way, and we memorize all the statistics that go with it."

"And the umpires are like judges," Gregor concluded. "They wear special dark clothing like judges—"

"And the ump is always right."

"Like men," said Alice. "You can argue, but they're always right."

"'Kill the ump!'" Ives continued. "We don't *like* transcendent authority. *We* want to make and interpret the rules. So the ump is a perfect target. He embodies the rules, and enforces them. For this, the punishment is death. Oedipal father-fortissimo-furioso. Every damn batter and every runner a litigator. Argue the calls, appeal to another umpire. It's a loud dumb show of our contradictions. I wouldn't be surprised if baseball winds up, twenty, thirty years from now, creating a land full of lawyers!"

"I'm sure these thick-necked patrons would like nothing better than a real fight on the field, some unconfined violence . . ." Alice was in gentle high dudgeon.

"It is ironic," Gregor said, "that these despised villains are the guaranteers of *Unbescholtenheit*—do you say integrity?"

"In America, freedom is more important than integrity," said Ives.

Gregor would have cause, often, to remember these words.


It was a day of wonders—on the field and off. Despite the outstanding hitting and fielding of a Princeton shortstop named Moe Berg, Yale took the game 5–1 to win the Big Three title. Charles Ives was too nice a man to crow about it. His only post-game comment was "That Moe Berg is too slow for a shortstop. He should learn to catch." And he invited Gregor to come visit him at Ives & Myrick if he got the chance. He gave him his card.

Gregor and Alice followed the crowd back to the El, and each stood quietly on the noisy ride south, straphangers reviewing the richness of the day. Instead of taking the shuttle at Grand Central, they walked west along Forty-second Street, the sun beginning to lower in the sky, many New Yorkers still out strolling in the cooling part of a hot summer day. Gregor took a small detour to inspect the lions at the Public Library, and Alice thought he looked "quite heroic" standing next to them. They sat in Bryant Park watching children perform their elaborate jump-rope routines.


"Those little girls," Alice mused, "what kind of a world will they have? When they get too old to jump rope, what happens?"

"The breasts will grow, and . . ."

"Even you . . ."

"You jump before you know what I will say."

"Sex. Sex and sex. The prison of male desire."

"I begin to say that the breasts will grow, the hearts will grow underneath the breasts, the minds will grow above, and maybe—when there are more people like you—the voice will come out from between the mind and heart."

"But it starts with the breasts."

Gregor knew he was in dangerous territory, but his admiration for his bench mate, and the sexual energy he felt around her, kept him going, his dorsal gland as wet as his wound.

"Tell me what you are doing. In Washington. What you do in Washington."

"I sit in an office. The National Woman's Party."

"Are you what is called a femininist?"


Alice Paul *was* feminism. She was the single person most responsible for achievement of women's suffrage, and an untiring inspiration to a generation of politically, psychologically liberated women. She was the general of the army, the chief strategist of the think tank, the first to be out on the streets, or hauled off to jail, the most convinced, the most forceful, the most articulate, the most clearheaded revolutionary currently walking the land. By thirty-five, she had forever changed the governing of the United States, and now, three years later, she was aiming to change its very being. Did she laugh at Gregor's question? No. She simply said,

"The word is 'feminist.' And yes, I suppose you could say I am."

"I thought so. I look at the contents of your journal."

"Would you like your own copy?"

"Oh, yes, very much, I do."

"I'll send one."

"Oh, one million thanks! But in the meanwhile, can you tell me simply what is a feminist?" Breasts. Heart. Mind. Voice.

"I wish it were simple. There are people who think I don't know what the word means."

"Truly? But you are editing a magazine . . . You must explain me about your Amendment, as I was not here."

"The men went off to war to fight for Freedom."

"And your great president's Fourteen Points. I read them."

"And what do the Fourteen Points say about women?"

"I must think. I can't remember."

"That's because they don't say *anything* about women. Our children were killed fighting for Freedom, and not one woman in this country was free."

"You mean free to vote election."

"That's the first of all freedoms. From elected officials come Law, and from Law comes culture and behavior. This is a country run by men, for men."

"So is Czech Republic, so is Austria."

"Do you think this is right?"

"To tell the truth, I did not think."

"Exactly. This has to change—all over the world. We decided to change it. Some nine years ago, my group began to picket—you know what that is?—to stand in front of the White House where the President lives, with signs asking President Wilson to help us get the vote."

"Surely he did, such a great man."

"Surely he didn't. But we were getting sympathetic newspaper coverage until the war fever began, and then we were attacked—by men in the streets, soldiers, sailors, little boys even, spitting, throwing bottles and stones. The police just stood there and watched."

"And President Wilson did not stop them—right outside his own house?"

"He ordered us to be put in jail."

"Why? What you did?"

"For blocking the street. We weren't blocking the street. The people attacking us were blocking the street."

"You really went to jail? You? This lovely woman sitting here?" Breasts. Heart. Mind. Voice.

"Seventy days."

"What did you do?"

"We went on a hunger strike."

"What is 'hunger strike'?"

"When you refuse to eat. You make the authorities—and everyone—decide if they are ready to kill you for blocking the sidewalk."

"Like a Hunger Artist."

"What's that?"

"In Vienna we had—I mean there was—a carnival with a man who would see how long he could go without to eat. There was a sign outside his cage of how many days it was."

"Was he protesting something?"

"No. That was his art. To be able to go without food. To be able to survive longer than anyone else in the world without food."

"They *made* us eat. They couldn't take the publicity if we had died."

"How did they do that? Make you eat?"

"They held us down on a table, six big men, and they forced tubes down our throats into our stomachs and poured some horrible concoction down."

"Oh no . . ." Gregor's heart went out to this thin, pale, large-eyed woman. He spontaneously reached for her hand. She pulled it away. Then, guilty at offending this gentle soul, she put it lightly back on his.

"It felt . . . dreadful. I couldn't breathe. My stomach retched and I vomited all over myself. Each time. They put me in the psychopathic ward."

The sun shone red in the library windows. Gregor's heart was so full of sympathy—sym-pathy, *Mit-leid*, with-feeling—he couldn't say a word. He covered her lightly touching hand with his other claw, and they sat together in silence, each absorbed in memory and longing.

"You are a beautiful person, Miss Alice Paul." Gregor could not contain himself. But then he did not know what to say. Alice stood up. "You are wanting to go," he said.

"Let's go back to the hotel. I'm getting chilly."

They walked the rest of the way in silence. While crossing Sixth Avenue, Alice took Gregor's arm to pull him along out of traffic's way. She held on for two long blocks, and did not let go until they had crossed Broadway and stood in front of the hotel. It was almost nine by the time this odd couple stepped into the ornate lobby. The bellhops stared.

As you might imagine, Gregor was both wary and excited about what the night might hold. A line from Rilke, his beloved countryman, kept running through his head: *Wie soll ich meine Seele halten, dass sie nicht an deine rührt?* How shall I withhold my soul so that it does not twine with yours?

"You must go?" he asked.

"I should. I have a meeting tomorrow morning with the one man who resigned from President Wilson's staff over the way he treated us."

"Who is that?"

"His name is Dudley Field Malone. A principled man. I appreciate his courage. We're putting our heads together about strategy."

Gregor wasn't sure about this putting heads together. A wave of jealousy ran through his thorax and thickened his throat. A desperate save:

"Would you mind telling me about strategies? It would help me better understand America. We can go in my room, and you meet Ulla, the manager of the hotel who lets me use her apartment."

"It wouldn't disturb her?"

"No. I'm sure she will be interested."

"And I'd be interested to hear from a woman managing a large hotel. Let me go to my room first, change my clothes, get a little something to eat, and I'll come in an hour. Will that be all right?"

"Oh yes. Very all right. Come to room 2016, on floor twenty. I will wait for you."


Ten o'clock. Fifty minutes to go. What to do? Fifty minutes, fifty years! He checked the dressing over his wound. Damp. He gave it a smell check with his right antenna. Better change it. He got undressed, peeled off the tape, and deposited the brown-stained bandage in the kitchenette trash. Ulla was used to this.

But what was that wonderful, heady smell? Oh, no! His dorsal gland was starting again to drip pheromone in anticipation. It may be a good thing that human noses are vestigial. Into the shower to counter secretions. Soapy, soap, soap. *Da ist noch ein Fleck! Fort, verdammter Fleck, fort, sag' ich!*

How our bodily fluids do inform against us! He was in love—was it possible after all these years and the oceans of water under God's bridge?

Granted, his emotions were extrapolated and premature, but that's what falling in love is all about. He had found a soul mate, and would mate with Alice's soul. Yet his physiology seemed to have its own thoughts. He wanted to make love with her rarity; his insect organs seemed to have other, more hormonal, plans. He shut off the hot water and invested himself in the cold.

Hypothermic but calmer, Gregor re-dressed his wound and wrapped himself in one of Ulla's bathrobes. Back in his bedroom, he surveyed the scene. 9:45. One bed, one chair. *If I sit on the bed, that will look too casual. On the other hand, if I take the only chair, then she is forced to sit on the bed, and that will make her tense. I can always bring another chair from Ulla's room. Now, clothing. Greet her in this robe? Why not? No. Too pushy. Too scary. But casual. Slacks and an open shirt. And perhaps slippers, for just a touch of* je ne sais quoi.

He dressed and slicked back his antennae. He sat down in the chair. 9:55. He stood up and retrieved his copy of Einstein from the bedside table. He sat down again. Nonchalant. Let her walk in and see me reading. 9:56. Nonchalant. 9:56 and a half. Calm down, old man. *Auf die Frage: "Warum fällt ein Stein, den wir emporheben und darauf loslassen, zur Erde?" antwortet man gewöhnlich: "Weil er von der Erde angezogen wird."* She won't come early, I bet. If she comes right on time, does that mean she's anxious to see me, or that she is just punctual to all appointments? Like a business appointment. If she comes late, does that mean she's trying to tease me? Maybe she doesn't really want to come. . . .

There was a knock at the door outside Ulla's room. *I'll let her knock a second time. Make her wonder just a little bit.* Come in? Come in! Gregor crossed his lower legs and remained nonchalantly seated.

"Gregor?"

"Yes?"

"It's Alice."

"Come in. I'm in here, through the green door."

Alice stuck her head into Gregor's room. He rose, as slowly and gracefully as he could, to greet her. The volume of Einstein clattered from his lap to the floor, losing its dustcover.

"Oh, dear," said Alice, and rushed to rescue the book. Gregor, remembering the recent retrieval problem at her door, allowed her to pick it up for him.

"Thank you. Do you know this?"

"*Über die spezielle und die allgemeine Relativitätstheorie.* No. I don't read German. But Einstein, yes, him I know. So does everyone. I didn't realize you were a scientist. I'm impressed."

"Have you been in Europe?" he asked.

"I did some graduate work in England—a long time ago."

"Now *I* am who is impressed. I call you 'Doktor'?"

"Alice is fine."

"Come sit down. Here, I'll from Ulla's room bring another chair."

"Where is Ulla? You said she'd be here."

"There was emergency with the chambermaids. Not serious, but they have a meeting she had to be."

"Will she be back?"

He pushed a small armchair through the door.

"I think as soon as it is over."

They both sat down.

"So." Gregor waited.

"You said you wanted to know more about our plans." As usual, Alice was quick to get down to business. "I'm here in New York because we just met at Seneca Falls to organize for a new amendment to the Constitution—"

"Another amendment! You and Mr. Ives. How things are quickly changing!"

"Mr. Ives, if I may say so, is a crackpot—you know what that is?" She banged on her head to demonstrate. "Our drive will be realistic—and successful. An amendment to guarantee equal rights for women."

"The name of your magazine."

"Precisely. I wrote the amendment text; it's simple: 'Men and Women shall have equal rights throughout the United States and in every place subject to its jurisdiction.'"

"Who would have one problem with that?" Gregor drew his chair closer to hers, the better to hear her answer.

"No one, you would think. But people will, I assure you."

"Your amendment would make it nothing different for women and men."

"Correct." Alice, soft but hard.

"Because they are equal."

"That's right." This discussion was not exactly what he had in mind.

"But women and men are not really the same," he said. "They are smaller and weaker, and often they need protection."

"It's men that need protection—from each other. Did women make the war? It's men who mismanage a man's world. Conflicts settled by violence, bloodshed, war, and militarism. When women are included in world affairs, things won't be that way."

"How do you know?"

"And, excuse me, 'protection.' Men's so-called protective instinct comes primarily from jealousy and self-interest. Women are 'good' if they are protected by a man, and 'bad' if they're not. Why the uproar now about unwed mothers? Because they defy male proprietorship, and act out their sexual freedom." Alice got up from her chair, looked at her host, and sat down on the bed. Gregor's knees perked up.

"You believe in sexual freedom?" he asked.

"I believe in a woman's right to determine what she does. Just like a man's. Equal. Equal rights."

"There are women who don't agree with you. The ones who think you know nothing about feminism."

"Some women, especially the younger women now—the flappers—oppose our program because they still believe women were created solely for the comfort and glory of men. Older women oppose it because they think anything new is scandalous. Some, young and old, oppose it because equality for women affects their selfish interests. Some oppose it because they don't think politically. But, for the most part those opposed or indifferent are opposed or indifferent because they don't know the facts and haven't been aroused to their responsibility to do justice." All this militant rhetoric was spoken slowly, in a gentle, deep voice. But Alice's eyes blazed dark fire.

"Do you mind if I tell you my reaction?" asked Gregor.

"No, surely not. I'm interested in a European point of view. Because this movement must be taken worldwide."

It wasn't clear to Gregor whether, under these conditions, honesty was the best policy—but at least it might be anodyne to his tachycardia, and the unrequested wetness of his dorsal gland.

"It seems that all those who opposes you is or reactionary, or selfish, or stupid. But maybe there is something correct about what they say, too. For example, do you have here the man pays the woman when there is a divorce?"

"Alimony. Yes."

"Do you think the woman should also pay the man, too?"

Alice was unflappable. "Some feminists want to do away with alimony."

"That will not be very popular with women."

"No. But instead of dropping alimony, the law could require that each pay the other an amount that would make up for earning capacity lost in marriage and family care."

"It is smart. The man does not get much, yet the law is equal."

"The point is that equality under the law precedes all else. Everything will follow from that."

Rather than pulling away from Gregor as a result of his honest critique, Alice felt closer to him. She began to recover that sense of connection that had developed during the day, especially in the park, but which had begun to wither in their current setting. Gregor sensed the warming immediately, perhaps with his antennae, perhaps with antennae more spiritual. He decided to press on with this new, seemingly successful, direction. Such are the uses of honesty.

"I am hearing a contradict. On the left side of your mouth you say that women and men are equal, and on the right side that women are better."

"Even though women are in many ways superior to men, all we ask is that they be considered equal under the law. There's no contradiction."

"How is the women superior?"

"Women value human life more, probably because they give birth to it. Last week in Wisconsin, a jury sentenced two youths to six years in jail—each—for stealing a watch. No woman would do that. Women should be allowed on juries."

"It appears you hate men."

"I don't hate men. I wouldn't go out with one, but I think the interests of all humanity are identical. Men don't know how to further such goals."

"Even Dudley Feel Malone, or whatever is his name?"

"Most men are bad at it."

"And animals."

"What?"

"Animals have interests, too."

"Yes they do."

"Even insects?"

"Of course."

"Even male insects?"

Alice got up from the bed.

"Oh, Gregor, don't be silly." She put her hand on his tegmen. "Let's stop talking about this. I talk about it all the time. Let's go for a little walk, and then I have to go to bed."

"Would you go to bed with me?" There, he said it! All or nothing. Whatever happens, happens. He was surprised by her response:

"Why?"

"You said you wouldn't go out with a man."

"And?"

"And I'm lonely. And I like you. And maybe you like me."

"What about Ulla? Don't you sleep with Ulla?"

"Ulla? No! Never. She lets me share her rooms."

"Why not—if you're lonely? Men will sleep with anyone."

"I can't explain it to you. Or I do not want to."

"But she'll come back from her meeting. What will she think?"

"I lie to you. She is not in a meeting. She is at her uncle's house, and will not be home tonight."

"Why did you lie to me?"

"I don't know. I told you she is here so you would feel safe and come."

Alice stood facing him for perhaps thirty seconds, then sat down on the bed and took off her necklace.

And here, gentle reader, the curtain must be drawn. The interactions of chitin and flesh are rare, and like many rare things—tropical orchids, Beauty's visits from the Beast, solitary woes—they are best left in darkness, unmolested. Suffice it to say that it was not a happy experience for either Gregor or Alice. Strangeness mixed with shame will spawn an unsound brew. Flesh is tender, chitin hard. How to play antennae with someone who has none? Some lips are made for kissing, others definitely not. Humans are the only mammals that mate face to face; one of our pair was not even a mammal. There are places where hooks are not appropriate. The one good thing that can be said was that they did not have to worry about birth control.

Some would-be lovers can brush off a traumatic night, or even a series of them. Some will try again, hope burning eternal in the sweating breast; some will seek couples' counseling, licensed or unlicensed; some will cast about for psychological, physiological, or pharmacological assists—or medical appliances. But this pair was too deeply wounded: she, because at thirty-eight, she had never imagined losing her virginity this way (she had never imagined losing it at all), and he, not for the first time, had given great pain to someone he loved.

First, he had sorely pained his family years ago with his change. True, his cruelty had been thrust upon him, but nevertheless, the very fact of him had rent the hearts of those closest to him, those he wanted only to help and to love. And here, now, once again, the pain. He had seduced this strange and lovely woman, manipulated her into his bed—and made her cry. Who was he? Was he doomed forever to be out in the cold, his beak pressed against the window of humanity? If not Alice Paul—the magnificent, munificent Alice Paul—then who could want him, who would have him, in his current condition?

And was he—doubly inhuman—up to his imagined task of helping humanize humanity? How could he, when his very physiognomy prevented intimacy with others, if his efforts to share what was best and most generous in himself were destined to yield only suffering?

He lay in bed, covered with her fluids—saliva, sweat, possibly blood. Worst of all—the tears. His own wound wept through the dressing on his back; he lay, despondent, in a cold, brown pool. Alice had left his room at two A.M., disheveled and dejected. When he called her at eight to apologize, he found she had checked out earlier that morning.

```
24 July 1923 with Alice last night very very bad experi-
ence. Grausam. I can not endure this way, without some-
one for intimate relationship. Things must change!!! I
```

```
see a plackard in the trollycar for plastik surgon. To-
morrow I go to look on trollycar for telephone.
```

This was a desperate decision for Gregor, considering how negative he felt toward the surgery developing in Austria and Germany during and after the war. Surgeons were becoming fabulously wealthy performing *Nasenplastik*—nose jobs—on rich Jews wishing to improve their images, their business prospects, their chances for intermarriage. Moishe Rosenbaum transformed into Martin Rose—Martin Rose of the aquiline nose. Nasenplastik, Mammaplastik—how scornful he was of this kind of chicanery, as if Mother Nature could be hoodwinked with a few thousand dollars and a scalpel. Yet here Gregor was, another Jew in search of metamorphosis, reduced to scouring public trolleys for a referral. Where would the money come from? That he hadn't considered, so needful was he in his agony.

The doctor on the poster appeared to be about thirty-five, a blond, clean-shaven, square-jawed, WASPy but friendly-looking man in a white coat. DO YOU HAVE A PROBLEM WITH YOUR APPEARANCE? FREE CONSULTATION. CALL HA-6984. Gregor made an appointment with a pleasant-sounding receptionist for his first day off.

Morning thunderstorms having cleared out a week of oppressive humidity, it was a pleasantly cool afternoon in early August. Gregor took a cab from the hotel up to 999 Fifth Avenue. Long walks on two legs exhausted him, and he was still unsure about scurrying along the streets of New York in a horizontal position. He hadn't realized what an expensive address 999 was, at Seventy-sixth Street, across from the park. But when the cabbie said, "Here ya go, bud," and he stepped out of the cab, he realized for the first time that he might be getting into something over his head. But the ad had said "Free Consultation," and he could always back out if needed.

Nine-ninety-nine was a large, gray townhouse sandwiched between two huge luxury apartment buildings. The doorbell did not identify its occupant. Gregor checked the slip of paper in his jacket pocket: 999—a hard number to read or write incorrectly. He rang the bell. The same pleasant phone voice greeted him: "Yes?"

"Gregor Samsa here. I have a four-o'clock appointment."

"Yes, Mr. Samsa, we're expecting you. I'll buzz you in. Take the elevator up one flight, and I'll meet you at the door."

Doors were always hard for Gregor. It was difficult for him to manipulate American doorknobs designed for hands, not claws. And especially when he had only the few seconds provided by a buzzer. But it seemed as if Dr. Lindhorst had had him precisely in mind, for this knob was actually a lever, as in Europe, which could be easily engaged: Gregor pushed down, and opened the door. Yet what a lever it was! He felt it before he saw it, a grotesque brass head with a long, protruding tongue. While the outer aspect of the face was that of a normal, even handsome young woman, with her lovely right ear at the axial center, the inner aspect, closest to the door, was a horribly mutilated quasi-face, as if its subject had been half-eaten by the most ravenous cancer. Her tongue was hyperextended, not as a convenience to Gregor, but in a cry of misery or repugnance. Strange, he thought, and shuddered.

A small, self-service elevator greeted our elevator operator, an ornate, mirrored cab with only one button, a sky-blue oval marked "HIGHER." Where was "down"? he wondered. There must be a separate entrance and exit, he thought, so patients will not have to be stared at. Clever. Thoughtful. He thinks of everything. Gregor pushed the blue button.

The elevator was completely silent, and extraordinarily, bizarrely, slow, taking perhaps two minutes to climb the twenty or so feet to the first landing. On the wall in front of the gate, the passenger could leisurely view a brilliantly executed collage of faces and figures from Brueghel and Bosch, Leonardo's "Five Grotesque Heads," Dürer's Horsemen of the Apocalypse, each horseman scattered solo, willy-nilly, among the madhouse of others, and all these multiplied, should one turn away, in what Gregor now observed to be subtly—and not so subtly—distorting mirrors. It was surely an extraordinary man who had planned such entertainment for his customers. One would never have imagined this, from the face on the placard.

The cab stopped in front of a plain, paneled door. A lithe young woman with glowing skin, but strangely wrinkled hands, opened it gracefully, and gracefully pulled back the inner gate.

"Mr. Samsa, how nice to see you. Come in." Gregor stepped into a small antechamber, perhaps a waiting room. "I'm Miss Mozart." Gregor's eyes lit up, prismatic. "No relation, I'm sorry to say. Won't you have a seat? The doctor will be with you shortly." She disappeared behind one of the three doors.

Gregor paused before the only chair in the room, a carved oak masterpiece, probably sixteenth century, as singular as all the good doctor's other artifacts: instead of the normal lion's paws, the arms of the chair ended in human hands, gripping globes, the globe on the left carved and painted with the map of the known world, on the right with the celestial spheres. Both featured monsters—of the depths and of the heights. On the middle digit of each hand, a ring with pearl of great price. The legs of the chair were shaggy and ended in cloven hooves, though of what beast Gregor could not say. The tapestries on seat and back were covered with a marvelous array of iridescent insects. He sat down—and felt a strange vibration course through his body, a sensation one might have if suddenly embraced by the hairy god himself.

The insect theme was continued on floor and walls. In this relatively small room were thirty or forty framed exhibits of butterflies and moths, arranged by subspecies. Set in pots and canisters were an assortment of plants Gregor had never seen before, in either the old or the new world—including a nine-foot tree in a huge golden pot—a tree whose reddish-brown bark seemed to be crying: aromatic fluid, the color of Gregor's, was seeping from its innumerable cracks, and hardening into tear-shaped globules that he could harvest, should he so desire. Several feet up, a split in the trunk revealed two bald labia, rimmed in bark, pushed apart by some pressure behind them. Were Gregor more sexually sophisticated, he might have recognized the female image they formed. Pressing out from the core of the trunk, as if straining to escape was—there was no mistaking it—the shaped image of a reaching hand and fetus face—a human infant trying to grasp its way into the world. This was not a carving, mind you. This was an act of playful Nature, dancing among the categories, crossing her own uncrossable lines. Gregor got up to more closely examine this freak of sculpting nature. Five fingers on the hand. And the mouth open as if uttering its first cry.

"Mr. Samsa, how wonderful to meet you!" Gregor jumped. "I've heard about you for years—good things, good things . . ."

A burly, stocky man, one human head shorter than Gregor, his dark red face haloed in white hair, his beetling eyebrows almost covering piercing black eyes, his enormous, blue-veined nose in colorful contrast, offered his huge, hairy hand to Gregor. He wore a gray European smock, covered in streaks of clay.

"You must forgive me for keeping you waiting. I had to finish up a little sculpture—oh, it's nothing, a trifle, but one in which a patient is most interested."

"Who are you?"

"Dr. Lindhorst. Who did you think? Maxwell Lindhorst. This being America, you may call me Max, since I feel we are already old friends."

"But Dr. Lindhorst . . ."

"Yes? I said call me Max."

"But Dr. Lindhorst is—more young. And he has a white coat."

"*I* have a white coat. I just don't scare my patients with it."

"But the picture on the trolley car."

"Appearances, appearances. All you Americans ever think about. Excuse me, I know you are not American—you are Czech, correct?—but it is Americans, by and large, who read the ad."

"You put up picture of you that isn't you?"

"Who said it was me?"

"The placard says, Dr. Lindhorst—"

"I beg to differ, my friend. The placard says, simply, 'Do you have a problem with your appearance? Free consultation.' You found my name only by calling the phone number."

"I guess that is true."

"I cut the picture out of a toothpaste ad in *The Saturday Evening Post.* 'Dentists prefer Pepsodent,' or whatever."

"You mean he isn't even a plastik surgeon?"

"He may be a plastic surgeon, for all I know, posing as a dentist. We mustn't worship at the shrine of appearances. Come into my office and you can tell me what brings you here."

Max Lindhorst ushered Gregor into his office, a high-ceilinged chamber, completely lined with books, many ancient, some to be reached only by ladder. Gregor was gestured to the large chair behind a combination desk and worktable, on which, lying on newsprint, was a clay mask of a noble male face, the carving tools beside it. The doctor took the only other seat in the room, the clay-dusty top of a small stepladder.

"Why am I behind your desk, while you sit on a ladder?"

"Because you are in charge, Gregor Samsa, and I am your servant. This is sometimes hard for a patient to understand, so I make it clear this way."

"How do you know me?" Gregor asked.

"I first heard of you several years ago from my friend Kaltenborn. He said he had seen your Roentgen act. Quite a piece of showmanship."

"It wasn't showmanship. It was to demonstrate that—"

"It was to demonstrate that the owner of your circus could use the newspapers to drum up a bigger crowd. *Nicht wahr?*"

"I don't know. Perhaps."

"But that's not how I really know you. In the last few months, my daughter Olympia has written of nothing but you. Her team was the winner of a Gregor Dance contest in—coincidence—Olympia, Washington."

"Washington! Does she live near the Capitol?"

"Olympia is the capital of Washington."

"No, of the United States. America."

"Gregor, there is a state called Washington—all the way on the other side of the country. Then there is Washington, the city, which is the capital of the United States."

"And your daughter lives in the faraway one."

"Unfortunately."

"Yes," the roach agreed.

"But why unfortunately for you? You don't know her."

"I have a friend in the capital of the United States."

"And?"

"I thought maybe your daughter would know her."

"You sound sad."

"I am tired. I did not sleep very good last night."

"Ah. This is no reason to visit a plastic surgeon."

"Dr. Lindhorst. This is but a consultation, correct? And it is free of charge?"

"Certainly. I never let money stand in the way of my patients' satisfaction. Besides, for you, the famous Gregor Samsa, all is free, everything. My compliments."

"You mean if we have an operation, I don't pay?"

"I am interested in your happiness."

"I don't pay?"

"You don't pay."

"You see, I have very little money."

"You don't pay anything. What can I do for you?"

There was a long pause. Strange as it may seem, Gregor had not previously considered an answer to this predictable question.

"Dr. Lindhorst, my situation is, do you say unique?"

"I know that, my friend."

"There are things about me, about my body, which stop me to do . . ."

He could not say out loud what he had so long held in secret: the name of his game, the title of his quest. It sounded too pat, simultaneously too megalomaniacal and too trivial: "I want to help the human race." Oh, I see. Tell me another one. But if he could not be intimate with another human being, how then to do? Publish a paper? Write the book of all books? What would he write?

"Why did you sleep poorly last night?" asked the doctor, cutting to the quick.

"In my bed I think of . . ."

"The woman from Washington."

"How you know?"

"I'm paid to know. Or not paid, as the case may be."

"Doctor, do you think I can be more attractive when I have the right number of limbs?"

"What is the right number?"

"Four. Four limbs. Two arms and two legs. Like you."

"Maybe you need more legs, not fewer. Eight, perhaps. Or ten."

"That will only make it worse. Then they will never allow me."

"Who?"

"Human people. A woman."

"A woman who could love you with four legs could just as easily love you with ten. Or twenty."

"Not true. Too many legs make difficult holding."

"You cannot sculpt your way to happiness."

"I want you to take off my middle legs."

The doctor looked at Gregor long and hard. He took a silver cigarette case from his smock, opened it, and offered one to his patient. Gregor declined.

"No thank you. The smoke makes my spiracles to hurt."

Dr. Lindhorst snapped the case shut and slipped it back in his pocket.

"Do you see that little statue on the bookshelf over there?"

"My eyes are not too good at far away."

The doctor got up from his stool, brought the piece over to the table, and plunked it down in front of Gregor's face. It was painted plaster of Paris, eight inches long, and showed a lovely, pink, naked woman—"stacked," as they say—modeling for a sculptor. But the sculptor was a pig, also pink, and the statue he was molding was that of a pig, a lovely, pink, naked pig in the same seductive pose as the woman's. His model had two red nipples; his sculpture had eight. In *bas-relief* along the base, Gregor could make out the word "Pig-malion," nipple red on pale green.

"I won this at Palisades Amusement Park. It took me three tickets worth of ringtoss."

Gregor was familiar with the game from his own carnival in Vienna. But he had never seen such a vulgar statue.

"Why did you want it?" He tried not to be judgmental.

"It reminds me of you. And of a lot of my patients who want to sculpt themselves in their own image."

"But you are the sculptor."

"I am only a servant, a pair of hands to do their bidding. Do you know the story of the real Pygmalion?"

"He was a sculptor who fell in love with his statue." Gregor had not taken six years of Greek and Latin for nothing.

"And what happened to him?"

"I don't remember. But nor do I remember anything terrible, and if something terrible would have happened, I would remember."

"No, you're perfectly right. Venus answered his prayers and turned his statue into a real and lovely Galatea who loved Pygmalion, her creator, with all her heart. Nine months later, they had a child. They both lived happily ever after."

"I thought you would tell me they were punished."

"Do you think they should be punished?"

"No, but . . ."

"No but yes. Why did you mention it?"

"Myths usually speak—you say transcressions, *vergehen*, to go estray?"

"Very good. What was the transgression?"

"Hubris." The Greeks, of course, had a word for such a thing: overweening presumption, irreverent disregard of human limits, the sin to which the great and gifted are most susceptible. Faust before Faust.

"So," Gregor wanted to know, "why weren't they punished?"

"Not every malefactor is punished—right away. Do you remember the rest of the story? *Metamorphoses*, Book Ten, the book of Venus Afflicted? Ovid, the egg of all changes? What was their daughter's name?"

"I think . . . I don't know."

"Paphos. She was so happy, they named a Greek island after her. She also had a son. He wasn't so happy."

"What was he called?"

"Cyniras. But his daughter Myrrha called him 'sweetest, dearest father.'"

"Why you say but?"

"Every father loves a doting daughter, but not necessarily a lusting one. When her mother was off on a trip, she weaseled her way into his bed and seduced him three nights running. On the third night, he realized this wasn't just some three-night-stand courtesan, but his own daughter. He grabbed for his sword to kill the unnatural thing, but Myrrha managed to escape with his child in her womb."

"You blame only her. But he was unfaithful to wife—"

"But this is not a story about unfaithfulness. It is a story about incest. *Blutschande*."

"Why you tell me this?"

"To help you understand the myth of Pygmalion. And we Doctors Pygmalion—you and I. Our Greek sculptor friend didn't just fall innocently in love with a beautiful statue. He is guilty of narcissism, onanism, and incest."

"What is onanism?"

"Spilling your seed upon the ground."

*"Ach ja, onanieren*—to jerk off."

"My, my, your idiomatic English is excellent. Where did you learn that?"

"From a bell-hopper in my hotel. He is teaching me words. But Pygmalion does not jerk off. I don't remember that."

With great delight, Dr. Lindhorst sprang from his ladder seat and retrieved a beautifully bound volume of Ovid from the shelf nearest his desk.

"Let's see . . . here . . . *'He gives it kisses'*—the statue—*'and fancies they are returned, he speaks to it, and takes hold of it . . .'* Here . . . *'He places her on coverings dyed with the Sidonian shell, and calls her the companion of his bed, and lays down her reclining neck upon soft feathers . . .'* Do you think that statue came out dry?"

"That is very beautiful. Maybe I need such a statue who does not mind how many legs I have."

"Masturbation, narcissism—you know what that is—and incest—those are the clarifying echoes, two generations away, from Pygmalion's original sin."

"And you say if I ask you to sculpt me—to be my sculptor hands—then I am doing jerking off and narcissism and incest?"

"I just want you to think carefully about what you are asking. I am a doctor who dispenses dreams, and you, dreamer of dreams, must be prepared for what they bring. I am your servant. Are you your master?"

"What happened to the daughter? Myrrha, is it?"

The doctor brought the book to Gregor and lay on the table in front of him.

"Read it. There. Kaltenborn says you're a great actor. Show me how well you can read."

"But this is English. I am not so good. I am better at Latin."

"You're an American now. Read."

"*'Gods, I accept my punishment gladly, whatever it is.'* This is Myrrha talking? *I offend the light and defile the darkness. I pray you, therefore, change me, make me something else, transform me entirely, clean me . . .'*"

"Excellent. Your accent leaves something to be desired, but very good. Here, I'll read you the rest: *'There must have been some god who heard her desperate petition and granted her prayer, for the earth now covered her feet, and her toes were rooting into the soil to support the trunk of her body, which stiffened as flesh and bone transformed themselves into wood, blood became sap that flowed up and into her branching arms, and skin became bark. Within her, under the wood, in her womb, a restless fetus moved, and the tree could feel it and grieve at the ruin of those fresh hopes that a baby's birth should imply. Tears flowed from the tree, miraculous fragrant tears of what we know as myrrh.*

*'And what of the child within her, that poor and ill-conceived half-brother and son? He seeks a passage into the light, a way to be born and live. The tree is swollen and contorted, and although it cannot call out, it appears to writhe in its pain. Lucina . . .'*—she's the goddess of childbirth—*'Lucina pities its tears and the plaintive sound of the wind in its groaning branches. She touches the wood with gentle hands. The tree cracks open, the bark splits, and the baby boy is born. . . .'"*

"Moment. There is such a tree in the room out there."

"I saw you inspecting it."

"Those drops on the bark were the tears. And there was a hand reaching out, and a face . . ."

"Adonis being born, a child, and then a youth, so physically handsome that Venus herself falls painfully in love."

"Ah, yes, Venus and Adonis."

"What happened with Venus and Adonis?"

"You must think I am stupid, but I don't . . . It is all quite vague."

"You would do well to take these stories more seriously. They're all about *you*. Adonis may have been good-looking, but he was a brat of little brain. A goddess in love with him? He'd rather go hunting."

"Maybe he was wise. Not to involve in a such unequal involvement."

"You mean a cross-species relationship? Gregor, you may be right. But if he was wise, you would never know it from the story. On the hunt, a wounded boar charged him and ripped his testicles off with his tusks. He bled to death from the groin, poor fellow. Not a happy ending."

"So what you say is the looking-like-innocent acts of Pygmalion the sculptor carried much evil within them."

"Enough to make one cautious." He put Ovid and Pig-malion back on their respective shelves. "Shall we still talk about amputation?"

"Yes."

"Really. Well then, let's talk about amputation. How will you support the middle of your body? I assume you still use six legs occasionally."

"They all come from my thorax close together. It should not make such difference."

"Let me see you crawl with your middle legs folded."

Gregor walked and ran, and even jumped along the rugs of Lind-horst's office.

"How about crawling up the walls and along the ceiling. Do you still do that? You'll have only two-thirds the stickiness."

"I still do it when I'm very happy."

"Are you ever very happy?"

"Not often."

"But you might be. Especially if your scheme works out. Give it a try. There's some free wall space between those shelves. Just don't knock down the moth."

Much to his surprise, Gregor found he was shaky, tentative, on a vertical wall. He did not dare the ceiling.

"Looks tentative, my hexapod friend. Are you sure you want to give that up?"

"I know this must have a trading off. I do not need to walk on the ceiling."

"Well, I'd like to be able to walk on the ceiling!" It had been a childhood ambition of young Max in the high-ceilinged apartments of Berlin. "What about back strain? Come over here." He put both hands on Gregor's back at the level of his still-folded middle pair of legs. "Let's take a short stroll." And he put his weight over his arms. They must have been a comical sight: the large cockroach with middle legs caressing his own thorax, and the short, thick, smocked doctor attempting to keep up, trying to maintain his downward thrust. They barely avoided knocking over the ladder. This went on for no more that thirty seconds before they were both exhausted.

"How did that feel?"

"Terrible. But you won't be doing that to me."

"Do you still want to be drastically modified?" asked Lindhorst, once again cutting to the heart of the matter.

"It may help me . . ."

Dr. Lindhorst stepped resolutely to the desk and pressed a button under the leg space. Miss Mozart stuck her blond head through the door.

"Yes, Doctor?"

"Miss Mozart, please prepare procedure T for Mr. Samsa here." Miss

Mozart nodded both her head and eyelids in a gesture that sharply brought Alice to Gregor's mind. The residue of hesitance was washed away in the sweet ache that rose from heart to throat.

"All right, my friend, Maxwell Lindhorst at your service. Maxwell Lindhorst, who lacks the knowledge, the wisdom, and even the right to decide what is best for his patients. Many consider cosmetic surgery an act of vanity. Some see Pride there, or Envy, or Gluttony for praise, or Sloth finding the easy way around, or Anger taking a knife to self instead of other. In your case, I suppose, it is Lust in the driver's seat. But I do not judge—because only you can know. This will all be free, gratis, as I promised. I merely ask you to sign this consent form. Don't worry. You don't have to sign in blood. I'm not interested in your soul."

The doctor took several sheets of paper from a desk drawer and placed them, along with a fountain pen, in front of him. Gregor drew his large reading glasses from his jacket and perused the pages. It was not clear what he actually understood: much of the document was in technical, medico/legal language.

"Can I die from this?"

"Of course. One can die from many things. Joy, for instance. Or love. However, it would be an extremely rare event."

Gregor took up the pen, but had trouble unscrewing the top.

"Here, I'll do that for you," said the obliging doctor. Miss Mozart knocked lightly, and again stuck her head into the room, this time from a door among the bookshelves that Gregor had not noticed. Her bun was gone, transformed into a stream of golden hair.

"The room is ready, Doctor."

"Thank you."

She disappeared behind the door.

"Shall we go?"

"Now? Right immediately?"

"There's no time like the present. Except the future. Except the future."

He walked to the bookshelf door, opened it, and beckoned his patient through. Gregor expected some sort of operating room, with huge lights over a surgical table, green tile walls and floors. Instead, he found a room more like a recording studio: a wooden chamber with acoustical tile and strategic baffling, in the middle of which a Bösendorfer concert grand faced the only seat in the room, a contraption quite like a dentist's chair, yet obviously far more comfortable.

Miss Mozart, now clad in embroidered Irish robe, held a hospital johnny over her arm.

"Mr. Samsa, will you step behind the screen, remove your clothes, and put this on?" She handed him the johnny.

"All my clothes?"

"Please."

Gregor, truly embarrassed, backed himself behind the four-paneled Chinese masterpiece. He could have sworn it had depicted a serene and holy mountain. But now, from behind, the image had transformed into a fierce mountain of a tiger, dismembering a small deer. He folded his clothes, placed them neatly on the floor, and slipped into the skimpy covering.

"I can't reach to tie this behind."

"Come out," said Miss Mozart, "I'll do it for you."

Gregor didn't mind showing this beautiful woman the smoothness of his tegmen. He strode more confidently out and presented her his open back.

"Oh!" She jumped back. He had forgotten his wound. With the day's already disturbing events, the bandage was more than saturated.

"What's the matter?" Dr. Lindhorst came quickly around to look. He held the johnny open at arm's length.

"Having a bit of a problem, there, Gregor? What's going on?"

"My wound, it . . ."

"What happened?"

"My father was frightened."

"Oh?"

"And he threw an apple at my back."

"I see. Mind if I take off the bandage? Miss Mozart, will you fetch some fresh dressing? Thank you."

This was the first time Gregor had ever shown his wound. It was the first time he had been asked about it. He rarely thought about it except as a hygiene problem, to be cared for like dandruff or body odor. Here was an unexpected benefit of his visit to the surgeon.

"Rose-red, in many variations of shade, dark in the hollows, lighter at the edges, spots of blood, small necrotic areas . . . and . . . we've got to clean this out."

"I clean it twice a day. It does not hurt me. I think it will not be cured."

Miss Mozart returned with a tray of sterile gauze and saline, and deftly cleaned and dressed the wound while the doctor spoke.

"We may be able to do something about this later, unless it's a somatization of a spiritual wound, which would be a serious category error to treat. The immediate issue is the amputation. Can you concentrate on what I'm saying while Miss Mozart works?"

Gregor drew his attention back from the light playing in her hair. Yellow light attracts insects. "Yes. I listen."

"You still want to go ahead, Herr Pygmalion?"

Gregor nodded.

"When Miss Mozart finishes, I am going to ask you to lie in this chair, and get as comfortable as possible. Then I am going to ask you for a vow of silence—complete silence—for one hour. We will be going through a preprocedure which brings our chances for success to almost one hundred percent. Other surgeons have a range of results; I do not. You have chosen the right pair of hands, Gregor, and the right strategist behind them."

Miss Mozart finished the final bandaging. A work of art.

"Are you willing to be silent for an hour, to concentrate entirely on what you hear?"

"I will."

"All right. Come lie in the chair. Miss Mozart will adjust it for you. Comfortable? Good. We're going to strap you in for your own safety."

There was a long silence during and after the buckling. An expectant tension filled the room. Dr. Lindhorst sat down on a small padded projection coming out of the chair, took hold of one of Gregor's bare legs, and spoke quietly toward its knee.

"All cultures except our own Western, sanitized, and scientized one have understood the intimate connection between processes of the body and those of the soul. When the soul consents, its physical shell will follow. Without that consent, there is unpredictability and chaos. My surgical results are more successful than those of my colleagues because, while they start by opening the skin, I begin—and end—by opening the soul.

"The eyes may be the portals of the soul, but they are exit portals only. Seeing is an important but finally trivial sense. Eyes can be opened or closed, objects can be visible or not, the world can be dark or light. Nature does not give central place to such a contingent sensibility. No, the chiefest and deepest connections are made through the ear—which can hear at all times, in the dark, around corners, when eye is blind. Today we are going to engage your soul—through your ears. I'm fully aware that in your case, the word is metaphorical. Insects have no ears, I know. But they have fine hearing organs at the leg joints. That is one reason I am reluctant to amputate: we are talking about partial deafness, reduced acoustic acuity, closing one third of the doors into the soul.

"I am willing to go ahead, Gregor Samsa, if, in your wisdom, you would so like. But I am aware that there is much still unsaid between us, and many consequences of the unsaid. I am aware of your sleeplessness last night, your *Bettschmerz*, as it were. I am aware of your mysterious friend in Washington, D.C. , and of your wanting to be loved.

"Gregor, Love is brother to his sister, Death. Eros and Thanatos, my friend. Longing always leads somewhere, and that somewhere is not always longed for. You must appreciate this—deeply—before you take an irreversible leap of mutilation in the service of love. If you understand and truly accept, your tissues will heal. If you do not understand, if you do not truly accept, you will carry yet another unhealing wound." He paused to let his words sink in. "Miss Mozart, you may begin."

The slim, intense woman took off her shoes and sat down at the Bösendorfer, barefoot. Smoothing back the sides, and reaching behind her neck, she encircled the long fall of her golden hair with her fingers, moved it from her gown, and let it fall loosely onto her half-bare back. Though Gregor could see every detail with his immense peripheral vision, he felt himself drifting back into a hazier space deep inside his cuticle. Long echoes of Lindhorst's hypnotic voice rippled slowly in circles of ever-softer sound.

Miss Mozart placed her right hand on the keyboard. The first gentle A reached up a plaintive minor sixth, and hung there, suspended in non-time, until its own weight eased it down to the supporting net of the note below—only to immediately fall through that net—oh surprise!—to the accented half step below, the awe-full D# of the Tristan chord, the chord of chords, that miraculous find of ambiguous, melancholy longing. Search was its name, and its mode, and its function. Search. But for what? The beauty of despair? The despair of beauty? What trembling question was being asked? In the long pause that followed, Lindhorst whispered, "Be in the silence, Gregor. Let the sweet pain soak in at your soft joints." Then he signaled to Miss Mozart to continue.

The second phrase, a step higher, infinitely slow, exaggeratedly, tormentingly slow, left Gregor hanging as did the first, the *Sehnsuchtsmotiv*, the leitmotif of longing, calling him from the vast darkness. His wound began to weep into its new dressing. His dorsal gland began to moisten. The meat at his leg joints began to soften, as if to bid welcome to the knife.

"Something is dissolving, Gregor. What is it? Don't answer." He couldn't have.

A third time the phrase called out, higher still, and longer, reaching upward by two more notes, as if its fingers were stretching from an already outstretched hand.

"It hurts, my friend, does it not?"

As if to answer, the phrase returned, hanging there, radiating in the silence—until beginning again, it pushed beyond itself, and with a final leap, reached beyond itself, above and below, to a land that could be footed, an almost safe place—an accented chord of F-A-C—but with a B above, a skyhook—which let gently go, and allowed the hearer—and the universe—to collapse down to a graspable flow of molten melody, the Motif of Love.

"Now you can swim, Gregor. Your wings are beginning to spread." And indeed, Gregor could feel pressure at his back, once associated only with sexual excitement, but now with something more mysterious, sexual in part, but as much larger as the sea is to the drop.

The clock had ticked off ten minutes, but there were no minutes here. The labyrinthine melody rolled on and on, reaching ever higher, falling back and reaching again, a melody of melting and surpassing tenderness, sweeping up in its wake the mists of the sublime—a world so far beyond perceptual grasp that our sense of its beauty is deeply mixed with dread. Alarming and reassuring both, it swept along in ecstatic prolongation, immensely complicated, dissolving tonal language—and any other, complicated, yet beyond complicated, and thus simple: exaltation, transformation, an intoxicating brew of idealism and lust, delirious forces striving to embrace, exchanging the Kingdom of Day for the Kingdom of Night.

With spidery fingers, Miss Mozart piloted this extraordinary tone poem back to its unsafe harbor, the *Sehnsuchtsmotiv*. The Prelude to *Tristan and Isolde* sank down to its embers.

"After such love, why is there still longing?" Lindhorst whispered, tears in his eyes. Miss Mozart turned quietly to the very last pages of the piano score and, in hushed tones, began Isolde's song of Love's triumph over Death. *"Mild und leise,"* Gregor knew the words, *"wie er lächelt, wie das Auge hold er öffnet . . ."* She sang beautifully, as extraordinarily well as she played, and not having to overcome an orchestra, she was able to evoke the most delicate nuances of emotion and inflection as Isolde gazes upon her lover, transforming his death into eternal, living life. In the intimate murmurings of the first serene phrases, slowly rising through unbelievable ascending passages of modulating sequences, wave upon wave, lyrical, rhapsodic, ecstatic, to climactic heights of passion and transfiguration, Isolde makes her decision to die, to melt with Tristan into ultimate ground of being, to leave behind the torment of the finite doomed to infinite yearning. Together they will be at home in the vast realm of unbounded night, borne on high amidst the stars, and then down, down, to where there is no down, and beyond that still, to . . . Release! Death powerless against the Inextinguishable—love's vast, immeasurable redemption. Yet even here, after this inspired surging of metaphysical perception, even here, in the midst of yes, even here, appear the ineffable harmonies of the *Sehnsuchtsmotiv*, longing beyond longing, even in final exhalation— longing! Then silence. Profound silence.

Miss Mozart sat still, staring at the piano, her wrinkled hands in her embroidered lap.

"Gregor, are you still there?" Dr. Lindhorst checked his abdomen for the rise and fall of breath. "Gregor, listen to me carefully. This music is all very well and good, but it is a paean to annihilation. Do you understand that? There is redemption there, and transcendence, but it is transcendence of individuation itself. Do you want redemption from Being and its torments? A fiendish redemption, that.

"And, Gregor, have you ever asked yourself how you got this way? What crime had you committed? What deal you are pursuing, you externalization of the beast in man? I know, I know, you're a nice person. They're all nice people. But why . . . you? For this"—here he rapped on the hardness of Gregor's thorax, at the level of amputation—"why you? Don't answer. I'll tell you why you. Because you ask too many questions, dream too many dreams, and embark on too many quests. I'd like to put all you questers in one large room and photograph you weekly in your Unreal City."

Perhaps it was because Miss Mozart was no longer there, perhaps it was the sudden stridency in Lindhorst's voice, but Gregor was coming around from his mind-altering polyesthesia.

"Gregor, because a lovely woman has stooped to folly; must you folly, too? Because there are people in a burning building who will not come out unless the weather is just right, must you be the one to rout them?" Dr. Lindhorst got up from his seat, grabbed the two handles protruding from the rear of the chair, and began to push Gregor toward the black door.

"I'm not ready."

"What?"

"Don't take me in there. I'm not ready."

"You're not? I thought you were."

"You mock me."

"Like hell I do."

"I want to get up. Please to unstrap me."

"With pleasure."

Nothing in Lindhorst's oration made the patient change his mind. Rather, it was an image from Dante that had flashed through Gregor's distended heart—that of a man carrying a light on his back to illuminate the way for others: the only way to accomplish that task was to plunge resolutely into the darkness.

Appropriate, this image, even heroic. Yet what prescient audacity on Lindhorst's part to invoke the proximity of Love, Death, and Culture, with its time-warped echoes of Germans and Germany, of the nearness of Goethe's Weimar to the crematoria not yet built at Buchenwald, those ovens that would burn fiercely, incessantly, like the blazing hunter in a fierce New Mexican sky.

## 12. *Of* DEATH *and* DEATHS, *and* LIFE *on* EARTH

As Gregor—with all his legs intact—was leaving 999 Fifth Avenue in the early evening of August 2, 1923, a first bulletin was streaking its way across the lights on the Times Building. By the time he arrived at Forty-third Street, the crowd in the Square had grown to hundreds. Gregor was too exhausted by his recent ordeal even to wonder what the commotion was all about. The next morning's headlines told the story: PRESIDENT HARDING DIES SUDDENLY; STROKE OF APOPLEXY AT 7:30 PM; CALVIN COOLIDGE IS PRESIDENT. The *Times* story was bordered in black:

> The Chief Executive of the nation, and by virtue of his office and personality, one of the world's leading figures, passed away at the time when his physicians, his family, and his people thought that medical skill, hope and prayer had won the battle against disease.

Yet Gregor, tutored by cynical bellhop colleagues, was "in the know" about other possible explanations: that the President had been poisoned by his wife, insanely jealous of his lover, Nan Britton, and their illegitimate daughter, his wife who had been alone with him at the time of death, and who would not permit an autopsy; that he had been murdered by his "friends," the legatees of the Teapot Dome and Veteran's Bureau scandals, and of fiscal shenanigans around a German metals company after the war. The KKK believed that Harding had been poisoned by Catholics.

Millions of Americans lined the tracks to catch a last glimpse of "Uncle Warren" as the funeral train made its stately way from San Francisco, through Chicago and Washington, to his home in Marion, Ohio. Meanwhile "the little fellow," as Harding privately described his vice-president, Silent Cal Coolidge, stepped forward from his home in the woods of Vermont, to lead the nation from "normalcy" to prosperity.

. . .

Up and down, up and down. Gregor's elevator paced out the sine wave of events, of men's fortunes, of human aspiration. Before that device, poorer patrons had huffed and puffed up the stairs to their sixth- and eighth-floor rooms. Now, the rich commanded views from new twentieth floors, and the richest, from thirtieth. Every elevator trip demonstrated the finest gradation of the American class system. By the end of the month, Gregor felt he could tell a twenty-third floor person from a twenty-sixth floor one if both were standing in a crowded lobby. And because he could continually test his hypotheses, he soon got quite accurate. People-watching in elevators as a technique for class analysis. He could have published a paper.

Shortly after eleven on August 31, Gregor left the hotel for a post-shift, nighttime stroll. As he turned the corner onto Broadway, he noticed a small crowd gathering in the street, reading the Times bulletin. His first thought—in anxious echo from a month before—was of a presidential assassination. Some anarchist or socialist had murdered Coolidge, and the police were swooping down on all progressive people. Let it not be, let it not be. But no—as he focused his ommatidia on the moving lights, he discovered that Japan had been hit by a devastating earthquake, and that Tokyo and Yokohama were incinerating in a great fire. He turned back immediately, took the elevator up to Ulla's, let himself in, and headed straight for bed without even nodding to his hostess. As he was undressing, she knocked on his door.

"You okay?"

"Yes."

"You look white as a sheet. Well, tan anyway."

"I don't feel well. You have heard about the earthquake and big fire in Japan?"

"Yeah. It was just on the radio. Is that what's upsetting you?"

"Yes. I think so."

"It's sad, but what's it to you? You got relatives over there?"

"No—not really."

"Can I get you anything?"

"No. I'll be fine in the morning."

But he wasn't fine in the morning, for the next day's *Times* reported, in great detail, the story of the "worst natural disaster in history." A hundred thousand dead, another hundred thousand seriously injured. Fifty thousand missing, a million and a half homeless, sixty percent of Tokyo and eighty percent of Yokohama completely destroyed. A population grown indifferent to the daily shivering of seismographs had learned the bitterest of lessons.

And when all was done, amidst the gruesome rubble of downtown Tokyo, only the Imperial Hotel stood tall, undamaged. The new Imperial Hotel, an experimental building by Frank Lloyd Wright, challenging the Japanese idea that structures must rest on solid ground. Instead, Wright had sunk his piers into seventy feet of mud, a "floating" approach to earthquake safety, unacceptable to local architects. Science had, so to speak, triumphed.

As he lay in bed the night before, Gregor knew none of this, yet still he was nauseated and could not sleep. Why? *Did* he have relatives there, perhaps in a former life? What was Tokyo to him, or he to Tokyo?

And then he recalled two objects belonging to Amadeus. The first was a framed print hanging prominently over the entrance to his Cabinet of Wonders as if it were a statement of purpose or mission. It was five feet long by two feet wide, a painting called *Dreaming of Immortality in a Mountain Cottage.* On a steep slope of rich foliage, a little hut, and in the hut, a man asleep at a table, his head on his arms. In front of the cottage, the mountain slopes sharply off into a cloud-filled abyss. And floating there, in the cloud, the soul of the sleeping man, beautifully robed, standing upright, on the Void, in the Void. Gregor had often dreamed of this image, and it came to him now, in waking state, an ever greater mystery. Who were these people, the Japanese, who could imagine such vast, symbolic landscapes, such self-abnegation, such desire to be joined with the Void, the Void as wisdom and highest goal? Whenever he looked at this painting, he felt within himself some delicious, mysterious vibration, which he could only call "The Sweet Shudder." It sometimes made his back wet.

The other object was to this as tool to vision: a carved sixteenth-century dagger, some eleven inches long, consecrated to one use only: *seppuku*, *hara-kiri*, ritual suicide. As a young adult, Gregor had gone with a school friend (actually, on a "date") to see a Kabuki play performed at the Stadtteater in Prague by the first touring Japanese company. He couldn't remember the name, but it was based on a true story about a lord forced unjustly to perform *seppuku*, and the revenge taken by his retainers. Gregor had found the scene of ritual suicide not so much horrifying as infinitely intriguing, and further reading had deepened his sense of wonder.

The early twentieth century was the golden age of European Orientalism, and German-speaking scholars had led the way—bringing out art, monographs, and translations, and enticing foreign companies to make their European debuts. Gregor read voraciously on the subject, beginning even before his attendance at *Chushingura*, the most popular play in the Kabuki repertoire.

But after *Chushingura*, the phenomenon of *seppuku* drew much of his attention. In addition to the act itself, often calmly performed, with expressions of gratitude for opportunity to enact such an honorable deed, two other details fascinated him. Early in the history of the tradition, the performer alone was responsible for his death; the killing stroke had to be his alone. In addition to the abdominal tear, more painful and symbolic than instantly lethal, he had also to cut through his spine or, later, his carotid artery. Before so doing, he would tuck the ample sleeves of his white kimono under his knees, so that when he fell, he would fall forward, in an honorable direction, and not backward, displaying his ghastly wounds to his superiors. Gregor would often meditate on this moment of tucking in. Having been a fabric salesman, he would imagine particulars of his own kimono, and such detail would draw him into the mental and spiritual state of the wearer in a most personal way. What would he, Gregor Samsa, do, think, feel, hear, see at this moment? It was a *Gedankenexperiment* that left him metaphysically gasping.

The other element that gripped him was the role of the assistant, or *kaishaku*. As the tradition evolved, it became important for the *seppuku* performer who, no matter his crime, in this act was an honorable man, to be spared as much pain as possible. Consequently, the coup de grâce became no longer his, but that of his assistant. After the performer drew the knife through his own abdomen, the *kaishaku* would decapitate him with one clean blow. Because the condemned had initiated the sequence, the beheading was understood as more honorable than the simple beheading of a common criminal. The *kaishaku* was often a friend of the condemned who, once requested for the role, trained assiduously for the fatal stroke. Only already accomplished swordsmen were eligible, but even the most accomplished secretly studied his friend's neck and practiced on various kinds of mockups. Imagine this practice, thought Gregor. He couldn't decide which was more courageous, the act of the performer or that of his aide. Both were almost incomprehensible to his Western mind. Even now executioners fire as a team, or push an array of buttons so that no man knows who has taken the life—of even a despicable stranger. But here it is friend to friend, I will do this for you. Thank you.

It was considered best not to cut the head off with one stroke, but to leave a layer of uncut skin and muscle at the front of the throat, so that the head would not roll offensively away, but rather fall forward, hang down, and conceal the face. The technique was called *daki-kubi,* or "retaining the head," and was a mark of the most excellent swordsmanship. It was this that required the most study and practice. After the master stroke, the *kaishaku* would make the last separation in a controlled fashion with his short knife. Awful. And awesome. The product of lifelong Buddhist/Samurai training. How far we are from this, ritual suicide, the thoughtful, thankful, courageous embrace of Friend Death.

Yet here was an earthquake making all irrelevant, an end-run around the vast mental and spiritual training of the race. Of all people—the Japanese—Buddhists aware of contingent existence, so capable of conscious, mindful choice—how ironic, how horrible, for that fine discrimination to be overwhelmed by the brutality of shock and fire. What an injudicious waste of sensibility—*that* is what nauseated him. What was the use of any attainment if it could be swept away by incomprehensible, uncomprehending forces?

He recalled Jewish weddings in Prague, the bride and groom under the *chupah,* in holy space, and their final act: crushing a fine wineglass under the heel. Jews! That Jewish vision, based on so much dreadful experience, that even in the happiest of times, even in sacred space, even surrounded by relatives and friends, the universe can simply shatter. Shatter in violence. In earthquake and firestorm.

.   .   .

Up and down, up and down. One of Life's great mysteries is that after only a few up-and-downs, a year has passed, and then more than a year. Gregor had done much reading, much people watching, had made a few appearances at dwindling dance contests (a fad is a fad, and the Charleston had for the moment won out), and had sampled the cuisine at every inexpensive restaurant and hot dog stand within a ten-block radius. He loved it all. Cockroaches are devotedly omnivorous.

A year and two months after the Japanese disaster, the day before All Saints, Gregor was up in his room, quietly weeping at the foot of the radio. Texaco, in Saturday generosity, had been presenting *Parsifal*, live from the Met. This story of a guileless fool, who knows not who he is or from whence he comes—this story had obvious resonance. Keeper of the grail. But what could that mean for him, for *him*?

As if in response to his aching confusion, the phone rang:

"Allo, Gregor Samsa here."

"Gregor, it's Alice. Paul." A long silence. "Alice Paul—do you remember me?"

"Yes."

"Is this a bad time to talk?"

"Yes. I mean no. I have my shift in quarter hour."

"It may seem strange to call you out of the blue, but . . ."

"You didn't answer my letter."

"What letter?"

"I send a year ago a letter."

"I never got a letter. Gregor, you can't trust the mail in America—it's not like in Europe. If it's important, you have to send a telegram, or call on the phone. Was it important?"

"I was thinking of you now before you call."

"Good thoughts?" Pause. "Bad thoughts? I've thought about you, too. But good thoughts, good thoughts."

"I am listening and reading *Parsifal*."

"I don't know it."

"Then never mind. Why you are calling me?"

"Gregor, you sound angry."

"No. Really. I am just surprised to hear you. Why you are calling me?"

"Your English is better. But you have to say, 'What's up?'"

"What's up? I will remember that."

"'What's up' is this. Do you remember Dudley Malone?"

"This is your friend, the lawyer, in Washington?" Gregor could feel his jealousy organ irrationally starting to glow.

"Yes. I told you about him. The man who publicly resigned from President Wilson's staff."

"I remember."

"Something intriguing has come up, and you may be able to help. I can tell you about it briefly, and if you're interested, perhaps we can all meet and talk further."

"Yes? Go ahead."

"There's a high-school teacher in Tennessee named John Scopes who's just been indicted for—"

"What is indited?"

"Charged with a crime."

"I see. What is the crime?"

"The crime is teaching his students about Darwin's Theory of Evolution."

"This is a crime in America?"

"It's a long story I can tell you later. Last year Tennessee passed a law against it—political grandstanding. No one thought it would ever be enforced."

"But someone enforced it?"

"It was actually some of Scopes's friends. They thought the law was stupid, and they wanted to test it, so they persuaded him to get arrested."

"He wants to be in jail?"

"He's not in jail, but he's scheduled to go to trial next summer."

"I still don't understand why someone would want to—"

"That's the way the system works here. Legislatures make laws, and if they're bad laws, someone breaks them, then argues the case in court."

"Why don't they think them out before the hand?"

"Beforehand. You can't always think of everything. It's not a bad system, provided the courts do their job, which is not always the case."

"So it's not a good system either."

"Gregor, you have to go to work in five minutes. Here's the point. Dudley has been asked by the ACLU—"

"ACLU, what is that?"

"Sorry. The American Civil Liberties Union. Dudley's been asked to take Scopes's case, and argue in court in Dayton. Tennessee. We were talking this morning—"

"You were visiting him? Where are you?"

"I'm in Washington. At home. We were talking on the phone."

"Yes?"

"We were talking about evolution, and I mentioned my friendship with you . . . are we still friends?"

"Yes."

"And we hit on the idea of your being a witness in the trial. Does that interest you?"

"What I witnessed?"

"It's not what you witnessed. It's what you are. You're material evidence."

"Alice, I must go. We talk about it later."

"But are you interested?"

"I don't know. Yes. I need more information. How long it takes. What I do . . ."

"Certainly. I'll be in New York next week. We can go to Dudley's office together and talk about it. I'll call you when I get in."

"I am going to see you next week?"

"If that's all right."

"Good. Yes. Very all right."

"Then I'll call you Thursday. It's nice to talk to you. Happy Halloween. Boo!"

"What is boo?"

"Boo. I'm a ghost. From the past. Ghosts say 'boo.'"

"*Ein Gespenst? Ein* Ghost*?*"

"Never mind. I'll see you Thursday. Bye-bye."


Gilbert Murray, the distinguished humanist and regius professor of Greek at Oxford, once called the Scopes Trial "the most serious setback to civilization in all history." Yet in public memory, the "Monkey Trial" was a simple icon, open and shut. In an hour and a half of sometimes sadistic questioning, Clarence Darrow reduced William Jennings Bryan—three-time Democratic presidential candidate, ex–Secretary of State under Wilson, beloved Populist—to intellectual rubble, made him the laughingstock of the intelligentsia, and the whipping boy of "real" Fundamentalists, for whom his wavering on the six days of creation was liberal heresy. At the same time, Scopes, Darrow, Malone, and their team lost the case. The jury found Scopes "guilty" after eight minutes of deliberation—as well they might, since he had admitted teaching evolution, and that was the only question Judge Raulston allowed.

The Dayton days and nights were brutal—searingly hot, sweatingly muggy, home weather for the mobs, but hell on the northerners moving briefly into town. The trials of the Trial were new to them, and such as to bring out a self-defeating hauteur, a pompous condescension toward the peasants and their primitive confines. There was an alarm, for example, about the floor of the courthouse cracking under the great weight of the crowd. So the judge adjourned to the courthouse yard, where a stand was erected and lumber seats provided. Behind the platform, a huge painted sign which said "READ YOUR BIBLE DAILY." Scholarly grumbling evoked ominous mumbling.

Most detested of all by the mountain men was the arrogant H. L. Mencken, darling of the urban intellectuals, covering the trial for the Baltimore *Sun*. For a week he reported on the Dayton "yokels" and "morons," until on Friday, July 17, he was visited by "some of the boys."

"We've decided that this here climate ain't too healthy for you, Mr. Menkin. See that big ol' tree in the yard? You do? You've got two hours to leave town."

"Gentlemen, that's one hour too long," he said, and left immediately, taking a taxi forty miles to Chattanooga, and then the train to Baltimore.

Since Judge Raulston would not allow the scholars to testify, there was only one last-ditch alternative for Darrow, a radical one: calling Bryan himself as a witness. The judge saw the impropriety of the request, and would have dismissed it, but Bryan begged to comply.

"Here's my chance to confront the unbelievers who would lead the current generation astray, my golden opportunity to lay the specter of evolution to rest."

At the end of the famous debate, when Bryan said, "You have no interest but to scoff and sneer at the Bible," Darrow yelled at him, "I have no interest except to explode your fool opinions which nobody believes." Word was that if Darrow had touched him he would never have left the platform alive. The judge knew the fierce mountaineer temper; he returned the trial to the steaming courtroom to risk the unsafe floors.

Many were put off by what seemed Darrow's personal vindictiveness. While he had good reason for his fervor, he seemed to enjoy flaying a trapped animal. Bryan, on the other hand, maintained his personal dignity, and was saddened by Darrow's performance:

"Mr. Darrow is the greatest criminal lawyer in America today. It is a shame, in my mind, that a mentality like his has strayed so far from the natural goal that it should follow—great God, the good a man of his ability could do if he would align himself with the forces of right instead of with that which strikes its fangs at the very bosom of Christianity."

The furor raised by the cruel debate prompted the judge to exclude all press—as well as the jury—from all subsequent argument and testimony, including Gregor's appearance. Excluded as an "expert witness," he was presented simply as evidence—that life forms can change from one kind of entity to another, and were not fixed at the moment of their creation.

He was hot under Dudley's overcoat "disguise," his neurons bouncing high-temperature signals off his will, twitchy, frustrated he could not show off more for Alice. His unveiling was dramatic enough, causing Judge Raulston's jowly jaw to drop and William Jennings Bryan to faint. But his short appearance left little mark on history. With the courtroom cleared of all attendees except the principals, with no radio or telegraph reports, no news photographers clicking away, the final moments of the trial were invisible to the public, recorded only in the archives of the ACLU and, with inconsistencies, contradictions, and exaggerations, in the correspondence, diaries, and notes of the few people remaining in the courtroom.

The disabled Mrs. Bryan was one of them. Wheeled each day into the courtroom, she sent "bulletins" to family at home—interesting, if partisan, accounts of the trial's events. The earlier events of the trial, especially Darrow's cross-examination of Bryan, are well known. But Mrs. Bryan's notes are one of the few extant documents also to cover Gregor's appearance:

DAYTON, TENNESSEE

JULY 25, 1925

BULLETIN NUMBER THREE (PP. 7–10)

. . . When the judge brought the court to order, the second dramatic event occurred. Mr. Malone, whose morals I wrote about in my last letter, requested to put a new witness on the stand. When questioned, he admitted this to be an "expert witness," and the judge ruled that unless the new witness could testify to details concerning Mr. Scopes, his testimony was irrelevant and should, like the others, be committed to writing and entered in the record. The defense went into conference, and Mr. Malone changed his request to something he admitted to be unorthodox—that the new witness be presented and entered into the record as "evidence." Papa looked at me quizzically, and even Judge Raulston seemed confused, but when promised it would not take long, he dismissed the audience (only those of us on the "teams"—I was considered on Papa's team!—were permitted to remain), the jury, and the reporters, and gave permission for the new witness—or evidence—to be presented. A man walked in from the lobby dressed in coat and hat in spite of the great heat. Mr. Malone wanted to seat him in the witness chair, but the judge ruled that he should stand at the table with the other evidence. At a signal from Mr. Malone, the man removed his hat and coat, and looked to be some kind of large insect. This was when Papa fainted, and of course the whole court was immediately taken up with that. After a few minutes, Papa was fine, drinking cold water, and the proceedings began once more.

I had thought perhaps this person, a Mr. Samsa, was some unfortunate, suffering from a rare disease, like people with elephant skin. But no, apparently, if one is to believe Mr. Malone, Mr. Samsa was a perfectly normal human being, a salesman living in Prague, Czechoslovakia, who one day evolved (or unevolved, as Papa says) into an insect. He took off most of his clothing and displayed his insect parts in a manner most convincing, though I suppose it could have been a human in a cleverly designed costume. At any event, the strategy backfired on Darrow and Mr. Malone, since Papa maintained, and the judge agreed, that Mr. Samsa, whoever and whatever he is, could as easily be an act of God as an evolutionary event, and these last proceedings were also stricken from the record.

The jury retired and were out of the room about five minutes, returning with a verdict of "Guilty," but left it to the court to determine the fine. Court then placed a fine of one hundred dollars and bail was fixed at five hundred dollars—the Baltimore *Sun*, the awful Mr. Mencken's paper, offering to be responsible. Scopes then appeared and recited a little piece which had clearly been taught him by the defense layers about his feeling that the law was unconstitutional and that he would resist it as long as possible, etc. When he had finished, he cast a sheepish eye at his counsel to see if he had said all that was required.

On the evening after the trial, students of Dayton High School held a dance in Darrow's honor. The sixty-eight-year-old man came, danced, and "even smoked cigarettes with them," according to Arthur Hays, a lawyer on the defense team. Adulation and second youth made for a heady evening.

Alice and Gregor left before the various festivities. They were both on the late-afternoon bus to catch the evening train to Washington. Because of Gregor's color, they sat in the rear, so as not to attract the driver's attention. Alice did call forth stares from passengers black and white, with her weary, pale face standing out among the dark ones back of the wheels.

Gregor spent the next few weeks sleeping under the couch in Alice's Capitol Hill apartment. On the first of August, bringing in the mail, he handed her a letter from the AnaKostia Kostume Kompany.

"What is this?" he asked. "I didn't think you were one interested in costumes. And that a right spelling?"

"I don't know what it is," Alice said. "Probably just a promotion." She opened the letter with her Boy Scout knife.

```
Dear Miss Paul,
    It has come to our attention that you are currently
cohabiting with a dark and foreign male. In the past, we
have appreciated your work for democracy, and would re-
spectfully suggest you end this relationship toot-sweet.
A word to the wise--and you are wise. Other-wise, we may
have to have a fashion show featuring some of our latest
Kostumes.
    Respectfully.
    O. E.
    Imperial Kludd, Grand Dragon, D.C.
```

"What's *that* all about? Who's O. E.? What kind of kostumes? What is Kludd?"

"Oh, my hard-shelled friend, you're so . . . you've got so much to learn. Mr. O. E. seems to be from some local branch of the KKK. What's the KKK? Do you know?"

Gregor shook his head.

"Well, they're a bunch of men—supported by their wives, unfortunately—who like to dress up in hoods and sheets, and make life uncomfortable for whomever they don't like."

"Who they don't like?"

"Oh, draft dodgers, union members, whores, pimps, bootleggers, gamblers, crooks—and anyone different from red-blooded, Waspy Americans. Sacco and Vanzetti, for instance."

"Waspy?"

"White Anglo-Saxon Protestant."

"Oh. I thought maybe they liked insects. But O. E. seems to like *you*. At least not until I come to visit."

"For one thing, I am a Wasp. A stinging one, perhaps, but a Wasp nevertheless. And a lady. Southerners *love* ladies. But more than that, there are KKKers deeply committed to America—just like me. They think crime is un-American, they hate crooked politicians and philanderers of all kinds. But since civilization is breaking down . . ."

"Spengler."

"Yes, Spengler, perhaps. They haven't read him. But since Western civilization is declining, people need punishment to keep them in line. Tar needs feathers, backs need lashing, necks need lynching, testicles need the knife. And un-American ideas may need fire to quench them . . ."

"Aren't you afraid what O. E. might do? To you?"

"The D.C. Klan is just a bunch of joiners without enough to keep them busy. Middle-aged grade-school graduates, oppressed by everything new going on, promoting one thing they're sure of—their one hundred percent pure Americanism—so they can be Guardians of Society. Great cure for inferiority complex."

"So you don't think they'll do anything to you?"

"If I were afraid of the KKK, I might just as well leave the country. If the Klan hates Jews, so do half of our good hotels. They hate foreigners like Nick and Bart? So does the National Institute of Arts. If they want to eliminate Negroes, so do all state houses south of the Mason-Dixon Line. They persecute and condemn just like half our churches. They're a secret society like the State Department. They hold their idiotic parades like policemen and mailmen and firemen. And they use the mails for shaking down suckers like the Red Cross. They even want to control private morals—just as Congress does. The KKK is your basic America, Gregor."

"And what is Sacco and Vanzetti?"

"Who are they, you mean? Sacco and Vanzetti?"

Gregor nodded.

"Where have you been?"

"In an elevator, usually."

"Taking the upper classes up to the upper floors, no doubt?"

"They come down, too."

"To what?" She took a deep breath. "Sorry. You seem hurt—I apologize." She closed the Boy Scout knife and put it back in its drawer. "It's just that I've become friends with Rosina Sacco. We've been writing. She lives like a sleepwalker, wandering through a dark world, much colder than Lombardy. She's thirty, but she looks like an old woman. She once had red hair and white skin and coal-black eyes. And now she's a hag in black, commuting back and forth to Charlestown prison."

She pulled an envelope from under the knife, withdrew the letter, and read:

"'The dear remembrance is still rimane in my heart'—she's talking about being back in Italy with Nick—'we both of us went in city town, and we went in a big stor, and I was all dress up and look beautiful . . . Those day . . . they was a some happy day . . .'"

Alice began to cry. The letter dropped from her hand. Gregor felt he couldn't reach her, garbed in his hideous ignorance. He picked up the letter and put it back on her desk.

"Just give me a moment."

Gregor waited. *Wie soll ich meine Seele halten, dass sie nicht an deine rührt?*

"You look so silly, standing there wondering what this is all about," she sniffed. "Look, five years ago, in April of 1920 . . ."

"Just before I arrive. You see?"

"Yes. Before you were here, somebody killed two people during a robbery. No one knows who the killer was. But witnesses thought it was two 'foreign'-looking men. Lots of different descriptions—the contradictions didn't matter. Nick and his friend Bart Vanzetti were picked up. They both had been seen elsewhere at the time of the crime, but did that matter? All their witnesses were Italian—so how could Americans believe them? They're scheduled to be executed. Electrocuted."

"But why them? Why Nicko and Bart and not any many others?"

"They were foreigners, different. Worse, they were anarchists, hoping to change the world into a better place, more tolerant, more just." She began to cry again. "But they were dark—like you—and they had an accent—like you—and they were something different—like you."

It was a minute before she could continue. Gregor walked behind her chair and put his claw on her trembling shoulder.

"You know what the judge said before they were tried? 'You see what I did with those arnychist bastards? I'll get those guys hanged.' This is American justice, Gregor. Maybe you should take some more time out from your elevator and head up to Boston to fight for them. . . . It could be you, Gregor, some dark and foreign male. They could be you."

. . .

The last event in Gregor's Washington stay was watching a parade with Alice on Pennsylvania Avenue. It was August 8, 1925, and forty thousand hooded Klansmen marched the broad thoroughfare from White House to Capitol celebrating their victories in the recent election, and their faith in America's future.

# 13. ALIENS *and* SEDITION

Gregor Samsa lay in bed.

*Handcuffed. Front and middle legs. The strap squad walks him briskly down the corridor, through a heavy door and into the execution chamber.*

*Massive piece of furniture—dark, shiny oak, angular, functional: wide arms, ladder back, vertical wooden slats for headrest, two hefty legs behind, two narrow ones in front, the timbers of justice. Tiny room, white walls, ceiling, white shiny floor. All dominated by the chair, a weighty sculpture in a small, bare gallery.*

*Union electrician, long leather gloves, fastening electrodes. Headpiece, aach—cold sponge against shaved scalp. If the warden were to order the prisoner to crawl under the chair and bark, he would gladly obey.*

*Who are you, why are you here? All you people in suits and ties. You with the notebook, what are you scribbling? Who are you? Why are you here?*

*A sudden, violent shortening of every muscle in the client body: inner flesh becomes as steel. Back pulled tight, head wrenched back, hooks and hairs clutching inward, splaying out. The current runs a cycle, from very high voltage to more moderate voltage, and as voltage abates, the body sags ever so slightly. Then—with a distinct click!—the cycle returns to maximum current, and the body in the chair jumps again, like someone dozing, awakened by the phone.*

*Step right up, ladies and gentlemen. Only two marks. The extra-special thing about this act is that the repercussions are incalculable.*

Gregor Samsa was given to disturbing dreams.

*"Hey, Greggo the Last, wanna take a look? C'mon. Know thy enemy."*

*11:11*

*"Now here's how we'd improve it—first of all, it needs a more comfortable backrest, don't you think?"*

*"I would thicken up the gauge," Klofac observes. "Wires won't get so hot."*

*"What about a drip pan?" Kramar suggests. "Make the cleanup easier."*

*"Besides," Soukup says, "they could use the fat in the kitchen. Present company excepted, of course. No fat on this boy."*

*"I think two leg grounds would be better than one, don't you?" Klofac asks. "In at the top, whoosh out through the bottom."*

*"And I'd put Jell-O on the patient's head, not just a sponge," Soukup says. "You like Jell-O, Greggo?"*

"Ave Westinghouse ad dexteram Teslii. Ave AC, gratia plena." *Kleagle crosses the air and genuflects in hosanna.*

*"Why a chair? Why not a bed?"*

*"But it's not a chair, Greggo, it's a throne, a royal throne," Kludd answers. "You're to be the king of the ball. Kings don't lie in bed. They're busy, busy, busy saving their people, making the deserts bloom. I hope you know how to dance. Oh, how silly of me. You* are *a dance."*

*"But don't you think the blade should be slanted, or at least convex?" Klofac asks.*

*The quarter hour rings. On Hanus's clock, Death pulls his rope. The moon throws the guillotine's long shadow far along the cobbled street.*

*"Field trip over. Time to go back home."*

It has been shown by exhaustive research that a current of 1 ampere passing through the brain or other vital organ of the body will in most cases produce death in only 1/240$^{th}$ of a second, far more rapidly than the speed with which the nervous system can register pain, thus ensuring a death that is both instantaneous and painless. Also in roaches.

*Down the slowly sloping hill, past warehouse doors, locked or chained. A sickly young girl stands at a pump in her dressing gown, gazing at Gregor while the water sings into her bucket.*

"Is that Grete's violin?" Gregor wondered in deep sleep. "Is she now a pretty young woman, stretching her body?"

*The isolation cellblock is reached by stone steps rising from the guttered street. "I'm likely to be pardoned. My advocate is working on it. He's optimistic."*

*"A man can't be too careful," Soukup observes. "Even while they're pro-nouncing the pardon the judges foresee the possibility of a new arrest."*

*"And old Greggo here isn't a man, anyway," Kludd says. "A man can inter-vene, make a plea for himself. But this one here, he's just a thing waiting to be done. It's* human *life that should be sacred."*

*Kleagle the historian: "'After walking eleven hours,' a traveler of the early centuries relates, 'without having espied the print of human foot, to my great comfort and delight, I saw a man hanging upon a gibbet. My pleasure at the cheering prospect was inexpressible, for it convinced me I was in a civilized country.'"*

The idea for an electric chair was the product of a business war be-tween Edison's DC system for commercial lighting and Westinghouse's AC design. The stakes were as high as they come: purchase of equipment and services for every major city in the world.

Early in the struggle, several people were killed by Westinghouse high-tension wires, and Edison seized on this to argue for his own DC. But the cheaper Westinghouse design was steadily gaining political ground. So Edison hired an engineer and turned him into an executioner. Across the country, he showed that Westinghouse wires could kill— horses, cats, and dogs.

"In Albany . . ." he thought.

"Where is Albany?" he thought.

"I don't know. In Albany, they passed a bill allowing execution by electri—"

*Klang. Klick. Klop.*

*"I have something to read you," the warden says—but the piece of paper in his hand, bordered in black, speaks for itself. Curiously bloodless: one dry "whereas" after another culminating in a businesslike "therefore."*

*"Please sign here. Any special requests for a last meal?"*

*What a curious thing to ask.*

In July of 1927, Gregor had gone up to Boston "for the duration," liv-ing in a collective house of ex–Gregor dancers, now dedicated to saving the lives of Nicola Sacco and Bartolomeo Vanzetti. He was proud to have translated a letter of support from Dr. Albert Einstein.

*11:19*

"*Okay, boys, cuff him up. Both sets of hands. It's time for the final walk.*" *Chief guard Kludd.*

"*This guy ain't so bad. He's for the little man, the workin' people. Like us.*" *The socially conscious Kladd.*

*Emil "The Professor" Knecht: "All social questions achieve their finality around the executioner's thrust."*

"*Leave him alone," Kleagle says. "He don't want to hear no lectures now.*"

"*C'mon, Sluggo, get moving!" Kludd yanks on his chain. "You gonna cry tears in your eyeballs. Last supper—a fine treat for the likes of you. We'll add a little dirt, a little soap in the soup.*"

*11:21*

*The bright red tumbrel moving at a walk through five locked gates to the outer edge of the prison. The outer edge and yet the depths. Gregor's escorts, in their ill-fitting black suits, with their pleats, pockets, buckles, and belts. Eminently practical, no doubt, though it's unclear what actual purpose the pleats and pockets serve.*

*Someone in the audience claps his hands high in the air and shouts "Bravo."*

*11:23*

*The guards who take him to the death room act as if they were going to a party. Their faces shine enough to light the evening mist. Children blow kisses, but one woman spits. Walking with the wagon, a bent old man lectures.*

"*Such sights are frightfully painful. The blood flows from the vessels at the speed of the severed carotids, then it coagulates. The muscles contract; their fibrillation is stupefying; the intestines ripple and the heart moves irregularly, incompletely, fascinatingly; the mouth puckers in a terrible pout. All this can last minutes, even hours in sound specimens. Death is not immediate: every vital element survives decapitation. We doctors are left with the impression of a murderous vivisection, then premature burial."*

*"Everything ready," a voice calls out. "Proceed with execution. Immobilize head with harness and chin strap."*

On August 28, six thousand protestors began to march, filling the street twenty-five wide, fifty thousand spectators falling in behind. South to the crematory, the March of Sorrow, six miles. Irish yelled "FURRINERS GO HOME." Police charged anyone with an armband. There was heavy rain to wash the marchers clean—so many people cleansed for two Italians! And a thin column of smoke rose from the crematory chimney. A thin column of smoke rose from the middle chimney, dark and straight into the graywhite sky.

*"Removed from this place . . . close custody . . . thence take at such time to the place of execution, there to be hung by the neck until dead." (Executions hidden not because they offend public taste, but because the public likes them too much.) But never on Sundays.*

*A minute after midnight, though, it's not Sunday.*

Gregor, almost awake, recalled Vanzetti saying, "If it had not been for this thing, I might have lived out my life talking at street corners to scorning men. I might have died, unmarked, unknown, a failure. Now we are not a failure. This is our career, and our triumph. Never in our full life could we hope to do such work for tolerance, for justice, for man's understanding of men, as now we do by accident. Our words—our lives—our pains—nothing! The taking of our lives—lives of a good shoemaker and a poor fish-peddler—all! That last moment belongs to us—that agony is our triumph."

Someone in the audience clapped his hands high in the air and shouted "Bravo."

*Kerko holds a carved dagger, some eleven inches long, just above Gregor's head. "Now I am to seize the knife," he thinks, "and plunge it into my belly." But his arms are bound.*

*"It is considered and ordered by the Court that you, Greggo Samsa, and you, Alice Paulo, suffer the punishment of death by the passage of electricity through your bodies within the week beginning on Sunday, the tenth day of July, in the year of our Lord 1927. This is the sentence of the law."*

*Judge Thayer: "DID YOU SEE WHAT I DID TO THOSE ARNYCHIS-TIC BASTARDS?" In the year of the Lord, 1927?*

*11:33*

*We must bow to the inevitable. Anus stuffed with cotton, mouth taped against vomit, we must be cosmetically acceptable.*

Most prisoners, they say, walk to their executions with surprising calm, in a state of dreary despondency, resigned, stars in a drama pandering to public fear and lust for vengeance, sometimes called Justice. But some fall apart during the last walk and have to be dragged, kicking and screaming, to their deaths.

It is strange that a man rarely faints during his final seconds. On the contrary, his brain is terribly alive and active, racing, racing, racing—like a machine at full speed. Imagine how many thoughts must be throbbing together, all unfinished, some of them irrelevant and absurd.

The executioner gets $100 a victim, just for throwing a lever.

Remarkable, the meekness of the condemned. They have nothing more to lose. They could choose to die of a guard's bullet, in a frantic struggle that dulls . . . Yet, with few exceptions, they walk passively toward death, and the newspapers write "the condemned man died courageously," meaning they make no noise, they accept their status as a parcel, and everyone thanks them for this.

Hundreds of persons offer to serve as executioners without pay.

Old Charlestown prison is built in the form of a cross. . . .

*A clock in Prague strikes midnight as saints process. Alice walks to the chair unaided, with the simple dignity she had in the worst of times. "Do not forget to show my head to the people," she says. "It is worth seeing."*

*Executioner Sanson, Warden Henry, and ten official witnesses enter the death chamber. Sanson puts a blood-red outer garment over his neatly pressed clothes. Gregor walks down a narrow concrete path to the door behind which twelve men are sitting to witness his death. His upper legs are lashed to armrests, his middle ones bound tightly around his thorax, his hind legs strapped to the chair legs, and his body to the chair so tightly that his thoracic-abdominal junction is like to snap.*

*The electrician attaches one of the electrical jacks to the metal plate inside the strap holding Gregor's tarsus. Too thin for good contact. Gregor wiggles around to show him. He clips the condemned's sensory hairs with wire cutters and moves the electrode mid-tibia. He reaches behind for the sponge-covered death implement sitting in saline solution, and slips the screw post into the death cap, specially wrought to contain antennae. If Gregor presses his elbows tightly against the wood, he can hear ravishing, humming vibrations. He decides to concentrate on these so that when his head falls, he may even be in doubt as to the event, feeling nothing more than a slight sensation of coolness.*

*The crunch. The mounting whine and snarl of the generator. Mouthparts peel back, the throat strains as if to cry, the chitinous body arches against the restraining straps as the generator whines and snarls again.*

*A thin column of smoke rises from Gregor's head and leg, and the sick-sweet smell of burning chitin permeates the room. The death chamber is filled with ghosts.*

Just inside the door Vanzetti paused near Warden Henry and said with great precision: "I wish to say to you that I am innocent. I have never committed a crime; some sins, but never any crime. I thank you for everything you have done for me. I am innocent of all crime, not only this one, but all, of all. I am an innocent man." With that he shook hands with the wardens, the doctor, two of the guards, then took his place in the chair. As the guard on the right knelt to adjust the contact pad to his bare leg, he spoke again, his eyes covered. "I now wish to forgive some people for what they are doing to me." 1,950 volts would suffice for this dreamer and man of words.

*"Warden, I pronounce this thing dead."*
*Someone in the audience claps his hands high in the air and shouts "Bra . . ."*

Gregor Samsa was given to disturbing dreams. But in August 1927, disturbing dreams ran rampant over five continents. On the night of the twenty-second, a tremor of panic shook the world.

—In Boston, machine guns on the prison roof were trained on uneasy crowds in streets below. Civil rights are playthings for quiet days, not for a day of death. Gregor was among those arrested.

—In New York, the entire police force was mobilized, and soldiers on Governor's Island waited for a signal to cross the river into the city. . . .

—In London, shortly before 5 A.M., the Death Watch walked in closed circles—coal miners, textile workers, longshoremen . . .

—In Rio, a little before two in the morning, crowds at the U.S. embassy shouted so loud, they thought they might be heard in Boston. . . .

—In Moscow early morning crowds swarmed around wall newspapers. "What time is it now in Boston?"

—In Paris, workers wept nightlong at our Embassy. . . .

—In Warsaw, as daylight broke, demonstrations were broken up even as posters appeared, calling upon Poles to make one final effort to save them. . . .

—In Sydney, it was mid-afternoon. Longshoremen went on strike. They marched to the American embassy chanting. . . .

—In Bombay, millworkers lay down their tools for an hour of silence and prayer. . . .

—In Tokyo, at midday, police attacked workers in front of the American embassy. . . .


Never before in all human history was there a thing like this: these floods of tears across humanity. But so as not to disturb the apparent calm, radio networks and newspapers downplayed reports of world reaction. Newsreel companies, too, took part in the conspiracy of silence. Two weeks after the flood, Gregor clipped and folded an article from *The Exhibitor's Herald* into his diary:

> The Sacco-Vanzetti case is closed, and that means as far as newsreel pictures of the events which terminated with the execution of the pair.

The case is closed on the screen, voluntarily. Executives of the newsreel companies were unanimous in their decision to eliminate all reference to the matter in their releases.

The announcement was made following conferences with representatives of Will H. Hays, after receipt by the Hays Organization of requests from overseas that the motion picture industry do its share in bringing the case to an end by ignoring it on the screen. Films in the vault will be burned.

It was clear to Gregor, and to those who participated with him in the struggle, that what they had been through was not, as was widely alleged, a miscarriage of justice. By 1927, he had seen enough of America to understand that this *was* justice here. And he vowed to help change it.

At that time, in the city of Boston, there was a club known as the Athenaeum, a club for Boston Brahmin, for university presidents and judges, a club that no foreigner, no first-generation rabble-rouser, no Jew or Negro, had ever entered.

On August 23, 1927, the morning after the execution, a slip of paper was found inserted in every magazine and newspaper in the reading room. On each slip were the following words, typed in capital letters on an old Remington Model One:

ON THIS DAY, NICOLA SACCO AND BARTOLOMEO VANZETTI, DREAMERS OF THE BROTHERHOOD OF MAN, HOPERS IT MIGHT BE FOUND IN UNITED STATES, WERE DONE A CRUEL DEATH BY CHILDREN OF THOSE WHO FLED LONG AGO TIME TO THIS LAND OF HOPE AND FREEDOM.

Someone in the audience, clap hands high in the air and shout "Bravo."

"Good *Morgen*, Mister Chollie."

"Hey, mornin', Mistah Gregor. How you are this fine Monday on Wall Street? Now I don't want you jumpin' outa no windows today. Lookee heah, the *Times* say 'Wall Street ready for heavy trading as orders pour in.' Things is lookin' up. 'Sides, gotta vote for Norman Thomas tomorra. Every vote count."

"I have no stocks, so I am not jumping out of windows. Besides, I can fly if I really want to."

"Oh, yeah, you a card, Mistah Gregor. But you gotta also watch out fo' other people flyin' who *ain't* got no wings. Dey fly right on yo' head, you jus' as dead. Like dem two las' week. Dese hea streets too narrow for dat kinda monkey business."

"I take my *Times*, and my *Vorwärts*."

"It always amaze me some people kin read dat Jewish writin'. Look like chicken scratchin' to me."

"I come from chicken land. Everybody reads it in the old country."

"You all chickens."

"Every final one."

"Well, have a good Monday mornin', Mistah Gregor. No suicidin' please, and you be sure to vote tomorra. Mistah Thomas, he our man. He gonna make things betta."

Gregor walked the three blocks to Cedar, feeling the heaviness of towering granite in the early morning November gloom. He glanced at the front page of the *Times*: yes, WALL ST. READY FOR HEAVY TRADING AS ORDERS POUR IN. Well, maybe things *would* pick up. He didn't really understand the market, but knew enough to know that when prices were low, people would buy, and prices would rise. Orders pouring in? That sounded good. Not even the main headline. Just one column. The big news—TAMMANY SEES BIG VICTORY. LA GUARDIA IN FINAL PLEA ASKS FOR THOMAS VOTES.

Maybe there will be upset. On the bottom of the page, a two-column spread: ELEVATED TRAIN STOPS FOR A DOG, IS RAMMED FROM BEHIND AND EIGHT PERSONS ARE HURT. Monday, November 4, 1929. New York. Would a train stop in Prague—or even Vienna? *Weiß nicht.* But in America it stops—and gets punished. Poor, sick country, suffering from its own strengths. The land of opportunity, everybody can get rich. And everybody can jump out of windows. Sick country. Like a sick eagle. Like a sick eagle looking toward the sky.

He thought of Mr. Ives's song. Mr. Ives was so nice to give him a signed copy of his book of songs. "To Mr. Gregor Samsa, my prize student. March 1929. Ch. E. Ives." That was his favorite, "Like a Sick Eagle"—he could sing it just the way Mr. Ives would like it. Even better. Mr. Ives wanted quarter tones, but Gregor could easily do eighth tones, sixteenth tones if he were careful.

"Like a Sick Eagle," a tiny masterpiece, a one-page study in descending tones, short phrases with weary, chromatic pauses between them. The score is marked "Very slowly, in a weak and dragging way," shining exhausted light on Keats's disheartened poem:

> *The spirit is too weak;*
> *mortality weighs heavily on me*
> *like unwilling sleep,*
> *and each imagined pinnacle and steep*
> *of Godlike hardship*
> *tells me I must die . . .*

*"Like a sick eagle,"* Gregor sang. *"Like a sick eagle looking towards the sky."*

Ives wrote it while his new wife, Harmony, was in the hospital, undergoing the hysterectomy that would render them childless, with an unhappy adopted daughter. What a way to start a marriage!

"What a way to run a country," thought Gregor.


Forty-six Cedar Street, Ives & Myrick, the foremost insurance agency in the country, perhaps the world. Gregor worked on the seventh floor, at a desk in a long room with a high ceiling and huge windows with dark, oaken frames. Mr. Myrick's desk was right up front, along with all the others'. But the shy and messy Mr. Ives had a private office in back, behind frosted glass, with its own elevator entrance, and its own unique chaos. Most of the time, the door was closed.

He had had enough of elevators, and slowly walked the stairs, upward, upward, twelve half-landings, like the twelve sissy half tones Mr. Ives was always belittling. From elevator operator to insurance scientist, he thought. It had been an upward journey in more-than-Minkowskian space. Back in New York after Dayton and Washington, he had been too embarrassed to ask again for his job at the Occidental. For once again, he had simply left—without notice—to attend the trial, and more important, to visit again with Alice. Up the stairs. Up the back stairs to Ulla's. He couldn't stay, he knew, but he asked her to keep his clothing and few possessions until he found another job, another place to live.

His rich journey, his "hidden years," hidden, at least, from the census. Up against the wall of New York, a city unforgiving even in boom times, he had been forced into a conceptual leap in order to survive: he had had to become—once more—a cockroach. A cockroach in New York City, a home as welcoming as Rome to the Pope, as the outback to the Aborigine. Yes! A New York City cockroach—what could be easier? His size might make for some hardship, but *Gott, ja!* what could have been easier?

The fifth half-landing. In the summer of '26, lodgings had been a minor problem—if necessary he could sleep out in any number of parks, alleys, or dark empty lots. Food was the primary issue: what do cockroaches eat if they're not sitting at table? Darn near anything and everything, that's what. "Bark, leaves, the pith of living cyclads, paper, woolen clothes, sugar, cheese, bread, blacking, oil, lemons, ink, flesh, fish, leather," wrote the British scholar L. C. Miall in his 1886 edition of *The Structure and Life-history of the Cockroach*. And in 1926 it was even easier: the dumpster had been invented a decade earlier.

At first, he had explored the back alleys of his old neighborhood. Lindy's, at Broadway and Fifty-first, had a huge output of half-eaten food. No pith of living cyclads for him when he could feast on the remains of hot pastrami sandwiches, cheesecake, and apple strudel. Every once in a while, when he had a yen to play the European dandy, he would head up to the Russian Tea Room at Fifty-sixth and Seventh, and nibble daintily on smears of caviar, or shards of sturgeon, perhaps from the very plates of Igor Stravinsky and his gaggle of emigré princesses. At the end of September, the air began to chill, and he set about looking for a place to stay. But why one place? Did he have to pay rent? Why not two, three, four places, one for every mood? He had to stop thinking like some poor human immigrant and start thinking cockroach. What freedom! No rogue and peasant wage-slave he. He had a small, cozy flat in an empty brownstone on West Sixty-first, a loft on Forty-ninth and Tenth Avenue, and a fantasy-space in an abandoned Chinese restaurant around the corner at Forty-ninth off Ninth. No pockets, no keys. He could slip through broken windows, or in at the bottom of kicked-in doors. He had his choice.

Food and shelter taken care of, he turned his attention to winter clothing. Seventh half-landing. What a relief it was to know that, as a cold-blooded animal, he had no need to maintain any particular body temperature. True, the colder it was, the slower he became, and should he reach "chill-coma" temperature, he would be completely immobilized. But as November came on, he found that intentionally exposing himself to lower and lower outside temperatures, he could acclimatize and lower the temperatures at which activity was still possible. He knew there must be some cold death point at which his internal liquid would fatally freeze, but in a civilized city, in the north temperate zone, such extremes could be easily avoided. In case of severe hypothermia, he could always bury himself deep within the composting heat of any dumpster.

With the basics of food, (no) clothing, and shelter taken care of, Gregor could afford to take in the city in all its cultural glory, a bohemian roach-about-town. One evening at the end of January 1927, he was approached on West Forty-third Street by a fur-wrapped, over-rouged woman. Eighth half-landing.

"Hey, Mister . . ."

"No, thank you, I—"

"I'll give you a good deal."

Should he, or shouldn't he? His last encounter, almost four years ago now, had been disastrous, and he had felt desexed ever since. The thought of a woman's soft flesh had become repulsive once more. He didn't know this person. He could get a disease. She was vaguely attractive. But wasn't this illegal? What if he were caught? Without papers, he could be deported. Still . . .

"They're great seats. Fourth row, center."

"What?"

"Fourth row, center. We have an extra ticket."

"Ticket for what?"

"Oh, forgive me. I thought you were heading for the box office."

And, in fact, Gregor had stopped to puzzle out the poster in the Town Hall display. PRO MUSICA INTERNATIONAL REFERENDUM CONCERT. What sort of referendum? Wasn't that when you voted on some proposal? Music to vote on proposals? What sort of proposals? He had just stepped away from his myopic inspection when the woman . . .

"Debussy and Ives. You never get a chance to hear this music."

"Ives?"

"Charles Ives. The insurance genius–composer. You've heard of him?"

"Is he about two meters tall, and he is writing an amendment for your Constitution?"

"I haven't met him, but it sounds like it could be."

"I think I have met him. Does he like baseball?"

"That I do know. My husband and he played together at Yale."

"Yale. That was the team of the game I saw."

"Then it was probably Charlie Ives. Don't you want to hear some of his music?"

"Yes. I would like to. But I have no money at the moment."

"Oh. Too bad. We do need to get something for the seat."

She took herself and her perfume over toward the box office, a benevolent spider awaiting her fly. But Gregor's curiosity was fired up. He would go to the concert, ticket or none. It was easy enough.

Ninth half-landing.

In the last months, Gregor had become expert at slipping in and out of buildings unnoticed, of caressing the shadows, and being caressed by them. He knew the midtown alleys like the claw of his pretarsus. He knew the back doors of all the major concert halls in town. He knew the ushers stood in them preconcert, in the coldest weather, to smoke. He had a black overcoat and a flute case for such occasions. Walk in quickly, authoritatively, nod the head, flash the flute case nonchalantly. They had never challenged him before, and wouldn't now. What usher wants to be dressed down for hassling some distinguished international musician? Then, up to the second floor via the stairs at the back of the hall. Slip into the auditorium as the usher seats another customer, and wait behind the curtain on the back wall. What a wonderful thing to be flat. Even six feet tall, Gregor could get behind an arras without making a bulge. In the dark, with two sticklike legs protruding at the bottom, he was totally undiscoverable. He had only to edge over and stick his knee outside the tapestry for excellent acoustics—even if he couldn't see.

He would go to the concert. Then afterward, he would visit Ulla, take some time, share the last months—and retrieve that card Mr. Ives had given him at the ball game. Yes, he'd get the card, and if he liked the music, he would call up Mr. Ives and tell him. And so it happened.

Tenth half-landing.

Gregor arrived at the back door of Town Hall at 7:25, walked right by two ushers finishing up their Chesterfields, and found his curtained place at the back of the orchestra. Not fourth row, center, but it would do. For now, the soft darkness.

If Gregor was given to disturbing dreams, he was also given to revelation. The smell and feel of his velour shroud brought back memories of Prague, of the plush seats of its theaters and concert halls. And earlier, still. He treasured the feel of the dark red couch on which he would lie as a boy and young man, listening to Grete practice. Bach. The Chaconne. His fan of memory opened out, even in this chink behind the curtain, ready for the imprint of some unanticipated truth.

Theater and music performances had always been supreme events for him, jewels on the path of the ordinary, moments of comprehension on the common course of imprecision, shoddiness, and unclarity he normally abandoned to moronic harangue. As in ancient Greece, there were hidden points that led down to the underworld, so were his history of performances attended—extraordinary trips to worlds from which dreams arose, to events that reached him like echoes heard from the darkness of a past life. From velour, the deep well of the past—but also a call to unfolding. Strong attending meant laying hands, now claws, on the future. Eleventh half-landing, and twelfth. He stood outside IVES & MYRICK, stood there, listening.

This concert of January 29, 1927, had been played by fifty musicians from the New York Philharmonic under the baton of Eugene Goosens, an up-and-coming conductor-composer. He had originally proposed to premier the whole symphony, but the Comedy movement took up so much energy, there was no time left for rehearsing the even more demanding last movement: only the first two would be played. Besides, Goosens couldn't make head or tail of the music, and thought his men would be lucky if they could just get through it. He didn't tell Ives.

Charles and Harmony had come to all the rehearsals but, in their typically bashful way, hid themselves in the green room where they could hear scarcely anything. Goosens had to come backstage to consult, so frightened were they to come out and face "the men."

Ives was last on the program, which began with Debussy's late, elusive cello sonata, a strange, otherworldly work in which the cello, chameleonlike, metamorphoses into violin, into flute, into even mandolin. The house was half-full, but the applause for Pierre Fournier, the intrepid young cellist, was thunderous. Gregor loved this work, and wondered he had not heard it in Europe—for it had appeared in the same year as himself, 1915.

Gregor stuck his head out during intermission, but decided to remain hidden and not mingle with the crowd. As the hall emptied, he spotted Mr. Ives and a woman—his wife?—sitting anonymously in the rear near the exit, positioned, he thought, to flee. He was curious what he might hear.

The hall lights blinked, and the audience took its seats for the major work of the evening, the opening movements of Ives's last symphony, finished thirteen years earlier, as Gregor was performing Rilke for his own audience. From the opening challenge of cellos and basses, he didn't know what hit him. This fierce question gave way to a distant choir of strings, flute, and harp, whispering fragments of the hymn "Bethany," *"Nearer, my God, to Thee."* Gregor didn't know the words, of course, but the feeling of intimate divinity was patent, all the more telling for the preceding, striding immensity. *"E'en though it be a cross that raiseth me . . ."* It would have been good for him to know the text. *"Still all my song shall be nearer, my God, to Thee."* It was too soon for him to know this, his cross, but there he was, behind the curtain, with such thought-forms swarming through him.

Ives must be on a quest, too, he thought, a quest for wholeness, a way to bring all this diversity together. This is a work of high mystery.

Not three minutes in, behold! a choir, out of nowhere, asking the question Gregor had been feeling:

*Watchman, tell us of the night,*
*What the signs of promise are . . .*

Gregor could hear the words, understand them. What about the night? And the answer:

*Traveller, o'er you mountain's height,*
*See that Glory-beaming star!*

Yes, but it is so distant, a mere pinpoint in a universe of darkness . . . The chorus, too, was skeptical:

*Watchman, aught of joy or hope?*

But the answer, unequivocal:

*Traveller, yes, it brings the day,*
*Promised day of Israel.*
*Dost thou see its glorious ray?*

All this within a rich fabric of orchestral sound woven from fragments of other hymns, gently polyrhythmic, polytonal—as is the world. And in less than five minutes, the movement was over, evaporating in the question *"Dost thou see its glorious ray?"* Dost thou, Gregor Samsa? Dost thou? Yes. Yes, I do.

What followed was one of the most extraordinary events in Western music, probably in all music—ever. Maestro Goosens, when questioned afterward about it, was quoted as saying, "My dear boy, I didn't know what happened after the downbeat."

What happened was all that ears could possibly hold, the damnedest racket ever to come out of an orchestra before or since. It's not clear how much Gregor "got," standing behind the tapestry at the back of Town Hall. But the main thrust was clear: there was a tiny voice that kept appearing, a hymn-singing, delicate voice. It would lift itself up in frailty and, harmonized in shifting quarter tones, would make sincere attempts at hymnody. But each time—it would be smashed, crashed, bashed, trashed by ever greater pandemonium, massive musical agglomerations of dizzying, polyrhythmic marches, ragtime piano riffs, secularizations of other hymn tunes, jingoistic clear-the-way for America, America on the march—even a foreigner, a less-than-legal immigrant, could hear that.

And when America marched, it was in a confusion of keys and meters, with ten different rhythms going at once, and half a dozen tonal centers at the same time—appropriate in a country where everyone seemed out for himself. Awash in a maelstrom of competing keys, the total effect was far beyond tonality, an utterly complex shaping and clashing of sound masses. It was the sound of the twentieth century, as even Gregor could understand, the roar of our cities and factories, the clash of our people, races, cultures, a satanic bellowing-out that added up to sheer madness. In such a context, old tunes seemed transformed: "Columbia, the Gem of the Ocean," once a song of joy, now roared monstrous power, monstrously applied; the old Stephen Foster tune—"Down in the Cornfield, hear dat mournful sound"—seemed here not about massa's death, but about the travesty of white supremacy in the racist South—and North. In short, the movement seemed a nightmare crushing of the inner sounds of yearning, hope, and vision, an intimation not of immortality, but of eternal punishment.

Poor little tune in the solo violin (it was "Beulah Land," unknown to

Gregor)—out there all alone, waiting for the inevitable, singing with your head in the guillotine. Why are you there? What are you doing in company such as this? You—fragile, sentimental, but undaunted, with your somber accompaniment and strange quarter tone noodlings. Did you come only to be trampled under our heavy industrial feet, crushed by the venalities of our small-town Babbitry with its blaring booster bands? Or is your presence ironic, a sweet reminder that religion shares complicity in our tragedy? Or are you just there, as truly you are, nine-hundred-lived, watching, waiting for the racket to die out on its own? At the end of the movement, Gregor did not know.

He did know he was shaken. He knew he had been present at a miracle of pedagogy—Mr. Ives was trying to tell him something about his new country, about himself, about his quest. He knew he would go see him, as he had been invited to, three and a half years before.

Watching the Iveses sneak out amidst the booing, he knew Charles Ives would be his teacher.

And his teacher he was, not least of all about the philosophical and loving basis of life insurance. Gregor went back that night to Ulla's room—not home . . . had she gotten herself a boyfriend?—let himself in, and rummaged in the left-hand pocket of his good brown suit still hanging in her closet—there it was, the card:

CHARLES E. IVES

IVES & MYRICK

The Mutual Life Insurance Company of New York

46 Cedar Street

Telephones, John 3663 – 3832

The next day he called, was put right through, and was amazed and flattered that Mr. Ives remembered him.

"'Course I remember you, sonny. How many people have never seen a baseball game before? And the lady with you, Miss Paul. She never did call . . ."

They had made an appointment for February 2, at the office. The talk ranged from philosophy to music. Ives was particularly interested in Gregor's experience of the Great War. He had never had a chance to speak at length with "the enemy." Together they bewailed man's inhumanity to man, and Ives showed Gregor a draft he was writing on One World Government:

> There is one thing in their work which the People's World Nation Army Police shall not do under any conditions—forever and ever—in any way whatsoever—and that is to use aeroplane bombs. Anyone who does shall be stoned to death—not buried in graves but in swill piles—and any man who ever says that bombing is right will be beaten on the jaw until the doorbell to Hell rings him in!

Gregor, of course, couldn't agree more, and supplied Ives with heartrending details of the aftermath of Allied bombing in Vienna. He was as good as hired. But when Ives popped the question "Who's your favorite composer?" and Gregor answered shyly but truthfully, "Until last week, Gustav Mahler, but now, if you will forgive me . . . you," the die was cast. Ives called him a lollygagging, suck-up flatterer, but was flattered nevertheless, and when Gregor described his experience at Town Hall, the old man was convinced he had met someone perceptive, visionary, courageous, and humane—someone worthy of working in life insurance. Gregor would start in training the very next day. He whistled and danced his way down twelve half-flights of stairs.

But today, November 4, 1929, things seemed darker, gloomier, like a sick eagle—more portentous. When Gregor opened the gabled door marked IVES & MYRICK, he found the other early arrivers away from their desks, gathered toward the rear of the great room, some ten feet from the door to Mr. Ives's office. He made his way up the center aisle.

"What is happening?" he asked Kathryn Verplank, Ives's personal secretary, whose desk was the center of the conglomeration.

"We don't know," she whispered. "Mr. Ives is in there. I think he's alone—he has no appointments. There's talking and yelling—I think it's just him, though. Today is always difficult for him, the anniversary of his father's death. But it's never been like this before. . . ."

From within: *"Jump, jump, jump, the boys are jumping . . ."*

This was enough for Gregor. He pushed his way out of the crowd, and with both his claws turned the knob and pushed open the door to Charles Ives's private office. The old man was standing on the floor leaning out the tall window, wide open to the cold November air. Snaking behind him, like some great tail, was all the furniture in the room: desk, three chairs, table, two small bookshelves, and a compact safe on wheels—in which he kept his manuscripts. He was still in his hat and overcoat, though he had been in the office for at least an hour.

"Excuse me, Mr. Ives."

"Come in, Mr. Samsa, come in. Close the door behind you. It's a little cold out there. *Come in to my Lord, oh come in . . .*"

"It is cold, Mr. Ives. Here, let me close the window," said Gregor, making his way quickly between his employer and the open space seven floors above the sidewalk. "There. Better. It will warm up in a short while."

"Tell me about the defenestration of Prague, my lad. It's a wonderful phrase, 'the defenestration of Prague.' Worthy of a short song, don't you think?"

"Why did you do this to the furniture?"

"Oh, you wouldn't know this, but today's my father's birthday, I mean deathday, and he and I always have some sort of party. Today we're playing trains like we used to. The old Ives Brothers Railroad. Father always comes to make the noises for Moss and me. Did you hear the noises? We had just gotten to the window. Did you hear the air brakes? They make us get behind, maybe two or three measures late. Tell me about the defenestration of Prague."

"Let's sit down, and we talk about it." Gregor arranged two of the chairs as far from the window as he could. "Here, I'll take your hat and coat."

"Thank you. You know, a man who tries to hitch his wagon to a star and falls over a precipice, wagon and all, always finds something greater than the man who hitches his gilded star to a mule who kicks him back into a stagnant pool, where he lives forever, safe and sound in his swamp, in his ecstasy of splashing mud on mankind."

"That is surely true, Mr. Ives."

"Defenestration."

"Yes. This is something we must memorize in grade school, so still I know the date: twenty-third of May, 1618. The beginning of the Thirty Years' War."

"The peasants against hog-mind. Good for them."

Gregor took Ives's hat and coat to the coatrack.

"Were you going to jump?"

"Where?"

"Out the window. Just now."

"No."

"You were singing about jumping. That is why I come in."

"I was thinking about jumping, so I started singing about jumping. Think-sing. But I wasn't going to jump."

Ives sank into his great leather desk chair.

"I'm not doing well, Mr. Samsa. I'm in a bad spell that won't say uncle."

"What uncle?" Gregor interrupted.

"Say uncle. That means you give up. It won't give up. The spell."

"Ah."

"The doctors say I have to go slow, I'm having a general running down, some kind of depression. My arms hurt so much, I can't touch the piano. My hands shake so much, I just leave snake tracks on the paper. Harmony and Edie have to rewrite my letters for me. Charlie Ives, hiding behind the ladies, will you get a load of that! It's my heart, polyrhythms, it's my diabetes kicking in hard, going for the extra point."

"You can still work on your music—"

"I can't even see the damn music! It's like little green dots crawling all over the page. I've got no energy to compose. Haven't written anything real in years. Not since the Concord. Not since the Fourth. I've just been cleaning house. . . ."

"Maybe you should take a vacation from work. What if you just stayed home? We handle things here. Lots of good people. And Mr. Myrick can help us stay in touch with you. . . ."

There was no response.

"Mr. Ives?"

"I'm thinking about it. Throw in the towel. Why not? I'm finished. Just taking up high-rent space."

Gregor pondered his next move.

"Mr. Ives?"

"Yes?"

"You know how in your symphony the chorus asks the watchman about the night? What comes after the night?"

"Watchman, tell us of the night."

"Yes. What does the watchman say?"

"There are no signs of promise."

"He says that there is a mountain to climb, and above the mountain is a glory-beaming star. He says to hope and make joy, because the night brings the day. . . ." And Gregor started to sing. In trembling, other-worldly tones, scarcely audible, but perfectly pitched, he sang,

*Promised day of Israel.*

*Dost thou see its glorious ray?*

"Stop it!" yelled Ives. "That's stupid. You want *real* watchmen? Mendelssohn's *Lobgesang:* 'Even though morning comes, the night will come again.'"

"That is a different story. Maybe it's the German Jewish story. But you are American. The American story is what you wrote."

"The American story is the eternal struggle against hog-mind! What do you think is happening out there? It's the hog-mind of the minority against the universal mind of the majority."

Ives got up and started pacing, working his way up and down the train of furniture.

"Mr. Ives, sit down and rest—"

"Hog-mind slowing down human progress."

"What is hog-mind?"

"Hog-mind! Hoggy-mind, the self-will of the Minority! Hog-mind and all its sneak-slimy handmaidens in disorder—superficial brightness, gallery thinking, fundamental dullness. Spreading suspicion, cowardice, and fear and then weapon-grabbing. It's all a part of the minority, the Non-People, the politicians, the bankers that own them, the antithesis of everything called Soul, Spirit, Christianity, Truth, Freedom, insulting us . . . Look out there."

He threw up the window again. Gregor jumped to close it. His *New York Times* fell to the floor.

"Look in that stupid newspaper you have. You want to learn something? Stop reading the damn paper, making America soft with its commercialism, with its mechanization, its standardized processes of mind and life, touting conventional ways, platitudes, dogmas, headlines, half-truths which confuse every issue and every ideal. Where's my chair? Mr. Smooth-It-Away, read all about it, Mr. Live-for-the-World, Mr. Scaly Conscience, sneak-thieving medieval-minded dictators with their sudden, underhanded, dark-age bossy gouging tricks displacing the direct will-of-the-people way, emasculating America for money! We're gradually losing our manhood! The Puritans may have been everything the lollers called them, but they weren't soft. They may have been cold, narrow, hard-minded rock-eaters, but they weren't goddamn effeminates. Where's my hat and coat? Oh, you hung them up. The majority of Americans own something—a few, too much; everybody knows that. But whatever they own, for the most part they've worked for it hard with their hands and their brains. And if some Minority bandit should sneak down the road and try to take away those Americans' homes, shops, farms, whatever they've laid up for a rainy day, for their children, a new version of the lion and the mouse will be staged and the Minority Hog would be too groggy to applaud many of the scenes. And let some hog-minded, self-willed Minority agent try to take away any of their natural rights or freedom, he'll find himself on the canvas from a blow which'll be heard on Mars!"

"Mr. Ives?"

"What? You wanted to know what hog-mind is!"

"Mr. Ives, you're so angry."

"Damn right, I'm angry. You know what I saw on the train this morning? An editorial saying, 'Not one in a million is troubled with a conscience.' 'Not one in a million is troubled with a conscience!' Hog-mind hogwash! Of the world's greatest lies, this is the greatest. Please get me a glass of water. That would mean no distinction between human life and life in the most luxurious pigsty. It would mean death was Man's only hope. . . ."

"Here's your water. Here, sit down in your chair."

"Thank you. Mr. Samsa, if there is one ideal social evolution's got to have, it's belief in the innate goodness of mankind. Innate goodness. That's why we sell insurance! If the majority want to put themselves in the timid hog-mind class for a while, all right. But a few men on Wall Street don't have the right to determine the quality, the courage, the generosity of the People. If Suspicion ever gets the lead, it's all over with the world. It's all over with me."

"Are *you* suspicious?"

"Me? No. I believe in the Majority. The People . . ."

"I'm not suspicious either. In this very office there are three not-sus-picious people."

"You and me and . . . ?"

"And the glorious Mr. Thoreau you lent me last month. Your Thoreau book, there, back on your desk. I read about his pond."

"He was a great musician."

"So are you. Do you remember how he ends the book? Do you re-member the story of the strong and beautiful insect which came out of a table sixty years, maybe a hundred years, after its egg—"

"Of course I remember."

"The farmer heard it gnawing away for a long time, trying to get out. Do you hear any gnawing? Listen."

"I hear gnawing."

"What is it?"

"I don't know. Gnawing."

"It's the winged life in *you*. It's still there, already hatched, gnawing. It will come. At unexpected time it will come. Don't give up. Just wait."

Ives sat quietly in his chair, listening. Then, "I will. Wait."

"Do you remember the very end?"

"Of what?"

"Of the pond book."

Ives reached over and grabbed the *Walden* on his desk. "'Only that day dawns to which we are awake. There is more day to dawn.'"

"There is more day to dawn."

"'The sun is but a morning star.'"

"Does that remind you of anything, watchman?" Gregor asked quietly.

"Promised day of Israel."

"Dost thou see its glorious ray?"

"But after the day the night comes—again."

"So?" Gregor helped him on with his coat, took Ives out, and walked with him, slowly, silently, all the way up to Grand Central, where he put him on the train for West Redding. Ives officially left his agency on January 1, 1930, but remained available, at home, for consultation. He spent his days hatching the insect egg within him.

# 15. SOMETIMES, *the* UNEXPECTED; SOMETIMES NOT

Gregor put on his new camel's hair coat on this frosty Ides of March, and scuttled down two flights of stairs into the morning sunshine. Eighth and C. The fabled Lower East Side, more than its image, less than its myth.

Once he was a salaried employee again, the Roach About Town had decided to settle in, gather his belongings under one roof—his own—and concentrate on building a life. True, the Wall Street crash had clouded things somewhat, but the mood at Ives & Myrick was upbeat, reflecting, perhaps, the sunny personality of Mike Myrick, and the hibernation of the confused and depressed Charles Ives. Gregor's $35 a week was more than ample for room and food—provided he live frugally in a low-rent neighborhood.

The Lower East Side was the obvious choice. For a being so dedicated to life, *L'chayem,* this was the core and center, the bubbling ur-soup of real-life life, tenement canyons and courtyards hung with laundry, bedclothes, people up and down fire escapes, bodies, always bodies leaning out windows, talking, calling, yelling. Inside, outside, the rhythm continued, the streets always alive with pushcarts and junk bells, cats yowling and beggars singing, dogs whining and babies crying, men, women, children talking, talking, always talking up a storm. Even the parrots could curse, constantly—in Yiddish. Talk, talk, talk, Jewish talk, up and down the airshafts, Semitic surf and symphony, untiring, counterpoint to the rattling of dishes, the squeaking of clotheslines, the plop and splat of peelings and fish heads tossed from above. On the street corners, soapboxed, seers and rebels, prophets and cranks, shouting God's fire and America's woes unto the sky. In Yiddish! Yiddish! A language he could understand without translation, words he could speak without accent. The Old World in the middle of the New—at last he belonged, truly belonged.

He belonged among the children who owned the streets and every smallest corner of alley or lot, every found piece of twisted junk, every stick of lumber, wheels off rusty prams, old dead clothing, who rejoiced in even the find of a dead, half-rotting squirrel, somehow escaped from Tompkins Square. The children! How beautiful these children. Like little animals with yarmulkes and braids, scouring the world for the few pennies they needed for a hot dog, or a cup of chocolate, halvah, knishes, pickles, or fifty kinds of candy, playing tag and tops and kites and stickball, skelly and ringeleveo. Swarming.

The children and the aged. The nobility of these gaunt, gray-bearded men, shuffling in black coats and hats to schul and synagogue, the same as in Prague. The same clothing, the same bentness, the visible, invisible weight of learning and dedication. The peddlers, old-timers—and new ones forced from their stores by the crash—managing the streets, filling them with infinite variegations of the material world. The "I cash clothes" man, the old and dignified scissors grinder with his huge, wheeled grindstone. Gregor loved to watch the sparks fly, fire from friction, swords into ploughshares. He loved hearing the names of angels and demons from every corner, seeing the babushkas and old fur hats, the riot of banana peels on gray pavement; he loved even the smell of urine. To a blattid, urine smells of life.

The sights and sounds, the tastes and smells of the Lower East Side were a continuous, multisensorial madeleine, bringing our six-legged Proust back to his bipedal youth in Prague in the decade before the "sanitization" of the Jewish quarter, Josefov. Though his upwardly mobile father had moved from ghetto to square several years before Gregor's birth, still, the square backed right onto the ghetto, and young Gregor spent much of his non-school day exploring the crooked alleyways, the dark tunnels with their "spittoons of light" as he called them, leading to interior courtyards of houses named "The Mouse Hole," or "The Left Glove," or "Death." Like the Lower East Side of the thirties, Prague's Jewish quarter of the previous eighties had suffered an exodus of the well-to-do. The more prosperous families had moved out of Josefov, leaving only the poorest of poor Jews, soon joined by multicultural ranks of the underprivileged: gypsies, beggars, prostitutes, and alcoholics. By the time Gregor's father, he of the apple, moved out of the ghetto, only twenty percent of its inhabitants were Jewish in this, the most densely populated area of Prague. The malodorous Josefov was seen as a blight upon the city, in the words of Meyrink, "a demonic underworld, a place of anguish, a beggarly and phantasmagorical quarter whose eeriness seemed to have spread and led to paralysis." No wonder Herr Samsa wanted out. No wonder the city fathers wanted urban renewal.

In 1893 they decided that Prague might become the jewel of the Empire, a beautiful, bourgeois world city like Paris. And so the old neighborhoods came down and were replaced with block upon block of opulent art-nouveau buildings, decorative murals, doorways, and sculpture. Along with gypsies and prostitutes, the Jews, too, were cleared out: the end of a community that had existed for a thousand years. Given the Nazi occupation forty years later, we might expect there to be no trace at all of Josefov today. But truth is stranger than fiction: the remnants of the old Jewish quarter had their savior, one Adolf Hitler, who chose to preserve what little was left of the ghetto—the Jewish Town Hall and the Altneu Synagogue wherein sleeps the golem, the Old Jewish Cemetery that is eternal home of the great Rabbi Lowe who created him, and five other synagogues with their contents—as the basic sites for an "Exotic Museum of an Extinct Race." Jewish artifacts stolen from all over central Europe were stored in these buildings, and now constitute one of the great collections of Judaica in the world. With friends like these . . .

Thus, the situation in the ghetto of Gregor's youth was much like that in New York fifty years later, and his new life had a deep and secret resonance that softened the edges of what someone more objective might see as desperation. For even the early days of the Depression had led to many evictions, and forced ever greater numbers of families to crowd together in unheated quarters with aunts and uncles, cousins, grandparents, and friends.

Late October in the northern latitudes is no time for an economic crisis, for the winter comes hard upon, winter with its dripping walls and airborne diseases. Poverty in winter, the collective suffering of a hundred thousand tenements, grimy, windblown junkheaps of rotting lumber and cracked brick. And in them, thousands, tens of thousands of tuberculars and paralytics, hunger, fatigue, a world of rotting livers and breaking hearts, babies screaming until breath stopped, pneumonia, influenza, typhoid.

Garbage trucks and hearses prowled the streets in ghastly competition. Multitudes were without work, and strikes, suicides, food riots pushed pious women to harlotry. The streets reeked with filthy slush, and the sun vanished in grayness behind the sky. Winter 1930.

Yet Gregor, eternal optimist, was wont to see the beneficent Janus face of adversity. Its precious jewel was that spirit of community where everyone knew everyone, complained and kvetched, but were there for one another when chips were down—as they almost always were. With any eviction notice came a collection from housewives up and down the block. In sickness, who could afford a physician? Yet people cared for one another, and the old witch doctor, Baba Schimmel, made her rounds, an old crone with huge varicosed calves, carrying philters in her knotted apron. That scene last week of children chasing the sightseeing bus, pelting it with rocks and garbage—and a dead cat—"Go home," they yelled, "Go back uptown!"—what else could Gregor conclude but that there was some enormous vestige of neighborhood pride, a sense of strength among the surviving.

On this sunny, cold March morning, Gregor overslept. He jumped into his clothes, did up his antennae as quickly as he could, put on his camel's hair coat, and heeding the pangs of mid-morning hunger, made the snap decision to go buy a bagel. He loved bagels—he always had. His mother used to make them, soft, warm, and chewy. He would watch them rise from the dead in the boiling pot and float, triumphant, carving out a tesselated honeycomb of circles on the bubbling surface. Now that he was older, he recognized in bagels the great symbol of Buddhist Nothingness, and the joyous O of O say can you see and O what a beautiful morning.

Perhaps even more than bagels, he loved going into Paddy's Bagel Bakery on Sixth Street, off Avenue B. The name was improbable enough, but the large brown bagel hanging out front, growing out of its intensely green four-leaf clover, broke the bounds of all rational construction. And the sign was just the beginning of the outlandish Paddy experience. Gregor would descend the short flight of stairs to a basement-level areaway piled with years of tossed-in trash, a genuine archaeological dig site. There was a narrow, almost clear path toward a door that over the years had carved a radial swing space in the mass of miscellany, and as he headed for his goal, Gregor thought how lucky he was to have six legs, in case he needed them. When he pulled open the door, a full body-caressing blast of steam greeted him, feeling um-um-good on a freezing morning.

Inside, the steam was thick, almost impenetrable, and the two 15-watt bulbs hanging from the ceiling served only to make it opaque as well. Bagels have to be boiled before baking, and here in this low-ceilinged basement storefront sans ventilation, it was the steam from two great vats that took front and center, above and below and behind. Shadows flitted and projected through the thick, atmospheric fog, but shadows of what— no one could tell. It could have been a whole hoard of Nibelungen dwarves, or more likely a large cohort of leprechauns jabbering away in Gaelic.

Yes. A bagel from Paddy's. He whizzed down the stairs and hit the streets running. But at the corner of Eighth and B, he was stopped short: a crowd of some sixty people was gathered around a little forty-year-old Jew and his wife, sitting at an enameled kitchen table, their four children around them, shivering in holy clothing, the youngest crying pitifully, as if he could foresee what was abroad in the world. All their worldly belongings were piled around them—a shrine, a museum, a mausoleum of objects: an old, bedbugged mattress with sagging, protruding springs; a stained, embroidered under-stuffed chair; a lamp with a burned-through shade. Around the family and the furniture, the small objects that constitute a life: a washtub packed with dishes, a box of bedclothes, a broom. What broom, Gregor wondered, could sweep this journey clean? A seven-year-old was idly rocking an empty carriage abandoned last month by her baby brother, a still-valued possession to cling to in an uncertain world.

With heavy heart, the wife reached into the washtub, retrieved a tea glass, and placed it on the table. Were they going to have tea? Gregor wondered. Where would they boil water? A neighbor woman close by placed a penny in the glass and mumbled a Hebrew prayer, and the husband stared at his hands laid flat on the table. From a twelve-year-old, another coin—and then, from many, many. Rosie the prostitute pushed gently through the crowd and placed a dollar bill into the glass half full of nickel and copper—an act her judgmental neighbors knew not how to judge. Incredible. Indigestible. The crowd parted to let her back through, and heads turned to watch her walk back into her shameful building. The husband still stared at his hands. "We are not beggars," he cried out, as he lifted his head for the first time. "We are respectable people!" And he drew back into his humiliation.

Gregor was about to put some money on the table, next to two apples and a banana, when there was a stirring at the back of the crowd, and a voice called out, "Okay, the cops are gone. Furniture back in the house!"

A woman ordered, "Form a squad and block the doors if they come back!"

The Young Communists were calling for volunteers. Such a family was entitled to a place to live. And people responded. Not just the young and daring, but small boys and girls, frail, elderly men, women with young children clinging to their hems. Gregor picked up the lamp with the scorched shade and marched it back into the apartment.

"Sheriff! Sheriff!" came the lookout voice, and a group of young men, well practiced, ran around the corner to kick over ash cans and bang with fists on parked cars, diverting the police so the uneviction might continue.

The ten or fifteen people who had declined to take part stood aside, watching the action. A child bought a pickle from an old, old man; Gregor came back out the door into the crowd of spectators. Sensing a ready-made audience, a dark, disheveled gnome of a man appropriated the last kitchen chair, pushed it over to the bystanders, and jumped up on its cracked seat.

"My dirty thief of a cousin, Herman Rothblatt, may his nose be eaten by the pox, he stole my shop, he stole my shop away from me!"

Before he could elaborate, a muscular young comrade with no coat, his sleeves rolled up in the cold, pulled the chair out from under him and tossed it to a comrade in the uneviction brigade. Herman Rothblatt's cousin picked himself up, dusted off his disheveledness, and walked silently away. Before rounding the corner of Eighth Street, he turned and yelled, "When the Messiah comes to America, he better come with a big car and a chauffeur and a full wallet, or people will think he's just another poor Yid, and he'll have to wash dishes in a restaurant!" Gregor saw him throw up his head in pride and disappear around the corner.

It was already eleven. He wouldn't be at work for half an hour. He thought of taking a cab, but in the midst of others' poverty, felt ashamed to do so. He walked quickly on Eighth Street and turned south onto Third Avenue toward the Bowery.

. . .

On his quickwalk downtown, having lost his appetite for bagels, Gregor was playing in his heartmind with the German language paradoxes of the *Unterüberwelt* and the *Überunterwelt.* Gregor lived in the *Unterwelt,* an "underworld" not in the Plutonic sense, but in the way the "underdog" is under. Nevertheless, his neighborhood underworld was actually an overworld, superior—at least morally—to the district he worked in, and thus an "over-underworld." Wall Street, his destination, was the inverse, an "underover-world" in which evictions, bankruptcies, and even suicides were private affairs, sometimes whispered about, but never collectively mourned. As he walked, he tried to feel the downward slope of moral descent on the absolute flatness of the physical path, and the class-ascent of the taller and taller, more resplendent buildings. Up, down, and level, all at the same time, a mysterious Trinity pervading most human affairs. He arrived at work tense.

It didn't help that he was three and a half hours late. When Kathryn Verplank, once Mr. Ives's personal secretary, now general site manager, appeared at his desk, he feared it was all over. Caught.

"Mr. Ives would like to see you in his office."

"Mr. Ives? Why is he here? Did he come all that way to personally fire me? I can just leave without disturbing him."

"He has something for you."

"Yes, ma'am."

Gregor rose slowly and inched his way toward the room behind the frosted glass. Something for me. A tin watch to honor my less than three years of service? He can be frightful when he is mad. It was one spooked employee who knocked tentatively on the great man's door.

"Come in!" came a voice, frighteningly firm, so unlike the last doddering hesitations Gregor had heard. Prepare for the worst.

"Mr. Samsa, how nice to see you!"

Ives got up from his desk and strode robustly across the room to shake Gregor's claw. What was going on? *Isn't he mad I was late? This is a trick.*

"Well, I did what you told me."

"What was that?"

"Give birth to the insect gnawing in the table. The table, that's me."

"You mean you wrote another symphony?"

"Sonata, my boy, a sonata. For the old *hammerklavier.*"

He went back to his desk and plucked a thick music manuscript from the top of a pile of unopened mail.

"Here you are. Take a look at the dedication."

SONATA NUMBER THREE FOR PIANO
THE INSECT SONATA
CHARLES E. IVES

"It's on the next page."

Gregor turned over the elegantly copied manuscript page.

TO MR. GREGOR SAMSA, BEST OF EMPLOYEES, FOR CONDUCTING ME, MA NON TROPPO, FROM MESTO ROTTENABILE TO ALLEGRO ONCEAGAINDO. WITH DEEP APPRECIATION.

C. E. I.

Gregor was dumbstruck. What could he say? He turned over the pages. A huge number of notes—and strange notation. First movement, "Creation"; second, "Revelation"; third movement, "Redemption."

"Thank you, Mr. Ives. I wasn't expecting this. I mean to say, I was expecting you to get better, but I didn't think I—"

"And here are two tickets to the premiere—April Fools' Day. I've already rented the hall. That'll fool 'em as thought I was a goner. You'll come with Mrs. Ives and me."

TOWN HALL
APRIL 1, 1930, 8PM
"THE INSECT SONATA," by CHARLES E. IVES
NICOLAS SLONIMSKY, piano
*The work will be played twice.*

Gregor did not get his tin watch. He did not get fired. But he did get confused. How was it possible that he, a mere insect, could have helped bring such a thing to birth? Was this the first evidence that he was truly on the path, that his quest had a realizable goal?

He took his lunch at the usual time, but couldn't go back to work. Concentrating on numbers, budgets, probabilities—impossible. He became aware of the wound in his back. It was not leaking but tingling—perhaps glowing. Dry. Electric. He called in sick from a pay phone on William Street. He *was* sick—sick with The Sickness Unto Life—but this he didn't tell Mrs. Verplank.

Gregor walked home slowly, out of the dark canyons of perplexed plutocracy, up the moral gradient. Up Broadway to the Park, over to Center Street, and then up to Houston. Turning east, high *Überland* now, he realized he hadn't yet eaten and stopped in to Yonah Schimmel's for a knish. Ah, the warmth of hot, spiced potato on a nippy day of not-yet-spring! He opened his mouth and allowed the knish to make smoke in the broad air. Now he was a fire-breathing dragon, a Fafnir guarding the secret hoard. Hoard of what?

Crossing Houston, always dangerous, better concentrate, he turned north on Avenue A. Just past the courthouse, he felt a tug on his left sleeve.

"I know you from this morning. I see you standing there before you take the lamp into the house."

It was the gnome, cousin of Herman Rothblatt, still disheveled.

"My cousin, may the worms find him, may he eat nothing but dry crusts, he stole my shop. He stole my umbrella shop. I own it myself. I work for myself. I live and laugh, I take him in as partner, he needs a break."

"You said that this morning."

"I didn't. I didn't say what kind of shop. I didn't say about partners."

"You are right. You didn't."

Gregor sped his pace, so that the manikin had to trot to keep up with him.

"He stole my shop, and now I will die of starving. A curse on Columbus, the thief! A curse on America, the thief! We live ... slow down! ... we live in a land where the lice make the fortunes, and the good people starve. May six and sixty-six black years fall on them, the lices have ruined the world with greed! When Messiah comes, he will change all this, believe me."

Gregor stopped. They had reached Eighth Street.

"Do you need money?"

"Yes."

"Will five dollars be enough?"

"Ten."

Gregor pulled two five-dollar bills out of his wallet and handed a third of his salary to his swarthy companion.

"Here."

"Thank you. You are not a lice. You are a good man."

"I have to go now. Thank you for telling me about you."

"God bless you. You are not a lice."

In fact, this little colloquy had quite taken the wind out of Gregor's sails. He had started uptown breathing in the bracing gradient of poverty, that poverty of spirit that will be blessed with the kingdom of heaven. But now he was breathing simple, wretched poverty, the poverty of theft and eviction and crafty, manipulative begging. He passed the corner of the morning's events, deserted now, eerily empty of its usual play. He reached his home—on the corner of Avenue C.

High, then low. It was no accident that his gaze was drawn to that stone in the courtyard, an early gravestone, broken and discarded, which some enterprising landlord had used to fill a hole in the paving.

THE 21TH. 1719 AG

ED 38 YEARS

HERE LIES ONE WH

OS LIFES THREDS

CUT ASUNDER SHE

WAS STRUCKE DEAD

BY A CLAP OF THUNDER.

Barely readable, but searing all the same.

Mr. Pinzer was chatting in the courtyard with Mrs. Grossman as she hung the laundry.

"From the Talmud one can learn anything," he assured her. "For instance, it takes the Angel Gabriel six flaps of his wings to come down to earth. The Angel Simon it takes four flaps, but the Angel of Death, him it takes only one flap of the wings."

It is wonderful to be learned.

Though Gregor had offered to meet the Iveses at the concert so as not to take them out of their way, they wouldn't hear of it: they would pick him up at seven-thirty at the corner of Eighth and C. Instead of April Fools' pranking, he had spent the day being fitted for appropriate attire. Via a call to Ulla, he had located a Jewish tailor from Kraków who, instead of following the migration north to the garment district, had established a tiny shop on Elizabeth Street, in the heart of Chinatown. His sign read EMANNUEL PINSKY, ESQ. ELEGANT CLOTHES FOR STYLISH MENS, with translations in Yiddish and Chinese lettered below. Perhaps it was more grammatical in Yiddish. Gregor arrived at ten in the morning and, after telling Mr. Pinsky about the evening's affair, received an enthusiastic "Oi, have I got just the thing for you!"

He was always hard to fit. It was no surprise that he didn't leave Pinsky's until four-thirty—famished—carrying a large white box containing a dark blue worsted tailcoat, a pair of gray pin-striped wool trousers with braces and cummerbund (the starry-eyed tailor reported that "pinstripes" were his invention, named after him), a pleated, pale blue linen shirt with a darker silk ascot, and to add a touch of what Pinsky called *"finésshe,"* a larger-than-life red satin carnation. "You'll be the hit of the show," he assured his doubtful and embarrassed customer. But Pinsky knew America better than he and was after all an acknowledged expert in stylish menswear. It said so on the sign. So Gregor went along with the enthusiasm of the master, and accepted the generous offer, "For you, special," to rent rather than buy.

Gregor was overdressed. When he climbed into the cab, he found Ives in his usual gray overcoat, over his normal brown tweed suit and brown tie, his daily fedora perched far back on his head. Harmony looked a bit more elegant in her black dress and light fur piece, but still . . . Gregor *was* overdressed.

Charles, always truthful if not tactful, said "Mr. Samsa, you look like the winner of the Nobel prize for Undertaking—Wouldn't you say so, dear?" Harmony thought Gregor looked just fine. The cab drew up on Forty-third Street, and the three got out, a singular-looking trio.

The lights were going down. There was a moment of rustling silence, and Nicolas Slonimsky—the extravagant Russian emigré pianist, composer, and conductor with a passion for modern music—walked on from stage right. Perhaps "staggered" might be a better word, for he had done nothing but eat, sleep, and drink this difficult work for the last three months, trying to get it into his brain and under his fingers. He was not a sissy. He drank strong samovar *chai*. Still, a man needs sleep.

But one can stagger and still be on fire, and Slonimsky, even punchy, was a force to be reckoned with. He bowed to the audience. Without a word of introduction, he walked upstage of the Steinway Concert Grand and returned with a large brick and two pieces of two-by-four, one 47¾ inches, the other 45½ inches, the longer painted in white, the shorter in black enamel. He put the wood on the piano bench and carefully leaned the cement block on the sustaining pedal. Climbing out from under the keyboard, he retrieved the wood and placed the longer piece, narrow edge down, along the white keys, and the shorter one, wider side down, along the black. He was ready to begin the first movement: "Creation."

Standing over the keyboard, the piano bench behind him, he took a huge breath and crashed his whole body weight, elbows first, down onto the wood. Some in the audience gasped, most jumped. The piano let out a sound such as had never been heard in any concert hall. At no time, ever, had all eighty-eight notes of a Steinway Concert Grand been simultaneously sounded and sustained publicly.

Quadruple fortissimo to start, the opening ultra-chord took a full two and a half minutes to decay into nothingness, though the absolute endpoint depended on each listener's distance and auditory acuity. Slonimsky stood above the keyboard, his eyes closed, and allowed his spirit to spread to the farthest physical and spiritual reaches of the expanding vibrations.

When he could hear no more (he was the last in the hall), when what he would call his etheric body had reached its maximum distance and had begun to contract significantly, he removed the two-by-fours, replaced them upstage, reached under the piano, pushed the brick to the side of the pedal, and took his seat at the keyboard. While it is nowhere indicated in the copious commentary in the score, it is clear that Ives's opening was also the first direct musical reference to the "big-bang" theory of creation.

The "Big Bang" had occurred in 1926 to the Belgian astrophysicist/ priest Georges Lemâitre in a religious vision. It accounted for Hubble's red-shift findings, and explained the recession of galaxies in the framework of Einsteinian General Relativity. He published his theory in 1927 in an obscure Belgian journal ("Un univers homogène de masse constante et de rayon croissant rendant compte de la vitesse radiale des nébuleuses extra-galactique," *Ann. Soc. Sci. Bruxelles,* 47A, 1927, pp. 49–56), which, in 1930, was "discovered" by a graduate student of Arthur Eddington's, who then announced Lemâitre's theory—just a few months before the concert—to the world. The public loved its alliteration, and its straightforward imagery of the "primeval atom," the "cosmic egg," containing all matter in the universe, whose disintegration marked the beginning of time and space—which may explain the general acceptance of this cacophonous moment. Without being told, people understood that the opening of a movement called "Creation" might consist of some kind of big bang. The actual experience, apparently, was something else.

Ives's big bang gave way to a world of vast, austere empty space. Out of silence, there appeared atomic fragments of pre-melodies, one note, three notes, two, a gentle report of almost-vacancy as the pre-melodies staked out their polytonal grounds. Punctuating the slow metamorphoses of individual capsules were quiet outbursts of tremolos at the seventh and ninth, creating halo-like shimmers of light. There were six such crescendo-decrescendos in the movement, clocking the six days of creation, after which there is rest. On the fifth of such presumptive days, the day when God said, "Let the waters bring forth abundantly every moving creature that hath life," the music thickened markedly. It now had enough mass for rhythm to emerge, at first simple syncopations, and finally a polyrhythmic cosmic dance, a combination of simultaneous musics, as Ives was wont to do, but here slower, softer, more anatomized, not the repulsing chaos of the Fourth Symphony "Comedy," but a far more inviting, massaging, soundspace enveloping the listener in a finally friendly creation. On the sixth presumptive day, with the addition of "creeping things" to the bestiary, a clear, easily recognizable rhythmic figure, a quarter note, a rest, and quick pickup to the next quarter: Gregor recognized the telltale rhythmic signature of an insect heartbeat, gathering.

The middle section of this ABA movement is marked "The firmament walks up a mountainside to view the firmament," an odd but evocative piece of topology. Slow, gentle, aggregations of kaleidoscope-massed chords and tone clusters, the total effect of which hit Gregor as an accompaniment to some still-absent melody. The bass tried out "Oh Maker of the Sea and Sky," only to have it fade away, incomplete. The tune returned again, "Creator Spirit, by Whose Aid . . . ," and advanced a few bars further before dissolving in its own accompaniment. In this middle section, the overall serenity was occasionally pierced by inexplicable explosions, surprising, sometimes barbaric, leaps of tone sequences from one end of the keyboard to the other. Wisps of quotations—Gregor recognized Handel's frogs and locusts, Mahler's lindens, Haydn's whales and worms, Beethoven's cuckoo, Carl Ruggles's lilacs, Saint-Saëns's, Tchaikovsky's, and Sibelius's swans—made fragmentary appearances, half a dozen notes, like the sprinkling of stars that form a constellation.

Then, as if from a different level of spacetime, the first mood returned, now enclosed in a trinity of superimposed sets of perfect fifths, a pedal point pervaded by heartbeat, giving birth, as if from a resistant hardwood table, to a hesitant, but slowly complete, chorale setting of "Watchman, tell us of the night," the melody floating in and out of tonality, sober, *maestoso*, "Watchman, tell us of the night"—here not an anxious question, but a humble entreaty, its feet washed in mystery. It was Gregor's gift to his employer to refocus him here; it was Ives's gift to Gregor to bring it thus to mind.

And with it, Slonimsky closed the movement, quietly, firmly, then placed his hands in his lap and waited the full three minutes requested in the score. For the first of these, the audience was completely silent, hypnotized by the evocation. In the second minute, people grew uncomfortable. Some worried that something was amiss, while others gathered their suspicions of a put-on. A small flurry of whispering was shushed out by the faithful, and the silence cycled around again on a deeper level.

The pianist opened his eyes and once again placed the brick on the sustain pedal. He stood by the side of the piano while two stagehands pulled pins from their hinges and placed the huge piano lid against the wall, stage right. The performer now had in front of him an enormous horizontal harp, ready to speak of "Revelation."

But not just a harp. A harp inside an enormously powerful, sophisticated structure, evolved over centuries, a structure capable of containing and supporting more than eighteen tons of amassed string tension. A structure of multiple strings in two overlapping fans. A structure of spruce and steel very like a coffin.

As a child, Gregor had studied piano until his father decided one music student in the family was enough. The Steinway rental was terminated. How often, though, had Child Gregor been attracted, amazed, and thrilled by the technical genius under the lid. And at the same time, he remembered the strong feeling of *coffin*, an ominous but somehow freeing impression. He wondered now if Ives had any sense of that in writing the second movement, if all its boisterousness was ironically placed inside a tomb and must be so understood. That was how Gregor listened.

The entire second movement, "Revelation," marked "*Scherzo* TSI-MAJ," takes place inside the case, and requires of the performer an utterly unprecedented technique, and of the composer an extended notational system to describe the rich sound palette of an undamped piano harp in a sophisticated sound chamber, urged by fingers that can pluck and stoke, flick and scratch, flesh, bone, and nail, by fists that can bang, and palms that can slap, by forearms grazing and elbows jabbing, and even by hair brushing lightly, across or along the strings. Add to these the percussive sonorities of various striking objects: the metallic echo of wedding ring on harp bolt, the ticking or tocking of chopstick and toothpick, the liquid rebound of strings released by soft dough. No description can communicate such aural complexity.

Because a performer would quickly be lost in a forest of undifferentiated stringing, the strings were colored black and white to mirror the familiar keyboard; though paint had been lost over the hammers, and in areas of maximum vibrational displacement, the visual effect was still striking. Gregor thought that certain combinations of vibrating strings, though each only black or white, can create short flashes of color. The physics of this is unclear. Perhaps it occurs only for the blattid nervous system, or solely in mosaic eyes.

Creation. Revelation. After the long silence of what must have been the Sabbath, the movement opened triple pianissimo, with a quietly pulsing, timeless E-flat, the same sustained note Wagner chose to represent the beginning of the world from abysmal depths. ("Mark my new poem well," he wrote to Liszt, "it holds the world's beginning, and its destruction.")

All of a sudden, there was a loud, old-fashioned, short fanfare, the kind of musical cliché that would invariably be followed by "And now, ladies and gentlemen . . ." and Slonimsky embarked upon the section marked "Feeding Frenzy, *Allegro Scrumptuoso,*" where an increasingly agitated rhythmic figure was mixed into the more and more dissonant sonic halo and the performer began what must be the most fiendishly difficult task in the repertoire. *"Antennae accelerando,"* Ives orders, and the music broke out into quick-march version of "I Hunger and I Thirst," and "Come Thou, Font of Every Blessing." Then, a clarion call from chopstick-struck strings: "Hark a Thrilling Voice Is Sounding," and the whole grand harp broke into a Yale Football March, with a tapped-out supra-melody of "Rush Down Boys." In the score is written, "All hands on deck!!!," and all hands were surely there, and knuckles and elbows, too, for a chaotic concatenation of barn dances, popular parlor tunes (with highly unpopular treatments), polka-dot polkas, cross-rhythmic children's songs, and devilish ragtime, *"allegro (conslugarocko)*—wag those knees," all swirled together in stubbornly original juxtapositions, "wrong note" harmonies, and polychords. In the dim light, Gregor followed his autographed score: here Ives had written "play adagio or allegro—very nice." Slonimsky had completely free choice about the sonic boom he was creating.

The pianist's manic disposition, fueled by months of caffeine, made this performance a never-to-be-equaled thrashing about in the cupboards of Americana and the annals of technical prowess. Honky-tonk whip-chords, sharp, unexpected jabs at irregular intervals, *"Presto con Blasta,"* *"Con Furyoso-fffff."* Again, an abrupt halt; in the manuscript: "Back to the hero—all good Opryettas got to have a hero." So, scratched out with fingernail on the thickly wound lower strings, we hear the belching song of an overstuffed roach, the theme of F, E, E, D —now revealing itself as the second phrase of "Three Blind Mice"—"see how they run," mice in this case metamorphosed into roaches running in mighty molasses motion.

Then, crash! the fastest and most difficult passage of all, a long section of rapid, sprawling chromatic chords, out of which the left hand pulled quintuplet dances of jaunty wild demons, while the right hand slap-accentuated every fifth sixteenth note, and the entire raucousness came to a vociferous climax in a repeated polytonal canon on "The Streets of Cairo," a belly-dance tune that emerged to dominate the scramble. In the manuscript: "EVEN HERBERT HOOVER WILL GET THIS,"—though some in the audience didn't. And "Revelation" ended with a section entitled "Southpaw Pitching," a left-hand solo recitative of highly improvisational character.

A revelation most ambiguous. Gregor knew from the Piano Trio that TSIAJ means "This *scherzo* is a joke." But what of the added "M"? "This *scherzo* is mostly a joke"? What is the non-joke meaning?

That intent became clear to him in the inspired last movement, "Redemption." As prelude, burly stagehands fitted the lid back on the piano and raised it to its full height.

In the score, "Bring Art into life and Life into art (no elite redemptive space!)" floats mysteriously above the movement title, in small letters at the right-hand top of the page. Then, "III. REDEMPTION," that short phrase announcing a gift to humanity as full of import as the "6. Der Abschied" in Mahler's masterpiece *The Song of the Earth*. Creation, Revelation, Redemption. Gregor was more than ready. "Allegro fortissimo with marked energy."

Back at the keyboard, the movement began, with a complex clarity fresh to the ears after the misty vibrations of an unrestrained piano harp. Ives kicked off with the most complex statement possible, with many subsequent motives elbowing for space in the first measure, enough germ material, Gregor thought, for an entire symphony. The Big Bang X-rayed, Gregor thought.

There followed an *animando* section, *crescendo*, with the upper choirs rising and the lower ones descending until they each dropped off into empty space, extruding the tenor duet out in front to begin the second section, an overlay of funeral marches incompletely metamorphosing one into the other, to an irregular, discordant accompaniment below that quietly growled. The funeral march from the Eroica changed its famous descending trochees into the steady, falling eighth note spondees of the Chopin funeral march. Accompanying this noble procession, like Sancho Panza alongside the Don, was a second line of burlesque commentary, the mock-funeral from the Mahler First, chirping along from above, while "The Worms Crawl In, The Worms Crawl Out" rocked deep below, like an ominous carved cradle.

Silence. Slonimsky glanced furtively at the crowd.

Then shocking surprise: the fierce opening of the movement exploded again, *"fortissimo possible,"* causing several members of the audience to wet their underwear or worse. Even Gregor jumped. As before, the sound grew richer as the choruses formed, as the contrary motion filled the space. But this time, the outer choirs did not fly off into upper and lower regions, but gave birth to a second, even greater, surprise—a voice.

This was Slonimsky's singing debut, for when are concert pianists ever asked to sing? "For God," he bellowed out, "is glorified in man," a line from Browning's long dramatic poem *Paracelsus.* As Beethoven had needed the human voice to bring the Ninth to culmination, so Ives had transcended the limits of the piano sonata. Some wonderful singer might have been engaged to enter here, as a flute player does at the end of the Concord Sonata, but no. Ives specifically notates "No helpers allowed!" as if to demand that any performer demonstrate—in his or her own person—the ability to metamorphose and transcend.

Slonimsky sang of Paracelsus, that German-Swiss physician and alchemist, a real-life Faust of the sixteenth century, who established the role of chemistry in medicine, a restless seeker after knowledge who would not stop until he discovered "the secret of the world." A proud man, brilliant but arrogant, "singled-out by God," he thought, "to be a star to men," Paracelsus was always at the center of controversy. He was deeply hated.

At the end of his life, he offered up a testament to the world, imagined and articulated by Browning in the long, inspired, final speech of his poem.

*For God is glorified in man,*
*And to man's glory vowed I soul and limb.*

*Yet, constituted thus, and thus endowed, I failed.*
*I gazed on power, I gazed on power till I grew blind . . .*
*What wonder if I saw no way to shun despair?*
*The power I sought seemed God's.*

So *that* was the meaning of the huge outburst at the beginning of the movement, the human counterpart and echo of the Big Bang: it was man trying to play God, a performance whose accompaniment must become a funeral march.

"I learned my own deep error," Slonimsky sang, in a new section, *andante molto.* "And what proportion love should hold with power in man's right constitution; Always preceding power, And what proportion love should hold with power in man's right constitution; Always preceding power, And with much power, always, always much more love."

Those last, deeply reflective words, "al-ways, al-ways . . . much . . . more . . . love." The two "always" drawn out in slow funereal iambs, the length and hesitation of "much" and "more," the final fall of a major sixth onto the long-held D of "love."

From the Big Bang of Creation, through the complex ambiguous Revelations of the manifested world, from the arrogance of the Seeker to the final simplicity—Love. This was Ives's gift to Gregor, the bug that crawled out of his table, his thank-you for being reminded of that glory-beaming star, the promised day of Israel.

It took the hearers a full minute of silence to begin a tentative applause. In that minute, wherever their souls were, they were unaware of one detail, known at that moment only to Slonimsky, Ives, and Gregor: After the final note with its long fermata, after the double bar, was written, in small letters, *vers la flamme.*

Then, applaud they did, wildly, with Bravos! Stamping and whistling. One enthusiast actually yelled "Encore!" but the indignant stares he got soon convinced him otherwise. "But the ticket says . . ." The ticket was wrong. No encore was possible.

Gregor was transported; the Iveses were ecstatic. Slonimsky returned for a bow, and indicated the composer at the back of the house. Used to slinking out of concerts amidst the booing, the old man was not quite sure how to acknowledge such acknowledgment. Harmony nudged him: "Stand up. Take off your hat."

The applause lasted for two more Slonimsky exits and entrances. Musical history had been made. How surprised our trio was then to find that only a few people came up to greet them. The center of interest seemed to be elsewhere—around someone in a wheelchair sitting in the aisle, keyboard side, toward the front. Gregor couldn't see through the crowd who it was. The composer and his wife were about to go backstage to congratulate Slonimsky when the wheelchaired figure pushed his way through his admirers, up the carpeted slope, and around the back of the hall to where Charles, Harmony, and Gregor were putting on their coats. It was the Governor, the Governor himself, Franklin Roosevelt.

Mr. Ives! Mrs. Ives, I take it? And you must be the subject! He reached out and shook hands with each, moved, and moving, with genuine gratefulness for his extraordinary experience.

Hold that shot, that handshake, that famous handshake, the handshake that would determine the remaining years of Gregor's life.

Gregor was a big hit at work. Kathryn Verplank, ever loyal, had posted the reviews on the corkboard outside her old boss's office—the room still untouched, waiting for his fabled return.

*The New York Times* was approving, if somewhat supercilious (as was its wont). Olin Downs could not even get the composer's name right in his note "concerning the Insect Sonata of a Mr. St. Ives (sic)." Still, even that grand old man seemed moved:

> The thing is an extraordinary hodge-podge, but something that lives and that vibrates with conviction is there, a "gumption," as the New Englander would say, the conviction of a composer who has not the slightest idea of self-ridicule and who dares to jump with feet and hands and a reckless somersault or two on his way. It is genuine, if it is not a masterpiece, and that is the important thing.

When Gregor walked in on Wednesday morning, he was cheered by the crowd at the corkboard. He took off his hat (a brown fedora in shameless imitation of his mentor), made a deep, stiff-backed bow, and spent a few moments describing the work and audience reaction to his colleagues, none of whom, except the Myricks and the Verplanks, had attended. All were especially impressed by Governor Roosevelt's reaction, and his actually shaking Gregor's claw.

His celebrity lasted about fifteen minutes, and then the office settled in to its daily routine, Gregor plugging away at his desk along with the hundred or so others. For the month the clippings stayed up he was bathed in the ever more mottled light of Ives's masterpiece, and then it was simply gray again, as even the glorious spring was darkened by a tightening economic disaster. President Hoover kept up his optimistic announcements, but they rang increasingly hollow—so hollow, in fact, that they led Gregor to look more deeply into the abyss.

At Ives's suggestion, and with his support, Gregor spent the next two

years developing a project that would make his name famous in certain circles, and catapult him, for a time, into the highest ranks of policy-making.
It is not given to everyone to invent a totally new science: Galileo, Pasteur,
Mendel, Einstein, Bohr, Wiener . . . the list would be a short one. And
while Gregor's seminal work on Risk Management is nowhere near as
crucial as that of his predecessors, it has had much impact, and has saved
countless lives in the six decades since its publication. More lives, ironically, than the quest he had chosen—for the grail of human kindness.

Yet he worked in obscurity. His colleagues at Ives & Myrick had no idea
what he was doing with those stacks of government documents on his
desk, or where he spent all that time out of the office. Mike Myrick knew,
of course, and cut him a great deal of slack. Where did he spend his time?
At the periodicals division of the Low Memorial Library at Columbia University, poring through the Memphis *Commercial-Appeal,* the Jackson
*Clarion-Ledger,* the Greenville *Democrat-Times,* the Chicago *Defender,* and
other black papers: the Pittsburgh *Courier,* the Baltimore *Afro-American,*
the Boston *Guardian,* the Louisville *News,* the Norfolk *Journal and Guide.*

Irrational as anyone else, he preferred the Low Library to the even
larger collection at Forty-second Street because it reminded him of Rabbi
Lowe, and their common home in Josefov. The rabbi was that wise man
of the sixteenth century who created a golem out of clay to protect the
Jews of Prague. Things did not turn out well.

Until Gregor's rethinking, the insurance industry was simply reactive,
making do with elementary actuarial analysis, trying to match its under-
writing commitments with statistical data on various types of loss. His
breakthrough was to imagine a proactive role for the industry. Insurance
payments did not really compensate for the loss of home, family, business, earning capability. Why could not an insurance company also help
reduce the risk, operate preventively, saving itself money and its customers untold grief?

The word "risk," Gregor discovered, comes from the Arabic *risq,*
which signifies "anything that has been given to you by God and from
which you draw profit." *Risq* has connotations of a fortuitous and favor-
able outcome. But as the notion migrated westward to Spengler's declin-

ing "evening land," it became more and more pessimistic. Gregor wanted
to return risk to its earlier, Eastern, more hopeful roots.

Estimation of risk is a tricky business, especially concerning low probability events. If the potential outcome is a possible disaster or catastrophe
that threatens the very existence of the individual, organization, or country, it cannot be ignored no matter how improbable it is. But what to do
if the probability is "effectively zero," yet the potential loss is thought to
constitute "an unacceptable risk"? No amount of rational analysis will resolve the issue of what is "unacceptable." Reducing risks for one group
may increase risks for another—and *this* is what brought Gregor to his
fateful study of the 1927 Mississippi flood—a rich paradigm of complexi-
ties and mismanagement, which set the last phase of his life in motion.

It was the most beautiful of spring days in April 1932. The trees on the
Morningside Heights campus were in outrageous blossom, and so were
the students, in shirtsleeves for the first time since the brutal winter. Gregor made his way through crowds of lovely Barnard coeds into the cool
dark of the huge library. Psycho-erotically, he was always poised on the
edge—his loneliness and longing vs. his natural disgust with soft external
parts, and painful memories of his misencounters, Alice chief among
them. To get through the gauntlet of breasts and hips, of smiling faces
and gay human flirtation, he would consciously push himself over, concentrating on the nauseating jiggling and chirping, the insipid puerility of
these couples. A little of that went a long way—far enough to get him to
his isolated cubicle in the stacks, where he settled into his deeper default
of hopeful, universal love.

At lunchtime, he brought back to the periodicals desk the huge stack
of newspapers he had been accumulating all morning. Standing in line
behind a foreign student with language difficulties and some complex
problem, his thin arms were almost buckling under the weight when a
deep voice behind him said, "Need some help?" He turned and saw a
handsome man in his mid-forties wearing an open-necked, white short-
sleeved shirt, his pocket bristling with pens.

"That would be most helpful, thank you," he replied, and his new good Samaritan lifted half the stack from Gregor's arms and perused the top front page.

"'Conscript Labor Gangs Keep Flood Refugees in Legal Bondage,'" the *St. Bernard Voice.* "What are you up to?"

"I am studying the flood from '27."

"Why?"

"I am seeing how it could have been better managed."

"By Hoover?"

"Yes, but not just Mr. Hoover. It shows a breakdown in the system."

"How so?"

At that moment, the student ahead moved on, and Gregor and his helper plopped their papers on the desk. The clerk checked them, and returned Gregor's library card. He turned to leave.

"Wait. Don't go. I'm interested in what you've found out. Do you have time for lunch?"

"I was just now going out for eating."

"Can we go together?"

"Surely."

"Where would you like to eat?" Professor Tugwell deferred to his companion.

"I go usually to Koffee Korner across the street."

"Fine for me."

"I go get my briefcase and I meet you here."


On Good Friday, April 22, one day after a huge crevasse had opened just north of Greenville and threatened to flood the entire delta, President Coolidge named his Secretary of Commerce, Herbert Hoover, to coordinate all rescue and relief efforts. It was the chance of Hoover's life: fortunes were being undone, farms and families destroyed, and here he was, cast in the role of savior, able to call on Army and Navy, the federal treasury, every state's banks and businesses, and National Guard—a no-lose situation, doing well by doing good.

He spent some sixty days in the flooded territory, touring with a railroad car full of reporters, issuing orders and press releases. He dominated the newsreels and radio waves. Every major metropolitan daily ran front-page stories about his brilliance and heroism. "The Great Humanitarian," they called him, "The Great Engineer."

Old Man River himself was offering Hoover a chance to realize his only unconquered frontier. At twenty-seven, the young Stanford engineer had helped find and develop fabulously profitable mines and became "the highest paid man of his age in the world." What was left to achieve? Power. The power of the presidency.

As if on cue, President Coolidge did nothing—in spite of much pleading, he would never visit the devastated areas to help raise consciousness and funds. The President did nothing; and Hoover did everything. For months, not a day went by without media images of Hoover saving American lives. Newsreels, magazine feature stories, Sunday supplements—his every word was news. Before the disaster, he was a minor player in Republican politics. Afterward, he was inevitable presidential timber. Hoover represented a new kind of man creating a new world order: he was an engineer. Not since the heyday of the early Enlightenment had there been so much faith in science. Engineering was the new gospel, and Hoover was the priest par excellence, rich, respected, "the engineering profession personified." He rode this wave for all it was worth—right into the White House in '28—a complex, driven man, a man with a plan.

Early on he was a blazing visionary, calling for "abandonment of the unrestricted capitalism of Adam Smith," condemning "the ruthlessness of individualism," and attacking the "social and economic ills" caused by "the aggregation of great wealth." "No civilization," he said, "could be built or can endure solely upon the groundwork of unrestrained and unintelligent self-interest." But to Roosevelt and his friends, Hoover was the enemy.


Gregor and Tugwell settled into their red vinyl booth and, without consulting the menu, the professor waved over the waitress. "I'll have a BLT on toast."

"What is that, BLT?"

"A sandwich. Try it. It's good. It's American."

"I have usually egg sandwich. But I try BLT."

"Make that two BLTs." The waitress nodded and left. "I'm Rex Tugwell."

"Ohhh—I've heard of you," Gregor blurted. "You are 'Rex the Red'?"

"Professor Rex the Red, please. Tyrannosaurus Rex, subversive revolutionary."

"This is what people call you?"

"Ignoramuses. I'm actually a conservative trying to save their damn profit system."

"I'm Gregor Samsa."

"I know."

"How you know this? I have never see you before."

"But I saw you. At a Town Hall concert a couple of years ago. You have a face that's hard to forget."

"Yes, forgive me."

"Nothing to forgive. Columbia has lots of strange folks around."

The waitress brought their BLTs.

"Look, Samsa," said Tugwell, "I'll get right to the point. I'm working with two other professors here—Ray Moley and Dolph Berle—on Governor Roosevelt's campaign. So tell me what you've discovered about the Great Engineer."

Gregor was not quite ripe for recruiting. He was wary of Tugwell's pushiness.

"So far I am concentrating on two big problems. I try to think how to managing risks better, so I am not precisely concentrating on Mr. Hoover."

"That's fine. What are the problems?"

"Wait. This is bacon. Jewish can't eat bacon."

"Go ahead. God will forgive you. BLTs aren't in the Torah. Tell me what you've learned about Hoover."

"First, how he treated the colored people, and how it made them not want to help with relief."

"Like what—treated the colored people?"

"This is most delicious."

"See, I told you so. Hoover."

Gregor shuffled in his briefcase for a moment.

"Here. 'Dear Mr. Hoover, It is said that many relief boats have hauled whites only, have gone to imperiled districts . . .' What is 'imperiled'?"

"Districts that are in danger."

"Ah. '... boats have gone to imperiled districts and taken all whites out and left the Negroes; it is also said that planters in some instances hold their labor at the point of a gun for fear they would get away and not return.'"

"They were scared of losing black labor who would work for little wages."

"*Klar.* 'In other instances, it is said that mules have been given preference on boats to Negroes.'"

"That's not the worst of it. We have reports that National Guardsmen were rampaging through the camps, beating anybody who threatened to leave, raping the women, stealing money ..."

"I'm sure Mr. Hoover must know about it, but I have not find him to do anything."

"What's the second problem?"

"Second is the sacrifice of the poor people below New Orleans—for psychological effect. There is no democracy in these decisions. All is decided by the rich people for benefit of rich people. They say they have to dynamite the poor people's levee to relieve pressure, but it was not so."

"Where is Hoover in all this?"

"I don't know yet details. He was perched on all information like a Spinne in his web, so he must know. Also they do not pay back any of the people they promise to when they flood the lands. I know the Hoover and the Red Cross refuse all responsibility. They say it is the New Orleans's business."

"They have too much faith in businessmen. Tell me more about Hoover's treatment of Negroes."

"Hundreds of thousands had to camp on top of the levees—the only dry land. Half of all farm animals are drowned, and when the waters go, they make serious disease. Everywhere is mud, and water is contaminated. Dogs all over, washed away from food and owners, frogs, and spiders crawl into homes and public buildings. Everywhere it smells of death."

"But cleanup was 'nigger work,'" Tugwell surmised.

"Oh, yes. Loading and unloading barges to feed hundreds of thousands people and animals—it was 'nigger work.' Reloading onto small boats, preparing food, sorting, distributing, cleaning, fixing, putting floors under tents, all was 'nigger work.'"

"So the shotguns stayed loaded, I'll bet."

Tugwell had struck a gold mine: a point man who had all the goods on Hoover.

"Hoover say—here—'No relief to flood sufferers by action of Congress is desirable, but rather all efforts should be concentrated on formulation and passage of adequate flood control measures.'" Gregor put the article back in his bag.

There it was, in Tugwell's focus! "No relief to flood sufferers." That was the line that needed attack, the line that would seduce large numbers of the southern black population away from their traditional Republican votes.

"You have mayonnaise on your—what do you call that?"

"What?"

"Here, let me wipe it off. What do you call that on your face?"

"Mayonnaise? *Mayonnaise*. Same."

"No. That part of your face."

"Oh. I don't know. *Mundwerkzeug* maybe. Mandible *auf Englisch?*"

"Mandible. Sure."

By now they had spent three hours going through his notes and clippings, and Gregor felt more comfortable with Tugwell's motivations.

"Can you get me details on Hoover's role in dynamiting the levee?" asked Tugwell, as he rose to pay the check.

"Let me pay half," said the blattid.

"No, no—I've just been promoted to full professor. I've got money to burn."

"Truly? Well then, very much thank you. And I will send you any information I find."

"Here's my card. You can call me at home or at school."

Gregor felt a little like a spy. Twice weekly, he called his information in to Tugwell, his handler, usually outside of work. His coworkers at Ives & Myrick were unaware of this aspect of his research. His classic, now famous work, "Fundamentals of Risk Management," had yet to be published, and was known only to Mike Myrick. For the others in the office, he was still the new kid on the block—a role that was getting somewhat old—the new, foreign employee, the subject of one of Mr. Ives's wackier piano pieces, a member-of-the-team doing different work from everyone else in the office. Yet in late July of 1932 he made a splash big enough to impress the most doubtful of his colleagues.

On March 1 of that year two-year-old Charles Lindbergh, Jr., was kidnapped from his parents' home in Hopewell, New Jersey. Aside from his dismay—a feeling shared with millions of Americans—Gregor took a professional interest in the event. The general uproar sidetracked his other investigations, and he devoted an intense week of July heat to the insurance consequences of an alarming four-year rise in kidnapping. He reasoned thus:

If money were of little import, the human risks associated with ransom would plummet. If Ives & Myrick were to create a kidnapping rider to their theft policies, victim families would be financially protected, and victims themselves be less threatened by desperate gambits based on financial fear. The fact of a kidnapping would trigger a quick, almost cut-and-dried response leading to the return of victims.

But what to charge for kidnapping insurance?—that was Gregor's challenge. In order to quantify the actuarial table, he needed a formula to gauge the probability of a person being kidnapped. After two intense nights of work, when others in his tenement were up on the roof trying to stay cool, he arrived at the following formula, now known in the industry as the Samsa Conjecture:

$$P_k = \frac{0.833nC(cW)(S)^2(J)}{A^{\frac{1}{2}}}$$

where

$P_k$ = the probability of being personally involved in a kidnapping; 0.833n represents the fraction 1.25n/1.5, the probability change due to the number of previous kidnappings, the 1.25 in the numerator representing the increase in risk as kidnapping momentum increases, and 1.5 in the denominator the decrease in risk as community concern, personal caution, and police protection rises. In addition, C = number of children in the family; c = the celebrity of the family or individual on a subjective scale of 1–3; S = the Index of Suffering, an original contribution of Gregor's, now in standard use among economists.

$$S = \frac{\text{(unemployment rate in percent) (inflation in percent)}}{1 - \text{(probability of situation continuing another month)}}$$

J = the Jahreszeit (Ger. *season*), a Germanism that has traditionally remained in the formula, and A = age of the victim in months.

Gregor spent the next two weeks checking the validity of his equation before mentioning it to Mike Myrick. He went through the entire *New York Times Index* ("kidnapping") for the years 1874–1932, and found that his formula predicted the kidnapping ($P_k > 0.75$) for 86 percent of all reported victims. With this information, he calmly went to his supervisor's office, knocked politely, and said, "Mr. Myrick, I've found something you may be interested in."

Interested? Myrick was delirious. It was an insurance industry coup, something current and hot, something no other agency had even dreamed of, and he quickly ran it past the actuarial department. Two days later he phoned *The New York Times* and *The Wall Street Journal*, and Gregor was once again a minor celebrity, though this time more permanently.

But the topping on the celebrity sundae, the whipped cream and the cherry, was the phone call he got on July 29, 1932. Mrs. Verplank, not too subtly, bellowed down the forty-foot aisle, "Mr. Samsa, Governor Roosevelt is on the phone for you." The office gossip knew no bounds.

The next day he was in Albany at the Executive Mansion, meeting with the Governor, and Professors Tugwell, Moley, and Berle. They wanted him to join the Brain Trust for the final push of the campaign. He was to be in charge of Hoover research and was more than welcome to join in brainstorming alternatives to current political structures. The group felt his European background would add a fresh perspective.

Both Ives and Myrick were happy to grant him a leave of absence, with pay, until the election, and longer if he needed it. If FDR lost, they would have their star employee back. If Roosevelt won, they would have a voice in Washington, close to the ear of the President. It was a no-lose proposition.


Gregor would not return to Ives & Myrick. He commuted twice weekly to Albany or Hyde Park, and then was kidnapped to Washington. Miss MacPherson, the quiet young woman at the desk across from his, was quiet and sad.

The roach was tireless. By Election Day 1932, working full-time and more, he had assembled a seven-volume dossier on Mr. Hoover: every damning phrase and paragraph from every article in every newspaper and magazine across the land—including his own words, so easily used against him. This was no negative campaigning, focusing voter attention on sensational, irrelevant distractions. No, Gregor's research was solid history, economics, politics, and sociology. It spoke truth about power to a population presumed intelligent. Tugwell and Moley and Berle spun this material out to the public until President Hoover was snared in his own undoing.

Roosevelt: 42 states; Hoover: 6. Electoral College: 472 to 59. It is true that almost any Democrat could have beaten Hoover, he of the "Hoovervilles," so frustrated and irate were the American masses. But the landslide was enough to give one pause. So much faith sits uneasily on any mere human being.

Yet FDR was at ease, apparently confident, during this most uneasy winter. Farmers brandished rifles when the tax men came to foreclose; apple sellers crowded the streets, but how many apples could "the common man" eat? People were hungry, marriage was rare, bank accounts were overdrawn. And on Roosevelt's fifty-first birthday, January 30, 1933, Adolf Hitler became Chancellor of Germany.

FDR, tanned and relaxed from a twelve-day cruise, disembarked at Miami. On February 15, he rode in an open car to greet a crowd of twenty thousand supporters at Bay Front Park. He rode in a blue Buick convertible, along with Raymond Moley, who had come down to Miami to report on the Cabinet search, and with Gregor Samsa, who had been rewarded for his Herculean labors with a Caribbean cruise on the *Nourmahal.*

Gregor Samsa on Vincent Astor's yacht! This child of the Jewish quarter of Prague, this circus freak, this erstwhile elevator boy and dumpster diver, this toiler in the innards of insurance. In America, anything is possible.

Seated in an open car, driving along a dark street on the way to the park, Moley observed how easy an assassination would be. But FDR was fearless. In the crowded, well-lit park, shortly after nine, Moley and Gregor hoisted the President-elect up on top of the backseat, where he could be seen. He spoke for two minutes to much laughter and applause, then lowered himself into the seat of the car to greet Mayor Anton Cermak of Chicago, who was visiting his father in Miami.

Suddenly, a popping in the air. Roosevelt thought it a firecracker, Moley a backfire. Gregor was the first to spot a short, swarthy man, standing on a rickety folding chair twenty feet away emptying a revolver in the direction of the President-to-be. After the first shot, a nearby woman had grabbed his arm, and subsequent bullets made their wild ways through the crowd. The gunman was tackled and subdued by bystanders and Park Police while Secret Service men bulled their way toward the center of the violence. "I'm all right! I'm all right," Roosevelt yelled.

But Mayor Cermak was not all right, nor were four others. The mayor's shirt was covered in red, and blood streamed from lung to mouth. Secret Service agents shouted frantically for the car to evacuate, but FDR ordered the driver to stop so the mayor's body could be lifted into this, the first vehicle that would be free of the crowd. He tried to find a pulse as Cermak slumped forward. "I'm afraid he's not going to last," he whispered to Gregor, as the car made for Jackson Memorial Hospital. The man from Hyde Park coached his friend from Chicago: "Tony, keep quiet—don't move. It won't hurt if you don't move."

"I'm glad it was me and not you," the mayor gasped.

There is honor even among politicians.


In the ER waiting room, Moley approached Gregor. "It would be good for you to visit our would-be assassin. Find out if he acted alone or if there are others. Get back to the railroad car by eleven-thirty."

Armed with a handwritten note from Roosevelt, Gregor took a cab back to the park and made his way to the twenty-first floor of the Dade County Courthouse, overlooking the scene of the crime. There, surrounded by Secret Service agents, was an unemployed bricklayer, one Giuseppe Zangara, thirty-three, come to the United States ten years earlier aboard the steamer *Martha Washington*. Italian anarchist. So much was Gregor told. He asked to be left alone with the prisoner, and Secret Service reluctantly retreated.

"Hello, Mr. Zangara. I am Gregor Samsa, a friend of Mr. Roosevelt."

"I am friend of nobody."

"Mr. Roosevelt wants you to know he is all right."

"Too bad. I am better kill him. Too crowded. Too much crowds."

"Why do you want to kill him?"

"Because rich people make me suffer and do this to me."

He lifted his shirt to show Gregor a large keloid scar on his flank and abdomen.

"Rich people make me to go out from school," he continued. "Two months I am in school and my father come and take me out and say, 'You don't need no school. You need to work.' Six years old, he take me out of school. Lawyers ought to punish him—that's the trouble—he send me to school and I don't have this trouble. Government!"

"Do you hate the government?"

"Yes," he answered, through clenched teeth. "Because rich people make me suffer and do this stomach pain to me."

Zangara was barely five feet tall. He had come to the conclusion that the real causes of exploitation—and of his constant stomach pain—were political leaders. He was going to kill King Victor Emmanuel, but he never got the chance. So he came with his uncle to America. He joined a union and saved his money. In the prosperous twenties, he sometimes made $14 a day. Then his uncle decided to marry, and Giuseppe had to move out of the apartment they shared. From that time on, he lived in complete isolation, an angry hermit who took no part in the Italian community around him. A stranger to wine, women, or song, his whole life revolved around his stomach pain.

When the Depression struck, he took his savings and traveled from city to city, winding up in Hackensack, New Jersey, where he lived in a ten-dollar-a-month room and rented the room next door to prevent anyone living near him. For the winter he moved to Miami.

By February 1933, he had less than a hundred dollars to his name, and his stomach was pure agony. He decided he was going to get even, and kill Herbert Hoover.

"I kill that no-good capitalist," he told Gregor. "He make the Depression. He make unemployment and the soup lines. He make burning in my stomach."

"But Mr. Roosevelt works *against* Herbert Hoover. He is your friend."

"Hoover and Roosevelt—everybody the same. Hoover too far. Washington too far. I have only forty-three dollars."

"So Mr. Roosevelt came right to you, to Miami."

"I read in the paper he is coming, and I don't must go to Washington. I make Roosevelt suffer instead. I want to make it fifty-fifty since my stomach hurt I get even with capitalists by kill the President. My stomach hurt long time."

Gregor was dealing with a nutcase. This man could only act alone. Who would act with him? He imagined a possible insanity defense.

"Did you know what you were doing when you shot at Mr. Roosevelt?"

"Sure I know. You think I am crazy? I gonna kill President. I no care. I sick all time. I think maybe cops kill me if I kill President. I take picture of President in my pocket. I no want to shoot Cermak, just Roosevelt. I aim at him, I shoot him. But somebody move my arm. Every American people mistreats me. You give me electric chair. I'm no afraid that chair. You is capitalist crook man, too. Put me in electric chair, I no care."

At the time of the interview, Zangara was charged with only four counts of assault with a deadly weapon. But three weeks later, when Mayor Cermak died, the charge was changed to first-degree murder. Only thirty-three days after the event, the wiry Italian got his wish. Strapped down in "Ol' Sparky" at the Florida State Penitentiary, he railed at the observers, "Lousy capitalists—go ahead, push the button." They did.

"Do you think this was a political act?" Moley asked the roach.

"He said he thought anarchism, socialism, communism, and fascism were stupid. Also religion, God, Jesus, heaven, hell, and any thought of soul. When I asked him if he believed anything he read, he said, 'I don't believe in nothing. I don't believe in reading books because I don't think and I don't like it. I got everything in my mind.'"

"Did you get any sense about what he did believe?" Roosevelt asked.

"I asked him that. You know what he said?"

"What?"

"The land, the sky, the moon."

The men and the roach sat in silence. Beyond the ticking telegraph poles, the moon shone full on the track back to Washington.

WASHINGTON, D.C.

## 20. DREAMING *of* IMMORTALITY *in a* KITCHEN CABINET

The White House was running over with Roosevelts. Plenty of cots were needed, too, when the whole Roosevelt kit and caboodle arrived together, or even in part, and the halls rang with laughter and childish screams, often provoked by the President himself, tickler, wrestler, and pillow-fighter extraordinaire. The stately dining room felt more like a crowded cafeteria, with so much hearty noise, the servants could do the dishes in the pantry next door (verboten before) without bothering a soul. What was an official building under the Hoovers had become a happy home.

What wasn't so wonderful was the kitchen. To be blunt, it was old and filthy, a facility unworthy of any middle-class household, much less of being America's "First Kitchen." The moldy, dark wood, with eight administrations' worth of grease and dust, was simply unscrubbable. The White House kitchen, with Taft's huge, outmoded gas range, boasted corroded sinks with rotting wooden drains, and a rusty dumbwaiter to hoist the precious china and silver. The refrigerator had a wooden interior, and smelled nothing short of evil. The room was lit by dangling overhead bulbs, and the electric wiring was frayed and dangerous. There were rats.

In fact, the whole basement of the West Wing—the service areas on both sides of the vaulted central corridor—was dark and shabby and somewhat surreal, with Dr. McIntyre's clinic neighboring on a pantry full of tin cans. FDR tried to put the best face on it, elegizing "the pleasant smell of groceries, spices, and coffee" as he rolled his chair through a makeshift route from Oval Office to living quarters, but Eleanor was not so enthusiastic. The idea that one had to raid a medical office to get the silverware was a bit much for her practical mind. Thus, one of the first and most radical innovations of the New Deal was a new kitchen—and an entire new service area—for the President's House.

What chaos! For months, all cooking was done in the midst of a dozen men with wheelbarrows full of dirt. You couldn't tell if you were in the White House or some mine or quarry. The kitchen was a far worse mess than before, with not infrequent periods sans gas or water. The service area became a maze of tunnels and pipes, as a huge cave was excavated under the driveway of the North Portico for 4,200 square feet of storage and workrooms. No more tomato cans in the clinic.

Rewiring circuits from DC to AC led to the discovery that all the White House plumbing was rusted; rotted pipes had to be replaced and more and more flooring and walls were ripped out—and not just in the basement. Plaster dust was everywhere. The heating pipes from the furnace were broken, with dust seeping in, distributed throughout the rooms. The First Lady's bathroom sewage left not by pipe but by trough, a menace to public health. There was much work to be done.

But finally all was gleaming and new, especially the kitchen, now suitable for public view. And Eleanor in fact invited the forty-nine young Homemakers of Tomorrow (one from each state and the District of Columbia) for the "first, last, and only tour of this part of the Executive Mansion," an event later written up in the *Journal of Home Economics*. The contest winners were quite keen on the seven spacious windows, the electric fan to draw off fry fat, the room's rounded, dust-preventing corners, the shiny stainless steel, the state-of-the-art electric ranges with red handles, the eight electric refrigerators, and, best of all, the new, electrically operated dumbwaiter replacing the old one pulled by a rope.

As might be expected, the new kitchen was more popular with the theorists and designers than with the help, who continued to use dishrags and towels, and left the dishwasher and dryer to themselves.

But there was one effect of the new kitchen that was entirely positive—at least for Gregor. Replacing the giant French gas range with the General Electric Industrial had opened up five and a half feet of wall space, and uncovered a vacant wooden closet, four feet wide, extending back ten feet into an adjoining room. Gregor, always comfortable with laborers, was the first administration figure to hear about this, and reported it immediately to the First Lady, the overseer of all renovation. The two of them, together with Missy LeHand, the President's private secretary, tramped down into the workspace to view the discovery.

"What do you think?" Gregor asked the women.

"Well, we won't be really needing the space when the storage chambers are done," offered Missy.

"But it *would* be a shame for such a lovely room to go unused," he said.

"You think it's lovely?" Eleanor was reflective.

"Whoo," shuddered Missy, "it gives me the creeps. I can feel the ghosts blowing through my bones."

"Do you really like it, Gregor?" the First Lady wanted to know.

"Yes, I do. It's dark and thought-provoking. It's close. It makes me feel protected."

"Why don't you take it, then?"

"What?"

"Take it. Move in. Where are you living now?"

"Near Dupont Circle."

"It must take you half an hour to walk," Missy observed.

"Twenty minutes."

"That's not bad," said Eleanor, "but wouldn't you rather live here in the White House—rent free—with us and Missy, and Louis?"

"And I would sleep . . ."

"Here, in this newly discovered room."

"But it's not a room, it's a closet. There are no windows. There's no light."

"Gregor, come with me," said Eleanor. "I want to talk to you. Missy, will you excuse us?"

Eleanor led Gregor eastward down the long vaulted corridor, the two of them dodging wheelbarrows, wires, and pipes, until they arrived at the small White House library. After brushing off the dust on his jacket, she invited him to sit down next to her on the Duncan Phyfe couch.

"Gregor, I don't know how to say this, but you know I always speak the truth, and that I have your best interests at heart."

His own heart sprang into his throat.

"What is it?"

"Gregor, you're a wonderful person. We value you greatly. But you are a roach person. There's no way around it. We ignore that, we treat you no differently from anyone else, we don't even have to work at it anymore— you're simply our friend, Gregor Samsa, trusted colleague—and roach person."

"I'm not denying—"

"Nothing to deny. But you may be denying *yourself,* denying yourself certain pleasures because of your human, forgive me, human imposture.

You know you are a roach. We know you are a roach. Why not feel free to act more like a roach? Franklin often speaks of the Four Freedoms. You use only three of them: you have freedom of speech, you worship as you will—I don't know if you do, but you could if you wanted to—you are free from want, at least relatively so compared with many. But you're not free from fear. What did Franklin say at the inaugural?"

"The only thing we have to fear is fear itself."

"Yes, and he believes it with all his heart. But do *you?*"

"I'm not afraid."

"You are afraid, dear Gregor, of being who you are. 'No windows, no light.' You pass pretty well as a human, but you're a roach, and you don't give yourself the opportunity to act roachlike, to experience the joys of a roach, to bring the blessings of genuine roachness to the people around you."

"People don't like roaches."

"That's only because they don't know *you*. Why don't you be you? Don't be afraid! You have so much to offer!"

"You want me to move into the closet in the kitchen—and be a roach? A roach in a kitchen cabinet?"

"You make it sound silly. But I know roaches like small, dark spaces. I know they like the close smell of food. And I'm not even a roach."

"That's true. You're not. And they do."

"Say *I* do."

"I do. I like small, dark spaces and the close smell of food."

"Well, there it is, Gregor—all yours. You can be around more, you can be more helpful to us and to the staff. They all like you. They trust you. You can play with the children at bedtime instead of going home. You'd *be* home. Consider it your own Fifth Freedom: the Freedom to Be a Roach."

So does the world tease us with metaphors, language revenging itself on reality. But the First Lady was never less than persuasive. Gregor gave notice at 1825 T Street, and moved into 1600 Pennsylvania Avenue.

"Let Gregor be Gregor." The children loved it. They began by just riding on his back, falling off in the carpeted hallways when he (intentionally) jerked around or accelerated quickly, and they laughed and laughed. Booker DuBois, one of the maintenance staff, rigged up a harness to stabilize the ride, and they were able to add "Bucking Blattid" to their hilarious games. But eventually the most fun of all was climbing the walls, and even walking the ceiling. It required much extra strapping, and was looked on with initial concern by the adults. But there was never an accident, and after a few days, the game took on the safe but exhilarating aura of a circus ride.

The East Room was best for "Roach the Roof," as little Anna had named it. It was the largest in the building, with the most uncluttered wall and ceiling space, and a marvelous view of the concavity of the great chandeliers. While Gregor's mosaic scan was somewhat fuzzy, the children were sharp-eyed as gulls. "Awk, awk!" little Elliot squawked his first time up. "Awk, awk, gawk, gawk, yech, these lights are disgustingly filthy." Gregor almost fell off the ceiling with surprise and laughter. But it was true. The cleaning staff had a monthly routine of cleaning the twenty-two thousand hanging pieces of glass in the East Room chandeliers. Percy would go up on a high ladder, hand piece by piece down to Arvid, midway, who would then hand the pieces down to a team of women who washed each one with alcohol, polished it with felt, and handed it back up the chain. It took days, even alternating chandeliers monthly. The glass did sparkle, but the other-than-glass—the interior brass, the porcelain sockets, and the electric bulbs themselves—were positively grimy. When Gregor brought this to Percy's attention, he said, "I know it, boss, but there ain't no way to get in there. You'd have to come in from the top, and the chandelier's too wide to reach in. I figure it's part of the museum—George Washington's grunge."

Come in from the top? Who better than Gregor, perhaps with a small helper strapped into the harness? In the egalitarian spirit of the early New Deal, he volunteered a seasonal cleaning of the chandelier interiors to the applause and admiration of the staff. And he had no more trouble recruiting assistants among the children than Tom Sawyer did finding help to whitewash his fence.

One thing led to another, and persnickety jobs began to fill in the cracks of Gregor's daily schedule. When his musical sophistication became known, he took over the onerous chore of deciding who was to perform at White House events. He sorted through fan letters to the President from people who wanted to give him something back for the hope he had given them: Mrs. Martha McGregor, whose husband earned $3.50 per week, wanted her little girl to dance for him; Hickey, "the Cowboy" Caruso, a young man with infantile paralysis, asked to sing "The Star-Spangled Banner"; Edward G. Alterman felt FDR would be inspired by a demonstration of the "Theramin Wave—a scientific musical mystery"; Georgette Ivers would entertain the President by playing the piano wearing mittens; Mrs. Emma T. White, a black mother, wants to come, with her family of nine who play by ear, with Rufus, her baby of eighteen months, conducting in perfect time; Fred Carlson and his little niece Suzette wanted to play "My Country 'Tis Of Thee" on their violins for the President—and at "every capital of the 48 states." It required his European cultural sensibility plus Solomonic wisdom to consider such requests. At least that's what he was told by those who wanted off the hook.

So tactfully did he handle these requests that he became the Unofficial in Charge of Difficult Mail. Like the bill from the haberdasher for two dozen ties sent to the President, unrequested, ties so awful they were discarded immediately. Or requests for souvenirs: "Please send me," one man wrote, "a wishbone the President has eaten on."

One afternoon, Gregor passed the President scooting down the second-floor hallway in his chair. FDR spun around and yelled at his back. "Gregor, come see me in the Oval Office at four."

*Oh no,* he thought, *what did I do now? Maybe one of the children got hurt playing Periplaneta. Swinging around by the arms—I knew it was not good. I talk to the children, get them to stop.*

However, the four-o'clock interview was not to admonish but to reward. When Missy LeHand showed him into the Oval Office, there was the President with Rex Tugwell and a man Gregor did recognize—but vaguely.

"Gregor, good to see you. You know Rex, of course. Have you met Henry Wallace, my new Secretary of Agriculture?"

"And my new boss," Tugwell added, having just been appointed Assistant Secretary.

Henry Wallace! Yes, that was the man from the party. Gregor was thinking back to FDR's birthday at the end of January when he had gotten just the slightest bit tipsy on Dvorak vodka, a large bottle smuggled in the diplomatic pouch by the Czech ambassador. Gregor could not resist a small nod to the man who had written the Symphony from the New World.

And in the consequent daze, he had met a man—this Henry Wallace, he was sure of it—who spoke of things not spoken of. Perhaps he, too, had been tipsy, but Gregor remembered words like "In the long run, karmic justice . . . ," like ". . . work out the spiritual foundations for a true creative expression for the American people." And here he was now, what was it? Secretary of Agriculture? Responsible for feeding the entire nation in this time of excess, dearth, and starvation?

Wallace stood up and offered his hand. "We've met, I believe. At the party."

"Yes," Gregor replied. "It is nice to see you again."

The President gestured for them all to sit down.

"Gregor, you've been hanging around in my kitchen cabinet long enough. It's time for you to become official. The Secretary, the Assistant Secretary, and I have decided to offer you the post of—what was it?"

Tugwell chimed in. "'Special Assistant to the Assistant Secretary of Agriculture in charge of Entomological Affairs.'"

"Will you accept?" the President asked.

Gregor hesitated. "What I do? What I will have to do?"

Wallace spoke of working with the department to develop a national pest control policy, perhaps working with the latest pesticide discoveries like DDT.

"First job, however, is to get rid of the ants in the kitchen," FDR injected. "They're out of control, I'm told. And there was a huge cockroach yesterday in the elevator—not you. I mean a real cockroach, one about three inches long. Scared the dickens out of one of the chambermaids."

So principled was Gregor Samsa that he actually hesitated here. A roach as an exterminator? Enough to give anyone pause. But after a few minutes' conversation, Gregor decided: "Better I should do it than them."

And it *was* better. Gregor's was the earliest voice—three decades before Rachel Carson—to speak out (in vain) against widespread use of organic poisons. He accurately predicted some of the uncontrollable secondary effects of pesticide use: the possibility of developing resistant strains, the death of natural predators, the possible explosion of even more destructive populations. And what about the effects of such poisons in human food? There were no answers—but the problems were already visible to insect eyes. The large chemical companies, of course, were not interested in such speculation. This was a time of emergency, and all strong solutions were deemed necessary. As usual, strength (and money) won out over caution.

But not in the White House kitchen. Gregor quickly got on the ant problem—most serious during large culinary affairs. He set the kitchen table legs in shallow plates of kerosene, but the ants soon contrived a path up the wall, over the ceiling, with an aerial drop to the kitchen table. The problem was now worse: the ants were still in the food, but now they were also falling from the skies into workers' hair and faces. And the meat tasted of kerosene.

Back to the drawing board. He lined the walls with salt, or soap flakes, or talcum powder, or baking soda. After weeks of experimentation, largely on himself, he finally hit on boric acid. He found that, while he could avoid ingesting it, still, small amounts were absorbed right through his cuticle, making him ill enough to want to avoid it. Diatomaceous earth also worked, its rough-edged particles becoming embedded in his waxy surface, opening avenues for infection and water loss. A thousand cuts. But he felt abrasions were too unkind, and he abandoned this line of research. Boric acid, odorless, non-staining: that was the way to go. For that alone, he should be honored by millions of New Yorkers.

During the time of his experiments, the New Deal also progressed. The famous first hundred days—Gregor found himself admiring, then awed by the leader behind them.

And so, by and large, was the nation. By May 1933, Washington was swarming with people animated with wonder and excitement, adventure, even elation. There had never been so much hope, as the new Administration, young, without political experience—or corruption—settled into gear, trying to put the country to rights. Conferences, hearings, briefcases bursting with plans and reports, men and women reorganizing agriculture, banking, the structures of business and industry. The capital, for the first time, really felt like the center of the country, a forgotten revolutionary center: the government, the President, truly vested with the will of a confused population—help us, save us. Even the business community looked to Washington for solutions.

At the same time, common people were moved to offer advice to the man whose voice came into their living rooms. Letters piled up in his "bedtime folder," and he read through them every night and morning. America was bringing itself to Washington, urging the immediate actions promised by the President in his inaugural address, and granting him extraordinary powers to bring them about.

In one hundred days he took control of the banking system, took the country off the gold standard, and embargoed gold exports; he began a complete reorganization of the Federal Government and the management of all farming. He undertook commodity price-fixing, reinflation of currency, government refinancing of farm and home mortgages, and regulation of securities. The railroad bill and the Tennessee Valley Authority programs signaled the nationalization of public services. A huge public employment program put unemployed men and women to work building bridges, growing forests, building roads, painting, writing, performing dance and music and theater.

The beginning of the end of Prohibition. And more important, the end of Hoover's prohibition of direct Federal aid to the needy. Strong, perhaps dangerous stimulants, all to urge the country from the Slough of Despond. One Hundred Days.

"This great Nation will endure as it has endured," he had told them, "will revive and will prosper. So, first of all, let me assert my firm belief that the only thing we have to fear is fear itself—nameless, unreasoning, unjustified terror which paralyzes needed efforts to convert retreat into advance." And they were not afraid as, in great detail, he enumerated a list of truly fearful things, the "dark realities of the moment" brought on by "a generation of self-seekers." Restoration meant applying "social values more noble than mere monetary profit," he had said, and learning that "our true destiny is not to be ministered unto but to minister to ourselves and to our fellow men." He would lead them. And so he did. Gregor, and many others, adored him.

Walking down third floor east one afternoon in May, Gregor heard a voice calling out from the Lincoln bedroom.

"Hey! C'mere."

It was Louis Howe, the President's cherished personal advisor, a wizened, asthmatic troll of a man who had used his personal pull to commandeer the famous room and turn it into a sick bay for himself and his oxygen.

"I want to see Franklin. What's he doing?"

"He's in a meeting with the British Ambassador."

"Tell him to come to my room when he's through with that bloke."

Just like that? Order the President around? Make him scoot around in his wheelchair like some crippled servant? Still, Louis had spoken. Gregor waited outside the Diplomatic Reception Room till the interview was over, and conveyed the request.

"Louis wants to see me? Where is he?"

"In his room, sir."

"I'll get right up there." And he swung his chair around and headed down the hall.

Amazing, Gregor thought.

That night, as he lay thigmotactically content in his kitchen cabinet, the smell of the next morning's bread wafting under the door, Gregor thought about the Howe–Roosevelt connection. Here was a brilliant, ugly little man who had fastened himself to FDR at a low point of his life—1912, the year of his typhoid fever—and stayed tightly with him even through 1921, the year of his polio attack, the year that had seemed likely to mark the end of his political career. Howe realized he could gain power and reputation only from behind the scenes, as an aide to a more acceptable and charismatic figure. He applied what he had learned as a seedy freelance reporter, studying politicians and businessmen at statehouse and racetrack, and had made FDR "his man," his puppet, his attractive front, planning his campaigns, his strategy, his tactics, writing his speeches, advising him on appointments, being teacher, psychiatrist, and priest rolled into one. Both Franklin and Eleanor counted on him for all advice, large and small. He had made himself indispensable.

Physically, he reminded Gregor of Amadeus, the secretive, moribund but powerful éminence grise of a public operation. Functionally, Howe operated as a kind of hideous anti-Lindhorst, a Mephistophelian sculptor of men, scheming others' ambitions into being, then claiming his due. "It is easier to be forgiven for being wrong than forgiven for being right," he had once remarked, apropos of nothing. Too acerbic. Gregor didn't trust him.

Yet what had he brought to pass that was in itself objectionable? Did not much of the President's extraordinary output originate with Howe? He had even written the "fear itself" line—inserted it at the last minute in the inaugural address. There was nothing wrong with being manipulative, Gregor thought, if the manipulation led to worthy goals. Why not adapt Howe's strategy, and use FDR's power to achieve his salutary goals? His wound began to tingle.

Gregor's ambition—not for himself, but for humanity—was great. So he would need great shoulders to stand upon, Newton's "shoulders of Giants." Even a cockroach standing on a giant's shoulders may see farther than the giant himself. Franklin Delano Roosevelt had giant shoulders, shoulders of a football player from his years on crutches, years propelling himself in a chair. His moral shoulders were huge with noblesse oblige. His spiritual shoulders? Well, he had Henry Wallace close at hand. And now he had Gregor. It was a plan. Why not? Insert roachwise into the crevices of government, earwig into appropriate ears, and do it! Already well placed, Gregor fell asleep to the sweet smell of steaming sourdough.

Christmas Eve 1935.

Gregor had been invited to the President's annual reading of *A Christmas Carol*—an event anticipated with pleasure by the large and ever expanding presidential family.

This was not some species of flattering the king, for truly FDR's was a classic performance, complete with stage voices, props, and dramatic business that kept the smaller children on the edge of their seats, squealing with fear and joy. And indeed, as in the earliest days of his parenthood, the performance was held in the presidential bedroom, with the smallest children piled on the bed, the larger ones on drawn-up couches and chairs, and the parents and guests sitting and standing against the walls. It was an event mirrored perhaps in other households around the country, but here achieving a perfection of technique and good feeling that must have been rare.

The Blattid Assistant to the Assistant Secretary left his cabinet room at six twenty-five that Tuesday evening and climbed the circular stairs to the first floor, where he checked his cubby for any late-arriving Christmas mail. Along with a Christmas card from the People's Bank, and a candy cane wrapped with pipe cleaner to resemble a thin, red-striped reindeer (cute), he pulled out a small package, brown paper, wrapped with string, with no return address. Since the hour was getting late, he stuck the items in his pocket and made his way upstairs to the West Wing.

The Christmas Eve reading was perhaps the only punctual time in the Roosevelt year. This was a long story, and by the end, the smallest audience members would be just about gone. Some would simply fall asleep, but others would begin to fidget and whine, so six-thirty—and no later—seemed the right time to start. Gregor entered an already packed room and found a good place for himself under a couch on the north wall. Under-a-couch brought him mixed emotions, memories of a confusing time in Prague, but it was the only empty space in an overcrowded room.

Eleanor Roosevelt, her usual charming self, called the event to order: "Friends, and wonderful family, we're delighted each of you can join us tonight—some for the first time, and welcome!—to hear this marvelous tale, so relevant in this time of hardship, when meanness often rules, and generosity goes begging. Have a cup of tea or milk or juice—there's post-Prohibition eggnog for the grown-ups—and settle in for what? the thirtieth? thirty-first? annual reading of . . ." and here she cued the audience, who all chimed in,

"*A Christmas Carol!*"

She took her seat, and out from the master closet came the President, in striped pajama pants, ascot, and dressing gown, his Dickens clasped, with crutch, in his right hand, doing his best imitation of John Barrymore for the applauding crowd. He sat down on the bed, scooted the littlest ones over, covered his legs with the comforter, and began his tale.

> I have endeavoured in this Ghostly little book, to raise the Ghost of an Idea, which shall not put my readers out of humour with themselves, with each other, with the season, or with me. May it haunt their houses pleasantly. Their faithful Friend and Servant, C. D., December, 1843.
>
> *Marley's Ghost*
>
> Marley was dead: to begin with. There is no doubt whatever about that. . . .

Through the cage of dangling feet, Gregor could watch the children on the bed, and those sitting on the far side of the bed, and the grown-ups lined up on three walls. He could see the President's left profile and gesturing hand.

> Mind! I don't mean to say that I know, of my own knowledge, what there is particularly dead about a door-nail. I might have been inclined, myself, to regard a coffin-nail as the deadest piece of ironmongery in the trade. But the wisdom of our ancestors is in the simile; and my unhallowed hands shall not disturb it, or the Country's done for. You will therefore permit me to repeat, emphatically, that Marley was as dead as a door-nail.

This was good! Gregor was expecting some treacly tripe, served up by Sentimentality, Inc., the thriving chief corporation in Depression America. Relieved, he settled in for a good time. But rolling on his right side, he found the package in his pocket digging into his tegmen, and after a minute decided he'd better move it, perhaps take it out of his pocket altogether.

Scrooge! a squeezing, wrenching, grasping, scraping, clutching, covetous old sinner! Hard and sharp as flint, from which no steel had ever struck out generous fire; secret, and self-contained, and solitary as an oyster.

It was hard to extract package from pocket in the tight space under the couch, and as he pulled it around, it gave out an embarrassing crackle, causing a child's face to appear upside down from the couch above. Gregor hushed him conspiratorially, and the face disappeared. He continued his move more carefully.

The fog came pouring in at every chink and keyhole, and was so dense without, that although the court was of the narrowest, the houses opposite were mere phantoms. To see the dingy cloud come drooping down, obscuring everything, one might have thought that Nature lived hard by, and was brewing . . .

There! Free at last! That feels better. Gregor looked for a moment at the rectangular solid, and though there was no return address, he noticed that the original handwriting was quite European. The package had been sent to E. P. Dutton, his publisher, and forwarded to Ives & Myrick, probably the last address Dutton had for him. Gregor recognized Mrs. Verplank's handwriting forwarding it on to the White House. His curiosity was piqued. *I can listen to the story and open this quietly,* he thought. *I'll just see who it's from, then deal with it later.*

"Bah!" said Scrooge, "Humbug!"

All the children began to laugh, so fierce was the President's delivery. Gregor used the commotion in the room to bite through the string and slip the contents from the wrapping. A book and a long letter . . . from? It didn't say, at least not on the first page. Berlin. Who did he know in Berlin? And the book . . . *Mein Kampf . . .* ah, yes, *Mein Kampf.* He'd heard about it, of course, but . . . He shuffled one-clawed through nine sheets of the long communication. Who would have time to write such a thing?

". . . what right have you to be merry? what reason have you to be merry? You're poor enough."

On and on. Last page . . . Amadeus Ernst Hoffnung! Amadeus! *Oh, how wonderful to hear from you. How are you? I thought you might be gone by now.* Those empty spaces on the mirror . . . Amadeus!

What to do? He wanted to listen to the President's story, but Amadeus, Amadeus had written! All those pages. It must be important. And so he did what any of us might have done in such a predicament: he tried to take in both, to be mostly present for the story, but also to get a preview of the news he would devour later in his closet.

```
Berlin
21 September 1935

Most Honorable Gregor Samsa,
```

. . . a kind, forgiving, charitable, pleasant time: the only time I know of, in the long calendar of the year, when men and women seem by one consent to open their shut-up hearts freely, and to think of people below them as if they really were fellow-passengers to the grave . . .

```
    I send this letter and Gift (observe the multilingual
pun) like a note in a bottle from the Less-Than-Happy
Duchy of Ditchland. My copy of Wo Sind Sie Jetzt? cred-
its you with the important Principles and Practice of
Risk Management, which the library of Humbled University
Across The Street lists (without owning) as published by
E.P. Dutton and Co., New York, which the New York City
phone directory lists at 124 Madison Ave.--and the trail
leads no farther. Dead. Which I hope and assume you are
not. So on this equinox, truly a time in which light
turns to darkness, I once again utilize my ever re-
```

sourceful father to scheme letter and poison into the
U.S. diplomatic pouch, to be trudged to you, via publisher, safely out of this once-great, now grating,
country.

... thousands are in want of common necessaries; hundreds of thousands are in want of common comforts, sir." "Are there no prisons?" asked
Scrooge....

Yes, Berlin is the manger for this letter, and Hum-
boldt University is across the street from the little
apartment to which I have betaken myself to be closer to
the cranky-house of the famous Herr Doktor Professor
Siegfried Werner, the very he of Werner's Syndrome,
though his interest in it seems merely scientific, even
prurient, but not personal: at eighty-six, he's healthy
as a dog. And I am not. But enough about me for the moment. Let me get right to the point.

... stooped down at Scrooge's keyhole to regale him with a Christmas
carol ...

I don't know that this letter will even reach you,
but if it does, Y O U M U S T D O S O M E T H I N G to
alert the American structure of Power to the real situation in Germany.

If he could only know where I'm reading this!

It seems you've become an important author, a theo-
retician of risk. Surely your word will be listened to.
I have been following the coverage of our events in
American papers, and I assure you that you have ab-
solutely no real information. Last week, at the annual
Nuremberg rally, Hitler announced the "Reich Citizenship
Law" and the "Law for the Protection of German Blood and

German Honor." So now we know who is "officially Jewish," that is, a member of the living dead, eliminated
from any kind of civil or social existence. People who
don't exist have a poor prognosis, especially here. The
living dead may soon become the dead—period.

... darkness is cheap, and Scrooge liked it. But before he shut his
heavy door ...

Last Monday, the day after the Party orgy, graffiti
denouncing the new laws was found on the Jungfernbrücke,
a few blocks from my apartment. The afternoon papers
gave it lots of play, and that very evening I heard
yelling in the street. Cat-curious, I went down to follow the crowd. Men and women, presumably Jewish--in any
case, patronizing Jewish stores--were being rounded up
and herded over to the bridge, where they were ordered
to scrub off the graffiti using river water and their
own clothing. When things got too dull, the SA boys borrowed whips from the cart-drivers gathered for the show,
and added choreography to the Gesamtkunstwerk. You ought
to see the Jews jump! Nijinsky would be jealous. One
young girl lost an eye. The police kept order--that is,
they kept the sightlines clear, and made sure no one
disturbed the performance. In the middle of the cleans-
ing, a car arrived carrying four old men, apparently
grabbed at some ceremony of their own. They were made to
polish the grimy metal with their prayer shawls--to great
cheering and howling. The sacred garments, now ripped
and filthy, were thrown into the Spree. Then the whole
cleaning crew was marched, drill step, all the way to
the Jüdischer Friedhof where, I hear, they were forced
to help with the difficult work of turning over grave-
stones. I have to admit I have a limited appetite for
such entertainment. I went home from the bridge to vomit
(I do this often) and begin this letter to you.

Gregor didn't know if he could go on reading. Perhaps he should just calm down and listen to the story, then read the letter later. But the roach couldn't concentrate. His eyes went back to the pages on the floor in front of him.

> Since God alone knows what you know (though you don't know what God knows), let me backtrack for the benefit of news-deprived Americans. Even before the Führer began to führen, there was "unofficial" boycotting of Jewish businesses, pushed by the bully-boys in brown shirts, who also punished those patronizing Jews in any way. So "because of Jews" "German citizens" had to suffer. Even talking to a Jew, having a conversation on the street, could get you accused of "race pollution" and "civic disloyalty," and lead to being paraded through town with a sign around your neck. The unofficial boy-cotts were peppered with equally unofficial vio-lence. Naturally, there was the same kind of police protection.
>
> With such "mandates" from the people, our governments began to act. A pastiche of wondrously creative local laws almost obviated the need for "unofficial" populist action. And now, after three years of this, Jews are no longer allowed in parks, in theaters, libraries, muse-ums, on beaches, or into any club. They can't be guests in hotels or get service at restaurants. One profession after another has unlicensed them. They can't open stores, or be allowed into workers' unions or any jobs they control. Needless to say, all the new business and job opportunities go to Aryans, who are ever more grate-ful to the regime. You wouldn't like it here.

A slight disorder of the stomach makes them cheats. You may be an undigested bit of beef, a blot of mustard, a crumb of cheese . . .

Gregor felt his stomach gurgle. He hadn't eaten dinner . . .

In areas where Jews are not yet banned, other ways
are found to shut them down. Sugar has been cut off to
Jewish bakers and candy-makers. Jewish newsstands can't
get newspapers. Jewish businesses can't put ads in di-
rectories, in newspapers, on billboards or the radio.
You don't read about these things in your papers. We
don't need to read about them in ours.

It's true. And I read more than most. The *Times,* the *Trib,* the *Post,* the
*Worker . . .* Nowhere do I read this.

"You will be haunted," resumed the Ghost, "by Three Spirits."

But not everything, dear Gregor, is bleak. Though
many jobs are no longer available, at the same time, to
balance things off, certain jobs have opened up for the
children of Abraham and Isaac: cleaning public toilets,
for instance, and sewage plants. Jobs at rag-and-bone
works are considered possibly "suitable" for Jews. But
outside of such work, they have to fend for themselves.

My God. The chosen . . .

And the stink! Yes, they smell, those Jews--when Jewish streets aren't cleaned, water is shut off, and no
municipal services are available. The police, when present at all, are an occupying army, attacking at will.

. . . incoherent sounds of lamentation and regret; wailings inexpressibly
sorrowful . . .

Because they are persona non grata, Hebrews need to
be easily identified, and our rush-hour passengers are
not about to put up with checking IDs. So in several
cities, including my own, pretty yellow stars are required, with strict punishment for forgetting. And

names. Lots in a name. So Jews can no longer name their
children with "Aryan sounding names" which might confuse
us. They all have to adopt "Israel" or "Sarah" as middle
names, and use them on all identification. Now you can
tell all bruchs by their covers.

Gregor was breathing hard.

We now have 53 concentration camps around the country, centers for imprisonment and torture of anyone anyone thinks might oppose the regime. And something new--we
have a certain GESTAPO--some post office employee's suggestion for a name--Geheime Staatspolizei--to run them.
Since the Night of Long Knives--do you know about this?--
guard duty is granted exclusively to Gestapo "Death's
Head Units." You can imagine. Under the good old brown
shirts, the camps were mainly there to give victims a
hell of a beating, then ransom them back to relatives or
friends for as much as the traffic would bear. Relative
paradise. But now, under the black-shirted Totenkopfver-
bände--we shall see.

"'I am the Ghost of Christmas Past,'" the delighted audience chanted
together with the reader. Gregor looked out from his cavern, his attention
momentarily diverted.

"Long past?" inquired Scrooge: observant of its dwarfish stature. "No.
Your past." . . .

He drifted back to Amadeus, reluctant, but driven. . . .

Oh, and to people the camps (we want to get our tax
dollars' worth), there's the new SD, the Sicherheits-
dienst. Security, Gregor, security. We now have 100,000
part-time, and 5,000 full-time informers directed to
snoop on every citizen in the land and report the

```
slightest suspicious remark or activity. You can imagine
how many petty feuds are being settled. No one can say
or do anything without wondering how SD microphones or
overhearing agents--your son, for instance, or your fa-
ther, or your wife or best friend, or your boss, or your
secretary--might interpret it.
```

Gregor stared blankly out in front of him, then drifted slowly into the here and now, the here and then, of Dickens.

He was older now; a man in the prime of life. His face had not the harsh and rigid lines of later years; but it had begun to wear the signs of care and avarice. There was an eager, greedy, restless motion in the eye, which showed the passion that had taken root, and where the shadow of the growing tree would fall.

Gregor, too, was older. Chitin does not age as obviously as skin, but from the inside he could feel a subtle cracking, a reticulation of scar tissue at once deadeningly sullen and incisively inscribed. The pattern approximated the look of roots, but where would such roots be nourished? His eyes dropped again to the papers.

```
Gregor, I tell you there is gathering death energy
such as has never been seen before, energy without any
control. There are no voices left to speak against it--
all rational people have fled, and their writings have
been banned. Last year, at the Opernplatz just outside
my window, Goebbels ordered a ritual burning of "immoral
and destructive" documents and books. Your favorite au-
thors, Gregor, and mine, were deemed too left-wing, too
Jewish, or just too un-German to continue living and
breathing. Up in flames went Thomas Mann, Rainer Rilke,
Albert Einstein, Sigmund Freud, and of course the sa-
tanic, bearded Karl himself--a fiery show specifically
designed to enlighten the liberals of Humbled Univer-
sity. Heine wrote that those who begin by burning
```

books end by burning people. His works, of course,
went to the flames. Old man Spengler, I believe,
survived, but I'm sure he's less than pleased with
the conflagration.

Spengler. It'd been a while—a dozen, fifteen years. His stomach began
to hurt as never before. Was it an ulcer?

Gregor, I repeat: there is only one power in the
world that can stop this insanity--the United States of
America. There will be a war--of this I am certain.
Hitler is committed to the destruction of all values and
institutions of Western Civilization--and he is capable
of carrying this destruction out. Compromise with Hitler
is impossible, because his objectives are irrational and
unlimited. Expansion and aggression are built into his
system, and short of accepting German domination in advance, war is unavoidable. Do you understand? If one
side does everything possible to avoid war, and the
other side glorifies it, actively desires it and pre-
pares for it, who do you think will win?

. . . for Tiny Tim, he bore a little crutch, and had his limbs supported by
an iron frame!

"Just like yours, Grandpa," shouted little Katie. Everyone, including
the President, laughed. Everyone but Gregor.

Only the United States has the economic strength and
the untested arrogance to call Hitler's bluff. Someone
has to alert the American government. Your President
Roosevelt may be able to understand the dynamics. You
must get to him somehow, make him listen--show him this
letter if nothing else. Make him read Mein Kampf. Make
him know that Herr Schickelgruber means every word in
it. He must understand that. You must begin now, build-

ing up material and moral force for a quick, overwhelming victory--or all is doomed. It sounds ironic and preposterous, but maybe the continuation of human, humane
culture is up to you, poor thing.

Gregor was not sure he could stand up against such force. He was not
sure he could stand up at all, not sure he could make any difference in
this deadly, vicious undertow of history. His heart was thumping fiercely.
His wound was leaking.

And let me return to one final dimension, Mr. Jewish
Cockroach. A glance at any page of Mein Kakampf will
demonstrate the centrality of antisemitism. You, Mr.
Jew, are everywhere, a convenient symbol for everything
hateful in an unfair world--not least its commitment to
the ideas of the Enlightenment and the French Revolution
which emancipated you, and made you so much more visible. You symbolize every conceivable villain: the hated
capitalist financier, the revolutionary agitator, the
rootless intellectual, every aspect of "the competition." You're too damn smart. You take a disproportion-
ate share of professional jobs. You're a foreigner--no
matter where--a loathsome insect. Besides which, you
killed Christ. Do you think you and yours are going to
get out of this alive?

I urge you, with this, my dying breath, to somehow
get to the President. This ancient pullet does not cry
wolf. The sky is falling. Cluck, cluck. Bawk, bawk,
bawk, bawk, bawk, bawk, bawk, bawk, bawk! Ssssssssss.

I suppose I owe you a few words about my condition. I
send this package without risk: my life is already for-
feit. I have at last played out a "typical" role: the
average age of death in Werner's Syndrome is forty
years. I am now exactly forty, the scene of a grotesque
race to the bottom. Which contestant will have the honor
of bringing down the beast? Forty years old, and ancient

as Corruption, a boy within a corpse. My skin is at-
rophic and sclerodermatic--that is, I look like a cross
between an elephant and the drought-cracked lands of
your midwest. Continuing the American tour, my nose is
dark and bubbled, somewhat like the black, volcanic
rocks of the Moon Craters Monument. My face is the
penultimate version of the picture of Dorian Gray, except that I am now completely bald, the better to see
the misshapen skull, my dear. General calcification is
turning me into one big bone, though not even the dog
seems interested. Cataracts keep me from seeing clearly
except in the strongest light--such as I am now shining
on this paper; I know what it's like to look fuzzily out
of a mosaic eye. Perhaps we are converging: my leg and
foot ulcers remind me of your wound, also unhealing.

But every cloud has its sulfur lining: I can hardly
walk around for the pain, and this, you see, is good,
since last year I broke my osteoporotic right hip exer-
cising my right to exercise. Ewing's sarcoma, I have
discovered, is a lovely little cancer of the tissue
around my left femur. Dr. Werner, the glad-hand, tells
me it's better to have this than meningioma. Thank God
for little blessings. My scleroderma is lately rejoicing
in the company of sclerotic arteries, though I can't say
my heart is as happy, especially at the insufficient
trough of the anterior descending coronary, now almost
completely occluded. My kidneys, not to be left behind,
are trying out their new act; "End-Stage Renal Disease."
Catchy title. The good doctor Werner-San is proposing I
become a human guinea pig for a new machine which will
suck out my blood, launder it, and give it back, presumably cleaner and unharmed. I think I will pass. The good
news is that my central nervous system has been totally
spared, the better to appreciate and reflect on life's
gifts. In short, my friend, I am a one-man Museum of

Pathology, soon to be closed to the public. How poetic
is Justice!

No need to write back. I enclose no address. The dead
are not known to be avid readers.

Remember me!

Amadeus Ernst Hoffnung


Gregor was in tears. Through his own silent moan he heard the distant voice of the most powerful man in the world. He listened as if hypnotized.


. . . a boy and girl. Yellow, meagre, ragged, scowling, wolfish; but prostrate, too, in their humility. Where graceful youth should have filled their features out, and touched them with its freshest tints, a stale and shrivelled hand, like that of age, had pinched, and twisted them, and pulled them into shreds. Where angels might have sat enthroned, devils lurked, and glared out menacing. No change, no degradation, no perversion of humanity, in any grade, through all the mysteries of wonderful creation, has monsters half so horrible and dread. Scrooge started back, appalled. He tried to say they were fine children, but the words choked themselves, rather than be parties to a lie of such enormous magnitude. "They are Man's," said the Spirit, looking down upon them. "This boy is Ignorance. This girl is Want. Beware them both, and all of their degree, but most of all beware this boy, for on his brow I see that written which is Doom, unless the writing be erased. . . ."

Agitated though he was, Gregor knew better than to threaten White House merriment with Amadeus's news. Still, he found himself greeting laconically the most merry wish of "Merry Christmas!" and reflecting obsessively on the wisdom of Scrooge's "Bah! Humbug! What reason have I to be merry when I live in such a world as this?" After FDR's reading, he retired to his closet, reread the letter, and wept himself to sleep.

On Christmas morning, when much of the world was rejoicing in comfort and joy, Gregor was taking a chilly walk alone down Pennsylvania Avenue toward Union Station, as if some unknown force were urging him to leave, to just hop on a train. But where to go? Where was the world acceptable? Back to starving protofascist Europe? Africa, throttled by imperialism? South America, run by plutocracy for personal benefit? Antarctica? Too cold. His legs would stop working. Ridiculous thoughts. Here he was, close to the ear of the most powerful man on earth, a man through whom . . . Too cold.

New York Avenue down to Pennsylvania, briskly homeward bound. But was this home, this beautiful white house, classical, symmetrical, standing behind iron fence in well-trimmed park—in the midst of general misery? The President and his wife were certainly aware of, even guilty about, the contrast. They had affronted Washington society by living more humbly than their predecessors. But home? Home it might be if the President would read Amadeus's letter. Home it might be if he would do something about it—whatever he could. Maybe this *could* be home. Gregor stiffened his resolve, clutched the letter once more, marched past the guard with only a nod, in through the North Portico, and down to his room. Plop. Onto the straw. Overcoat still on. To stare into the darkness and wait.

It took him three days to apply to Missy for an appointment. Though he wanted to honor FDR's indulgence in Christmas, he knew, as did everyone else in Washington, that on January 3, the President was to address a joint session of Congress, the first such gathering since Woodrow Wilson's call for war nineteen years before. If any statement about Germany were to be made, it would have to be discussed now. So on December 28, 1935, at 3:58 in the afternoon, Gregor made his way up to the Oval Office, Amadeus's letter in hand.

The President was looking well after his brief Christmas respite. Though his family and friends had been worried about his sagging energy, this afternoon he was nothing short of perky.

"Mr. Herr Doktor Samsa!" With some difficulty, FDR stood up to greet him. "So you survived my Christmas reading?"

"Not survived. It was . . . you say bang-up? Everyone loves it."

"They're just flattering me."

"I have seen the great actors, in the great theaters of Europe, and—"

"And you decided it would be more interesting to read your letter. I saw you there under the couch."

"No, I . . ." Gregor felt suddenly defensive. FDR's teasing had missed its self-deprecatory point.

"I'm sorry, I didn't mean to accuse you. I'm sure the letter was important—more important than the millionth reading of sentimentalia, well written though it may be."

"Actually, the letter *is* interesting. And important. It is why I come to see you now."

"Oh?"

"I have a friend from Vienna, Amadeus Ernst Hoffnung, the owner of the circus I escape to from Prague."

"With a name like that, he *should* be interesting. God-loving, serious, hope. That's what we need."

"He is not your average circus-owner charlatan—you say charlatan?—type of person. Very, very smart he is, well-reading, interesting in many things. Also he is dead-sick, maybe even dead by now. The letter took some months to get to me. I do not heard from him in thirteen years."

"I can see why it would be hard to concentrate on Dickens. What did Amadeus Ernst Hoffnung have to say?"

"I am hoping you can have time to read the letter."

"Well, let's give it a look."

Gregor handed over the sheets.

"It came with a book, *Mein Kampf*."

"Ah, yes. I've heard of it."

"You must read this book. I lend it when I am finished."

"Here." FDR picked up some papers from the desk. "You read this while I read your letter. These are notes for my speech to Congress next Friday."

They both settled into chairs. Gregor could not believe what he was reading. For several years, he had been aware of all the carping from the left: FDR was trying to save capitalism; he was legitimating banks and big business, asking for their help; the New Deal was just the Old Deal in sheep's clothing. But this speech, the opening salvo of next year's campaign, this speech was . . . revolutionary!

I've given big business its chance with the NRA and the RFC, and it has resisted all my pleas, has denounced every measure to help the desperate and the hungry as socialistic or some kind of effort to "Sovietize" the US. Now big business must be clearly identified as the enemy, as a discredited special interest.

The enemies of progress are clear: business and financial monopoly, speculation, reckless banking, class antagonism, sectionalism and war profiteering rule America.

Never before in all our history have these forces been so united against any one candidate as they stand today. They are unanimous in their hatred of me—and I welcome their hatred. I would like to have it said that in my first Administration the forces of selfishness and lust for power met their match. For my second administration I want it said that those forces will have met their master. I throw down the gauntlet.

Gregor felt the tingling in his husk that passes for sweating in blattids.

Every item of reform has had to be fought for inch by inch, and now the fight grows harder as recovery proceeds and renewed business profits can be poured into lobbies, control of mass communication, resistance to change of any sort.

He looked over to the man in the chair, the "Leader of the Free World," his crutches at his side, his braces showing below his cuffs. As if conscious of being stared at, FDR looked up from his reading.

"Gregor, this isn't the first time I've heard things like this. I've had two letters this year from Bill Dodd, our ambassador in Berlin, which talked about similar things. Not so focused on Jews. More on the general spirit of aggression. Is Hoffnung Jewish?"

"No. I don't think so. I never actually ask to him. But he knows much about Jewish thinking and Jewish history."

"He writes well. This is a very sad letter."

"You finished?"

"No. What I've read so far."

"It's saddest at the end. Saddest about him."

"I'll keep reading."

Gregor could not concentrate further on the President's notes. He skimmed them through to see if there were any references to Germany or Jews. None that he could find. There was this:

A point has been reached where the people of the Americas must take cognizance of growing ill-will, of marked trends toward aggression, of increasing armaments, of shortening tempers—a situation which has in it many of the elements that lead to the tragedy of a general war.

We need a two-fold neutrality that would bar the sale of military supplies to aggressor nations. Our help to other nations threatened by aggression must be confined to moral help. They can't expect us to get tangled up with their troubles in days to come.

That certainly would not satisfy Amadeus, nor speak to his predictions. Gregor and the President would talk about it. That is why he was here.

"Terrible. Just ghastly." The President put the sheets down on the end table. "It makes me feel lucky to be simply paralyzed. I hope the poor man will be able to rest soon, God bless him." He had tears in his eyes.

"Mr. President, what can we do about it?"

"Do? About Hitler? Not much. Germany is a sovereign nation; it does what it likes."

"But making concentration camps—"

"Concentration camps? So do we! Remember last year—Governor Talmadge in Georgia, rounding up labor organizers, keeping them for months behind barbed wire outside Atlanta? Gregor, we've got to deal with our own issues before we can go messing with others'."

"Yes, certainly," said Gregor. "But we need also to help the Jews in—"

"Help the Jews? We're already called 'the Jew Deal.' We've got Lehman, and Morgenthau, and Brandeis, and Cohen. And Frankfurter, with all his brilliant 'hot dogs' inserting themselves in every roll of government. We've got eighty-two percent of American Jews behind us. How much more can we help?"

"And don't forget the niggers!" Louis Howe poked his head in at the door. He had been listening at the keyhole through FDR's last tirade. Howe, too, was now in a wheelchair, dragging two green tanks along with him, with oxygen mask at one hand, and a pack of Sweet Caporals at the other. A great stench of incense and stale tobacco came with him through the door. Smaller than ever, eyes sunken, more wizened, more simian than ever, Howe spat out crazy lines between coughs, wheezing, pulling in enough breath to continue, his voice coming as if from the far side of the grave—where in four months the rest of him would abide.

"The niggers your wife sleeps with. The nigger commies she sodomizes." FDR began his roaring laugh, perhaps remembering more newspaper madness they had shared.

"Ah—listen, Gregor Samsa, listen to his insane laugh. This is not the laugh of a simple paralytic. No, this is the laugh of a crazed syphilitic—"

"These are all quotes, Gregor, genuine, recorded opinions—"

"That's what they say: So poisoned with mercury treatments as to be a mercurial playboy, a cynical fomenter of class hatred, a power-mad dictator, agent of Soviet Russia, a very traitor to his class, the most destructive man in all of American history! Marx without a beard. Lenin without a mustache. A slick old thimble-rigger building a huge political machine in Washington paid for with waste and extravagance, and your tax dollars, a hog-jowled, weasel-eyed, sponge-columned, jelly-spined, pussy-footing, four-flushing, charlotte-russed Commonist! What can you expect from such a man?"

FDR was doubled over in laughter—which made this misshapen homunculus, this eccentric, guiding genius, cough even more, trying to contain his own. The President calmed down, sighing, and brought his mentor up to date.

"Gregor wants me to do something about Hitler, about his treatment of the Jews."

"Mr. Samsa, a man like this"—he indicated the President—"cannot carry your banner. A man like this . . . why even, did you see, the American Jewish Committee opposes any suggestion of Frankfurter going on the court? They don't want to 'fan the fires of anti-Semitism,' as they say. Have you heard Coughlin lately? Enough already with the Jews!" He broke into an uncontrollable cough.

Gregor picked up Amadeus's letter, and waited for him to stop.

"My friend in Berlin assures me we must go to war with Herr Hitler. We must prepare. He send me copy of *Mein Kampf.* You have read it?"

"Read it?" Howe sputtered. "I read it on the toilet, and wipe my ass with it shit by shit. We know it well, my ass and me."

"Could we make our references to Germany stronger?" the President asked.

"Franklin, what's in there is enough. The speech will cover aggression, increasing militarization, the threat of war. But we're not going to war, remember? Congress won't buy it. The voters won't stand for it. They won't stand for *you* if you stand for it. Did you see the petition that came in yesterday?"

"No. What petition?"

Howe shut down his oxygen, waited one two three four five seconds, and lit up a cigarette. "A hundred and fifty-four thousand students from all over the country: 'I refuse to bear arms in any war the United States Government may conduct.' Signed. Name and address. That's the tip of a very big, very cold iceberg, Franklin. You think the Great War vets will step in and take the place of their kids? Besides, supposing you could get the country behind you, and you could recruit an army, and you did go to war with Hitler—or Franco, or whoever—you know who would be president? All your friends who control steel, oil, shipping, munitions, and mines. When the war is over your government will be in their hands."

"What do you think of that, Gregor?" the President asked.

"I don't know what I think. But I think I have to go. My appointment time is finish. The smoke is making me hard to breathe and think." He didn't mention the wound weeping in his back.

"Labor, Gregor," the President said. "Let's choose our battles. For the moment, labor versus capital. If we win this, we'll have seventy-five million more voters behind us, and next term, we can do what needs doing about Hitler. Keep me informed. Whatever you find out."

"I will." He felt dizzy and confused, and left the two men behind closed doors to finalize the speech and plot the second presidential campaign. He crept slowly down three flights of stairs to bury himself in tears amid the alien straw.

## 23. The WOUND and the BOW

He awoke to

*Scent of magnolia, sweet and fresh,*
*And the southern smell of burning flesh*

Maybe he wasn't awake. That song going round and round in his flaccid sensorium, *the southern smell of burning flesh and the southern smell of burning flesh of burning flesh* . . . the six million six million *strange fruit hangin* the six million down giant nerve fibers six million burning flesh . . . fiber! fire!

He sprang out of his straw nest and flung open the door to the early morning kitchen. Henrietta Nesbitt, the head housekeeper, was standing, unflappable, grim, at the smoking door to the electric oven.

"Good morning, Gregor. You're up early."

"What's burning? I smell something burning."

"I'm burning the feather dusters. Go put something on."

"What?"

"Go put something on. I don't talk to strange naked males."

"What? Oh. Oh, I'm so sorry."

Gregor went back in his room and put on his kimono.

"I thought I smelled fire. What do you mean you're burning the feather dusters?"

"Just what I said. I told the staff two months ago I wanted no more feather dusters. They just lift up the dust and throw it around to settle right down again. Vacuum cleaning only. We have the new Hoover vacuums. Do they listen? Even after they've been warned? So I'm burning the feather dusters."

"Maybe they don't use anything called Hoover. Is it the same Hoover?"

"No. I don't know. In any case, it doesn't matter. It's ongoing insubordination."

"It makes a terrible stinking."

"That's why I'm doing it at four-thirty in the morning. The smell should clear by the time the six-thirty shift arrives."

"I thought it was—I don't know what. In my dream. A lynching. Isn't that strange? Then I thought it was six million piglets tossed into the fire."

"If I were Mr. Wallace, I could never live with myself. Killing those pigs may be good economics, but what kind of a man . . ." She shook her head.

It is one of the more tasteless ironies of history that in 1933, and for half a dozen years after, the phrase "the slaughter of the six million" was connected to a most unkosher cohort of piglets that Wallace's Department of Agriculture had ordered killed.

"I'm sorry if the smell disturbed you," the housekeeper semi-apologized, "but the kitchen is not a place most people sleep. I forgot you were in there."

"It's good I get up. I have much to prepare for the children that come."

"Yes, I do, too. Fifteen cots on the second floor. Toilet accommodations for seven in wheelchairs. Oxygen for three."

"And I have stage to set up. Including somehow the appearance of a deus ex machina—and we have no machines."

"What are they doing?"

"Sophocles' *Philoctetes*."

"I mean what do they need machines for? What kind of machines? We have plenty of machines. The machine shop can . . . "

"This is a play. They do a play."

"Why does a play need a machine? What sort of play?"

"A Greek play."

"Why don't they do an American play?"

"This is a play about someone who can almost not walk."

"That's hardly appropriate in this White House."

"It is famous. A good choice. You come tonight and see. I think the President likes it."

"Let me know if you need any machines."

"Are the feather dusters done? They don't smoke anymore."

. . .

Gregor spent from two to six P.M. with fifteen seventh- through twelfth-graders from Montgomery and Arlington counties, who, under the auspices of the new, FDR-inspired National Foundation for Infantile Paralysis, soon to be christened "The March of Dimes," had come together to form a company called Leaping Hart Theater (as, I suppose, in Isaiah's "Then shall the lame man leap as an hart").

Fifteen crippled children. One writer's rule of thumb was "If you have a terrible story you need to save, put in a crippled child. If it's *really* terrible, make it a blind, crippled child." Well, nobody was blind, but the crippled-child strategy, conscious or unconscious, made this troupe a winner. They could have performed the fiery end of *Götterdämmerung* with no singing and only a cigarette lighter, and still have wrung hearts of stone.

The full range of morbidity was represented. Nine children manifested the popular image of the disease: flaccid paralysis of various muscle groups resulting from destruction of spinal motor neurons with associated atrophy of unused musculature. Five children had mild to moderate breathing difficulties due to viral attacks on the upper spinal cord. Two of these had to use mechanical ventilators to push air through a tracheostomy into their lungs. In one child the virus had attacked the brainstem and the nerve centers that control swallowing. He drooled constantly and his voice sounded as if it came from the bottom of a swamp. There was a spittoon attached to his belt, and a tube that reached his mouth. The collective wisdom of the group (there seemed to be no director) was such as to cast him in the role of Hercules returning from the dead to order Philoctetes back to war. He was vocally quite convincing.

At seven forty-five, the guests, having eaten a simple meal in the State Dining Room, were admitted to the East Room for the eight-o'clock show, and Gregor took his seat among them. Nine Roosevelts with six Roosevelt children were in attendance. The entire Cabinet was there, with spouses, along with Louis Howe, Dr. McIntyre, Missy LeHand, Mrs. Nesbitt and her husband, Henry, and the British Ambassador with two of his aides. Forty-four chairs were taken by twenty four parents and twenty siblings of the actors. But none, most likely, was as keyed up as Gregor.

He had spent the afternoon helping the children set up, marinating in their oddness and their resulting strengths. That he, himself, was a bit odd, is given. But he was fully functioning, in command of all his forces. These beings were not. They called forth pity, and yes, terror, as if their energy came from somewhere back of the beyond. Before the show began, Gregor was already on the edge of tears, oppressed by his very normality, while the children showed absolutely no recognition of limits. It was inspiring, of course, but entirely disheartening. Gregor, hypersensitive to performance, was here in this arena of most extravagant events, and he was ready to explode.

At 8:10, the President rolled his chair in front of the platform.

"My friends, I want to welcome you here tonight, partly as your official host, but more importantly as an authentic representative of the disabled people in our country. I am pleased to present to you this project of our new National Foundation for Infantile Paralysis, our very own neighbors, the schoolchildren of the Leaping Hart Theater Company, in a performance of . . . someone help me out here . . ."

"Sophocles' *Philoctetes*," stage-whispered the wheelchaired stage manager.

"Sophocles' *Philoctetes*," echoed the President. "I have to be frank—I don't know the play, and I'm greatly looking forward to experiencing it. Ladies and gentlemen, the Leaping Hart Theater."

Grand applause from a most friendly audience.

Citing their disabilities is not to patronize the performers. As one can't ignore a rhino in the bedroom, one must acknowledge such obvious encumbrance. But according to Gregor, these children were extraordinary in more ways than one. They performed this text as if they meant it, almost as if they had written it. Daring directorial decisions had been made—such as placing a budding fifteen-year-old girl in the role of

Odysseus, and a tiny, oxygen-supported seventh-grader as Neoptolemus—which added resonances not normally encountered. It was one of those performances too odd to ever forget.

The stage manager wheeled herself over to the light switches at the south door and plunged the room into curtained darkness. A short chorus of off-stage breath evoked the sound of wind and sea. Odysseus entered, identified the scene, *"This is the sea-encircled, sacred isle of Lemnos,"* and described to young Neoptolemus, Achilles's son, how ten years earlier, the Greeks had abandoned Philoctetes on this remote shore. Their countryman had been bitten on the foot by a sacred serpent, and his malodorous wound and agonized screaming made him unacceptable company on the war voyage to Troy. Traitorous abandonment. (Gregor felt dampness under his shirt.) And now the deviled detail: oracles had proclaimed that the Trojan War could not be won without Philoctetes and his invincible bow, gift to him from Heracles. But how to obtain help from one so cruelly betrayed? Cunning, Odysseus urges. Cunning will be needed, for, as Odysseus observes, Philoctetes has become a maniac in hate.

*A maniac in hate.* Formidable expression. Only several hours earlier, six time zones to the east, Adolf Hitler had been firing up a crowd of forty thousand in München. Philoctetes, however, had other reasons for his ravings: desertion by friends makes for resentment-twisted souls. Odysseus reminds Neoptolemus that the old sailor's arrows are inevitably lethal, and that a battle would be futile. Trickery is the only way.

NEOPTOLEMUS
    But is not all of it a pack of lies?
ODYSSEUS
    Nay, necessary, boy; but necessary.
    The little shameless thrift we use today
    Earns us the life of honor and renown.
    We shall be called saviors of the State.

As a little blip of brown fluid moved from Gregor's back, through his bandage, to his shirt, Neoptolemus was persuaded to take part in the deception. Just one little lie from him today, and afterward all will be honest. Many a man has footed that muddy slope. Having set loose his plot, Odysseus hid and left Neoptolemus to do the dirty deed.

Philoctetes was heard coming closer, with groans of pain and bitter grief. Again, a daring directorial decision: a strapping, seventeen-year-old young man, with no visible deformity, save for the stain on the left foot of his flesh-colored tights. His symptoms consisted entirely of debilitating pain, like Philoctetes's, but though he looked sound, his courage must have been immense.

The chorus jumped back when they saw the wounded man, yet Philoctetes was drawn to them, overjoyed to hear his native tongue!

Neoptolemus told him of the war and won his confidence by sharing a feigned scorn of the Greek leaders.

Gregor's wound began to soak through his jacket and onto the yellow upholstery of the uncomfortable East Room chair. He slid forward in his seat.

Having been confirmed in his opinion of the Argives, Philoctetes pled with his new false friend to take him home to Greece "as freight," to store him in the hold where he would least disturb the crew. The young man, moved, but duplicitous, accepted. The trap was laid: Philoctetes and his unerring bow would be aboard Neoptolemus's ship; he would be carried to a Trojan battlefront, with or without his knowledge or consent, to win the war for his enemies. A theater of cruelty production.

Just as they were leaving for the ship, the only "special effect" occurred, and a remarkably well done one it was. A small balloon, hidden at the dorsum of Philoctetes's foot, under his tights, was slowly filled with beet juice from a bulb/reservoir affair surreptitiously pumped at the actor's hip. The audience could see an abscess begin to pulse and swell, and Philoctetes dropped, screaming, to the ground:

> Alas, my child, the pain again! Ai! ai!
> We're lost—ai! ai! By heaven, it eats me up!

Hast thou no sword, good youth, to shore it off?
Lop off my foot at once and spare me not.


And so on. Harrowing. Clearly, the cracked-voice screams were authentically remembered from the young actor's very own pain. They did not scan in neat iambs, but drew themselves out at excruciating length. His father clenched in his East Room chair, and his mother wept quietly.

For Gregor, the combination of betrayal and wound was unbearable. To stop the rushing up of vomitus, he clamped his tibia against his face and ran out of the room, his mouthparts wet with dinner. Dr. McIntyre sprang out of his chair and followed Gregor out the door to the corridor.

"Gregor, wait!" the old man yelled, but the Assistant to the Assistant Secretary of Agriculture ducked into the men's room without heeding him. The doctor followed, and found his colleague inside a stall, hunched over the toilet. He waited for the retching to stop.

"Something you ate? Do I have to worry about forty more cases of food poisoning?"

"I don't think so. It was the play. Seeing the play."

"That bad, huh?"

"No. Good."

"Really? Well, we're missing the end."

"I know the end."

"What happens?"

"Heracles orders from the heaven that Philoctetes go and slaughter Trojans for religion sake. I think that is what makes me—you say up-czech?"

"Upchuck. What about that stain on your back?"

"It's nothing."

"It's enough for a two-hundred-dollar upholstery repair at taxpayer expense. Why don't we go down to my office and take a look?" He helped the roach down the east spiral staircase to the ground-floor clinic near the kitchen.

"Still feeling sick?"

"No. I am better."

"But something is still juicy back there. The stain is growing. Take off your jacket and shirt, and let's see what's going on."

Gregor felt confident caring for his wound, and normally did not seek medical help. Still, McIntyre was so friendly, and so forceful, that Gregor followed his instructions. The doctor removed the dressing.

"Impressive. Six- or seven-centimeter wound, friable, weeping, raised borders—"

"It tells me of my mortality. And my task."

"Very medieval. What's brown? The fluid itself seems clear." He smelled his wet finger.

"I don't know. When I am cut elsewhere, I bleed water."

"Haemolymph, I believe, if I remember my sophomore entomology. How'd you get this damn thing? How long have you had it?"

"I have it since 1915—twenty years."

"And it's never healed?"

"No. Is a reminder."

"Of what? More mortality?"

"My father. He throw at me an apple. An apple. In my back. I don't like to talk of it. Maybe brown is from the apple."

"Still?"

"It reminds me."

"A useful wound! But it's not like this all the time, is it? What makes it worse? What makes it weep so?"

"Different things. Various."

"What brought it on tonight? What in the play?"

"When the boy is tricked and made to be not true to himself. And it gets worse when the play is so cruel. And the children are so hurt. It almost make me cry, but my wound cries instead."

"And the vomiting?"

"When the God is going to make him kill people with his bow . . . when he himself is so wounded . . ."

There was silence as the doctor opened a white wall cabinet.

"What do you think this play is about?" McIntyre asked, pulling sterile gauze pads and tape from the shelf. He swabbed the wound with hydrogen peroxide.

"I think it is about ways to betray."

"I think it's about a person poisoned by narrow, fanatical hatred," the doctor averred. "Isn't that a line in the play? Something about fanatical hatred?"

"A maniac of hate." He began to weep.

"Gregor, calm down. All right if I re-dress the wound?"

"Yes, go ahead."

The doctor packed the moist crater with folded gauze.

"Philoctetes was a bit much, with that metaphorically smelly wound," he said. "He was a stinker."

"What is stinker?"

"Someone you don't want to be around."

"All right. Yes," said Gregor. "He is a stinker. But so is everyone else."

"But Philoctetes is a *necessary* stinker. They can't win the war without him. They can't just use his bow—they need the stinker himself. With the stink. A bad character who is also indispensable . . . This size adhesive tape okay? It's all I have."

"Yes, okay."

"A hero with an incurable wound"—he went on bandaging—"like yours, my friend, perhaps like yours. His strength was inseparable from his wound."

"If he hadn't been bite in the first place—"

"Ah, but he was. And by a sacred snake, no? Sacred. Not some old rusty nail with *Clostridium tetani* on it. This was no accident. It was a lesson. For you. For us. This horrible stinker, Philoctetes, with his smelly, shit-filled wound, is also the master of a superhuman art. Genius—and disease. We normal people need genius. But we have to take the smell that goes with it."

"Do we need such children?"

"I don't know. But we've got 'em. There, you're all clean and neat. Except for your shirt and jacket, which I suggest you launder thoroughly. Want a johnny to get you to the kitchen?"

"No, it's ten meters. I go home semi-naked. Mrs. Nesbitt is still upstairs."

"Gregor, I'll tell you how I think things are." The doctor was washing his hands. "I think we live in a world where above fuses with below. You can't have a divine weapon, a sacred tool, without its abominable owner vomiting curses and fouling his nest." He dried his hands and opened the office door.

"And we can't have human without wound." Gregor stepped out into the hallway.

"Hey," the doctor called after him, "you told me what made it worse. What makes it better?"

Gregor turned around and faced the old man.

"Forgetting. It makes it better when I forget."

As March sunlight gilded their breakfast tables, Washingto-
nians read in their morning papers that in about two weeks
the Japanese cherry trees around the Tidal Basin would be
in full bloom. The same day Kansans breakfasted by lamp
light and read in their morning papers that one of the worst
dust storms in the history of their State was sweeping
darkly overhead. Damp sheets hung over the windows, but
tablecloths were grimy. Urchins wrote their names on the
dusty china. Food had a gritty taste. Dirt drifted around
doorways like snow. People who ventured outside coughed
and choked as the fields of Kansas, Colorado, Wyoming,
Nebraska and Oklahoma rose and took flight through the
windy air.

(Time magazine, April 1, 1935)

And after the dust clouds came the locusts. The sky would blacken in-
termittently, this time with hungry living creatures, their habitats
parched—living, swarming creatures, leaving no flora behind them—a secondary plague perhaps, not as well remembered as the dust, but for those
whose lives and livelihoods were decimated, the straw that broke the dying camel's back. In 1936, various species of "devastating hoppers" were
reported to have destroyed U.S. crops valued at over $100 million. The
Department of Agriculture took a serious view of the situation and set
about to avert the worst. In the depth of the Depression, vast crop and in-
come losses were not propitious for recovery—or for reelection. Among
others, Gregor was tapped to serve.

Insects researching Insectiva—a wise move: it takes one to know one.
Gregor had already been named "Entomological Consultant," Assistant to

the Assistant Secretary of Agriculture, Rex Tugwell, and had brilliantly solved the White House ant problem using boric acid as a nontoxic insecticide. It was inevitable that he be asked for help keeping locust swarms from California. The problem to solve was this:

On the one hand there is the charming green and yellow grasshopper, of Grasshopper and Ant fame, "always jigging ajog, hoppy on akkant of his joyicity." On the other, there is the swarming locust—not a different species, but the same species transformed like a mutant teenager in Halloween black and orange, with shorter legs and longer wings, ripe for swarming. What makes the green, chirping Jekyll transform into death-dealing Hyde? *That* is the question.

Food shortage has something to do with it, as post-drought swarming attests. But swarming also occurs under excellent conditions, when population expansion leads to crowding. Was crowding itself the key, drought forcing large numbers into small habitable areas? And if crowding were the stimulus, how might the response be aborted; how might individuals be preventively dispersed? Entomological researchers, Gregor among them, stood at this crossroads.

There are several ways to think about the problem. Modern science would council rationality—controlled experimentation on isolated elements of the puzzle. Henry Wallace advised Gregor to avoid interpretive political metaphor and get out the Bunsen burner. He even provided a budget to convert a small White House pantry into a basic laboratory in which Gregor might perform repeatable, reportable experiments. Keep must be earned. So Gregor was forced by social, cultural, and political pressure to perform the famous—if merely "scientific"—experiments that bear his name.

His famous experiments for the USDA were directed at two areas:

1. Finding the factors that produced gregarious, swarming behavior in populations of what were once solitary individuals; and

2. Exploring techniques to prevent such metamorphosis and such behavior.

The work on the first group was typical of the simplicity of groundbreaking science. Experimenting with immature, wingless hoppers supplied to him by the department, he noticed a tendency for them to gather thigmotactically in the corners of their cages, and therefore introduced circular containers to eliminate clumping. He divided the floor into thirty-six sections, put in hoppers eighteen at a time, and recorded their positions after they had settled down. Non-swarming hoppers, including migratory locusts reared in isolation, ended up two or more to a section 35 percent of the time. But hoppers "reared crowded" ended up two or more to a section 50 to 70 percent of the time. Conclusion: hoppers used to crowding crowd.

Was the learning visual? Gregor placed individual hoppers in small celluloid cages set down in crowds of other hoppers. When freed, they did not then tend to aggregate. But when they were placed directly in among the crowd, they did learn to aggregate. Blinded hoppers (Gregor made little hoods), also became gregarious. Touch seemed to make the difference.

While humans, for instance, might be moved by the touch of a loving hand, they are often repulsed by similar stroking from a claw. Gregor knew this well. Did touch for locusts have to be from another locust, or would other kinds of touch do? Gregor found that a cage full of roly-bugs—terrestrial crustaceans, not even insects—could turn locusts gregarious. What else might do so? In a fit of inspiration, after having witnessed a riotous tickling scene with the Roosevelt kids, he invented his celebrated "Heuschreckekitzelapparat" (Fig. 1), a jar with many fine wires and threads turned by a paddle wheel. The White House staff found it most amusing to discover 16-ounce mayonnaise jars, each with its engine and insect inhabitants, installed under leaky faucets—all thirteen of them—throughout the Executive Mansion. The experimental results? Wire-tickled hoppers became gregarious: Gregor was homing in on an answer.

It was the "vision vs. touch" series that led Gregor to his most important work, the discovery of what he called "smelltrons." How could he be other than the pioneer? How could humans, with the nasal sensitivity of a fire hydrant, possibly notice such a factor? His crucial experiment was as follows:

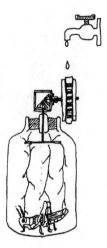

Fig. 1. Heuschreckekitzelapparat (Locust-tickling apparatus)

In the tunnel leading to the Executive Office Building, Gregor set up two parallel runs of glass tubing, 10 meters in length, with setups as in Fig. 2.

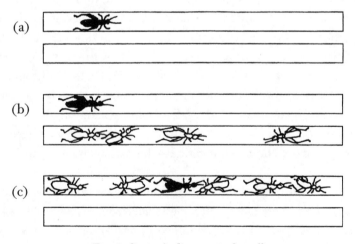

Fɪɢ. 2. Gregor's discovery of smelltrons

The test locust in (a) marched 30 percent of the time, in (b), with visual stimulus, 34 percent of the time (statistically insignificant), and in (c), with visual and tactile stimulus, 84 percent of the time. Predictable.

The surprise came when Gregor repeated the experiment, replacing the glass tubing with rolled sections of fly screen. This time, (a) produced 31 percent marching, and (c) 82 percent, as before, but (b) produced 55 percent marching, a significant increase. Some new stimulus, not visual, not tactile, seemed to be at play. The numbers were similar no matter what kind of wire was used, though in (b), marching decreased very slightly as the gauge of the mesh decreased. Evidently, something small was being carried in the air between compartments.

Unlike his human colleagues at the department lab on Constitution Avenue, Gregor could smell something going on. In fact, for him, the odor of a gregarious colony was quite different from that of an equal population of individual hoppers, and became more intense as the colony prepared to swarm. It was the difference between a sunny, placid F major (as, he said, in the opening of the Pastoral Symphony) and a slightly acrid, antsy C# minor (as in the opening of the Mahler Fifth). The change from individual to swarming colony was for Gregor an olfactory modulation as sweeping as anything in Wagner. Almost every member of the White House staff—including upper-level administration—was asked to smell the two extremes: no one could tell the difference. "Just smells like bugs to me" was the typical response.

He postulated the existence of "smelltrons," a species of volatile chemicals secreted in minute amounts that might be responsible for anatomical, physiological, or behavioral change. Perhaps the name was unfortunate; it was replaced in the fifties by the now common "pheromone."

Gregor's assumption of intraspecific chemical communication was not without precedent. About ten years earlier, Karl von Frisch had demonstrated a similar phenomenon. Having marked a minnow with an incision near its tail, he was surprised to see its schoolmates fleeing when he reintroduced the wounded fish among them. Philoctetes, of course, comes to mind. Frisch assumed that some "alarm substance" was being emitted, warning the school away from a potential threat.

Then, with his invention of the Elektroantennograph (Fig. 3), Gregor contributed immeasurably to the investigation. Gregor thought—why not use the smell organ itself as a biological conductor, and measure quan-

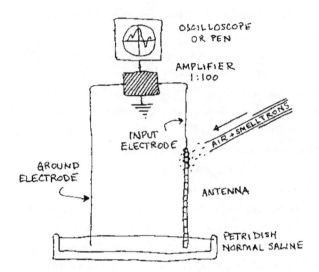

FIG. 3. Elektroantennograph. Filtered air containing test samples is blown over the antenna, which responds electrically to bio-active materials at picogram amounts ($1 \times 10^{-12}$—one trillionth of a gram) undetectable by the human nose.

titatively the activity of potential smelltrons? With the invaluable help of James Johnson, a White House electrician and ham radio enthusiast, Gregor was able to set locust antennae into a circuit that, suitably amplified, would write its enthusiasm, or lack thereof, on a cathode ray screen, or moving piece of paper. He amputated only one antenna per hopper, and honored his experimental subjects as war heroes in the battle of Science vs. Darkness.

The electroantennograph enabled him, and other later investigators, to test thousands of compounds, organic and inorganic, even complex, difficult to analyze mixtures such as vacuum cleaner air or used alcohol from chandelier scrubs. After a year of painstaking work, three compounds stood out as being especially provocative—in a class by themselves:

1. An ethanol extraction of the bark of the Guatemalan trey bush. Depending on concentration, it could either attract or disperse. The material was too rare and too politically hard to come by to be of much practical use.

2. An acetone extraction of thorax chitin from young, dead male swarmers. A disperser, perhaps related to von Frisch's "alarm substance." Gregor was against the kind of large, frontally aggressive activities necessary to acquire sufficient quantities.

3. Human female axillary sweat. An attractor. This seemed to have the most promise, especially in warm regions where the locust problem was greatest. Just a simple absorbent pad taped under each armpit between the months of June and early September—from White House staff alone—might have contained enough smelltronic activity to protect all of Montgomery County.

The operative phrase is "might have"—because there was no big locust outbreak in 1937. Nor in 1938. And with the recession of '37–'38 came slackening enthusiasm for WHIRL (White House Institute for Research on Locusts), and a drying up of meager funds. It was not until April 1939, fully eight months after Gregor had dismantled the mayonnaise jars, and incidentally had ordered all leaks fixed, that an unusual infestation of grasshoppers appeared in the Big Smoky Valley of Nevada. But by that time, Hitler had invaded Czechoslovakia.

## 25. LARGE THINGS
## and IRRATIONAL

From coast to coast, the dams, the parkways, the public buildings had been built. One could drive majestically across a Golden Gate Bridge. The Jefferson Memorial proclaimed FDR's idol, the man whose words "I TREMBLE FOR MY COUNTRY WHEN I REFLECT THAT THAT GOD IS JUST" now stand in foot-high letters overlooking the Tidal Basin. In cities throughout the country, there were housing projects for the poor and the black, there were more hospitals, firehouses, schools, and airports, and the blind now had talking books. Inner-city youths were roaming the forests with the CCC, planting trees and not suspicion. Writers were paid to write, painters to paint, actors to act.

Yet after five years of activist government, unemployment was essentially the same, the large-business community was still ferociously opposed, plotting its revenge, and again the seeds of political reaction were sprouting.

Gregor was spending much time at the Museum of Natural History, his second attempt, this time as biologist, to compass the scope of animal, vegetable, and mineral. It was not yet the era of "interactive" museums. Many exhibits seemed right out of Fischer von Waldheim's *Zoognosia: Tabulis synopticis illustrata, in usum praelectionum Academiae Imperialis Medico-Chiurgicae Mosquensis,* that huge leather volume, with tables and illustrations of every known species of animal—his first reading assignment from Amadeus.

Yet it was one particular beast that had initiated his visits, a creature far from Insectiva, a party at the large-size end of Animalia that called to him. It was Harold Ickes, he recalled, who had first spoken to him of *Moby-Dick*—this in regard to Gregor's study of English. The head of the Public Works Administration thought he might be ready for this torrent of high-and-mighty speech. And lo, the very day of that encounter, Gregor felt a copy calling to him from the library shelves at the end of his hall, the Rockwell Kent edition it was, one of the proud productions of the WPA. "Call me Ishmael," he read.

Standing in the middle of the small, cream-colored library, with its green rug and chandelier once owned by James Fenimore Cooper, Gregor knew he would spend his next year with this book.

Of course, it was the Cetology chapter that took him to the museum for the first time. No sperm whale there, but a model of the biggest of whales, the blue, the principal kill of the present day. Blue reaches its full size, 100 feet, at eleven years, lives twenty to twenty-five years, and weighs 150 tons—four times the estimated weight of the biggest prehistoric monster. Gregor would sit in the huge, balconied room from whose ceiling the whale was suspended, looking up. When what neck he had began to hurt, he would view from the balcony—but he preferred the lack of distance from below, the sense that any moment he could be crushed—like a bug. His early visits were done, Melvillian Baedeker in hand, for purposes of study. But after study came—what?—prayer?

He was on his way from White House to museum one drizzly late-April day, walking slowly, already in a meditative space, when he felt something whop down on his head, and found himself looking out of a net. Standing at the other end of a five-foot handle was a man in a gray municipal uniform, accompanied by a burly, armed member of the Park Police.

"All right, just take it easy and nobody'll get hurt," said the gray one. "Department of Animal Control."

Taking something of a chance, he let go of the net handle with one hand and reached around to his back pocket for his wallet. Shiny silver-badge-with-blue-center Gregor couldn't read.

"Just come with me. Truck's over there." White bakery-type van with appropriate municipal markings.

"What's going on? Get this off me!" Gregor was screeching unsympathetically. The cop drew his pistol just in case. Handcuffs too large.

"We've had a complaint. Several complaints about you. We've been watching you."

"I work at the White House. I live at the White House. I'm an Assistant to—"

"Tell it to the Judge!"

"Tell it to the Judge!" the blue one echoed, more profoundly. In these days, things were tense around Washington.

Gregor knew resistance would be catastrophic, so he followed his captors to the getaway van where he was de-netted and strapped onto a wheeled gurney borrowed from the morgue. Much of the trip was spent with the cop in the back of the van trying to keep the gurney from crashing into the walls at each deceleration and turn.

The van headed south to Anacostia, once site of the Bonus Encampment, now also home to the main animal impoundment center, euphemistically known as a "Shelter," as in "Food, Clothing, and Shelter." Gregor was off-loaded by dogcatcher and cop, wheeled into the front office, briefly questioned, name rank and serial number, then into the back, a great room full of wheeled cages.

"Wait a minute," Gregor shrilled. "Don't I get a phone call to my lawyer?"

Such a request had never been made before. Catcher, cop, and clerk conferred, and wheeled him back to the office.

"What's the number?" asked the clerk.

"I can dial it myself," the insect averred.

"Not unless we unstrap your things there," the cop observed, "which we ain't gonna do."

"FE4-2200."

"F-E-4-2-2-0-0." The clerk had to say the numbers out loud in order to get them right. Hand over the mouthpiece: "She says it's the Department of Agriculture."

"Hey," growled the cop, "I thought you worked in the White House."

Gregor left a message with Rex Tugwell's secretary, and was wheeled back into the local Bedlam—the barking and yowling of an unplumbed circle of Dante's hell.

Gregor wrapped his Burberry (a Tugwell hand-me-down) around his poor knees, which brought the input down from that of "a plane at takeoff" to only that of "raucous music; the subway"—somewhat more bearable. But distraction, distraction, what to do? what to read? Partly exposed in coatpocket by dint of unusual wrap-around, two envelopes, forgotten stash of Thursday's post. A bill from Fischer Scientific—the centrifuge, no doubt—and a letter from KMM at Ives & Myrick, 46 Cedar Street, New York City, N.Y. But who was KMM? He tore into the envelopes, first the bill—business before pleasure—then the thicker packet from . . . he shuffled the pages through to the end. "Yours forever, Katherine (MacPherson)."

Katherine MacPherson. Katherine MacPherson. It must be Miss MacPherson. Miss MacPherson who sat at the desk across the aisle. He never knew her first name. What could she have to say?

```
April 5, 1939
```

That was three weeks ago. Is the post kaput?

```
Dear Mr. Samsa,
    It has taken me four years to write to you, I've been
in such agony, unsure whether to take the chance. But
Gregor (may I call you Gregor?) I shall never be able to
forget you or master my love for you.
```

What?? (Gregor had yet to discover that life was truly stranger than fiction.)

```
    I have your picture (the one from the jacket of your
book) in my desk drawer, and every day I sneak many
glances at it, pretending to be looking for envelopes or
something.
    I know what you must be thinking: who is this woman?--
I never even noticed her. And it's true. I sat next to
you for years, too bashful to even glance across the
aisle except in secret, too frightened to speak to you
who knows so much about so many things.
    When you left I thought I would recover. "Out of
sight, out of mind," we say in America. But we also say
"Absence makes the heart grow fonder," and almost every
day I found my mind wandering, thinking resentful
thoughts about Mr. Mullen, who sits unworthily at your
desk, less and less able to do my work. Last week I
```

found myself pacing the office, thinking only of throwing myself on your neck and smothering you with kisses. I knew then it was time to write.

Perhaps you think I am too forward. What right have I to make such assumptions that you would be interested in me? Let me assure you that I am a respectable and honest woman in all senses of the word. Our first kiss would be my first kiss--and to no one else in the world, for after you, I no longer wish even to look at anyone else.

Mr. Samsa, Gregor, I am not a frivolous or gullible girl. I have done much thinking about intermarriage and its dangers. I know that those of the Jewish religion do not like to marry outside their race. So for the past two years, I have been studying Judaism, and I can tell you it is a moving and impressive religion. I was brought up to think of the Old Testament as "old," replaced by the "New" Testament, interesting as history, but no longer really important. But now I have read the "Old" Testament two times all the way through, and I can truly say that it contains a lot of wisdom. If we were to be married--even before, if I even knew you were interested--I would be willing to convert to your beautiful religion. I think Katherine Mary MacPherson would be a funny name for them to see in their class. (Ha ha.) I would be a good, kosher wife, and no longer just a "shiksa." (You see, I have been learning Yiddish, too, out of a book of common expressions.)

My mother and my father (especially my father) I know would object to my marrying a Jew. But they were both killed two and a half years ago in an automobile accident in Illinois, where they live, so there is nothing to worry about that they would make trouble at a wedding or anything else. Their death was also something that freed my mind and heart to think more seriously about you, I mean about you and me.

Maybe I'm just "meshugga" (I'm joking), but I really

believe in Love. I believe that when your heart tells you something so strongly, even if your head laughs, that some larger truth is speaking, and you must at least listen and consider very carefully. And Gregor, even if you don't hear the same voice, the truth may be speaking for you too, for it is a judgment on the possibility of Katherine and Gregor--both of us together.

   "Mr. Samsa," I am dying of longing to see you once more, to sit and quietly talk--though as usual, I would probably be struck dumb. But this I know with all my heart--I cannot live any longer without you. Farewell, my dear one. If you knew how I suffer . . .

   Please write to me what you think. I anxiously await your answer.

   Yours forever,

   Katherine (MacPherson)


Gregor checked the postmark on the envelope. April 20. She must have hesitated to post it, he thought. And then he thought, *Gott in Himmel! What I am to do now? She will kill herself, with me to blame.* He reread the letter several times amidst the awful barking.

Tugwell arrived at the pound late in the day, worked something out in the front room, and took Gregor back to the White House in a taxi. He studied the letter all the way up Fourteenth Street, and handed it back to his despairing colleague. "ER," he said. "This is a problem for ER. She's the queen of thank-you notes."

And indeed Eleanor Roosevelt was concerned and helpful. She assured Gregor that this was not a suicide note—it was far too full of hope. She instructed him in the use of phrases such as "Thank you so much for your kind letter," and "Unfortunately, I am not available for a serious relationship," the "unfortunately" added to save Miss MacPherson's self-esteem, the "presently" (Gregor's suggestion) subtracted to indicate closure. She advised him to take time to describe his current activities (supportive of her worth and right to know), while emphasizing that he was much too busy to undertake a serious writing relationship. The finished letter was a masterpiece of tact, checked and rechecked. But where to send it?

The Library of Congress is housed in two massive buildings east of the Capitol. It contains phone books from every city, town, and municipality in the country. There were six Katherine MacPhersons listed in Manhattan, seven K. MacPhersons, six and eight in Queens, four and four in the Bronx, three and four in Brooklyn, and three K's in Staten Island. Gregor spent the next week making phone calls: several K/Katherines were unreachable, and none of the others was right. Quite a few sounded suspicious of the caller. Unpleasant. Given her letter, he imagined she wouldn't be listed under a husband's name, or a parent's.

Failing in New York, he repeated the process for Boston, Chicago, San Francisco, Los Angeles, and then, fearing she may have moved to the Washington area to try to find him, for the District of Columbia, and nearby cities in Maryland and Virginia. Nothing. He didn't know which might be worse: finding her, or not finding her. About to go on to second-order cities—it was an overwrought education in American geography if nothing else—he realized (June!) the new phone books were not yet out, so any recent listing would not be . . . Doomed! The search was doomed! Had he killed someone? He might never know. Not salutary for one inclined to guilt.

The silver lining in the cloud was that he became a habitual user of the Library of Congress. The cloud inside the silver lining was that the Library of Congress subscribed to every newspaper published on earth, and Gregor became acutely aware—in all details, in several languages—of the dismaying events unfolding off the coast of Cuba, and now Florida.

On May 13, the Hamburg-American Line's luxurious cruise ship, the *St. Louis,* had set sail for Cuba, carrying 930 Jewish refugees, among the last allowed to leave Germany. Göring thought it a good way to export some rich swine—after confiscating all their goods and property; Goebbels found it good propaganda to create a liberal Nazi image, and the Hamburg-American Line saw it as a way to bolster their declining earnings. Each passenger had paid a steep ticket price (especially steep after having been relieved of all their wealth) and a large fee for an official landing certificate (fraudulent, as it turned out) signed by Colonel Manuel Benitez, Cuba's Director-General of Immigration. Only a few days earlier, they had been anxious victims of ever increasing Nazi terror. But on board—surreal!—they were treated as human beings, cruise passengers entitled to the luxury that normally accompanies such bookings. None was aware that a few days before departure, Cuba's President, Frederico Bru, victim of domestic pressure from anti-Semitic groups, and furious at not being given a cut of Benitez's scam, had announced his intention to invalidate their papers. Ersatz "landing certificates" would not be considered valid: they would need regulation visas approved by three separate Cuban Departments.

Conversation, deck games, dances, chamber music, and elegant meals were heady experiences for these lucky members of a recently despised race. Then, on May 23 Captain Schroeder received a telegram from Hamburg-American: MAJORITY YOUR PASSENGERS IN CONTRAVENTION OF NEW CUBAN LAW 937 AND MAY NOT BE GIVEN PERMISSION DISEMBARK. Fears returned with clutching intensity. On the twenty-seventh the *St. Louis,* now a floating prison, docked at Havana. Only twenty-eight passengers were allowed to leave the ship—twenty-two who had hired high-priced lawyers in Europe to obtain regulation visas, a Cuban couple, and six visiting Spaniards. Nine hundred and eight passengers remained on board. Their distress became a front-page story in newspapers throughout the world. Would they be sent back to Germany to die in ghettos or camps? There were many details to the dickerings.

At five P.M. on June 2, the roach was in the President's office.

"What would you like me to do?"

"Whatever you think of. What about temporary visas? Or a president directive—you call it finding?—concerning this special case? Or at least to register a protest! If we can't come to their physical aid, what about their moral aid?"

"And when 'President Rosenfeld' is destroyed by the anti-Jewish lobby, who will stand up to Hitler? Neville Chamberlain? Who will protect your people from American anti-Semites? Have you heard Father Coughlin lately, his fireside chats? Thirty million listen—every week."

"And a hundred million don't."

"Furthermore, my friend, there are legitimate security concerns. Do we know who all these people really are? Three or four spies, some saboteurs among the nine hundred? Nazis threatening to kill their families back home unless they do their dirty work?"

"The political mind," wrote Calvin Coolidge, "is a strange mixture of vanity and timidity, of an obsequious attitude at one time and a delusion of grandeur at another time, of the most selfish preferment combined with the most sacrificing patriotism. The political mind is the product of men in public life who have been twice spoiled—spoiled with praise and spoiled with abuse. With them nothing is natural . . ." Gregor had independently come to similar conclusions.

On June 6, at 11:40 P.M., under orders from Hamburg-American, and with no resolution in sight, Captain Schroeder turned his ship to the northeast and set course for Europe. His telegram arrived four days later:

REGARD THESE PASSENGERS AS DOOMED ONCE THEY REACH GERMAN SOIL STOP WANT TO BE ASSURED NO SINGLE POSSIBILITY OF ESCAPE SHOULD FAIL

TO BE GIVEN UTMOST CONSIDERATION STOP TIME IS OF ESSENCE BOAT HAS
COMPLETED MORE THAN HALF OF TRIP

Roosevelt was silent. For the entire week Gregor had been on the phone with Department Secretaries and underlings, with negotiators still working in Cuba and with the Joint Distribution Committee handling things in New York. On June 12, as the French Minister of the Interior was accepting 250 refugees, and the British were about to match that number, Gregor, more than slightly bitter, sat down with a wary President of the United States.

"It's good some of the refugees will be accepted," Gregor began, "but because we here don't do anything, already the *Völkischer Beobachter* claims we agree with their anti-Jewish policy."

"I'm sympathetic to the victims, but you know we can't risk being labeled 'pro-Jew.' I want us to be known as 'anti-Nazi.'" The President poured himself a sherry and offered some to Gregor.

"No, thank you. This is too narrow choices," Gregor insisted. "Something is much beyond normal polities now, something which leads the entire world to a condition where people and State are set at terrifying odds, where no person can trust any other person. This is not a world you or I can want to live in. I would like to talk you of my Jewish experience, both here and in Europe of my youth. I do not pretend to be a pious—"

Louis Howe rapped his signature "shave-and-a-haircut" knock. Gregor shook his head no.

"Come in, Louis," FDR called out.

The mischievous troll hobbled in, right on his own, maximally disruptive, cue, pushing his oxygen cart, and wheezing at a cigarette.

"Gregor was just going to give us the Jewish point of view on the *St. Louis* business."

"The Jewish cockroach view?"

"Nu, so vat else?" asked the President. The two chums laughed. "Sorry, Gregor, just teasing, and practicing my President Rosenfeld accent."

"It's all right. Jews are cockroaches, in a way. They must become hard on the outside from so much kicking around. But they are soft on the inside."

"Granted," Howe allowed. He, too, was softer than he seemed.

"Like cockroaches, Jews represent everything not to be digested, everything otherness, everything getting in the way, everything that will not be expelled—just like other poor people, Orientals, Negroes—like cockroaches. We always reopen the wound of all-not-accomplished-by-society. So we are fit for only one thing: extermination."

"That's a little exaggerated, don't you think?" the President asked.

"At the moment, Herr Hitler calls only for Jewish expulsion from German-Europe. If he extends his control, there will be more and more refugees to expulse. But his actions will grow to a demand for extermination: I need no crystal ball here, or especially smart. Anyone who reads *Mein Kampf* would come to the same judgment. Once that limit is breeched, there will be no hope: first the Jews, and then all the others. The slaughter machines will gear and no one different will be safe anywhere. Society will be controlled by the strongest members, moronic and selfish. There will be no 'Jews' left to question things, to confront the community, to bless it with creative discords rather than just legitimize and propagate. There will be no more art except art which glorifies the State. The world will collapse into an ice age of Fascism. The Jews will be dead, and humanity as a whole will be dying. There will be no more past to haunt the present, and no more future. There will be just Power."

"Gregor . . ." both the President and Howe began simultaneously.

"You first," Howe offered.

"No, go ahead," said FDR.

"I agree that things may get worse over there before they get better. But they'll never get that bad here. Even Father Coughlin—"

"Mr. Howe, I see the ads: in hotels and clubs, whole professions closed to Jews—just as in Germany. I look at Help Wanted ads, even in our *Washington Post.* In today's paper I find thirteen ads containing 'Christians' or 'Protestants only need apply.' These are from a utility company, three banks, a publishing house, an engineering and an industrial company, a hospital, and three law firms. This is how Germany began. I see apartment buildings in Bethesda with signs 'Jews and Negroes Need Not Apply.' How do you live when you have more and more no place you are allowed? I go to Georgetown Law School the other day, for a talk by a big law-firm man about hiring. You know what he said? 'Brilliant intellectual powers are not essential.' This is Jews he is talking about. 'Too much imagination, too much wit, too great cleverness, are quite as likely to impede success as to promote it. Our best clients are apt to be afraid of those qualities. They want as their counsel a man who is primarily honest, safe, sound, and steady."

"Oh, come now," Howe chided. "How do you know he was talking about Jews?"

"Mr. Howe, if I may be allowed some too much cleverness, let me ask you to think more deeply. There are literal Jews, and there are symbol Jews, and there is anti-Semitism growling at both. It is like ritual murder—the community must be cleansed of Jewish filth of all kinds. Power without power can—must be blotted out. Many American histories make open to fascism: our City on a Hill, our 'real' Americans, our independence from the rest of the world—everywhere carryover of force and violence from the pioneering day—all this makes for some explosion.

"I have read in Walter Benjamin: 'The world is simplified when tested for its worthiness of destruction.' We like simple in America. Please excuse my bad English. The one opinion I want to say, Mr. President, is that if you feel a political need to not talk about Jews, you must decide how not to talk about them in a better way. Excuse me."

And Gregor got up and walked out. Walked out on the President, and on his gray-green eminence. You don't get brownie points for such behavior.

The neutron. Now there's an entity a politician can love. Electrically neutral, bipartisan as it were, generally shoulder-to-shoulder with the gang, but heavy enough to throw its weight around at the behest of others. A well-placed tool in the pantheon of power.

And the perfect tool it was to slither past the electric fence of the nucleus: where a cyclotron might hurl a positively charged particle past nuclear repulsion using tens of millions of electron volts, a neutron can simply amble in at ten thousand, there to nuzzle or destabilize to its heart's content.

In late 1931, when Gregor was at Ives & Myrick developing risk management, there *were* no neutrons. Twentieth-century atomic theory held that there were only two basic building blocks: heavy, positively charged protons in the nucleus, and light, negatively charged electrons, largely spinning round, planets in the nuclear solar system.

But after January 1932, thanks to James Chadwick, there *were* neutrons, heavy as protons but without a charge, neutrons out there in public consciousness, and neutrons swirling in the head of one Leo Szilard, Hungarian physicist skulking around London. In mid-September '33, he had a vision at an intersection, a green-means-go vision that drove him through the next six years, and drove human history into a potential abyss:

> As the light changed to green and I crossed the street, it suddenly occurred to me that if we could find an element which is split by neutrons and which would emit two neutrons when it absorbed one neutron, such an element, if assembled in sufficiently large mass, could sustain a nuclear chain reaction. I didn't see at the moment just how one would go about finding such an element or what experiments would be needed, but the idea never left me.

Here was a fateful intersection of concepts: both "nuclear chain reaction" and the "critical mass" needed to set off and sustain it, for only with many atoms close together could the particles attain an ejaculatory cascade. And what would come from a furiously expanding neutron burst? More neutrons, radiation, heat—and energy—explosive or controlled. The splitting of atoms. The world is headed for grief, the Hungarian thought.

Why would anyone want to split atoms? Well, as Fred Allen once said, someone might need half an atom. Gregor didn't want half an atom. He wanted power, beneficent power. He remembered his Einstein studies back in 1917. Using $E = mc^2$, Gregor had once calculated that 1 kilogram of coal, if converted entirely into energy, would yield 25 billion kilowatt-hours.

While Gregor dreamed of metaphorical power, Szilard was pondering how to bring that actually about, spending six unfruitful years wooing investors for trials splitting beryllium, indium, and thorium with neutrons. So when in January '39, at the Carnegie Institution in Washington, Niels Bohr announced Hahn and Strassmann's neutron splitting of uranium in Berlin, Szilard, now at Columbia, slapped his forehead and jumped on a train to get a firsthand report from his countryman Edward Teller.

Early in the afternoon of a cold, sunny Sunday, the day after the "Fifth Washington Meeting on Theoretical Physics" had ended, Gregor was lying on his back, taking in the sun on the institution's spacious grounds, unconcerned with the turmoil that had been released on Saturday. He had given himself the day off to celebrate Mozart's birthday. As he lay on a rock, absorbing the healing rays, playing the painful Masonic Funeral Music in his head and speculating on the mysteries of life in death, he heard voices coming closer, speaking—what was it?—Hungarian! He had spoken a smattering of that mysterious tongue in his European days, and sounds with meaning began to penetrate the Mozart and fatigue.

Szilard and Teller were walking the path along the edge of Rock Creek.

"He was mumbling and going on as usual," Teller reported. "One got only the general drift. But then Fermi took over and gave his usual elegant presentation of Meitner's notion of uranium splitting."

"Did Bohr agree?" Szilard asked.

"Yes, he did," said Gregor in Hungarian, as he sat up on his rock. *"Azt hiszem, igen."*

The physicists jumped, and the insect was embarrassed at surprising them.

"I'm sorry. It was in the *Star* last night. A report on the conference. It said Bohr and Fermi agree."

"Who are you?" Teller asked in English, tactfully moving the language away from Gregor's attempt at Hungarian.

"Oh, I am sorry again." Gregor jumped down off the rock to offer his claw. "Samsa, Gregor. I am pleased to meet you. And you."

"Leo Szilard."

"Edward Teller."

"Are you in physics?" Szilard wanted to know.

"No, I am researcher working at the White House." This, Gregor had decided, was the term that best described his sundry duties. Szilard's ears pricked up.

"The White House of President Roosevelt?"

"Exactly so."

"What do you research?"

"Slightly this, slightly that. Momentarily I am working on whales."

"Ah, a biologist."

"Whales in the White House?" Teller wanted to know.

"In the Natural History Museum."

Teller inspected Gregor, bushy brows over black eyes, and decided to change the subject.

"What else did the newspaper say?" he asked.

"It said the new discovery has no practical use for power source."

The two physicists looked at each other.

"Good!" exclaimed Szilard.

To evade Gregor's inevitable "Why good?" Teller thought it best to talk of something else.

"Why are you here, Mr. Samsa, at the Carnegie Institution?"

"It's one of my favorite spots. I like this rock very well. I come here for special things."

"And today's special thing?" asked Szilard.

"I am ashamed today's special thing is not today. I pretend this is January twenty-seventh."

They both looked at him quizzically.

"Mozart's birthday. I always celebrate."

Teller flew into an unexpected rage.

"I cannot understand, simply cannot understand why otherwise sane adults—presumably sane adults—and excuse me, I have no reason to suspect you are sane—or not sane—why these people—so many people!—why sane people worship this man and his trivial music, count him among the great treasures of the human race!"

"You don't like Mozart," Gregor summarized.

"I like running my fingers up and down the scales, the arpeggios, the stupid spelled-out chordal basses. The actual process of playing them is very enjoyable."

"Dr. Teller is a first-class pianist," Szilard commented.

"But you don't like chordal basses," Gregor allowed.

"Oom-pah-pah-pah, oom-pah-pah-pah predictable boring. A genius, perhaps, but no talent, absolutely no talent."

Gregor was stupefied.

"He is a Beethoven pianist," Szilard explained.

"You prefer Beethoven." Gregor was still catching up.

"Imponderable, Beethoven . . ." Teller commented. And he began to drift away in a strange decrescendo of ever-stronger, but ever-sparser, adjectives.

"Blunt . . . determined . . . tense . . . combative . . . belligerent . . ."

In the pauses one could hear the creek, and the occasional *cheer-up, cheerily, cheer-up, cheerily* of some early robin.

"Doom-foretelling . . . no concessions . . . not a concession . . . explosive . . ." Pianissimo now.

"Explosive . . ."

Gregor thought he had gone into some kind of semi-trance. Szilard, used to Teller's fanaticism, ignored the whole event.

"Grand, central fury . . ."

The three had begun walking southward without ever deciding to do so, strolling along the rambling banks of Rock Creek, peripatetically present at a madman's monologue. Teller's eyes were focused into psychic space, as if detoured into some difficult problem in quantum mechanics.

"Low predictability quotient . . . zero point one perhaps . . ."

Was he still on Beethoven?

They walked on in silence, the beginning of a four-mile stroll toward the Potomac in Georgetown. Teller came to and continued the interrupted conversation as if nothing had happened.

"So you are friends with the President? You get to talk with him?"

"How did you get this job?" Szilard inquired.

Over the next several hours, Gregor spun out his story to the intently curious scientists. And in exchange, parking themselves on a bench at the Tidal Basin, the Hungarians related a layman's version of "The Story of Nuclear Physics." Beginning with Becquerel's 1896 papers on radioactivity, and on through Curie's discovery of radium, Lawrence's cyclotron, Cockcroft's splitting of the atom, Chadwick's discovery of the neutron, and with his own conceptions of chain reaction and critical mass, Szilard, with Teller accompanying, played out the findings and errors that had led humanity to its fateful crossroads. The conversation paused at this pause in the world, and the three watched in silence as the steam-driven crane hoisted the last marble block of the day, pink with sunset, high up on the almost finished Jefferson Memorial. After a minute, Teller announced abruptly, "I'm cold. I have to go home." And to Szilard, "You are coming?"

The two men got up.

"Nice to meet you, Mr. . . . Samza, is it?"

"Thank you. It was nice to meet you, too."

Teller hailed a cab to take them to his Garfield Street home. Gregor sat for another hour till the sun went down, and street lamps came on in the approaching darkness. Then he walked across the Mall and through the Ellipse back to the White House.

As spring of 1939 put out its feelers and warmed toward the glory of cherry blossoms, Gregor noted with interest that the public was being bombarded with mixed messages about uranium fission, touted as "the greatest scientific discovery since radium." Science Service, a respected news agency, played down the risks:

> Physicists are anxious that there be no public alarm over the possibility of the world being blown to bits by their experiments. Writers and dramatists have overemphasized this idea. While they are proceeding with their experiments with proper caution, they feel that there is no real danger except perhaps in their own laboratories.

Also dismissed or minimized were "forecasts of the near possibility of running giant ocean liners across the Atlantic on the energy contained within the atoms of a glass of water," or of replacing steam engines with "atom-motors"; or suggestions that "the atomic energy may be used as some super-explosive, or as a military weapon." It was as if the greatest scientific discovery since radium had little or no import.

But Gregor had taken on Szilard's concerns: news from Europe indicated that German military expansion might soon overrun Belgium, whose colony in the Congo was the principal uranium source of the entire world.

Szilard's campaign for secrecy had few American targets: in the United States, almost no fission work was going on, and no research at all of the possibility of a nuclear chain reaction. Yet the Hungarian's fears were well founded: French disclosures did prompt German action. Once Joliot's "Number of Neutrons Liberated in the Nuclear Fission of Uranium" appeared in the April issue of *Nature,* the president of the German Bureau of Standards urged buying all uranium in Germany, banning exports, and negotiating contracts with Czech mines. In Hamburg, physical chemists alerted the War Office in Berlin to "the newest development in nuclear physics, which will likely make it possible to produce an explosive many orders of magnitude more powerful than conventional ones." Germany became the first country to study nuclear fission as possibly applied to weapons. In September 1939 her greatest remaining physicist, Werner Heisenberg, was exploring how the metal might be made to explode. There was definitely something to worry about.

At Columbia, Szilard begged and borrowed what equipment he

could to do rudimentary experiments in radiation physics. Among other experiments, he irradiated frankfurters and salami, and left them for months in a lab refrigerator, checking now and then to test their appearance and taste. While salami is a far cry from weapons, he was again years ahead of his time.

On Tuesday, July 11, 1939, Gregor's phone rang at seven-thirty in the morning.

"Samsa here."

"Szilard. How are you? Ready for a little trip?"

"Szilard! Where are you?"

"At the cyclotron lab. At Columbia."

"What kind of a trip?"

"We go hunting."

"I don't like hunting. I don't kill things, any kind of animals."

"That's good, Samsa, but this is man-hunting, and I guarantee you'll enjoy it. Pack a bag for a couple of days, and be out on Pennsylvania Avenue at two o'clock. Teller will pick you up. You'll be driving up to Princeton and stay overnight at Wigner's. He's a great mathematician. You'll like him."

"What man do we hunt?"

"Tomorrow morning you and Wigner and Teller will pick me up at my place, and we'll drive out to Long Island . . ."

"Yes?"

". . . to visit an old friend of yours, the Professor."

"I don't know professors on Long Island."

"I didn't say you knew him, I just said he was your friend. Trust me, Samsa. I'll see you tomorrow morning early."

And he hung up. A typical Szilard move, the kind that made him an outcast in polite society.

At precisely two P.M., the precise Edward Teller pulled over to the curb in front of the White House gate. Gregor threw his small cardboard suitcase in the backseat and climbed in. They headed north on Fifteenth Street.

"Where are we going?" the passenger asked.

"Wigner's."

"I mean where are we going tomorrow?"

"To meet with Einstein."

"*Albert* Einstein?" He was afraid of another Izzy.

"You know any other Einsteins?"

Gregor could barely contain his excitement. His early admiration for the scientist and thinker had grown into worship for the philosopher and humanitarian, the socially committed, self-sacrificing, generous, and idealistic mensch.

"Why . . . are we going? Why to Long Island? I thought he was at Princeton."

"Wigner called his secretary and wheedled his vacation hideout. The old man needs better protection."

"Why am I going? Who am I to . . . ?"

"You're going because you know the President. You're our in–White House expert."

"Expert on what? I'm expert on nothing."

"Expert on what the President is like, what he listens to, what kind of thing will get his attention."

"Why do we need his attention? Is this another idea of Leo's?"

"We are going to trump Hitler on the bomb."

"What is trump?"

"You don't play bridge."

"Is it a card game?"

"Yes."

"No."

"That's because you're not a physicist."

"What is trump?"

"Trump is when you get the better of someone. Surprise them."

"We are going to surprise Hitler?"

"And ourselves. You'll see. Be patient."


Teller switched on the radio as they drove north through Chevy Chase and Bethesda. They heard the tail end of the Beethoven First Symphony.

The driver seemed impassive, so Gregor ventured, "I take it you don't like scales. Too predictable?"

"Don't be stupid. Was that predictable?"

"No."

"Don't insult Beethoven."

Gregor sulked. Though he had no high regard for his own intelligence, he was not used to being called stupid. *Eine Kleine Nachtmusik* came on.

"Now *that's* stupid," Teller remarked as he switched off the radio.

"It may not be ultimate profound, but how you can call it stupid? What is stupid?"

"Not the music. It's stupid to play *Nachtmusik* at three o'clock in the afternoon. They think Mozart didn't know what time it was?"

Gregor vowed never to engage Teller on music again.

Baltimore. Wilmington. Philadelphia. Trenton. Gregor was fascinated by the signs, the changing landscape, the surging traffic. Turning off Route 1, they swung east through dark, lush woodland and pulled into Princeton Junction. Teller called Wigner from a pay phone for directions to his house. The exhausted travelers were trundled, with little ceremony, into guest-room beds. They had to be up early.

Five A.M. Change cars. Through the Jersey woods and flats in Wigner's light blue Chevy. Over the George Washington Bridge to the Upper West Side and Leo Szilard's hotel near Columbia. It was a sparkling morning, already hot, as they drove across the new Triborough Bridge and past the New York World's Fair with its seven-hundred-foot-high Trylon representing "the finite" counterposed against a two-hundred-foot perisphere representing "the infinite." As the others made no lascivious comments, Gregor, too, was silent.

Szilard went into a hilarious monologue concerning his visit to the fair on opening day in April. "Building the World of Tomorrow." Never, he said, was American inanity so succinctly displayed. A brave new world of corporations. A display of air-conditioning by the Carrier Corporation in—what else?—a 100-meter-diameter pseudo-igloo. Many missed the point of Dupont's "Wonders of Chemistry" displayed in nylon on the shapely legs of half-naked models. Pickle pin souvenirs at the Heinz Pavilion, and "Mickey's Surprise Party," a cartoon about a mouse with gloves shown by the National Biscuit Company, followed by mouse crackers, of course. There was the Life Savers parachute tower, a triple mixed metaphor, and a pavilion where you could place long-distance calls for free, except no one knew anyone else's long-distance number. There was a Westinghouse robot that swept a floor, pushing the dirt around and around, including candy wrappers thrown by children, and twenty-one model homes, none of which would last more than five years, nor would you want to live in any of them. And most depressing and moronic of all, "Futurama," a depiction by General Motors of the world as it will be in 1960, if people will be able to breathe that long, given all the cars. Szilard had come away with a souvenir pin that said "I have seen the future." The funny thing was—he had.

Two Hungarians and a Czech. Both driver and navigator had IQs one and a half times higher than their weights, so naturally, once out on the Island, they became hopelessly lost. Driver and navigator confused the Indian names and drove to Patchogue on the south shore, instead of to Cutchogue, on the north, a detour that took two hot, sweaty hours. Finally in Peconic, their secret destination, they drove around asking vacationers in bathing suits the way to "a Dr. Moore's cottage." Strangely enough, no one seemed to know.

"Let's give it up and go home," Szilard whined from the backseat, a far cry from yesterday morning's mischievous enthusiasm. "This is fate. It might be a terrible mistake obtaining Einstein's help to apply to the government. Once the government sets its claws on something . . ."

Gregor felt indicted.

Wigner insisted they go on with their quest. "This is ridiculous," he said. "Every child knows Einstein." Szilard, perhaps cynical, perhaps consulting the child within, had a bright idea: "So why don't we ask a child? There's one over there. Pull over." A sunburned boy of seven was standing at a drugstore corner intent on tying a float on his fishing rod. Szilard leaned out the window:

"Sonny!" The boy looked up. "Do you know where Dr. Einstein lives?"

"Of course." He looked at them with scorn for the generic stupidity of adults, and pointed the way around the next corner.

The strange musketeers drove up to a two-story white cottage at the terminus of a dead-end lane and saw Einstein out in back, in torn undershirt and rolled-up pants, pulling a small dinghy onto the backyard shore. Friendly hails in German. Gregor was introduced, his heart beating madly in his back, like that of any teenage girl breathless with adoration. "I am honored to meet you," the great man said. Gregor gave a bashful smile and felt faint.

The Professor invited his visitors to a cool screened porch overlooking the Sound, and brought iced tea for all.

"So, gentlemen, what can I do for you?"

Szilard, Teller, and Wigner presented a short seminar on the latest advances in nuclear research to a wild-haired, undershirted elderly man who had not been *au courant* for years, a man whose attention was directed solely at the mathematics of his unified field theory. They told him how neutrons were behaving these days, how uranium bombarded by neutrons had been made to split or "fission," and how this might create nuclear chain reactions and nuclear bombs. $E = mc^2$. His reaction was classic Einstein:

*"Daran habe ich gar nicht gedacht."* I haven't thought of that at all.

The Professor had believed atomic energy would not be released in his lifetime, that it was only "theoretically possible." He puffed on his pipe.

His next utterance was philosophical: "If this works, it would be the first source of energy that does not depend on the sun." The others nodded dutifully.

The talk became political. Hitler was both lubricant and catalyst. Within half an hour, pacifist Einstein had reluctantly agreed to sound some kind of alarm about atomic bombs to beat Nazi Germany to this frightful weapon. "You cannot create peace by preparing for war," he warned. But Szilard was convincing: "If we make the bomb, and Hitler knows we have done that, he will be afraid to use his, and we will not have to use ours."

"What shall we do? I could warn the Queen about the Congo mines."

"Good, but not enough," Szilard urged. "You must write to President Roosevelt to warn him. We have to begin large research. Industrial size. Only the government has enough money."

"This will be expensive," Einstein offered.

"More expensive than pencils and pads." Teller's bitter jibe at theoreticians.

"What am I to write?"

Szilard picked up his briefcase from the side of his chair. "I brought along some drafts, in case you were willing. I have a short letter and a long letter—just to give you an idea." They held their breaths. The old man was not offended.

"Let me see."

He carefully read both, while his visitors discreetly followed his expressions.

"Will it be better to send a short letter or a long one?"

Here Gregor was able to offer some expertise. "My suggestion is you write to catch the President's attention, short, and if he is interested, you make a full presenting with all facts. That is how he likes working."

It sounded good to all of them.

"What about others, other physicists?" Einstein asked.

"Everyone is afraid to make a fool of himself, to initiate any kind of action. You are not."

"That is because everyone knows already I am a fool."

"So," Wigner observed, "your position is unique."

They all laughed.

Einstein agreed to write something and submit it to the group next week for approval, and the crusaders left with elevated heart rates.

Back in Princeton, Einstein requested another meeting the following week. Teller and Gregor went up; Szilard came down. Over the next month drafts were sent back and forth to develop a compromise document, shorter than long, but longer than short. Physicists have a deep need for data. At least experimental physicists. The final, famous document began as follows:

```
Albert Einstein
Old Grove Rd. Nassau Point
Peconic, Long Island
August 2nd, 1939


F. D. Roosevelt,
President of the United States
White House
Washington, D.C.

Sir,
   Some recent work by E. Fermi and L. Szilard, which
has been communicated to me in manuscript, leads me to
expect that the element uranium may be turned into a new
and important source of energy in the immediate
future. . . .
```

It imagined a possible nuclear chain reaction in uranium, which might lead to the construction of a new type of bomb. It suggested large-scale government work to investigate this possibility before the Germans did. It spoke of watchfulness and recommended quick action. It set a ball slowly rolling that would gather speed enough to shatter worlds.

The next step was to find a carrier, since Gregor warned that mail often got lost in the huge, but overstuffed, in-box. Who would be best to hand-deliver it? Only Einstein + Hungarians could come up with the idea of Charles A. Lindbergh. He was famous. He was a hero. The President would not overlook a message from him. So Szilard wrote Lindbergh a letter: They had "once met at lunch about seven years ago at the Rockefeller Institute," he reminded the flyer, "but I assume that you do not remember me, and I am therefore enclosing an introduction from Prof. Einstein." Intriguing beginning. Einstein's note asked Lindbergh "to receive my friend Dr. Szilard and to consider carefully what he has to tell you."

The crusaders waited impatiently for an answer. Five weeks passed. Like most Americans, Szilard tuned in to Lindbergh's first major radio address, hoping to glean some hint of his intentions. Carried by all three networks, Mutual, National Broadcasting, and Columbia Broadcasting, this analysis of the international crisis was heard by the largest audience ever for any single speech—and in it, Lindbergh denounced Roosevelt as a warmonger for his efforts to amend the Neutrality Act in order to sell arms to the beleaguered nations abroad. After listening, Szilard called Einstein with his rueful conclusion: "I am afraid he is not our man."

Who else? Compton at MIT? No. Too proper. He would be put off by Szilard. Who then? After more wrangling about academic politics, they came up with a compromise dark horse: Gregor. After all, he lived in the White House, he was on a first-name basis with the President, he could stay on top of the matter to see that it was not ignored.

Some have greatness thrust upon them. Gregor argued that he was just a lower-level functionary with nowhere near the clout of any of the other candidates, and that he was already in trouble with the President over their differences concerning Jewish refugees. In fact, he thought he was possibly "on the outs"—his most recently learned idiom. No matter. There were few other choices. He accepted his assignment.

It was October 11 by the time Gregor made his way to the outer vestibule of the Oval Office for his five forty-five appointment with the President. Fifteen minutes, just before dinner. He had better talk quickly. But instead of ushering him immediately in, FDR's aide, General Edwin ("Pa") Watson, asked to see the materials Gregor was lugging. Then he got on the phone and summoned two ordnance experts, Army Colonel Keith Adamson and Navy Commander Gilbert Hoover, to join them in the vestibule. The military men looked over the documents, then all four were ushered into the Oval Office. It was already six-ten. Good thing the Roosevelts were always late for dinner.

"Dr. Samsa, what are you up to?" the President asked, looking at the folders cradled in Gregor's four arms. He seemed to have forgotten, or at least forgiven, their last major encounter. Gregor had never seen FDR so tired; he was alarmed by the grayness. He imagined the exhausting struggle of moving from bed to wheelchair. Dozens of times a day this huge man had to heave his aging, crippled body around in the unending burdens of office: a constant stream of people to be seen, decisions to be made, correspondence to be read and answered, newspapermen to persuade, all this in the ever present context of prolonged depression, and global problems of unprecedented scale. Roosevelt looked tired unto death.

"What bright idea have you got now, my friend?"

With his chin, Gregor pushed Einstein's letter off the top of the top pile of folders, dropping it unceremoniously on FDR's desk.

"Sorry, that was awkward. I didn't mean to be rude."

"Believe me, I know what it's like to have my hands full."

One could see in this response why the President was so well liked—unless he was hated. Gregor handed the upper pile to Colonel Anderson, and the lower to Commander Hoover, who each began perusing them as FDR read Einstein's message. When the President finished, he looked up at Gregor. In his role as staff scientist, Gregor launched into a well-rehearsed but poorly delivered sermon on nuclear fission. After several minutes, Roosevelt interrupted him:

"Gregor, what you are after is to see that the Nazis don't blow us up."

"Precisely."

The President got on the intercom and asked his secretary to bring some brandy all around. When the general had served the four and poured a snifter for himself, Roosevelt, indicating the letter on his desk, said tersely, "Pa, this requires action. Call Briggs at Standards, get a committee together to study this uranium business."


The Uranium Committee Report arrived on November 1. It noted that "if the reaction turns out to be explosive in character, it would provide a possible source of bombs with a destructiveness vastly greater than anything now known," and recommended "adequate support for a thorough investigation." The President read it carefully and put it on file—and on file it remained, until well into 1940. Roosevelt had other things on his mind, political matters—like the November election. It had been a huge decision whether to run for an unprecedented third term. And for the first time in his career, he was in serious political trouble. While America did not want to go to war, Roosevelt—perhaps in part because of Amadeus's letter—privately thought it inevitable, a dynamic that did not escape his enemies.

## 28. WARS *of the* WORLDS III: *Of this* WORLD *and the* NEXT

Elections bring out the worst in people—the duplicity of dignitaries, the gullibility of the electorate. Will Rogers noted that "no party is as bad as its leaders." Franklin Roosevelt and Wendell Willkie were both extraordinary men—still, when chips were down and each thought he might come up short, cigar smoke vied with mirrors, and tactics became devious all around.

In 1940, FDR chose to run against Hitler (with Willkie a poor third), and as President-During-International-Crisis, he defined the territory. Willkie, though equally committed to defeating Nazism, ran as a "peace candidate," accusing FDR of sneaking the country into war, while the President, knowing war was coming, promised to keep the peace. The spin-meisters were whirling like dervishes, and Gregor was disgusted. The radical thrust of the New Deal was forgotten as the powerful flexed their muscles, and a gullible public gorged on confusion.

By the week before election, Gregor needed a place to hide. October 27 was the closing day of the World's Fair, and ever since hearing Szilard, the roach had been curious about "The World of Tomorrow"—the official version. On that closing Sunday, he took the six A.M. train to New York and got to the fairgrounds shortly after one. It was a cold, wet, gray day, but, as expected, the most crowded day of the fair.

Crowded, but melancholy. The fair had opened in brightest hope, and was now closing amidst crises and fear of war. It had been a financial failure, too, with much money owed, and as Brecht observed, in America, this is the greatest crime. For all the razzmatazz, later attendees felt flustered in a flustered land.

For Gregor, it was another performance, a static one, where only the audience moved. Initially suspicious, Szilard still in his ear, he found himself pleasantly surprised, even excited, perhaps even thrilled by this hollow-filled space with its still, large voice. Compared to his other worlds, this seemed to be life in a new region, a death-night perhaps, pace Szilard, but a brightly illumined one, boasting of clairvoyance.

. . .

On this closing day, lines were impossibly long for all the major exhibits: it would be hours before Gregor could get into Futurama, and he had to leave by five to catch the last train back at seven. So he stood for a long time, just taking in the scene, thinking thoughts as gray as the day. He was facing the courtyard of the Westinghouse building, a huge affair, an omega lying on its side, the last letter of the Greek alphabet opening its legs to a penetrating central tower. It was as if the whole fair had been designed by Frat Boys for Freud.

Omega, why omega? Ah! The symbol for electrical resistance, the ohm. Westinghouse. Electrical. Omega for ohm, the resistance, say, of a human body in an electric chair. But perhaps it wasn't for ohm. Perhaps it was just what it was, an omega, the last Greek letter, the end. From the first day of the fair, the building lay there warning: In the beginning is the end. Prepare.

He shook his head and pressed his sides with his middle arms to force a spiracular sigh. "This is silliness thinking. It's only a courtyard-making shape." And with the shaking off, he noticed the crowds of people peering at something on the ground.

Gregor wandered over and sifted through to center. The "something" was a hole, just a hole, somewhat under a foot in diameter, a dark hole into the earth. Ah! The Time Capsule! He had read about this. Several articles. He pulled back to the outside of the circle and looked around for some explanatory words. And there they were, surrounding a cutaway reproduction in a Plexiglas tube. Gregor studied the text. In September 1938, this metal cylinder had been installed in its "Immortal Well," there to rest for five thousand years, until 6939. 6939! Fingers twitch at writing such a date, and so did Gregor twitch and shudder, casting his thoughts in that direction. So much trivial was lodged therein, just as Szilard had said. A Mickey Mouse cup, a rhinestone clip from the five-and-dime. Was a mouse clothed and shod the symbol of our civilization, a central artifact for future anthropologists? Gregor bought a copy of the beautifully printed instructions for finding and interpreting the capsule. On its title page:

THE BOOK OF RECORD OF

THE

**TIME CAPSULE**

OF CUPALOY

DEEMED CAPABLE OF RESISTING

THE EFFECTS OF TIME FOR FIVE

THOUSAND YEARS. PRESERVING

AN ACCOUNT OF UNIVERSAL

ACHIEVEMENTS. EMBEDDED IN

THE GROUNDS OF THE

NEW YORK WORLD'S FAIR

1939

SEPTEMBER 23, 1938

In The World of Tomorrow, a freezing of the Cherished Now. Gregor sat down on a bench and leafed through his purchase, increasingly amazed. A little girl tugged on her mother's arm: "Mommy, look at the big bug reading a book!" Mommy shushed her and pushed her on into the courtyard.

The Book of Record began with a quote from Job, in small italics centered on the page: "All the days of my appointed time will I wait, till my change come. Thou shalt call, and I will answer thee." Gregor stared, almost shattered. His mouthparts dropped. Why this? Why this quote? Me. This book is aimed at me.

He carefully turned the next page. On the left, a drawing of the omega, with an outsized capsule pictured deep under the ground between its feet. On the right, a red, gorgeous, illuminated initial "W":

W HEN WE SURVEY THE PAST and note how perishable are all human things, we are moved to attempt the preservation of some of the world's present material & intellectual symbols, that knowledge of them may not disappear from the earth.

For there is no way to read the future of the world: peoples, nations, and cultures move onward into inscrutable time. In our day it is difficult to conceive of a future less happy, less civilized than our own. Yet history teaches us that every culture passes through definite cycles of development, climax, and decay. And so, we must recognize, ultimately may ours.

Who wrote this? Spengler's ghost? Surely this book was not a corporate message of—what did Szilard call it? American inanity in a Brave New World?

Gregor spent the next three hours in Talmudic study of this thin volume—as if it were holy writ, a cabalistic coding of mysteries. He read of the PREPARATION OF THE CAPSULE, of the consultations with "archaeologists, historians, metallurgists, engineers, chemists, geophysicists, and other technical men of our time." He marveled that Cupaloy had been created, non-ferrous and extremely hard, an amalgam which "in electrolytic reactions with ferrous metals in the soil, becomes the anode and therefore will receive deposits, rather than suffer corrosion." Science! This marvelous metal had been cast in seven segments (the mystic seven!) seven feet in total length, seven segments containing a Pyrex glass envelope to enclose its artifacts in an atmosphere of nitrogen:

> The materials inside the crypt have been selected for permanence and have been treated, so far as possible, to give them resistance to time. Material which would ordinarily be published in books has been photographed on acetate microfilm; a method that not only promises permanence but also makes possible the concentration of much information in small space. Metal parts which might be subject to attack by moisture have been coated with a thin layer of wax. No acids or corrosive substances are included in the crypt's contents or in the materials with which the Time Capsule is sealed, nor are any materials included which are known to decay or dissociate into corrosive liquids or vapors.

There it was—the secret of human striving, the quest for immortality, live burial with not only hope, but instruction for resurrection. And next,

RECOVERY OF THE CAPSULE, speech across the millennia to those who will read no English—if they read at all. My God, what presumption, what chutzpah to suppose that someone in the appointed year—"the 6,939 year since the birth of Christ, year 10,699 of the Jewish calendar, the 36th year of the 160th Chinese cycle, the 6,469th year since the birth of Mohammed the Prophet, the 7,502nd birthday of Buddha, the 7,599th anniversary of the first Shinto emperor, Jimmu Tenno"—what magnificent gall to order that world (should there still be a world) around.

When to dig, you ask? You future beings. Why, when the heliocentric longitudes of the planets on January 1 match the listed table, a combination of astronomical events unlikely to recur for many thousand years.

Where? Where to dig, should you care to dig? Latitude 40 degrees, 44 minutes, 34.089 seconds north of the Equator; longitude 73 degrees, 50 minutes, 43.842 seconds west of Greenwich, coordinates "accurate enough to locate an object one-tenth of a foot or less in diameter at a particular position of the surface of the earth.

"When it has been brought up out of the ground, let the finders beware, lest in their eagerness they spoil the contents by ill-considered moves." Ill-considered. Will there still be such a notion? "Let the Capsule be transported with the utmost care, at once, to a warm, dry place. Cleanse the outside of mud, slime, or corrosion. Then cut off the top carefully at the deeply scored groove which has been left to guide the saw. Should gas rush out when the saw penetrates the crypt, let there be no alarm, for this is a harmless gas enclosed as a preservative." The hortatory subjunctive. This is how we address our savior-heirs.

The tension was building, page by lovely page. What, thought Gregor, what other than Mickey Mouse will represent us to our accommodating friends? Ah, THE CONTENTS OF THE CAPSULE.

WITHIN the limitations imposed by space, the problems of preservation, and the difficulty of choosing the truly significant to represent all the enormous variety and vigor of our life, we have sought to deposit in the Time Capsule materials and information touching upon all the principal categories of our thought, activity and accomplishment; sparing nothing, neither our wisdom nor our foolishness, our supreme achievements, nor our recognized weaknesses.

And these were microfilmed books and pictures showing how and where we live; our offices and factories; machines that write, compute, and tabulate. Arts and entertainment were represented, newspapers and magazines, cartoons and comics. And not to be forgotten: descriptions of the world's principal philosophies, the educational systems for inculcating them, and a copy of the U.S. Constitution.

Gregor read, with special interest, how

> Our scientists have measured the speed of light, and compared the distances of the planets, stars, and nebulae; they have fathomed the ultimate composition of matter and its relation to energy, transmuted the elements, harnessed earthquake, electricity, and magnetism; they have shifted the atoms in their lattices and created dyes, materials, stuffs that Nature herself forgot to make. The stories of these achievements have been set forth in the Time Capsule.

Forgot, he pondered. How relieved she must be that someone has remembered. He read how

> Our engineers & inventors have harnessed the forces of the earth and skies and the mysteries of nature to make our lives pleasant, swift, safe, and fascinating beyond any previous age. Over wires pour cataracts of invisible electric power, tamed and harnessed to light our homes, cook our food, cool and clean our air, operate the machines of our homes & factories, lighten the burdens of our daily labor, & work a major part of all the complex magic of our day.
>
> We have made metals our slaves, and learned to change their characteristics to our needs. . . .

And lines from *Faust* came charging his giant ganglia, just as his pamphlet described: "We speak to one another along a network of radiations that enmesh the globe, and hear one another thousands of miles away. . . ." Hello? Goethe here.

> *Da steh ich nun, ich armer Tor!*
> *Und bin so klug als wie zuvor;*

And here, poor fool! with all my lore
I stand no wiser than before,

and then,

*Es irrt der Mensch, so lang er strebt*–Man errs whenever he strives. But the Capsule pamphlet forgot to mention that.

> All these things, and the secrets of them, and something about the men
> of genius of our time and earlier days who helped bring them about, will
> be found in the Time Capsule.

Gregor sampled the products of farms, he was informed of plants never seen in nature. A love song there was to "the many small articles we wear or use that contribute to our pleasure, comfort, safety, convenience– articles with which we write, play, groom ourselves, correct our vision, re- move our beards, illuminate our homes and workplaces, tell time, make pictures, calculate sums, protect property, train our children, and prepare our food. There were specimens of modern cosmetics, "and one of the singular clothing creations of our time, a woman's hat." He had never seen Alice wear one.

There was silliness in all of this: certainly enough to evoke Szilard's scorn. And yet, and yet . . . Was not this place of corporate power still, and even more, a place of love? Always, always much more love? Was it not a prophesying place, a place of dreamlike representation? In our country's state of obscurity and fear, is there not also, all around, some condition of expectancy? Gregor remembered a trenchant melody from Kierkegaard: "If I were permitted one wish, I would wish for neither riches nor power but for the passion of Possibility; I would only wish for an eye that was eternally young and eternally glowing with the desire to see Possibility." Here it was, milling and being milled around him. Look at the eyes on that little boy staring up at the Trylon . . .

> Each age considers itself the pinnacle & final triumph above all eras
> that have gone before. In our time many believe that the human race

has reached the ultimate in material and social development; others, that humanity shall march onward to achievements splendid beyond the imagination of this day, to new worlds of human wealth, power, life, and happiness. We choose, with the latter, to believe that men will solve the problems of the world, that the human race will triumph over its limitations and its adversities, that the future will be glorious.

## TO THE PEOPLE OF THAT FUTURE
## WE LEAVE THIS LEGACY

Time Capsule. Seismograph of self.

*Verweile doch, du bist so schön.* Gregor found himself weeping. "Stay awhile, you are so fair"–the one thought forbidden Faust, the thought that would trigger his eternal night.

For Gregor, too, it was an outlawed fantasy–that this world, with its petty vagaries, its conniving souls, all teeth at throat, that this vale of tears was worthy of love; that human life–solitary, poor, nasty, brutish, and short–was to be honored and obeyed. Why bother? For Mickey Mouse? And yet he wept. He wept for the sewer of uncertainty and terror that was his life and the lives of those around him and of those across the seas; he wept for an ungrateful biped resistant to transformation; he wept for the metamorphoses that might never come about–not so much for their absence as for their potential to sweep all this away–the wires and the comic books, the Bible and the cars, the "many small articles that we wear and use . . ."

Vanity, all is vanity, and yet not so. He looked around at the sad yet marveling crowd, and he found them lovable, all lovable in their sadness, and lovable in their awe. He thought of George Orwell. 1984 was forty-five years away, not five thousand: "If you want a picture of the future, imagine a boot stomping on a human face–forever."

"No!" he screamed out, and the crowd at the hole turned around and stared–but only briefly. There was nothing he could do but leave.

.  .  .

On the subway to Penn Station, he looked at the other passengers and leafed listlessly through the little book that had brought him so high and so low. At the end, a section called "Messages for the Future from Noted Men of Our Time." There were only three short statements: Robert Millikan thought that "if the rational, scientific, progressive principles win out in the struggle against despotism, there is the possibility of a warless, golden age ahead for mankind." More science, less war: Gregor was doubtful. Albert Einstein was something less than cheery: "Present production and distribution of commodities is entirely unorganized so that everybody must live in fear of being eliminated from the economic cycle. Furthermore, people living in different countries kill each other at irregular time intervals, so that also for this reason anyone who thinks about the future must live in fear and terror." It was Thomas Mann who spoke evocatively of a strange continuity with the citizens of the future, people who "will actually resemble us very much as we resemble those who lived a thousand, or five thousand, years ago. Among you too the spirit will fare badly—it should never fare too well on this earth, otherwise men would need it no longer." Something glimmered in Gregor's ganglia, but he was too exhausted to fan the flame. His trip home was indolent and slack, a small hibernation against the chills.

The next day, October 28, at Madison Square Garden, Roosevelt, self-styled Man of Peace, took full credit for the neutrality legislation of the 1930s, laws he had fought ferociously to block in Congress.

In Boston, two days later, he said, "And while I am talking to you mothers and fathers, I give you one more assurance. I have said this before, but I shall say it again and again and again: Your boys are not going to be sent into any foreign wars."

"That hypocritical son of a bitch!" Willkie exclaimed. "This is going to beat me!"

On Monday before the election, Henry Wallace, with Roosevelt's approval, made the following remarks: "Every sign of opposition to the President leads to rejoicing in Berlin. I do not wish to imply that the Republican leaders are willfully or consciously giving aid and comfort to

Hitler, but I do want to emphasize that replacement of Roosevelt, even if it were by the most patriotic leadership that could be found, would cause Hitler to rejoice."


Votes: for Roosevelt, 27,243,466; for Willkie, 22,304,755.
States: for Roosevelt, 38; for Willkie, 10.

## 29. WARS *of the* WORLDS IV:
## ORIENTALIA

On the morning of December 7, 1941, in ancient samurai tradition, Japanese war planes bombed American forces at Pearl Harbor. It was the most brilliantly conceived and executed surprise attack in the history of warfare, killing more than 2,400 American sailors, marines, and civilians, wounding 1,178 more, destroying 149 planes, sinking the battleships *Arizona, Tennessee, West Virginia,* and *California,* capsizing the *Oklahoma,* and running the *Nevada* aground—all at the cost of thirty Japanese lives.

The next day, following an address by the President, it took only thirty-four minutes of debate for Congress to declare war on Japan. Three days later Germany and Italy declared war against the United States, and Congress reciprocated.

The following weeks were truly frightening for Americans. The day after Pearl Harbor, Japanese forces attacked Guam and Wake Island, strategic U.S. protectorates, and within a week, all resistance had been defeated. On December 10, British carriers were sunk, and on Christmas Day, Hong Kong surrendered to Japanese military. Two days later, Manila was occupied, and U.S. troops were forced to flee to the fortress of Corregidor on Bataan.

Panic reigned. A Japanese invasion of the West Coast seemed imminent; there were nightly rumors and alarms. Cities and towns from San Diego to Seattle were blacked out; antiaircraft guns fired sporadically. In the five days following Pearl Harbor, the FBI rounded up some sixteen thousand "subversives" on the West Coast, most Japanese, some 1,200 German and Italian seamen. Gregor was most upset. "It is one thing," he thought, "to protect against sabotage, but much another thing to throw out of work honest and loyal people who are of another accident of birth. In fighting fascism, we must not let fascism happen here." And he told this to the President.

The President agreed. But others did not. Continuing Allied losses in the Pacific fed national paranoia; fears of a Japanese invasion increased.

The press fed all fires, left and right. The *Los Angeles Times* editorialized as follows:

## THE QUESTION OF JAPANESE-AMERICANS

A viper is nonetheless a viper wherever the egg is hatched. A leopard's spots are the same and its disposition is the same wherever it is whelped. So a Japanese-American, born of Japanese parents, nurtured upon Japanese traditions, living in a transplanted Japanese atmosphere and thoroughly inoculated with Japanese thoughts, almost inevitably grows up to be a Japanese, not an American in his thoughts, in his ideas, and in his ideals, and himself is a potential and menacing, if not an actual, danger to our country unless properly supervised, controlled and, as it were, hamstrung.

Needless to say, such media exertions took their toll. There were many attacks on Japanese men, women, and children. Law enforcement was reluctant to take up their cause, or even protect them—sheriffs had to run for office next election. State and local government urged the Administration to take action, in order to avoid vigilante activity. Congressmen pressed for forced evacuation.

The result was the famous—infamous—Executive Order 9066, issued on February 19 in which the President authorized "the Secretary of War, and the Military Commanders whom he may designate, to prescribe military areas in such places as he or the appropriate Military Commander may determine, from which any or all persons may be excluded." In addition, "The Secretary of War is hereby authorized to provide for the residents of any such area who are excluded therefrom, such transportation, food, shelter, and other accommodations as may be necessary in the judgement of the Secretary of War, or the said Military Commander." In other words, all Japanese in the western half of all coastal states would be "provided" with relocation and internment centers for the duration.

Gregor was horrified. It was yet another version of the *St. Louis* story, paranoia and selfishness run rampant. In a handwritten note to the President on February 20, he wrote,

```
I am heartbroken over your decision concerning the
Japanese Americans. It is two days until George Washing-
ton's anniversary. What would he say?
    Discouraged,
    your friend,
    Gregor Samsa
```

The very next day, there was an answer in his mailbox:

```
                    THE WHITE HOUSE
                    WASHINGTON, D.C.
Dear Samsa,
    I am sorry you are so disturbed by the Executive
Order, but I am a practical man. What must be done to
defend the country must be done. Public opinion seems to
be behind this, so there is no question of any
substantial opposition which might tend to disunity. We
are all doing the best we can.


    FDR
```

For the next days, Gregor took his angry despair to the monuments of the Mall. On Friday, he visited the whale again at Natural History, on Saturday, the Greco paintings at the National Gallery, and on Sunday, Washington's birthday, the Monument. Gazing southeast from the windows at the top, he scanned the buildings along Independence Avenue: Agriculture, the Smithsonian Castle, the Freer... The Freer! Why hadn't he thought of it before? He skittered like lightning down the stairs, beating the elevator by fifty feet.

The Freer Gallery in the thirties and forties held the premier collection of Oriental art in the United States, perhaps in all the West, works collected by Charles Freer, freightcar magnate, and donated to the government in '23. Gregor would drink in the wisdom of the East, a most apt balm for his current weeping of wound and soul. He made his way through the arcaded corridor to the Western galleries, turned into the room marked JAPAN, and was immediately dazzled by the gold leaf and pigments of Yeitoku's mystical screens. In front of *Pines on Wintry Mountains,* he heard in his inner ear the pregnant opening of "Der Abschied," last and greatest song in his favorite of favorites, *Das Lied von der Erde.*

Afflicted with a soon-to-be-fatal heart disease, having finished his colossal Eighth, haunted with the terminal history of ninth symphonies, Mahler had written these songs to forestall his fate. Into them he poured his threshold vision of life in transit to death. "Der Abschied" was the goodbye, the one-way journey up the mountain, the transition to eternity. Such thoughts sent shivers through Gregor's heart. *Pines on Wintry Mountains* . . . he could hear the *"ewig"*-singing clouds. He stood there for forty-five minutes, coming to balance.

Enough. He turned to go. At the doorway of the screen room his eye caught sight of—what? a monk? a Buddhist monk?—anyway, a young man in a saffron robe, meditating on something in a corner cabinet across the hall. Drawn by the monk's gaze, he tiptoed over to see the object. The robed figure was so close to the cabinet, Gregor had to peer delicately over his shoulder while trying not to interrupt his communion.

Beautifully mounted on green silk was a piece of parchment about four inches wide and eighteen inches long. Six fiercely painted characters—Chinese or Japanese, Gregor didn't know—ran from top to bottom, bold, assertive, each ideogram calling out its unique being while still evoking the chain of which it was a part. Gregor peeked around the meditator's waist to check the brass plate on the display:

CALLIGRAPHY ATTRIBUTED TO FU SHAN (1607–1684)

Not too helpful. Sounds Chinese. Is this the Chinese room? Is this a Chinese monk?

Having a large cockroach peer in around one's waist might be enough to break concentration of the deepest meditator, and the man moved aside with a gesture signifying "Your turn."

"Oh. Oh, thank you," said Gregor. "I didn't mean to interrupt."

"You can't interrupt. It's all one piece."

Gregor felt he was being offered the edge of some great wisdom—but it was awkward to inquire in this public setting.

"I'm sorry. I pushed you aside."

"Perhaps you need to see this."

"Maybe I do, but—I can't read it. Do you know what it says? I recognize that character, 'heart'—it looks like a heart, but I don't know the others. Are they Chinese or Japanese?"

"They're Chinese, classical, seventeenth century, but most are quite similar in Japanese. No problem reading them. Especially after three years, Chinese Studies major at UCLA."

"You? What is 'UCLA'? A temple?"

"Hell no, it's a big university. University of California–Los Angeles. You're not from here?"

"I . . . I'm living here now fifteen years or such, but I have not been to California or Los Angeles. And since we are talking so much, maybe I should introduce myself. Gregor Samsa."

He held out his claw. The yellow monk student placed palms together and bowed deeply. Gregor wasn't sure if he was serious or making fun.

"Yoshio Miyaguchi. You can call me Josh. Novice at Nipponzan Nyohoji Temple, on Sixteenth Street. Forty-nine hundred block. Where are you from?"

"Here. In Washington. I live on Pennsylvania Avenue."

"Where on Pennsylvania?"

"Sixteen hundred block."

"Sixteen hundred block? There's nothing there but the White House."

"That's were I live. In the basement. In the kitchen."

"Are you a cook?"

"No. I just live there. I help out what's needed. Sometimes the President doesn't like my work."

"You know the President?"

"Of course I know the President. We live in the same house."

"I mean, he talks to you?"

"It would be uncomfortable if he didn't."

"Could you give him a message from me?"

"I suppose. He gets many messages."

"He may listen to this one."

"What is it?"

"I'll tell you. But first let me tell you what this poem says."

Gregor had almost forgotten the calligraphy.

"Oh. Oh, yes. What does it say?"

"The six characters are"—he pointed to each one—"NATURE, PEACE, MEET, HEART, NATURALLY, and FAR."

"What does that mean?"

"It means something like: if one's inner nature is at peace, heartmind—that 'hsin' there is a combination you don't have in English—if one's inner nature is at peace, heartmind naturally meets—or blends with—the universe in its farthest reaches."

"And it seems you find this very interesting."

"I do."

"A possibilitarian"

"What?"

"You want your inner nature to be at peace."

"I do. I'm working on it."

"That's why you were studying this calligraphy."

"That's part of why."

"What's the other part?"

"To give myself courage."

"For what?"

"My father just committed suicide."

"Oh. I'm sorry."

"It's not your fault. Stop apologizing, please."

"I'm sorry. Oh. I'm sorry. I mean, whose fault it is?"

"It's your boss's fault. Or your landlord's. Or whoever he is."

"Who?"

"The man in the White House. "

"Roosevelt? Why is it his fault? Does he know your father?"

"Not at all. That's what makes it worse, Samsa-san."

"I don't understand."

"Nor do I. Have you heard of Terminal Island?"

"No."

"It's just off Los Angeles. My father owned a pharmacy—the Ishi Pharmacy. Regular medicines and Japanese medicines. It took him and my mom seventeen years to build up the business. There were four kids. He sent two of us to UCLA. My little sisters are in high school. They want to

go to college. And now—BOOM! Evacuation. Just like that. Give everything up. Everyone. Not just my parents. Everyone."

"I was in a meeting about this. There was nothing I could do."

"We had six days to move, then we had thirty days, then forty-eight
hours. The junkmen came around like vultures. They offered my mother
five dollars for a five-hundred-dollar set of china. You know what she
did? She broke the plates, one by one, right in front of their eyes. My father had no time to clear the shelves or make any contacts for selling
stock. The junkmen told everyone the government was going to seize all
their household goods."

"That's not true."

"Yes. But they said it was true. They were buying up refrigerators, radios, stoves, furniture for two or three dollars, loading up their trucks and
driving away. We were left with nothing, not our homes, not our gardens,
not our cars, not our fishing boats, not our nets. What good were nets
where they were taking us?"

"What happened to your father?"

"He left a note, then swallowed a whole jar of morphine. Might as
well use it as abandon it. Want to know what it said in his note?"

"No."

"Thank you."

"Why?"

"For being discreet."

"You are brave to face all that. I hope the calligraphy helps."

"I don't need to be brave to face all that. I need to be brave for something else."

Silence.

"I am going to perform *seppuku*. In protest of what the man in the
White House is doing to my people."

"With a sword? With a friend chopping off your head?" Gregor was
alarmed.

"No, Samsa-san. This is 1942. I am going to be modern. Gasoline.
Texaco. I will follow the great path of self-immolation."

It took Gregor a while to respond. Was he joking? He seemed like a
regular college kid, Josh, Josh in a yellow costume. Granted, he was Oriental. Perhaps "inscrutable," as everyone said. Gregor probed gently.

"How will you do this?"

"On the first of March, I will go to the Capitol steps . . ."

"Why the first of March?"

"It's my birthday. It will give me time to prepare."

"Why not the White House?"

"It's not just the President I hold responsible. I read the papers. I go to Congress to hear the speeches. It makes me ashamed to be American. I want to be at the Capitol, the symbol of this country. I want to gaze at the library across the parking lot, the Library of Congress. I want to think how much nobility and wisdom is there, how much there is to respect in the world, how much is being ignored."

"Aren't you afraid how much it hurts?"

"I'll show you how I'm working on this. You may need to know. I want you to stand right there and stare at those characters. Remember: NATURE, PEACE, MEET, HEART, NATURALLY, and FAR. Just keep looking at them and listen to me. This is what I tell myself as I look at them."

Josh positioned Gregor directly in front of the calligraphy and moved around behind him to whisper in what he thought was his ears. Gregor was used to this mistake. He moved his right knee out to the side and allowed Josh to speak into the bug.

"Death is not the end of life, just a brief transition to another state before rebirth. You agree?"

Gregor tentatively nodded.

"So I understand my suicide is not an escape, but simply an act of compassion. Compassion for my father, and compassion for the silliness of the world."

"I thought you said it was protest."

"Quiet. I'll get to that. My task in the next week is to become truly selfless, desire-less, and enlightened enough to prepare for the moment of passing. Those I leave behind—my mother, my brother, my sisters, even the world at large—will respect what I am doing. I tell myself that. They won't resent it, they won't reject it, they may not be ready for such an act themselves, but Samsa-san, you will see, they will not grieve—but praise. They will understand that choosing one's own time and place and manner of death with peace of mind is the most important thing, more important than length of life. They will know my father's clarity as well as my own. They'll compare their own clarity, and if they find it lacking, they'll be stimulated to think more clearly, to be more mindful. If the man in the White House becomes more mindful, the world will be spared much agony. To this degree, my immolation will be an act of protest, hopefully not in anger, but as a goad toward greater clarity."

"But burning alive is so . . . destroying."

"Samsa-san, I told you—and you agreed—there is no creation and no destruction. Conservation of mass-energy-intention. Read Einstein. Why then fear death? Personal extinction is irrelevant. We are absorbed into collective consciousness, the Great Totality. You will be, too, someday. You will be a no-longer-mere-entity, you will be aware of every other entity in the universe, free from the constraints of time and space, without beginning and without end."

"I would be afraid to burn myself."

"You'll get used to it. And to help you, your new friend Josh is going to make a very special request. Will you do it for me?"

"What? Do what?"

"You have to agree first. Then I'll tell you."

Gregor continued to stare at the six characters. Then, "Yes. I agree."

"Good. I knew you would. I want you to be my *kaishaku.*"

"The helper who cuts off the head? I can't. I—"

"No cutting off of heads. This is 1942, remember? When the samurai speaks to the *kaishaku* before or during *seppuku,* the standard response is *go anshin.* Say it. Say it."

"*Go anshin.* What does it mean?"

"Say it again."

"*Go anshin.*"

"Good pronunciation. It means 'set your mind at peace.'"

"*Go anshin.*"

"Excellent pronunciation. You're a natural. Next Sunday, when we go up the Capitol steps—"

"We?"

"Of course. The *kaishaku* accompanies the celebrant—always. When we go up the Capitol steps, I want you to watch me very carefully, sensitize your antennae, and if you feel me getting unclear you must say . . . ?"

"*Go anshin.*"

"Precisely. And then I can do it. Aren't you glad we met?"

"No."

"You will be. It's my gift to you, and the gift of the Gods. Goodbye, Samsa-san. I will see you at seven P.M., a week from today, east side of the Capitol, in time to illuminate the twilight. Wish me well."

Gregor was speechless.

"All right then, don't wish me well."

He turned to go.

"Wait," cried Gregor. "What is the message for the President?"

"I thought you'd never ask. Tell him to set his mind at peace."

He took Gregor by the shoulders and gently turned him back to the glass case.

Yoshio Miyaguchi walked out of the Freer Gallery, leaving Gregor to stare at Fu Shan's characters, NATURE, PEACE, MEET, HEART, NATURALLY, and FAR.

## 30. WARS *of the* WORLDS V: *Of* FIRE *and* ICE

"Perform what? Sepukoo? Does he need any help from us?"

Roosevelt was propped up in bed, the phone tucked under his chin as he ate his English muffins.

"What? To death? At the Capitol? Why?"

(Long pause.)

"Well, I don't see how that accomplishes anything. Have him come see me. Four tomorrow. Well, find him, goddam it. Check his monkery or what have you. Look, Samsa, we can't have the press on this. You're the point man. Whatever resources you need, you've got them. Call the FBI, call the Capitol Police, call the Fire Department if necessary. You stop this maniac or you're out of here! I mean it!"

The President was not as genial as he had been three minutes ago.


Temple Nipponzan Nyohoji had not seen Yoshio Miyaguchi since the weekend. He had not returned to his apartment. The FBI and the District Police were on his case—nothing all week.

On Sunday, March 1, from six-thirty in the warmish, springlike evening, Gregor waited in the parking lot at the east façade of the Capitol. No yellow-robed monks. At six fifty-five he was approached by a short, potbellied, new-bearded, somewhat seedy-looking Oriental man wearing a blue New York Yankees jacket and cap.

"Got a match, bud?"

"Uh, no—no, I don't smoke. Sorry."

"That's okay, I have a lighter. Follow me in five minutes. Not before."

Gregor had been fooled.

*"Go anshin,"* he whispered.

"My mind is at peace."

The Yankee fan joined the tourists scattered on the steps, long-shadowed in late-day light. He walked all the way up under the portico to inspect the head of Washington, flanked on the left by an angel with a pen, on the right by an angel with a trumpet. Pen and trumpet. So be it. He stood for a moment at the Columbus doors—those Ghiberti-like portals, here transformed from Gates of Paradise to Gates of Hell—for the Red Man. The tourist in the blue New York Yankees jacket with its white insignia turned and took in the dome of the Library of Congress, green oxidized copper, the red light streaming over the shoulder of the Capitol finding its hidden glow. He stood for a minute, breathing deeply through his mouth, then walked slowly down eighteen broad steps to the second landing. Standing there a moment, looking directly at Gregor below, he gave him a tiny, dismissive wave with his right hand, as if to say, "It's okay. Stay down there. I don't need you." Gregor's eyes sought out his face. Yoshio Miyaguchi gave him a wink.

Then, with a well-practiced, lightning gesture, he popped open his jacket, turned the gas can over onto his chest, flicked his lighter, shot up in flames, and sank to his knees in *seiza* posture, perfectly centered, perfectly framed. Gregor's first thought was "How beautiful he looks!"

But then the helper panicked, and looked wildly around for the police, the FBI, all the agents he assumed would be prowling. And indeed, they were coming, running from north, south, and east, tricked, as he had been, by a simple, unexpected costume—too late. The puffing crowd of law enforcement stopped at the first landing, eighteen steps below the flames.

Miyaguchi's roommate Ken Seiji, the real *kaishaku*, caught the scene with his Leica—the photo that became the famous *Life* magazine cover of March 6, 1942. Gregor ran up the steps to the group and shook the first policeman he contacted.

"Help him. Can't you try to help him?"

Miyaguchi's charred body fell forward, as was proper in *seppuku*.

"Cool it, buddy. The guy's a crisp. Besides, the only good Jap is a dead Jap."

It has been shown that blattid giant neurons acquire a slow, rhythmic pulse when stimulated consistently two, four, or eight times a second. The output frequency is approximately three per second, a metrical march irrationally related to the input, and still a mystery to insect physiologists. But such a phenomenon might account for the habitual creative reverie Gregor experienced when riding the railroad. Was it the rhythmic flashing of telephone poles or ties, or perhaps the clicking of iron wheels over intermittent temperature gaps? Experiments have yet to be done.

It was Saturday, June 12, 1943. Gregor was seated mid-coach, left side, staring out the window at the verdant Maryland morning. Normally myopic, he was slipping into fuzzier territory yet as the alpha rhythm began to prevail. It had already been the strangest of days, leaving the White House at six A.M., the First Family asleep, exiting unheralded like some hotel guest with an early checkout. The White House had been his home for more than a decade. He had seen its babies born, its children grow up and leave for college. He had witnessed the ever increasing distance between Eleanor and Franklin, as she became more empowered and liberated, and he weaker and more enslaved.

The last four years had been the worst: the war had brought the President and his blattid guest to loggerheads, and what was once a blossoming friendship had now become—what?—a toleration at best, a loss of interest and respect. The President did not need moral superiors to criticize or lecture him on behalf of the Jews or the Japanese. Gregor, on the other hand, didn't need heroes with moral feet of clay.

Yet who can easily exit such a setting? A free home at the seat of power. A fly's view of the people behind the roles. An embarrassed Roosevelt, for instance, wheeling impulsively in on a—surprise!—naked, dripping Churchill emerging, cigar in mouth, from his bath. "The Prime Minister of Great Britain has nothing to hide from the President of the United States," intoned the Englishman. Priceless. And unreported in *The*

*New York Times.* Only Gregor had witnessed it, passing by chance along the third-floor hallway. It was something to tell his grandchildren. So he stayed. Perhaps longer than he should have.

The last two years—maybe more, maybe since the *St. Louis* incident—had felt like a marriage gone stale, with neither party wanting to admit the change, each holding on to the formal daily round to avoid facing up to acid emptiness. Gregor felt the point of no return had been his failure to stop Yoshio Miyaguchi from committing *seppuku.* For all the controversy surrounding the New Deal, that single, almost irrelevant event had been the Administration's scandal. In the weeks following, Gregor expected at each moment to be called on the carpet, to be punished according to the enormity of the crime. But—nothing. The waiting was grievous. He reread and obsessed on that passage in *The Idiot* about the unutterable agony of certain impending death—but there was no priest to hold a cross to his lips as he mounted the imagined scaffold. At the same time, just as Dostoevski described, he became aware of the immense value of each moment of life, of the infinite importance filling every conscious crack and surface of his existence. He waited in this heightened state through the entire month of March and into April, but no remonstrance seemed forthcoming, and as spring faded into summer, the incident seemed swept into the dustbin of history, present at first only in its absence, as a bright light will leave a hole in visual space, then fade to a vague dissonance.

For his part, the President had suffered what was to be suffered, and had let the blaming largely go: he was big enough to forgive, and small enough to forget. Gregor imagined Eleanor playing some role here, counseling her husband to turn his attention to the real war.

Gregor had lived through a numbing '42 and '43, like Walter Benjamin's Angel of History, watching the world crumble around him.

There is a painting by Paul Klee called *Angelus Novus.* It shows an angel who seems about to take leave of something, something at which he is staring. His eyes are wide, his mouth open, and his wings outspread. This is what the Angel of History must look like. His face is turned toward the past. What looks to us like a chain of occurrences appears to him as one great catastrophe incessantly piling wreck upon wreck and hurling it at his feet. He would very much like to stay, to waken the dead and make whole what has been shattered. But a storm is blowing so strongly from Paradise that his wings are pinned back: he can no longer close them. This storm drives him irresistibly into the future, to which his back is turned, while the pile before him grows. What we call progress—that is the storm.

And now, Dr. New Deal had metamorphosed into Dr. Win-the-War, a man who wanted to be introduced as "Commander in Chief," rather than as "President." The 1942 State of the Union speech: goal—60,000 planes, 25,000 tanks, 20,000 antiaircraft guns, 6 million tons of shipping. The 1943 State of the Union: goal—125,000 planes, 75,000 tanks, 35,000 guns, 10 million tons of shipping. The creation of a military-industrial complex. This storm is what we call progress.

The train rolled on through Harpers Ferry, and Gregor was becoming dizzy, dizzy in ganglia, dizzy in heart. He tipped his hat down over his eyes and let the planes, tanks, and guns grind their way off the stage, transubstantiated beyond ploughshares into the thinnest air.

Slowly, as if from a great distance, a drone added its voice to the monotonous clicking of the train, a droning melody, the most trivial, the barest of tunes. Ah, yes, the newspaper boy from this morning. It's his tune. The ancient-looking organ-grinding newspaper boy in Lafayette Park—under the gnarling, cancerous tree, the willow-oak weeping. Standing on a pool of ice in the middle of June, the only ice around, under his feet, an inexplicable frozen puddle. Barefoot. A dog barking over the tune. Should I *not* go west? *Leiermann,* should I stay with you? What kind of a song is still left to sing? My song? Will you play my song? Why was no one else around? Why newspapers and hurdy-gurdy? And ice, why was there ice? I dreamed it. No. I bought a *New York Times,* a real *New York Times* for a real ten cents. Here, I have it here.

Gregor whipped his hat off his eyes and pounced upon the *Times* lying on the seat next to him. He tore open the paper as if to test its reality. On page four was a summary of the week's events in Los Angeles:

ZOOT SUIT RIOTS CONTINUE

Gregor did not know what a zoot suit was.

Now in their tenth day, disturbances between sailors and Mexican youth continue to make life in the City of Angels more interesting. This week, civilians were joined by servicemen in chasing, stripping, and occasionally beating zoot-suiters or non-zoot-suit-wearing Mexican Americans and blacks. On Monday evening, June 7th, thousands of Angelenos, in response to twelve hours' advance notice in the press, turned out for a mass lynching. Taxi drivers offered free transportation to the riot areas.

He still wasn't sure what a zoot suit was. But it didn't sound good. He recalled sheets and hoods parading down Pennsylvania Avenue, and thought again of Alice, the lovely antennalike hair of Alice Paul. All these years together in Washington . . . where did the friendship go? *Ou sont les neiges d'antan?*

For all the President's reluctance to confront, it was he who had finally broken their impasse and shattered the ongoing vacuum of politeness. At the '42 Christmas party, the President took Gregor aside and asked him if he were up for a special assignment and a little adventure. He could give few details, but he could assure Gregor it would make maximum use of his many skills, would probably change the world, and would be of great benefit to humanity—Gregor would just have to trust him. Trust, of course, was the principal victim of the last five years, and Gregor was leery, even suspicious. The icons "benefit to humanity" and "change the world" were moving, but their resonance had been muffled by the disappointing realities of the last years, and evoked in his thorax only muted strings, *pianissimo, da lontano.* Still, the embers flared when the President whispered, "Without you and Einstein, this might never have come to pass." Putting two and two together was easy compared to putting Gregor and Einstein together. *Myself and Einstein,* he thought—*in the same motion, in the same sentence!* The letter he had delivered. The lecture he had given—bad as it was. Perhaps something had come of them after all. Samsa and Einstein—benefactors of the world.

"This has something to do with a science project?" he asked.

"Risk management. I understand you wrote the book."

"Risk of what?"

"If you take the assignment, you'll learn what. I can't tell you more just now."

"Like a sacred mystery."

"I suppose you might say that." The President was weak on sacred mysteries.

"Let me think about it and I'll let you know." In his heart, he already knew.


Had he any doubts about taking the assignment, they would have been settled by a remarkable coincidence. Seeking counsel, he phoned Leo Szilard. Three times he called, only to be greeted by busy signals. Giving up, he got ready for bed; the phone in his cabinet rang as he was slipping into straw. It was New Year's Eve. Who could be calling?

"Hello, Samsa here." (He had never lost this European habit.)

"Samsa, Szilard here."

"Leo! I was just calling you. Three times. Your line was busy for the last hour."

"That's because I was calling you. Three times. Your line was busy for the last hour."

"How peculiar! What do they say? Great minds think alike?"

"Only mediocre minds think. Great minds don't think at all."

"Um . . . yes. Well, mediocre minds think alike, then."

"Speak for yourself."

"Leo, does your great mind know what I was calling about?"

"Of course."

"What?"

"The same thing I was calling you about."

"What is that?"

"Going to Site Y."

"What's Site Y?"

"You mean the President hasn't asked you to go?"

"Well, he did ask me to go on an assignment—an adventure—but he didn't say where."

"I want you to go. Wigner and Teller agree. Teller is going himself. Wigner will consult."

"Go where?"

"Site Y."

"Where is that?"

"I can't tell you."

"Do you know?"

"Of course. But I can't tell you."

"Well, what is Site Y?"

"About that, I can tell you even less. But we want you to go."

"Why?"

"You'll see."

"Does this have something to do with . . . what we went to Peconic about?"

"What's Peconic?"

"Einstein."

"Oh, yes. The Peconic State Parkway. We got lost. It has little to do with Einstein."

"Would he go? Einstein?"

"No. And they wouldn't want him."

"Leo?"

"Yes?"

"I think I should go."

"Great minds think alike. Let me know how things develop."

Click. As usual, Gregor was left staring into the phone.

On Saturday, January 2, 1943, Gregor sent a note to the President agreeing to take the assignment. The following Wednesday, at a chance encounter in the West Wing, FDR, whizzing past at ten feet per second, waved briefly from his wheelchair and yelled out between cigarette-holder-clenching teeth, "Got your message." Gregor heard nothing further for several months. The subject never came up. There was a note in mid-April from Szilard:

```
Samsa,
Be warned about Site Y. No one will be able to think
straight. Everybody who goes there will go crazy. Stay
sane. That's why we need you. LS
```

A month later, two railroad tickets arrived in his box via interoffice mail: for June 12, The Capitol Limited to Chicago, and the Super Chief from Chicago to Lamy, New Mexico, coach, no sleeping cars. Was this a trusting gift, or an easy-out invitation to leave? By May, Gregor was excited enough to think of it as gift, to put out of his mind the impish fact that *Gift* in his mother tongue means "poison." He had three weeks to settle his affairs and prepare to go off "for the duration," a phrase he took to mean "the duration of the war." It turned out to be for quite a bit longer. Probably eternity. But of this, he was not aware.

That evening, pulling out of Cleveland, Gregor's daze was rudely interrupted.

"Did that *New York Times* pay full fare?"

"Huh? What?" Gregor pulled his cap off his eyes.

"So, Mr. Bug-eyes, did that paper pay full fare, it should take my seat?" The speaker was a short man of about sixty, in a rumpled, shiny blue gabardine suit with a hideous "modern" purple tie, Coke-bottle glasses sitting awry on an enormous nose, and a feathered fedora abnormally adorning his bald head. He removed his hat, but not out of politeness.

"Oh. Oh, I'm sorry. I didn't know this was reserved."

"It vasn't. But now it is." The man plunked his hat down on the newspaper-vacated seat, took off his suit jacket, folded it less than neatly, and shoved it in the small rack above. He began to lower his lumbago carefully into the seat next to Gregor.

"Your hat!" the roach yelled.

"Just testing. To see if you vas a Landsmann. A goy vould let me sit on it."

"Well—I *am* Jewish—but anyone would—"

"You know something?"

"What?"

"You don't look Jewish."

There was a pause. Gregor was savvy enough to know it was a joke—

but was he suppose to laugh? He *didn't* look Jewish. His seatmate stared at him. Maybe this was a serious comment.

"You know something else?"

"What?"

"It's a good ting you don't look Jewish. It's Jews that got us into this war—"

"That's not true . . ."

The man began to stage-sob effusively.

"Mine poor husband . . . dying of kencer, my only son about . . . to be killed in Nort Efrica . . ." Other passengers were staring. "Oi, veh is mir!" he called to the ventilator in the ceiling.

"Your husband?"

"That's vat they say. It's the Jews. You like my ecting?"

This is the seatmate Gregor had been waiting for? All the way to Chicago with him? He's probably going to Lamy, New Mexico.

"You don't believe me? Here, come vit me." He pulled Gregor up by the sleeve out into the aisle, and pushed him along to the end of the car. "In there."

"That's the restroom."

"Go in there."

"With you?"

"Vat do you think, I'm some kind of a funny? I vant you should see something."

Gregor entered with great hesitance.

"Look!" He pointed to the urinal. Though there was some kind of wetness on the floor under it, the urinal itself was reasonably clean. "Vat do you see in there?"

"Pee?" asked Gregor, doubtfully.

"No! Vat are you talking? There's no pee—it's clean. You need glasses? Vat do you see?"

Gregor was panicking. He was always nervous at exams.

"'American Standard'?" The brand name was glazed in blue at the bottom of the urinal wall.

"You're getting varmer. Vat else do you see?"

"'American' is in regular letters and 'Standard' is in gothic letters?"

"Oi. He's so observing! Vat's at the bottom, dummkopf?"

"Drain holes for the water."

"And the pee."

"Drain holes for the water and the pee."

"And?"

Gregor stared at the drain holes. He had never looked at them before. He usually stared at the wall. They were arranged in the shape—of a Star of David! Two intersecting triangles of holes forming a Jewish Star.

"Aha. The light is dawning."

"Well, I can't believe they did that on purpose."

"Vat, you tink the Mogen David fell in there by accident? Vat color is pee? You hoid of the yellow star? You hoid of Hitler? Vat is the message of this urinal?"

"Urinals don't have messages."

"Against stupidity," the analyst exclaimed, "God himself is helpless. The message of this urinal is 'Piss on Jewish.' Get it? And vat is the next message?"

Gregor stared at this odd man, his heartmind spinning.

"'Flush them down the toilet.' That's the message of the urinal. Okay? Class trip dismissed. Ve go back to the seats."

Gregor fairly staggered back down the aisle, nudged along by his would-be mentor. It was not the first time he had encountered cultural anti-Semitism, but, specious or not, this example was uncommonly striking. The two sunk back into their seats.

"So vat are you, bashful, Mr. Bug-eyes? You don't introduce yourself?"

Though Gregor thought it might have been up to the newcomer to introduce himself, he reflexively apologized.

"Oh, excuse me. You just took me by surprise. I was dozing. I was . . . Gregor Samsa, here."

"Schwartz C. Leon. The 'C' is for 'Comma.' You can call me 'Mr. Schwartz.' In America ve use first names. Equality. Fraternity. Vere you are headed?"

"New Mexico."

"Vy not Old Mexico? Don't they have big cockroaches down there?" He burst out singing. "La cucaracha, la cucaracha . . ." Again, the other passengers turned and stared. They had never heard the song with a Yiddish 'r.' "How does it go after that? Ve didn't speak Spanish in Varsava. Or am I not supposed to talk cockroaches?"

"You are from Warsaw? I am from Prague. But I have been many times in Warsaw. In fact, I left my appendis in Warsaw with one Dr. Bong. Do you know him?"

"A terrible man, a terrible man. I don't know him, but vat else vith such a name? I didn't know your people had appendises."

"It was before, when I was twenty-two. What's bad with his name?"

"A Bong by any other name vould smell like feet. Before vat?"

Gregor realized he was unpracticed in the arts of avoidance. What would he do if Mr. Leon asked about his destination?

"Before the war. You got on in Cleveland?"

"My daughter had another baby. Five breeding daughters I have. I can't keep track of the grandchildren birthdays. But you're again changing the subject."

"No, I . . . what's the subject?"

"The subject is the murder of the Jews. You know vat's happening in Chicago? You ever been in Chicago?"

"I haven't. What is happening?"

"Very suspicious, someting very suspicious."

"What?"

"Vat a nosy you are! In the university . . . I live near the university, Fifty-seventh and Voodlawn . . . in the university there's an football stadium, Stegg Field, right around the corner from me."

"I don't get to American football."

"*Machts nichts*. Neither does Mr. Hutchins. They stopped doing football years ago. Too much brawns, not enough brains."

"So?"

"So vat do you think they are using this football stadium for?"

"I don't know. Baseball? Graduation ceremonials? Isn't June when is graduation?"

"Graduation ceremonials vit barbed vire and guards vit guns?"

"What do you mean?"

"Since last October I am vatching the trucks, the men vit coats and ties going in and out. I wrote down names. Sterling Lumber Company from the city, Goodyear Rubber Company—all the vay from Ohio on the license plate. A big truck from National Carbon Company, in and out, in and out, a closed truck, I couldn't see vat vas in there, but it vas lots of it, I'm telling you. Listen, the Mallinckrodt Chemical Voiks all the vay from St. Louis, in Missouri. In and out. About thoity-four gengsters, Back-of-the-Yard Boys ve call 'em, probably from behind the stockyards they look like. Every morning in, and every night out. You vouldn't vant to meet them in a dark alley. Crowbars, some had, and helmets. A car, big, black, Dupont four on the plate, vit fancy people in it. Tvice in and out two veeks apart. And the barbed vire. Early on, barbed vire. And if you listen outside the vest stands, you can hear them singing. Drinking songs. And the guards—outside at the barbed vire. First they are building fires in oil drums to keep varm, then they are getting portable fireplaces hooked up to gas. Then fur coats they get, raccoon fur coats for all the guards. You know vat costs a raccoon coat? Dis is big bucks, let me tell you. Raccoon fur coats and tommy guns. You think I'm telling a story?"

"No, I believe you."

"I could make such monkey business up?"

"You have a sharp eye."

"Vat the eye doesn't see, the heart doesn't feel. So Mr. Bug-eyes, vat do you see, vat do you make on it?"

"They must be building something there in the stadium."

"Brilliant. But vat? In the vest stands, under them. Vat you think?"

"Wood, rubber, carbon, chemicals . . ."

"I think they are going to round up the Jews and kill them. They are building some kind of a death camp in there."

"That's impossible. Who? The university? The government? They don't do things like that."

"You remember December, early December, the government said two million of our people had been murdered in Europe?"

"The State Department Report. And five million more were in danger."

"Mr. Bug-eyes reads the newspaper."

"I work in Washington."

"So?"

"What do you mean, 'so'?"

"So vat do you know, Joe? Vat do you know about vat ve're doing about it?"

"Nothing."

"Ve're not *doing* nothing, or you don't *know* nothing?"

"Roosevelt has decided not to do anything about it."

"And vat vill the Jewish community do about that?"

"I don't know. Demonstrating? Striking? Not vote for Roosevelt?"

"Not if they're in prison—or dead. Vat happened vith the Japs? You think ve don't round people up if they're a threat?"

"You think the government is going to round up Jews and kill them?"

"You think they aren't?"

Gregor reviewed everything he knew about Breckinridge Long and the anti-Semites at State, about FDR's sometime cowardice and vulnerability to political pressure, about the militarization of his thought, and the general mood of the white-sheeted, zoot-suit-burning electorate—and though he would like to have answered "No!," he wasn't so sure.

"I need to go to the bathroom," he said. "Please excuse me." He squeezed past Mr. Leon, walked back up the aisle, and after a two-minute wait for a little boy and his father, was able to lock himself in and think. After some minutes alone, he felt able to face his tormentor, prepared to rationally discuss what he knew and what he thought.

When he returned to the seat, he found a note scrawled over a light men's sport shirt in a Barneys ad on page seven of the *Times*: "May you have a happy next Passover with the Angel of Death passing over you. But check behind your neck for unexpected markings. Next year in Jerusalem. Selah. SCL."

Chicago, Union Station. Filthy arching glass roof, high up, far away. Corinthian columns. Dark wooden benches the color of his tegmen. Shiny. Smooth. Oh, to rub against them. Find the Santa Fe Chief to Lamy, New Mexico, wherever that is. Thirty-six hours—if all goes well, no floods or fire.

Track 22. Gregor could not see the engine, many cars ahead, a new, state-of-the-art diesel, yellow and red. Up into the coach car. Halfway down the aisle. Suitcase up on the rack. He thought how comfortable that rack might be for a long and drawn-out night. Instead of propping himself upright, being careful of his seatmate, he could just stretch out in the baggage rack if there were room. American luggage racks offered no privacy—a symptom of democracy, he supposed. Still, he lay his suitcase flat, next to another similarly disposed, and thought he might use that expanse as a bed should the need arise. These preparations made, he plopped down into a velveteen seat, next to an ancient Negro who nodded minimally and resumed his snooze. Gregor heard the hurdy-gurdy tune deep in his knees and legs. Then, something like sleep. Watchman, tell us of the night. "Princeton, Illinois," "Fort Madison, Iowa."

He fell into disturbing dreams, dreams of insectlike men, indifferent to life, men more thing than living-thing. These humanoids streamed in and out of churches, worshiping yet more things, different things—steam irons, steak knives, a box of matches. In the darkened nave of a large cathedral, a girl-child was selected, a human girl-child—was it Alice? child Ulla? his sister Grete?—selected to be queen. Several insectmen carried her carefully to an altar in the choir and held her down while streams of cohorts emerged from side aisles and chapels, carrying objects, things, a mass of items from "The World of Tomorrow"—cameras, portable radios, electric percolators, vacuum cleaners, plastic dishes—and buried the child and her captors under their weight. As the pile grew, it was circled by dancers and musicians, croaking and scraping their legs, whistling through spiracles, ticking polyrhythmically. "To Death," they sang, "To Death,"—hellish yelling intermingled with angelic counterpoint.

"La Plata, Missouri," the conductor called out, as early-morning-gently as the roaring of Bottom's suckling dove. It woke Gregor, saved him from the final hoarding of the objects, and the revelation of crushed, gashed corpses beneath them.

Newton defined force as the product of mass and acceleration. Simone Weil defined force as the ability to transform a man into a corpse. And by Kansas City, Gregor came to understand the ultimate polarity: not day and night, not male and female, but the polarity between those who have the desire, and thus the power, to kill, and those who do not. The killers were things and the lovers of things, entranced with all that is mechanical like themselves, perpetually ready to transmute organic to inorganic. Men of having, not of being, men who must possess or die. Men of abstraction, quantification, bureaucratization, and technique. Men not afraid of total destruction. Where would such men lead us? He sat up starkly in his seat and watched the dawn grow slowly in the Kansas sky.


In Prague, at Altneu, Rabbi Tsanck, he remembered, all the children gathering for stories of the Lamed-Vovniks, the thirty-six Just Men, indistinguishable from the rest of us, the thirty-six for the sake of whom God lets the world continue. The Lamed-Vovniks are often unknown, sometimes unknown even to themselves, and for these "unknowns," the spectacle of the world is an unspeakable hell. "When an unknown Just Man rises to Heaven" the rabbi said, "he is so frozen that God must warm him for a thousand years between His fingers before his soul can open to Paradise." But if just one Lamed-Vovnik were lacking, the rabbi had said, the sufferings of mankind would poison the souls of even infants, and humanity would asphyxiate, clawing at one another in agony. Because the Lamed-Vov are the hearts of the world, sink and drain for all collected grief.

One legend he told—that one of the thirty-six is the Messiah. If the age were worthy of it, He would unveil himself. The Messiah! Maybe the conductor. Maybe my snoring seatmate. Let us worship, let us pray. In the seventh century, Andalusian Jews prayed to a teardrop-shaped rock they thought was the soul of an unknown Lamed-Vovnik, petrified by suffering. Other Lamed-Vovnikim are said to have been transformed into dogs, even insects. Be on the lookout. Worship! The Messiah! The Messiah who will come only when He is no longer needed. But was it Xenophanes? "Were cattle to postulate a god, it would have horns and hooves." The satanic fury of Hobbes: "Men, Women, a Bird, a Crocodile, a Calf, a Snake, an Onion, a Leeke, Deified!" The Messiah.

Such were the thoughts skittering through the ganglia of a Czech Jewish blattid as he rode the Santa Fe Chief through Kansas and Colorado, and on into New Mexico, en route to the unknown. Was this trip, he wondered, yet one more flight from an implacable, gruesome "benediction"? Or was the western desert to be a grail scene of transcendence? The clicking rails whispered no answer.

Leaving Las Vegas, New Mexico, forty minutes from Lamy, Gregor put into operation the plan that FDR, master of intrigue, had scribbled for him on a White House napkin. Carrying his suitcase, he walked forward through the train to the baggage car, entered it using an FBI skeleton key, and located the wooden crate he had sent to the station ahead of him. Opening the padlock, he, with suitcase, climbed in, closed the lid, fastened it from the inside, and waited, cozy and thigmotactic after his disturbing, exhausting journey. At Lamy, he was loaded, gently ("FRAGILE SCIENTIFIC INSTRUMENTS. HANDLE WITH CARE. THIS SIDE UP"), onto a cart and left standing under the station portico in the evocative, early-evening light.

# LOS ALAMOS,
# NEW MEXICO

Being buried alive is a common and terrifying nightmare, but some among us have other thoughts about tight, dark spaces. Those fifteen thigmotactic minutes given to Gregor turned out to be world-changing, worthy of discussion in the dark light they deserve.

Blattids, as we know, have a predilection for pressure, a strong need to be touched on all sides at once. In the wild they find joy in the crannies of peeling tree bark, the moist cracks in limestone caves, or the wet layers of leaf litter on the rain forest floor. For the more civilized, there are the interstices of kitchen cabinets, gaps between bathroom tiles, all sorts of chinks in baseboards, window frames and trim, and the inscrutable architecture of water heaters, refrigerators, and stoves.

For outsized Gregor, the crate was a rare chance to indulge an appetite rooted at his core, and to encounter the insights of this ecstatic state. He lay there in the box, sensible of the darkness, yet for that very reason, all the more aware of the crepuscular light pouring in through three breathing holes at his head onto the mosaic of his eyes. As the light poured in, he felt himself pouring out, sucked into the vast, arid nakedness of the Galisteo valley. "The expansive power of extreme compression," he thought. He remembered Ives and his explosive quarter-tone harmonies, recalled the expansive conciseness of Chinese ideograms, with which a few characters might translate into an entire English paragraph. "NATURE, PEACE, MEET, HEART, NATURALLY, FAR."


Gregor began his Los Alamos career with a briefing from the top. In July of 1943, things were still relatively easygoing, and so both Bob Serber, "Indoctrination Czar," and J. Robert Oppenheimer, head of the lab, were available to take him around for orientation. They met at Fuller Lodge, the old Ranch School's dining hall, a huge log building with a magnificent view from its patio overlooking the Sangres. "Jemez to the west,

Sangres to the east," Oppie exclaimed, "the most important structures we've got."

"Why Sangres?" Gregor asked. "Doesn't that mean blood?"

"Not just any blood," Oppie explained. "The blood of Christ. I'll leave it to you to discover why. You'll have plenty of opportunity to hike in this beauty. There'll be cars available on weekends for mountain trips and jaunts into Santa Fe. I have to warn you, though, to always bring a saw and shovel. There's no road maintenance."

They passed the commissary, and Bob Serber commented, "There's lots of good, cheap food you can buy, or you can eat well at the army mess, if you can stand the noise."

"And every now and then a group goes to Edith Warner's teahouse, down at the river. I promise you a treat."

They walked around Ashley Pond—named, comically, for the old school's founder, Ashley Pond—and visited the hospital and commissary, the PX and rec building. The quiet latent in this site high on an isolated mesa was everywhere shattered by the deafening noise of a rising war factory. When they got to the housing area, Gregor was oddly reminded of the Lower East Side: children everywhere, a huge confusion of people, washlines with laundry flapping, telephone poles—if no telephones—and wires, all kinds of wires. Wooden walkways floating in the mud of last night's rain. The housing was "government issue—plain functional," apartment units built of green wood, filled with pitch. "And there aren't any fire escapes," Bob pointed out.

"If you need a bath, you can come to my house back behind the lodge," Oppie offered. "There are three bathtubs in this whole town. So feel free." They came to a heavily armed guardhouse.

"By the way," Oppie said, "I apologize for all the barbed wire. It's not my sense of the karma of this place."

"Did you know they call it 'The Devil's Rope' out here?" Serber asked.

"Blood of Christ, Devil's Rope . . ." Gregor mused.

"Yup, podner, you're in high theology country." Oppie tipped his porkpie hat and raised his eyes to the sky. "I'm going to let Bob take you around the Tech Area and give you an overview of what's happening with the work." He checked his watch. "I've got another meeting in three minutes. Be sure to come see me if you have any problems."

He walked off into T-Building, 130 pounds of fine-muscled intelligence.
"He means it," said Bob. "You can count on his support."

Serber got Gregor through the guardhouse, and together they surveyed the Tech Area, an inner barbed-wire region in an outer barbed-wire town.

"That's T-Building where Oppie just went. 'T' for 'theoretical': offices, administration, the theoretical physics group, library and classified documents—my wife, Charlotte, is the librarian—conference rooms, a photo lab, and a drafting room. That's V-building—the shop. And those going up are X, Y, and Z—specialized labs to house the Van de Graaffs, the cyclotron, the cryogenics lab, and over there, a small accelerator.

"This, over here, will be D-Building—metallurgy for uranium and plutonium. It will be air conditioned and as dust-free as we can make it. Radiochemistry, analytical chemistry, purification chemistry, and the metallurgical and analytical groups to fabricate the stuff into various shapes."

Bob Serber had just finished teaching the five-session orientation course for new arrivals. His less technical presentation to Gregor lasted two hours. Uranium vs. plutonium was the crucial topic:

"We need $U_{235}$, not $U_{238}$—a 'contaminant'—0.7 percent. Since they're isotopes, we can't chemically separate them. And since they're so similar in weight, it's very hard to do it physically. The natural mix is pretty bland, explosion-wise. But we'll see what comes in from Hanford and Oak Ridge. With enough $U_{235}$, or enough $Pu_{239}$, we can tickle the Einstein equation to climax."

How very unlike the quiet, shy Bob Serber, this last expression was. *Atomic energy brings out peculiar things in people,* Gregor thought.

"You still with me?"

"Yes," Gregor asked, "but why doesn't the $U_{235}$ in the earth explode?"

"Ah. Szilard had one other key insight: critical mass." Serber lit up his third Lucky of the tour. Gregor could deal with this outdoors. "The reason all the uranium on the planet doesn't set itself off and explode is that it's too dilute: should a stray neutron split a uranium atom, the secondary neutrons produced would fizzle out before they could split another atom, so—no chain reaction."

"I see. Obvious."

"Same with plutonium. But—what if those atoms were concentrated in a small space? Then the secondary neutrons might penetrate their neighbors, and tertiary neutrons theirs, and the chain would begin to rattle."

"How much uranium," Gregor asked, "how much plutonium would you have to pack into how much space for critical mass?"

Serber shrugged. "When the stuff comes, we'll try to find out. Last year, we had only unseparated uranium to play with. So Fermi built his pile—in a stadium."

A light bulb lit in Gregor's head.

"In a squash court under the stands at Stegg Field at University of Chicago, around the corner from Mr. Schwartz C. Leon's apartment on Woodlawn Avenue?"

"Amazing. How did you know? Stagg Field. Really. Security. How did you know?"

"I met someone on the train who lives around the corner. He was—you say spooked?—by all the mysterious doings. Like a lot of other neighbors. Could Dr. Fermi have blown up the entire Chicago?"

"Possible, but unlikely—according to his six-inch slide rule. 'Fermi never makes a mistake'—you've heard that? Forty physicists held their breaths, and hung out on the balcony to watch. History's most exciting squash game. Chicago didn't know anything about it."

"So everything material and intellectual is in place to make a bomb. But do we *want* to make a bomb? *Should* we make a bomb?" Gregor was asking *the* prior question, a question rarely asked.

Serber looked disturbed. He shook his head.

"I don't know. No one does. Scientists here from Europe think Germany has already begun developing one."

"German thought, German art, German philosophy . . . The atomic bomb is the legacy of Beethoven?"

"The legacy of Einstein. Most people here think we have to play catch-up. That's the catalyst for this whole thing. Planck is there. Von Laue is there, Hahn is there, Weiszäcker is there—Heisenberg is there. All you need is one Heisenberg. This is a double race, Gregor, both with Germany and between two fissionable metals. Which will be ready faster—a uranium bomb or a plutonium one? No telling, so we're pursuing both. There are huge Fermi piles at Hanford, Washington, trying to come up with purified plutonium, and a gigantic diffusion plant at Oak Ridge, Tennessee, trying to separate out $U_{235}$ from tons of ore. Whatever they get, they'll feed in here."

There was a minor ruckus at the guardhouse as some scientist tried to get into the Tech Area without his pass. His swearing at the MPs in German did not help. Serber shook his head and chuckled.

"If we can keep from going to war with General Groves, we'll try to design and build a weapon that can be carried in an aircraft and, when dropped, might actually explode. The theoreticians are making performance estimates for two weapon designs. The experimental guys are trying to get nuclear data so the chemists and metallurgists can work the materials into size, shape, and purity. And the ordnance experts will try to carry out the engineering design to create the supercritical mass, and to ensure its various components can be assembled into an operational weapon." Fourth Lucky. Serber needed calming. "And finally—I guess this is where you come in—the health personnel will try to minimize hazards. Good luck. Catch you at lunch!"


The first scientist Gregor met, post-orientation, was Seth Neddermeyer, a young physicist from Cal Tech, recently arrived, whose slouched demeanor would make a drill sergeant tremble (and there were several drill sergeants on site). Gregor was attracted to his tall, stooped figure, his narrow, insectlike shoulders supporting an enormous head, his thick, black-rimmed glasses and unkempt beard. He had probably been considered weird all his life, and even here, among the largest collection of crackpots ever seen, he was an outsider—the perfect friend for Gregor. On the evening of July 2, about three weeks after Gregor's arrival, the two of them were walking among the Sundt apartments—green (as was every building), two-story, four-family dwellings—when into the darkening sky there drifted the lush strains of a lovely piano melody.

"Do you know that piece?" asked Gregor.

"No," replied Neddermeyer, "I don't know music. 'Don't Sit Under the Apple Tree,' I know that. 'I'll Be Seeing You.'"

"You leave a girl behind?"

"Girls don't like physicists."

Gregor changed the subject.

"That's the Brahms Intermezzo, A major." They stopped to listen for a moment. "I love this. This is a tiny works which cram in everything, all of Brahms to a nutshell, extreme compression . . ."

In one Neddermeyer ear and out the other. It wasn't the Mills Brothers singing "Paper Doll." But the combination of the evening light and the idea of extreme compression evoked in Gregor a rush of his Lamy epiphany, never far from consciousness, but now intensified by the Brahms, and perhaps tamped by the uncomprehending consciousness off which it reflected. Gregor began to describe his experience, explained thigmotaxis, and the sense of power coming at him, into him, out of him. He described himself as a hollow vessel, a being in a shell, compressed and intensified by the celestial light focused on his core.

Neddermeyer lit up. Gregor had planted a seed: the implosion bomb idea was born between them, a rough beast still, and slouching.


The next day was spent gathering materials for an experiment they cooked up. Some TNT "borrowed" from the crew blasting out the basement for the cyclotron, several lengths of two-inch cast-iron sewer pipe from the "free" bin at the salvage yard, and a number of stovepipe sections from Eric Jette's porch (with his permission), a relic of the despised Black Beauty stove the Jettes had replaced with a hot plate. Fifty yards of primacord fusing, two tuna fish sandwiches, two apples, and two bottles of Ballantine completed the picnic preparations.

The following morning, the Fourth of July 1943, Gregor and Neddermeyer set out on a trek down the steep side of the mesa, into the Los Alamos Canyon, and wound up nestled among the caves and rocks of the mesa wall four hundred feet below, a mile and a half north of the main laboratory area. The world above them was celebrating the Land of the Free and the Home of the Brave in the midst of a war. An observer might have mistaken Gregor and Neddermeyer for large boys having fun, playing with matches and firecrackers on Independence Day. By the time they had chosen a safe-looking spot, shielded by overhang to minimize the noise, it was eleven A.M., and already 93 degrees. They downed the sandwiches and most of the Ballantine, and saved the apples for after the test, code-named "Gregor at Lamy."

Neddermeyer placed the two-inch pipe inside the stovepipe, and the two of them packed the cylinder with TNT, symmetrical around the inner pipe. Gregor then strung the detonator wire seventy-five feet to behind a large rock that they would use for protection; Neddermeyer saw to the connections, one at either end of the cylinder, 180 degrees apart. After checking the system, and the placement (careful not to have the results buried by exploded rock), he joined Gregor and the detonator behind the boulder.

The physicist picked up his beer and handed Gregor his.

"Here's to extreme compression."

"Extreme compression," echoed the roach. The clinking brown bottles sounded sharp in the dryness of the rocks.

"Would you like to press the lever?" asked Gregor.

"No, no. The inspiration was yours. I would say you get to press the lever."

"You are sure?" Gregor was nothing if not considerate. "This might be a great moment in history."

Neddermeyer made a sweeping comic gesture for him to go ahead, and they both crouched down behind the barrier. Gregor plunged the lever.

BOOM! Then BOOm, BOom, Boom, boom, as the sound echoed in the canyon. When the dust cleared, pipe and stovepipe were nowhere to be seen.

"Damn!" said Neddermeyer. "How can we do this experiment if we can't find the results?"

"Let's try it again," said Gregor, "over there, in that angle. I think the walls will hold."

They packed another length of stovepipe with pipe and TNT. Again Gregor ran the wire while Neddermeyer made the connections.

This time the explosion was better behaved. The plumbing pipe flew out above the cloud, bounced off an overhang a hundred feet above, and clattered down the side of the cliff calling obvious attention to itself and its landing. The stovepipe had again dispersed into the unknown. Neddermeyer ran out to claim the prize.

"Yow!" he yelled, burning his hand on hot metal. Gregor joined him. They inspected the twisted, bent, now-solid rod lying on the ground.

"I would say we did it. Extreme compression. Hollow no longer."

*"Reculer pour mieux pauser,"* punned the roach. Neddermeyer did not speak French.

"What?"

"Pull back, the better to pause."

"What does that mean?"

"We should stop and think about this."

"Hell, no. We should take this right to Colloquium Tuesday. I think we've got the gun design beat. You can't possibly fire a missile down a gun as fast as you can collapse a hollow vessel from all sides at once. We got it made!"

He grabbed Gregor by the upper legs and swung his light body around in a circle amidst the debris of the explosion, a gawky physicist, unwontedly frolicsome.

"Stop! Stop! I get dizzy," screamed the blattid. He didn't mention that his legs might come out.

As if in a demonstration of angular momentum, Gregor's body dropped down toward the ground, and within two decelerating turns, his bottom legs scraped the dusty tuff.

"Sorry," said Neddermeyer. "I was happy."


On July 6, Seth Neddermeyer brought his twisted rod to the weekly meeting at which scientists from all divisions—much to General Groves's discomfort—shared their work and thoughts. The colloquium was Oppenheimer's great victory over Groves's military fetish for compartmentalization and secrecy. Without it, the "long-hairs," as the general called them, would not have felt they were doing "science"—exchanging ideas in open community—and might have left. Groves was pragmatic enough to see that.

Neddermeyer took his turn toward the end of the meeting, the last of three speakers from O-division (O for Ordnance). He presented his plan in terms of a hollow sphere of subcritical material, to be compressed to criticality by a jacket of explosives. The pipe was a first effort, using simpler geometry. Gregor sat at the back of the gymnasium, which doubled as Theater Number One—the one with cushions on its benches. The metaphysical origins of the crushed pipe were never mentioned, nor was Gregor's role as lab assistant and drinking partner. That was all right with him: he felt that being too closely identified with any particular operation might compromise his "neutrality" as Risk-Management Consultant.

But he was not prepared for the scorn and derision voiced by this community of scholars and scientists, everyone supposedly colleagues and friends. Admittedly, this was a proposal "from left field," as Ives had taught him to say. Nobody else was thinking about implosion. The gun method was the method. Period. There was, to put it mildly, overwhelming skepticism.

Captain Deke Parsons, the director of O-division, thought it was a joke, pronouncing the idea "clearly unreliable," and a potential diversion from the more urgent program of designing and testing the gun assembly.

Others joined in the denunciation, though more politely:

"If the explosive doesn't produce an entirely even shock wave around the central hollow sphere, then wouldn't it be destroyed before it went critical?"

"Just a tiny imbalance would tear the sphere apart."

"How can you possibly make a perfect, spherically symmetrical shock wave?"

Richard Feynman summed up the group's opinion of Gregor and Neddermeyer's scheme: "It stinks"—an opinion he would subsequently be too ashamed to mention.

Though Oppenheimer was initially one of the scoffers, as the ridicule intensified, he began to doubt its wisdom. He had been wrong before: best not foreclose any possibilities. He took Neddermeyer aside, along with Gregor, who was consoling him, and said, "We'll have to look further into this." A crucial change of heart: for good or ill, had Neddermeyer's work been stopped, there would have been no atomic arsenal—at least till long after the war.

And Gregor would always know that without his vision at Lamy, there would never have been an implosion bomb. In his ever discerning heart-mind, neutrons of familiar guilt began a slow chain reaction.


On July 16, unknown to the mesa, the Nazis rounded up thirty thousand Parisian Jews and transported them to concentration camps. Twenty survived.

In September, the aspens, *los álamos,* turn color, a quivering vibrato of golden-yellow leaves, a living mountainside, calling.

Two legends are told about the aspen. One holds that the Saviour's cross was made from its wood, and that when the tree realized the purpose for which it was being used, its leaves began to tremble with horror and have never ceased. The other legend, diametrically opposed, is that when Christ died on the Cross, all the trees bowed in sorrow except the aspen. For its pride and sinful arrogance, its leaves were doomed to continual trembling.

Gregor, the Prague-schooled Jew, preferred the first. Although his eyes suffered from blattid insensitivity in the yellow range, because of his ability to see in the ultraviolet he was acutely aware of what some would call "aura": for all of the aspen's visual aggressiveness, its etheric impression was far from arrogant. Rather, he thought, it was much like himself—sensitive, making up for shyness with apparent éclat, caressing in a bashful, tentative way. He felt a brotherhood there. About the Cross, who was he to say?

But aspen-guilt or not, crucifixion was inescapable on the mesa. The blood-red sunsets on the Sangre de Cristo Mountains, rising thirteen thousand feet, thirty miles across clear desert, were unspeakably evocative, and not of any old sangre—rather, say, of soldiers at Ypres or Guadalcanal, of the blood of Bluebeard's wives, or Pharaoh's waters. For splitting the front of Truchas peak was an immense natural cross—cleft down the mountain face, with two horizontal fissures, slightly disjunctive. Throughout late spring and early summer, the only remaining snow would be packed into those enormous crannies, appearing white against granite during the day, and turning albedo pink, then preternaturally red at sunset, a ten-thousand-foot, blood-red crucifix.

And between the Sangres and Gregor's mesa was the canyon, an intimate nudity of landscape with only shadows to cover its private parts. It was a landscape bathed in luminous air, as if on the bright edge of the world, an atmosphere that Willa Cather had felt as "something soft and wild and free, something that whispered to the ear on the pillow, lightened the heart, softly, softly picked the lock, slid the bolts, and released the prisoned spirit of man into the wind, into the blue and gold, into the morning, into the morning."

That, and the crucifixion.

In the canyon there were no newspaper headlines, no books of opinion, no blaring radios with their undercurrent of panic. There were only the great sky, the air, the ancient rocks, with tiny wildflowers blooming, and rarely, the sound of a rill, whispering seductively to its opposite, the sand. Time seemed on hold, and war seemed far away.

But above the canyon, on the mesa between the mountains, the clock was ticking, the minute hand drawing ever nearer the putative midnight when Hitler would call the world to attention with nuclear weapons. Experimental blasts from the side canyons gave notice to the old timelessness that a new age had come.

Those blasts were heard in the pueblos along the Rio Grande. As were other blasts, like the whistle blast calling Pueblo men and women away to the buses that would carry them up the hill to be ditchdiggers, and maids for scientists' wives; like the blast of cash on a barter economy, the cultural blast of the mesa that turned practical pot making into factory production to satisfy the Hill's artistic tastes, and its acquisitive demands.

In the summer of 1928—while Gregor was still aching from Sacco and Vanzetti, and learning the insurance business from Charles Ives—a rich, young polymath named Julius Robert Oppenheimer moved out to New Mexico to hasten a cure from TB. In the foothills of the Sangres he bought a rough-hewn log cabin, two rooms downstairs, two up, with a staggering view of rolling, pine-clad slopes, flower-covered fields in summer, and snow-capped peaks in winter. He called it (mysteriously) *"Perro Caliente,"* the hot dog, and spent every summer there for the next forty years, exploring and riding in the mountains.

When, fourteen years later, he was chosen to head the lab, he prevailed upon the Manhattan District to choose the area he knew so well for its most crucial site. Remote yet accessible, the setting was also prodigiously beautiful, a crucial factor, he thought, to attract and retain the personnel he would be seeking.

Much the same reasoning determined his need to buck security by encouraging senior scientists to have an occasional meal off base, at Edith Warner's "teahouse," down the hill at Otowi Bridge. A frequent visitor, he could attest to the power of Miss Warner's to nourish the heart, break the tension of work, and keep uprooted people human, a high priority for Oppie, but trivial to Project Director, General Leslie Groves.


Edith Warner had found at Otowi the inner peace she had been seeking. From 1928, she welcomed tourists with home cooking and vegetables and fruit grown in her garden. The meals she cooked on her woodstove were always simple: stews flavored with herbs on big terra-cotta Mexican plates; posole, an Indian dish of parched corn; lettuce in a black pottery bowl from San Ildefonso; fresh-baked bread; a bowl of raspberries; or her renowned chocolate cake for dessert. The house had no electricity; the only light in the two small dining rooms came from the fireplace, and from the candles on each table. The fragrance of burning piñon mingled with the smell of baking bread, a feast for the nose to garnish the feast for eyes and tongue. The food and atmosphere made her a treasure for Hill residents, and she was soon besieged with requests for reservations, weeks ahead. In mid-1943, for security reasons, Oppenheimer asked her to serve only Los Alamites, closing her small restaurant to outsiders. He could not tell her why, except to say that their work was crucial to the war effort and top secret. She asked no questions and prepared dinner every day for ten people.

Gregor was a guest on the evening of September 14. Edith was not only cooking, but also serving that night.

"Where's Tilano?" he asked the Bethes, his table companions.

"I think he's dancing today," Rose Bethe responded. "It's Turtle Dance time. They chant all day a song that calls to the rain or snow to come, and the earth to open after summer thirsting. The same song the ancients prayed when they lived up in the caves. You should see the dances. It's like another world. You've been to the ruins?"

"No," admitted Gregor.

The front door eased open, and as if on cue, Tilano trudged in, waved two dead rabbits wearily at the guests, and disappeared into the kitchen.

Gregor imagined doing a Roach Dance for the Indians as his ticket of admission, a genuine "Gregor," no teams, only one dancer—the real one. How astounded they would be.

"I never forget a dance we see at Taos pueblo last spring," Rose went on. "The gray branches along the fields, the willows beside the stream, the silent vegetation, the guardian mountain . . . I thought, no wonder we white people watch these ceremonials with such envy. If we could only dance our dreams like that. . . ."

"It was like modern man and all his works was not yet dreamed," added Hans. "It's why Miss Warner, for all her close to pueblo people, can never really *be* them. *Sie tanzt nicht. Sie scheint oft so einsam.*"

"At the end, we will all dance," said the roach. His tablemates nodded, each with his own interpretation.


But Edith Warner was not lonely. An adopted daughter of the Pueblos, her spiritual devotion to the land, her life of poverty, and her gentle ways made her different from the other Anglos. And with such an image, she was not long at Otowi before an Indian of indeterminate age—fifty, sixty, seventy?—long black braids swinging down his back, arrived to help her run her tiny place, rented from the pueblo. It was Tilano, "Uncle Tilano," Atilano Montoya, he of the waving rabbits, come to build, come to visit, come to stay, an extraordinary man, gentle and deep, but always jovial, his face reflecting kindness, humor, and a network of wrinkles that seemed more a product of laughter than of age.

Edith and Tilano became companions, and shortly, housemates. He built her a fireplace, helped with the garden, did much of the heavy work, set the traps, and tended the cow and the chickens. He spoke a language of seasons and rocks, of bones and shells, of deer and eagle, of thunder and streams. He saw things Anglos don't see. He was grateful for everything, forgave everyone any trespass, and was humble before the life he had been given.

. . .

But it was an exhausted old Tilano who waved the rabbits at the guests and insisted on serving dessert and coffee. Impersonating the animal-gods, exchanging quotidian reality for a time-world as old as the zodiac, suspending human thought so that a surge of divinity might come streaming through him—and then, at day's end to become Tilano Montoya again, a five-foot, four-inch man, heavy with years—this was exhausting. His hand trembled as he poured Gregor's coffee and set down his cake.

"I heard you were dancing today," said the roach.

"You've seen the dancing?" asked the dancer.

"No."

"Hot stuff. I take you next time."

"I want to study up my anthropology before I come." Gregor, ever the scholar.

Tilano guffawed, interrupting the quiet conversations in the room. "You scientists!"

"I'm not a scientist. I'm a risk assessor."

"What kind of risk?"

Gregor was caught. Nothing to do but be honest.

"I can't tell you."

"I know what you're up to. It's no secret. It's all over Santa Fe."

"What?"

"You're planning a submarine base in that pond up there where the ducks swim, and those blasts—you're building a secret passage to connect it with the Rio Grande, and then out to sea."

From the next table, Dick Feynman yelled out, "He's caught us! He knows about the ducks!"

The whole room burst out laughing: in July, Feynman had convulsed a community meeting with an impromptu lecture on the thermodynamic-military potential of the ducks in Ashley Pond.

Tilano whispered to Gregor, "You come with me tomorrow. I'll show you some of *our* secrets. More powerful than white man's medicine."

"What kind of secrets?"

"If I told you, it wouldn't be secret. I'll pick you up at the East Gate tomorrow at two. You can come?"

"I'll make time."

"Good. I want to show you something special."

Edith came up behind Tilano and took him by the ear.

"That's enough, now. It's bedtime for all turtle dancers."

"Oh, Mommy, do I have to go to bed?" the Indian whined, winking at Gregor.

"Off with you, before you spill hot coffee all over our guests. Sufficient unto the day . . ."

". . . is the goodness thereof, " returned Tilano, as he shuffled off with an exaggerated pout.

Edith Warner was a strong but soft-spoken woman, naturally reticent, a woman whose silence had increased with the secrecy of the war years. Like Oppie, she was driven west by ill health and found her healing home in this desert country in her little house by the Rio Grande. She became a fixture of the region, and finally went native—hoping to absorb a landscape where mesas were "ancient beings who have seen much." Such were her fantasies, come to life.

Siren call of the spirit: the Los Alamos mesa that rose above her home had already been occupied by another redemptive fantasyland—Ashley Pond's "Los Alamos Ranch School for Boys." A sickly child like Edith, Pond, too, had come west to build his health, and to found a school where "city boys from wealthy families . . . could regain their heritage of outdoor wisdom at the same time that they were being prepared for college and the responsibilities which their position in life demanded." His boys wore shorts and slept outdoors even in the harsh winters. On camping trips, they were sometimes ordered to ride, work, and sleep naked. One wonders exactly what was going on.

All this came to an end when yet a third redemptive fantasy alighted on top of the mesa-which-had-seen-much, and was to see much more. On December 1, 1942, the Los Alamos Ranch School received notification that it was to be closed, and its lands and buildings taken over by a secret army facility. By mid-December, the road up to the school was being transformed, as hundreds of bulldozers, ditchdiggers, and earth-moving machines broadcast deafening noises to the mesa above and the valley below. Pueblo dwellers saw sacred burial grounds upturned, and hunting areas emptied of game. Anglophile Tilano was seen by some as a turncoat. But large redemptive fantasies, especially of huge mass, have huge momentum.

Gregor was waiting at the East Gate at two P.M., as instructed, under a cloudless, blindingly bright mid-September sky. Two-fifteen. Two-thirty. Had he heard wrong? Had Tilano been only joking? Was this an example of the "Indian time" he had heard about? He was sorry he hadn't brought something to read.

The agonized putt of a weary engine, climbing, became perceptible, came closer, and then in the distance, on the relatively level road to the gate, Gregor glimpsed the sky-blue '34 Ford pickup chugging toward him. Tilano pulled up and leaned over toward the open window.

"Why don't you ride in back?" he suggested. "It'll be more fun. It's only a few miles down the hill."

Gregor had never ridden in the back of a pickup truck, except inside a crate. Now he sat on a pile of old tires. The wind blowing through his antennae created a veritable symphony of sunshine, sensation, and scent.

Ten minutes later, they pulled off the road at a little gate. TSANKAWI CLIFF DWELLINGS AND RUINS, the sign said, 0.2 MI. Gregor jumped out of the back and looked around. Nothing spectacular apparent. Tilano opened the gate, and the two of them hiked down a little hill, then started to climb.

"So tell me about this," said Gregor. "Be my guide."

Tilano didn't answer, but kept trudging ahead.

"When did the Indians live here?"

"Five hundred years ago. My people. The Anasazi." He was a little out of breath after the short climb. Maybe that's why he's not talking, thought Gregor. He's getting old.

"Left because the rain stopped. Moved down to the valley and built the pueblos."

They climbed up a narrow trail worn half a foot into the rock and emerged on a plateau with a breathtaking view of the Jemez and the Sangres, the Pajarito plateau between them, with its lowlands of piñon-juniper, and occasional ponderosa clutching at the sparse damp of arroyos. They stood together at the edge of the cliff and breathed in the view.

A little over a million years earlier, 300 million years after the Carboniferous appearance of cockroaches, huge eruptions of the Jemez volcano had covered the area as far as the eye could see with thick volcanic ash called tuff. The Pajarito plateau was sculpted by streams, leaving the thrilling geography of mesas and canyons staring back at them.

"Is this the way it was then? The climate? The vegetation?"

"It was always dry. But not too dry to live. Then it was too dry to live. We came down from the mesa."

"Why would they want to live on top of the mesa? Where did they farm? Where did they get their water?"

"Down below. Climbing up and down carrying water six times a day is good for you. And they could see invaders coming. Not like us, in the valley—we didn't see you Anglos coming. But there's something special I want to show you. The secret."

They tracked back from the edge of the cliff and returned to the deep-worn trails leading upward. At one point they had to walk sideways to traverse a path worn shoulder-high between two rocks.

"How would you carry water through this?" Gregor asked.

"Strong arms. You couldn't do it. Arms too skinny."

By the time Gregor decided not to be insulted, they had reached the top of the mesa. Again, a heart-wrenching view. After walking awhile, Tilano pointed out the ruins of a three-hundred-room apartment complex surrounding a huge courtyard. *"Sic transit gloria,"* was, strangely, all he had to say. Where did he learn Latin? his companion wondered.

At the edge of the mesa, Tilano sat down and stared in the direction of San Ildefonso, his pueblo, eight miles to the northeast. He was often inclined to carve out a "moment" for himself, to call a halt to his activities in order to sit and ponder on the great, unanswerable yet utterly necessary questions.

"Why are we stopping? Is this the secret?"

Tilano just sat there, staring, not responding. Gregor, feeling ever the foreigner, resigned himself to the idiosyncracies of his guide, and lay down on his back in the late-afternoon sun. After half an hour, Tilano said, "Edith is not playful enough. She doesn't like it when I pinch her behind. But it's good for her."

An unanswerable comment.

"Laughter is from the gods."

Gregor could only nod his head, unobserved.

"Why don't you two have a phone?" he asked, feeling non sequitur was the order of the moment. "We always have to send someone down to set up dinner schedules."

"I have been in homes and heard those phones ring. The church bells are more to my liking. They call you to prayer, but they are polite and not in such a hurry. The phone is like a knife; it lunges at you, then it lunges again: no mercy, no consideration, only determined to make you bow to its wishes. Edith agrees. No phone."

"Is Edith your first wife?"

"What makes you think we're married?"

"Oh, I'm sorry, I just—"

"Everybody suspects us of hanky-panky. We have our separate beds, you know."

"I didn't mean—"

"My wife died in childbirth. I raised Domingo all by myself till he left home."

"Your son."

"Yes. Then I got lonely."

That was all for the next quarter hour.

"It's almost time for the secret." Tilano sprang up and headed down the trail.

Now it was Gregor's turn to stop and be silent. He looked out from the side of the cliff onto a landscape as different from Prague as could be imagined. Prague, magic, golden city, flowing with Vltava's liquid energy. Here, instead, was yucca, sand, and saltbush. Yet floating over this alien environment was the figure of his father, with his loud voice and his belt—that whooshing sound!—ever ready to wound and punish. Tilano was forty feet ahead before he sensed Gregor standing, staring.

"Come on," Tilano yelled. "The light is right. You have to see the secret."

They walked another quarter mile on a trail along the cliff side, and stopped in front of a tall rockface inscribed with a six-foot standing figure, a man with a head, two arms, and two legs. Tilano gestured at it.

"That's it."

"What about it?"

"It's a petroglyph carved five hundred years ago just for you."

"Why do you say that? It's nice, but . . ."

Tilano glanced at the sky. "You're going to sit here, quiet, for the next two hours, and watch that man up there. Don't argue."

Had he had any objections, they would have been useless, so Gregor leaned back against a boulder to begin his assigned vigil. It was a while before he could really focus. In the beginning, he was most aware of Tilano's silence. He is not silent, Gregor thought, because he has nothing to say. He is silent because he knows that words and more words won't do much to make the world better.

That being settled in his mind, he began to focus in on his assignment. Petroglyphs are far from frozen in their rocky settings. They were probably the first experiments in kinetic art. Some lines are cut deeply, some are shallow. The former can be seen in full light; the latter only when the sun angles across them. The most shallow lines can be seen only at the extremes of dawn and dusk. And so a petroglyph transforms throughout the day.

At about five-thirty, the figure on the stone began . . . to grow . . . antennae! Gregor was doubtful at first, but as the sun sank lower, there was no doubt: two lightly feathered antennae slowly appeared from the previously unadorned head. Next—*guck mal!*—a third pair of limbs, growing high out of the thorax, reaching in praise for the sky! The final touch—at six thirty-five—little hooks appeared at the ends of all limbs, and a set of cercae emerged at the bottom of the abdomen. Six forty-five—the metamorphosis was complete: a man had turned into an insect!

"Well?" Tilano inquired. "Ready to go?"

Gregor was speechless.

"Not ready to go?"

"Is it . . . my ancestor? My father? My real father?"

"It's not mine."

"My father in the New World . . ."

"Seems more like the Old World to me. Very, very old."

Gregor pushed himself away from the boulder and swayed, not quite able to balance. Then he did something he rarely did in public: he dropped to all sixes and scuttled on ahead of his guide. Tilano simply watched without judgment or surprise. As the trail snaked around to the beginning of the loop, Gregor, his face only a foot off the ground, came to an abrupt halt. Half buried in the earth, there glistened a piece of carved obsidian, red light reflecting off deepest black. He stopped and dug the object out. Such noncrystalline symmetry could only have been fashioned by the hand of a man.

He turned back to Tilano. "Arrowhead?"

"It's a spearhead," said the Indian.

"From?"

Tilano shrugged. "From your father. It's a gift."

Gregor held the object in his claw and saw two of his hooks through the black volcanic glass. For the first time since his change twenty-eight years before, he felt he was not alone.

A lizard jostled a bush on the valley floor, six feet below the path. The spell of recognition was broken, and it came to Gregor that he was holding a token of war. The Los Alamites were not the only ones to create death and suffering. Still, the ancient spear-maker had invoked his gods in beauty, called them forth with soaring voice, dancing body, and solemn prayer.

And now there was a new group of warriors in the very same world, intent on invoking forces deep within ubiquitous dust, calling forth with new voice the powers of the universe.

"If our hearts are right the rain will come," the first group sang. "If we can beat the Germans we can win the war," chanted the second, "heart" having dropped from the equation. Gregor knew that his was the group of the ancients, and not of his colleagues. And yet, the energy in the atom—was it really different from that which lurked in the dormant seed, which sprang from the crashing wave or the ardent fire? Long ago men had learned to call forth such energy by making themselves one with the need of earth for sun or rain. These transformations were his birthright.

.  .  .

That night, under full moon and clouds, it snowed on the mesa. And as the snow fell quietly to the waiting earth, it seemed to Gregor like a transfer of soft white down from eagle's breast to earth's breast, sent by the gods to those who remembered how to ask, as well as to those who had forgotten.

Tilano liked to tell stories:

*After stealing the sun and the moon from the Village of Light, Coyote came back over the mountain to his own Village of Darkness. He went right to the Chief's home with a crowd of people following him, and lay the two bags down on the ground. The chief poked at them with his feet and said, "I don't trust anything coming from over there on the other side of the mountain."*

*Coyote didn't say a word, but opened the sun bag and let it out to speak for itself. Everything turned bright. The Chief shielded his eyes. "Too bright. It could make us blind. Take it away." But the people paid no attention: they were happy to have light.*

*Then Coyote took the Moon out of its bag. "And this will shine in the night." The people went "Oooooh!" But the chief grumbled. "This is not as bright, but is even more dangerous. People will go out at night instead of sleeping. They'll make love all the time, and be too tired to hunt or gather food."*

*But the people loved the stolen sun and the stolen moon, and they made Coyote their new chief.*

Richard Feynman liked to tell stories, too. Like about his letter exchange with his beloved Arline, dying of TB in her Albuquerque hospital bed. As anything associated with Feynman was bound to be out of the ordinary, so were these love notes, written in code. Naturally, they were one of the first targets of the new Censorship Office, which notified Feynman of Regulation 4(e): "Codes, ciphers or any form of secret writing will not be used. Crosses, Xs, or other markings of a similar nature are equally objectionable." So much for kisses. Feynman, of course, refused to comply, citing his sick wife's mental health and need for entertainment. They asked for a key to the code. He said he didn't have a key—it would spoil his fun. Treading lightly, the censors said that if Arline would enclose a key for their benefit, they would remove it before the letter reached Feynman. Good enough.

But Arline's sense of mischief had been piqued. Informed (somehow) of Regulation 8(l), requiring censorship "of any information concerning these censorship regulations or any discourse on the subject of censorship," she began sending letters with sentences such as "It's very difficult writing because I feel that the [deleted in black] is looking over my shoulder." Dick would respond with erudite red herrings such as "It is interesting how the decimal expansion of 1/243 repeats itself: .004 115 226 337 448 . . ." and the baffled censors would go scurrying over the numbers as possible cipher for important scientific secrets. They never cracked the code—as there was none.

Before coming to the Hill, he concentrated on his science, and on enjoying life in topless bars, drumming on the beach, and telling jokes—usually at other people's expense. He thought, *If I am very good at understanding something and developing a new kind of knowledge for the world, then that's what I should do. There are plenty of other people who are better at ethics.*

That was certainly true. Feynman had the moral development of a charming four-year-old, seducing bar girls, undergraduates, colleagues' wives. Take any political position? "I haven't been following things closely enough." It is amazing how of all the notable scientists who passed through Gregor's life—Einstein excepted—it is Feynman who has achieved most public affection. Vulgar of speech, abrupt, capable of the most vicious disparagement in the spirit of self-aggrandizing play, a would-be con man as morally shallow as he was intellectually deep, he somehow succeeded in cultivating an entranced following, consciously generating amusing anecdotes and "Feynman stories." He was the most competitive person on the site. He had to be the best in the world at whatever he chose to do. Aggressive and loud as a New York cabdriver, he debunked anything he thought was "hokey-pokey."

Like everyone else, Gregor was attracted to him. As classically cultured and morally discriminating as he was, Gregor still found Feynman amusing, stimulating. And after a few months on-site, he found himself slipping into the role of Feynman's playmate and partner-in-crime.

The main issue that provoked them both was the hyper-inflated and self-important security apparatus on the mesa. It drove the all-too-similar Feynman up the wall. It had begun, reasonably enough, with the general secrecy of the project: railroad tickets to an unknown destination, no general talk about the nature of the work, etc. It already had some silliness attached, given the guarded isolation up on the mesa: fake names for the more famous people—Enrico Fermi became Henry Farmer (though Mr. Farmer would never respond to paging); Niels Bohr was Nicholas Baker, and so forth. Everyone's address was "Box 1663, Santa Fe, New Mexico"—children were even born in that box on their birth certificates.

But just before Gregor's arrival, the whole security thrust had begun to escalate to heights that seemed offensive and ridiculous to the international circle of scientists long used to open communication. Military mind was off in high gear. A memo in November initiated a new level of chaos with a wholesale clampdown on language:

```
Since employees must necessarily talk with one another
concerning problems related to the work in the perfor-
mance of their duties, it is advisable to invent ficti-
tious terms or code names, which are not descriptive,
for reference to secret or confidential matters which it
is necessary to discuss. The invention of such language
is left to the individual organization so that the terms
used will not be uniform throughout all phases of the
general project.
```

So atoms became *tops*. Bombs became *boats*. An atomic bomb was a *topic boat*. Uranium fission was *urchin fashion*. Uranium, however, was also called *T*, from its code name, *tube-alloy*. $U_{235}$ was $T_{235}$, or sometimes *tenure* ($2 + 3 + 5 = 10$; uranium = ure). Only Feynman's hilarious parodies could top the resulting babel.

Driven by General Groves's penchant for military secrecy, a "Loose Talk" campaign was begun with ubiquitous signs, posters, literature, even inserts into the dials of rotary telephones, warning residents to "HEW to the line," attempting to inculcate a general paranoia in which even family should be viewed with suspicion. "MUZZLE UP! There are at least three occasions when the mouth should be kept shut—when swimming, when angry, and WHEN OUR COUNTRY IS AT WAR!!" "Security Education Officers" spread out on the mesa to promote the campaign, each instructed to be "tactful" and yet to "sell himself and his work to all concerned."

Groves's goal was not just to bottle up military secrets but to make Los

Alamos completely invisible to the outside world. And so in October, the *Daily Bulletin,* crammed by GIs into kitchen doors, contained the following.

```
It is deemed necessary in the interests of security to
institute censorship over all personal communications to
or from any personnel at Site Y. Censorship will accord-
ingly be instituted, effective immediately, over all
such communications under provisions of paragraph 3D of
War Department Training Circular No. 15 dated 16 Febru-
ary 1943, which provides as follows: . . .
```

Groves was no poet. Because traditional military means of censor-ship—punched letters, censorship stamps, envelopes with flaps resealed—would call attention to the Project, residents were henceforth required to censor themselves. All letters were to be sent unsealed, then read, sealed, and sent on by the censor. If contents did not meet with censor approval, a letter would be returned to the writer with comments and instructions. Nella Fermi, thirteen, had a letter returned in which she had written a friend about studying fissioning amoebae in her biology class. The word "fission" was verboten.

In early December, Gregor received a letter from Colonel Peer De Silva, the Chief Intelligence Officer at Los Alamos, informing him that se-cure naming had been expanded to a second level of Site Y personnel, and that henceforth, he would refer to himself as George Samson. Being by nature far more law-abiding than Feynman, he went into baptismal angst. Samson. Why Samson? he worried. Did he want to be identified with a biblical hero who slayed thousands? Or was it because of his fatal attraction to . . . what? Would that there had been a Delilah in his life! Delilah. Delilah from *lilah,* "night" in Hebrew? What was the night he loved, the night that would cut off his strength and undo him? That very afternoon he betook himself to the small collection of books up on the balcony of Fuller Lodge, which must have been the remains of the Ranch School library, and there found a nineteenth-century Bible, dusty and un-used in this world of Science.

He read through the story of this *Übermensch,* a loner, a one-man scourge of the hated oppressor Philistines, a Nazarite, "one who is separate," one marked off from ordinary human beings and devoted to the spiritual life. Surely that fit, though the Biblical Samson was more like the Feynman of wine-women-and-song than like Gregor. Divine selection had always been murky at best.

Why do men need Delilahs? he wondered. Why now do they need bombs? Because they are glamorous and exciting? Because men yearn to be swept away by some passion beyond reason? Because men want to be present at the Fall? Because anger is aphrodisiac? Because they would know Death?

With quivering claw, Gregor returned the Bible to the shelf. As he gave a punctuating, spiracular sigh, his ommatidia registered the thickness of the book to its right, a timeworn gray-green volume with a faded, indistinct title. It took left and right claws to draw it from its space, and open to the title page:

*Theodor Benfey*
**A Sanskrit–English Dictionary,**
with references to the best editions of Sanskrit authors and
etymologies and comparisons of cognate words chiefly in Greek,
Latin, Gothic, and Anglo-Saxon.
London, Longmans, Green, and Co., 1866

His excursion with Samson had fired up his ancient history; his sharing a namesake's story had stroked his desire to know *Atman* as *Brahman*. In any case, quasi-exhausted from his tryst with multiple Delilahs, he decided then and there to learn Sanskrit. If Oppenheimer could do it, so could he. Confident from the dust layer that no one else would miss it, he tucked the book under his arm and went for a walk in the early December snow.

The Feynmans had been having fun with their codes until the censors, completely infuriated, had tossed in the trash her cotton sack containing a love letter written on the back of a disassembled five-hundred-piece picture puzzle of St. Basil's Cathedral. She had been reading *Anna Karenina* and, exposed to such passion, had fallen head-over-heels in love again with her handsome, funny, attentive young husband. She had procured this puzzle, express mail, from a catalogue, spent four days assembling it, carefully turned it over (with the help of a nurse) between two chest films, and spent another two days pouring her heart out onto the gray cardboard back. The censors, recognizing the onion domes, were distraught with the possible Commie plot. The puzzle was destroyed, and Arline's message with it. She was devastated—and Dick was incited to riot. He left his office in the Tech Area and went for a plotting walk in the early December whiteness. He bumped into Gregor at the northern edge of Ashley Pond between the Tech Area and Fuller Lodge. Feynman noticed the fat book under Gregor's arm.

"Whatcha got there, Samsa?"

"Samson. Do you mean Mr. Samson?"

"Oh yeah. New names."

"What's yours?"

"Mrs. Delilah. Wanna dance?"

He grabbed Gregor by the collar and spun him a little too roughly onto the snow.

The white-faced scholar checked his arms, gathered up his Sanskrit dictionary, wiped it carefully on a dry section of his overcoat, and asked, "What's the name of that dance?"

"It's called the 'I'm Gonna Get Those Fucks Samba.' You like it?"

"No. What fucks?"

"The goddam censors. Know what they did?" He launched into the story in vituperative detail.

"So what can you do about it?"

"I'll sue the bastards. I'll lean an open bottle of piss on their door and ring the bell and run away. Or maybe I won't run away." He took a swig from a lab bottle of ethanol in his coat pocket. "I'm gonna give 'em hell. I just haven't figured out how yet. What's that book?"

Gregor handed it over.

"Been over to Oppie's?"

"No. I got it from the Lodge."

"Why?" He took another swig.

"I don't know. It called to me."

"You need medical attention, Samson? You hear voices often? Tell me about your mother."

"I'm not joking. It's time for me to know some Sanskrit. I don't know why."

"I know why."

"Why?"

"Because me and you are gonna play a good trick on the boss."

"Why do you want to do that?"

"Just to get him for setting up this censorship bullshit."

"He didn't do it. Groves did."

"Groves doesn't know Sanskrit. It'll have to be Oppie." He took another swig of ethanol. "I'm unna go for a walk and scheme this thing out. I'll meetcha at your place at seven." And he was off, kicking up snow and shaking it off the trees at the side of the pond.

Gregor went back home—a renovated chicken coop in a field near Deke Parson's house on the north end of Bathtub row. At the housing office, he had offered to take any existing substandard unit, and the housing officer jumped at the chance to save a room. A short walk around the site revealed the perfect place. The Corps of Engineers even got it insulated before cold weather set in. While insulation is not crucial for a blattid, it does make for a more productive day.

Seven o'clock came and went. So did eight. No Feynman. At a quarter to nine, Gregor heard out-of-tune singing and rhythmic bashing of flowerpot on frying pan. It could have been "Don't Fence Me In," but he wasn't sure. When he answered the complex, extended knocking, he found Feynman sitting on the ground in front of his door.

"I gotta give up this alcohol. It's ruining my drumming."

"Do you want to come in, or would you rather sit in the snow?"

"Um unna give up alcohol. And cigarettes. Yup. And cigars and coffee."

Gregor helped him up, marched him in, and sat him down on a bale of hay.

"You think if I give up all that stuff I'll get moraller and moraller? Thas no good . . ."

In less than a minute, he was asleep, draped over the bale, like a pathetic rag doll. The smartest rag doll on earth.

. . .

The next morning Feynman was up at six, the crack of a late dawn.

"Hey, Samson, ass outta the sac. Let's work out our plan."

The plan involved safe-cracking, lock-picking, and breaking and entering—using the full array of Feynman's infamous techniques. This job,
however, had a new, ingenious twist. The physicist pulled a folded piece
of paper from his coat pocket, ink all running from the last night's snow.

"I woulda done this myself, except some damn bastard stole the Sanskrit dictionary from the library."

On the paper—a blank back-of-page from the *Daily Bulletin*—he had
scrawled a verse in his arrested adolescent handwriting:

> *Roses are red,*
> *Violets are blue,*
> *The Sanskrit Mole*
> *Is You-Know-Who.*

"I want a translation by four-thirty. Into Sanskrit. Think you can do it?
Sure you can do it. I have complete confidence in you. Then, you know what
we're gonna do? Tonight we're gonna plant this message in Groves's safe, in
Parson's file cabinet, in Bethe's, in Serber's, in Teller's, in every goddam
group leader's most secure lockup. And guess who's going to get blamed?"

"You."

"Nah. I don't know Sanskrit. Who knows Sanskrit around here? Who
gets intellectual points for knowing Sanskrit?"

"Oppie."

"You betcha."

"So what's the point?"

"Why does there have to be a point? Oppie gets blamed, that's all. The
place gets shaken up about a mole. You know what that is? A spy. Maybe
our leader, Dr. Director, is a spy. It's funny. Laugh."

It seemed innocent enough. Clearly no one would blame Oppie: he
would never pull such a prank. Besides, it might be instructive to jump
right into Sanskrit on a poem that could hardly be ruined. And to spend
tonight sneaking around with Feynman—this would surely be . . . instructive.

"Put it there, pod'ner," he said, imitating a phrase he had heard on the radio. He held out his claw.

"You Raven, kimosabe, me Coyote, ugh," said Feynman, who saluted, Indian-fashion. Gregor bowed back, Sanskrit style.

"Raven and Coyote, kimosabe?"

"Raven and Coyote heap big tricksters, blockhead furriner. Get 'em to tell you Coyote stories next time you're down at the pueblo. I'll be back at four-thirty to check your work. And I warn you, I'm an expert on Sanskrit, so it better be good."

Western culture has never been prone to honor Tricksters: they bring chaos and topsy-turvy strife; they shatter boundaries and break taboos. But even a cursory search among Western heroes will find them—from Hermes and Prometheus to Brer Rabbit. André Breton being taken to the cemetery in a moving van. Judge him as you will, Feynman came from such a utopian world, a world whose exchange value consisted in images, not dollars. The name "Prometheus" means "forethinker."

Gregor spent all day on Feynman's verse—on company time. The problem was that Benfey's *Sanskrit–English Dictionary* was just that: Sanskrit to English, and not vice versa. It took a great deal of insect patience to turn through six hundred–odd pages of nonsense script hoping to find each of the ten or so words in the poem. In addition, he could never find the word "violets." Maybe he just missed it. Maybe there are no violets in Sanskritia. So he substituted "lilacs"—without telling Feynman. Close enough for government work. Though a native speaker might guffaw, the written poem, in broken Sanskrit, looked quite beautiful:

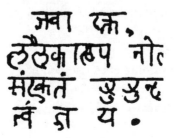

He came at four-thirty as promised, and was overjoyed at the work, hot off the Sanskrit press. They hand-drafted eight more copies for distribution, and headed for the dining hall (it was steak night) and then to their nefarious business. It was the first time they had spent any extended time together.

Feynman was quite nonchalant about breaking and entering. "You look so worried," he said. "People do it all the time," he assured Gregor. "Get stuff out of other people's offices. It's okay. We're not even taking anything. We're just putting."

Using paper clips and a small screwdriver, Feynman could get into any room within two minutes. The locked file drawers took somewhat longer, and the safes somewhat longer than that. But Feynman was often able to check a notebook he carried, and then concentrate on finding only one out of the three numbers needed for a combination. Sometimes he didn't need any.

"Where did you get the combination?" Gregor asked after Feynman went right up to Cyril Smith's safe and opened it.

"I've been in Smith's safe before. He's a physical constant man. I tried $pi$, 31-41-59, that wasn't it. I tried $e$, 27-18-28, and that wasn't it. But Planck's constant worked like a charm. 66-26-07. And anyway his secretary has the file combination on the lip of her desk drawer. See? A lot of them do."

"No sandpapered fingers? No listening for clicks?"

"That's what everybody thinks. They get it from the movies. But they don't read the safecracking books Arline sends me. It's all psychological. Or they use drills and nitro—which we don't wanna do here. It wouldn't be no fun."

Gregor was feeling more relaxed as lock after lock opened, and the Sanskrit lyric was distributed. After a while, he simply tried to make conversation, as Feynman tried various combinations.

"What have you thought of Cairo?"

"Ain't been there."

"I mean the Cairo Conference last month."

"Don't know nothin' about it. Should I?"

Feynman didn't listen to the radio and didn't read newspapers. History didn't really exist for him. Very American. It was also the secret of his seeing everything with fresh eyes.

"FDR, Churchill, and Chiang Kai-shek decide to wipe out all the Japanese Empire. They accept nothing but total, unconditional surrender. No mercy."

"Yeah, well, it serves those buck-toothed, yellow-bellies right. Bright, though. They're bright. Gotta say that." Gregor dropped the subject.

Groves's office was last on Feynman's list.

"I've got a special little present for his royal Fatness. Arline suggested this."

He handed Gregor a letter pulled from his jacket pocket.

```
Dear Sgt. Groves,

 For twelve years I have been working with cock-
roaches at my lab at Columbia University in Bogotá.
Because I am fearful that we are destroying the planet
with irreversible pollution and nuclear radiation. In
order to survive, I believe the cockroach, which has
been around for about 350 million years, has the answer.
I have now proved it, and I would like to make my dis-
covery available to you and the soldiers under your
command.

    I have developed a race of superman cockroaches by
feeding chemical pollutants and radioactive toxins to
them for three years, and my roaches developed immuni-
ties to the pollutants and toxins. I then extracted
their hormones and made a cockroach vitamin pill which
cures acne (for your troops), menstrual cramps (for the
WACs in your charge), arthritis (for you), and makes
everyone invulnerable to nuclear radiation. I have been
taking cockroach vitamin pills for over a year now, and
my colds and coughs have almost all disappeared.

    Sgt. Groves, you and I both know that mankind is de-
stroying the planet, and it is important that you and
your men be spared. Roaches are a race above.
```

Please call me at PU9-4244, Santa Fe, at your conve-
nience to set up a meeting.
Sincerely,
Dr. Joseph Stark, Ph.D.

"It's funny, but . . ."

"Funny? It's a goddam riot. It'll send him up the wall. Sergeant
Groves? He'll have a fit. Arthritis? Only someone on the inside would
know that. And all the radioactivity stuff . . . plutonium 94, atomic weight
244? He'll go drooly."

"But won't he think it's me?"

"You? Why you?"

"Well . . ."

"Does he think you're stupid enough to incriminate yourself? No. You've
got to gauge your enemy's intelligence, Samsa. He'd never suspect you."

Gregor, in spite of his leeriness, found himself getting into the game.

"I think the name ought to be more Latin American, like somebody
from Bogotá."

"Like what?"

"How about Simón Bolívar?"

"That don't sound Latin American. It's gotta end in a vowel."

"But Simón Bolívar *was* Latin America. The Liberator. The George
Washington of Colombia, Venezuela, Ecuador, Peru."

"You mean he's a real person? We'll get sued."

"He died a hundred years ago."

"But it already says Joseph Stark."

"Who's that?"

"He owned a hardware store on Central Avenue. Stark's. When I lived
in Far Rockaway when I was a kid."

"Simón Bolívar is funnier."

"What if he doesn't get it?"

"Don't they teach military history at West Point?"

"But it already says Stark. I'm gonna have to type it over."

"So?"

"But we're here now. In his office."

"So come back tomorrow. He's not even on-site. He's in Washington this week."

"Believe me, he'll hear about it as soon as the first of these Sanskrit things gets discovered."

"Even better. He'll think it's just those damn civilians who don't know how to maintain security. Then when he gets back, he'll find something in his own safe."

"A-plus for Samson, or whatever your name is. I'll do it. Simón Bolívar it is. B-o-l-i-v-a-r?"

"Exactly."

*Rabbit was carrying a large pack on his back. "What's in the pack?" asked Coyote. "Nothing you would want," Rabbit answered. "Okay, then let's see that nothing," Coyote demanded. "No," said Rabbit, "You won't like it. You'll be angry." "I'm already angry," Coyote yelled, and he tore the pack off Rabbit's back and ripped it open. Out jumped a cloud of fleas, right onto Coyote's back. He ran off scratching and howling. "I told you you wouldn't like it," Rabbit called after him.*

These are the stories Tilano liked to tell.

Christmas 1943 brought a spate of musical performances from Site Y's talented crew, among which was a sonata for trumpet and piano by Olivier Messiaen, which Gregor found at once sinister and transcendent. Otto Frisch on piano, and a hitherto unnoticed private first class, one Rudi Schildknapp. The program choice was obviously Frisch's; Rudi's groove was jazz.

Frisch was more than just the Project's best all-around pianist. Behind his gentle, cultured exterior was a man bitten by the bug, a scientist driven to quiet lunacy by the question of critical mass. Exactly how much uranium would it take to explode? He had it almost pinned down on paper. Would the material world confirm his calculations? At one Tuesday night colloquium, perhaps stimulated by his discussion with Gregor about hazardous experiments, he rose to make a confession to the congregation.

"You know I've been playing with my blocks out at Omega Nursery School," he said in his Austrian accent, "and soon Papa will be able buy us enough blocks for a real test."

He was referring to the small cubes of uranium hydride he had been stacking in a tiny pile to measure neutron production. The hydrogen acted to slow down fast neutrons so that the uranium became more sensitive—responsive to both fast and slow. Purification of $U_{235}$ was increasing now, and Oak Ridge was starting to ship workable quantities.

"Last Wednesday, so attracted was I by Lady Godiva"—his name for the naked uranium assembly—"that I leaned over her to see better her intimacies. Ah, the vulnerable naivete of men. She was subcritical, of course, but as I was peering into her cracks, out of the corner of my eye I saw the little red lamps on the monitors—they had stopped flickering, they seemed to be just glowing. I thought maybe the flicker had speeded up so much it could no longer be perceived, so I reached out and swept four hydride blocks onto the workbench, and the lamps went back to flickering. Question for the group: what happened?"

The audience yelled out without raising hands, like the gang of smart kids they were.

"You were acting as a tamper."

"You were tampering with a naked woman."

"You reflected neutrons back into the pile."

"With your molecular hydrogen, you watery beast."

In the pause after the storm, "Gregor the Risk Consultant" raised a troubled voice.

"How long were you exposed?"

"I don't know. Maybe two seconds."

"Can anyone calculate the approximate dose?"

Four and twenty slide rules sprang into operation. Feynman (no slide rule) yelled out, "Only one full day's permissible load. You'll need twice as much to be killed."

The slide rules seemed to agree. Wartime standards were more radiation-generous than they would be today.

"So I must be still alive," Frisch continued, "and therefore I want to propose an experiment. When enough tenure arrives, I want to make a real explosive device, full-size by my calculations, but leaving a big hole with the center missing so enough neutrons can escape before a chain re-action will develop. But—we make the center, too, and we drop it fast through the hole so for a split second we have real conditions for atomic explosion. And we see what happens."

There was silence in the room.

"We see if experiment fits theory," Frisch announced.

Feynman broke out in loud laughter. "That sure would be ticklin' the tail of the dragon."

Sinister and transcendent, thought Gregor.


1944. A new year, the last complete cycle in Gregor's life. One mid-January day, Rudi Schildknapp invited Gregor to a rehearsal of the Schildknapp Six, his snappy GI jazz combo. When the project risk consultant walked into the afternoon-dark theater, the band, forewarned, broke into its own version of the current Xavier Cugat hit "La Cucaracha," with Woodward switching over to concertina and Loach to maracas.

*La cucaracha, la cucaracha,*
*Ya no puede caminar;*
*Porque no tiene, porque le falta*
*Marihuana que fumar.*

"Hey, man, you know this song?" Rudi yelled out, as the band continued behind him.

"I don't speak Spanish well," Gregor answered.

"*Cucaracha*—that's you, man," Rudi pointed out. "It's pertinent. Listen up. Dig it. The old roach can't get on with it, 'cause he's got no MJ."

"MJ?" asked Gregor

"Marry-juana!" the band chorused out, and laughed, and continued to play, as Rudi jumped down off the stage into the dark house.

"Nice to see you, man. These are the real words. Gutierrez taught 'em to us. No Xavier Cugat bullshit. Marijuana to smoke, that's the scam. You ever smoke?"

"No . . . it's hard for me . . ." Gregor indicated with a sweep of forearm the contents of his thorax.

"Oh, yeah. Right. Well, we can maybe do something about that."


After the rehearsal, Rudi invited him to the party at San Ildefonso the following Sunday, after the festival. Gregor did want to see the dances, so he said yes, and spent the night with his beginning Spanish book, *El Camino Real*. "*Qué es el burro?*" it asked on page one. "*El burro es un animal. El burro es un animal importante. El hombre pobre usa el burro. El hombre rico no usa el burro. El hombre rico usa el automóvil.*" True, thought Gregor, too true.

Sunday, January 23, was the saint's feast day, the high point of the year for the San Ildefonso pueblo, a typical crisp winter day of dazzlingly blue sky, the snow-capped Jemez range to the west, the Truchas to the east, and the mysterious black mesa to the north, all looming beyond the roofs of the immaculate square. But for Gregor, it began in the dark, before sunrise, much as his last day would begin, eighteen months later, two hundred miles to the south. Late Saturday, the dancers had gone up into the hills behind the pueblo to metamorphose into animal gods. All during the night, the sound of chanting voices could be heard up high, and the faint sound of drums from deep in the village kivas. When Gregor arrived at five A.M., the stars were singeing the icy wind with their brightness.

The pueblo itself seemed deserted, not a footprint to be seen in the bare-swept plaza, as the great cottonwood kept watch over the sleeping houses. Toward five-thirty, small groups of Indians began walking along the road that borders the pueblo on the east. A small woman came up behind Gregor.

"Soon they come from over there," she said, pointing to the arroyo in the cleft of the hills. "All kind of animal—deer, buffalo, other kind, I know not how you call him. You watch. You stay there. Soon they come." And she continued on her way.

Suddenly the sound of a deep-throated Indian drum began pulsing in the semidarkness. Gregor could barely make out the group of four old men gathering at the entrance to the pueblo. They seemed not to be in any costume; they looked like uncles or grandfathers from anywhere except for their braided hair and headbands. They began to sing—and the world became transformed as the earth spirit rose up with the power of life in the trusting voices of these four men. Somehow it was clear: they were invoking man's kinship with the gods, and with the spirit of all living things.

Behind the chorus, women and children gathered quietly, looking toward the east, toward the morning hill. The sky behind grew lighter, the light began to contract around one particular point, calling the singing and drumming toward it, upward. A tall, dark Indian appeared at Gregor's side. He was dressed in regular Western clothes, and was apparently a visitor from another pueblo, another tribe.

"Indian sing for *all* men," he said, deeply earnest. "He sing for good things for this pueblo, for Indian, for all people everywhere. He sing for rain to come so summer fields grow. He sing for *everybody, everywhere.*" Over and over he kept repeating this as though he thought it something Gregor might not believe. "Indian singing for *everybody, everywhere.* That what the song say. He telling them animals bring good things, not just for this pueblo; good things for everybody, for you, for me, for this people, for all people in the whole world."

Suddenly, with blinding intensity, the first small segment of sun broke over the top, and a plume of dark smoke began to rise from the head of the arroyo high between the hills. The landscape seemed to give birth. Small figures could be made out, moving along the dark dots of juniper. On the crest of the hill two deer/men lifted antlered heads in a great nodding of yes, then made their way toward the square, dancing a zigzag trail down the slope of the hill. The Buffalo men hunched slowly down the arroyo, naked to the waist in the coldest part of winter, their bodies painted with symbols, their magnificent headdresses built ingeniously from green twigs and horn. Antelope children pranced carefully behind them. Gregor couldn't believe it: there they were, antelopes, in yellow-dyed long underwear. In spite of their comical costumes, these little ones were vastly skilled at their job, calling forth the heart as powerfully as the head dancers they followed. In the village, a chorus of Hunters had gathered in opposing lines close to the drums and old men, wearing evergreens at wrist and knee. Together, they sang and gestured an ancient ritual, renouncing hatred and enmity toward all creatures, promising to take life only for the sake of need. The Animals approaching were prayed to as gods, and asked to lay down their lives for the sake of all the living.

Once inside the square, the Sacred Animals wove their way through the groups of onlookers. Little Pueblo girls pushed in shyly to be closer, while their baby brothers and sisters peered intently from the blankets that wrapped them. Little boys in faded overalls and store-bought winter jackets looked as if they were spying on Santa's reindeer. And very tiny children hopped about, uncannily imitating the steps of the dancers. As they passed nearby, the waiting Indians threw sacred cornmeal on them—corn, the grain that flourishes only through human endeavor.

The sun was now up in full splendor, and the dancers disappeared into the ceremonial house on the South Plaza. They would come out to dance many times during the day, as the plaza filled with visitors and a myriad of booths for the display and sale of the Pueblos' famous pottery.

Not every member of the Los Alamos community who wanted to attend was ready to brave the cold of the predawn opening—cold is harder for mammals than for blattids. But by 9 A.M., the square began to mill with spectators in carnival mood. Gregor's mind went back to Vienna, the circus, Amadeus, Tomzak, Violetta, George Keiffer, Katerina Eckhardt . . . He could almost smell the popcorn and beer. But his heart was still coming down the arroyo with the animal/human gods. Who more than he knew of that intersection, that interface, that haunting doppelgänger? Who more than he yearned for animal-men to be able to emerge in an atmosphere of enjoyment, even relief, and not of horror and dismay? Why, he could probably pull rank if he wanted to. He had the strangest urge to embrace himself, half from shyly valuing his own split being, half from fearfully trying to hold it together.

The party that night was scheduled in the largest hall in the village, a long, chilly, adobe building whose walls were hung with evergreen boughs, and whose broken windows were artistically covered with beautiful Indian blankets and rugs. Clusters of crepe-paper streamers—red, white, and blue—had been tied to the rafters. The walls were lined with benches that soon filled up with shy Pueblo families dressed in fiesta clothes, looking like postcards of "Indians of the Southwest." As each woman entered, she headed for the table with a large tray of edibles balanced on arm or head, and the table piled up with simple offerings: stewed meat and pinto beans hot with chile, salads with pineapple, cabbage, apples and raisins, and several baskets of warm round-loaf bread, with plenty of butter and jam.

Then came the Yankee invasion. Crammed in among Indian offerings: hot dogs, hamburgers, and buns brought by wives in fur coats over slacks and jeans, their leather-jacketed men lugging ice chests and cases of Coca-Cola. The Europeans, especially the British, were more elegant than their American cohorts, in their overcoats, suits and ties, and more dressy dresses.

Because there was no electricity in the hall, an electronics team from the Hill set up a generator and connected the record player from Fuller Lodge. But for all the Ph.D.s involved, they could never get it to work right, and the evening's music would consist of Indian drums and chanting, and offerings from the Schildknapp Six. About seven-thirty, the pueblo chief made a welcome speech, first in English, then in Tewa, and the motley group settled down to a friendly, bicultural meal and evening.

The Indians opened the post-food festivities with a Comanche war dance accompanied by drums and a chanting men's chorus. The Hill countered with the Schildknapp Six doing their own versions of "Would You Like to Swing on a Star?," "Mairzy Doats," and "Is You Is or Is You Ain't My Baby?" At one point during a fast break in "Paper Doll," Dave and Kay Anderson broke into a jitterbug to the wild applause of the Americans. The band fed off the energy, other couples joined (it was a young crowd up on the Hill), and the Indians watched with smiles and giggles to see white thighs flashing under swinging skirts. The Indians answered the Anglo shenanigans with an elegant Dance of the Braided Belts, with its intricate movement from the men, and graceful, acquiescing answers from the women.

After a break for coffee and Coke, the Schildknapp Six went inappropriately risqué with a slow-dance version of "Bésame Mucho." No Spanish-speaking Indians went cheek-to-cheek, and since there was no alcohol, neither did the scientists, thus setting the tune as an oddly-awkward concert piece. But now the band was high in Latin transformation, and on came "Brazil" and "That Old Black Magic," with maracas and sticks. Suddenly, Rudi cut the band off and picked up the PA system mike.

"Ladies and gentlemen," he began, "please join with us in wishing a happy fortieth birthday to our favorite health and safety advisor, the great jitterbug himself, Mr. George Samson."

While the Indians responded with light applause, it took a few seconds for the Los Alamites to remember the codes and figure out just who was being congratulated. But when the band broke into a spirited version of "La Cucaracha," there was no more doubt: the spotlight was on a most-surprised Gregor. It was not his fortieth birthday. It was not his birthday at all, as far as he knew, either his original birthday, July 3, or his born-again day, sometime in the summer, he didn't know just when, he only knew it had been hot.

The crowd—at least the Americans, and some Spanish-speaking Indians—followed the band into the familiar chorus, though the Indians were bewildered and amused by the change of text from *fumar* to *bailar*—smoking to dancing.

Gregor, filled with the animal-god energy of the day, was half ready to accede to the request implied by all the little shoves and murmurs, to take center stage and do or say something. It was not the first time he had thought of performing a Cockroach Dance, the Gregor behind "the Gregor"—which dance-craze this crowd was probably too young to remember. Why, in a state of relative undress he could spin and fly, and skitter all over the ceiling. Wouldn't the children love that? But something held him back, perhaps simple bashfulness, perhaps the instinct of a proper guest not to upstage his host. Perhaps it was caution called up by "That Old Black Magic," wariness of a too-shocking exhibition that might bring out the latent but strong hatred/fear of witches Tilano had mentioned—witches who could transform themselves into animals for evil purpose. So he simply waved modestly and withdrew into the crowd and himself until the moment had passed.

Though the Indians were prepared to party all night, as was their custom, the denizens of the Hill had to be at work by eight. So at exactly eleven (musicians' union hours?) the band shut down and packed up, and a general white-skinned exodus began. Gregor approached Rudi.

"It's not my birthday. And I'd hate to tell you how much older I am than you said."

"Really? You don't look a day over forty. We needed an excuse to play 'La Cucaracha' since we rehearsed it. And also, just between the two of us, the *marihuana que fumar* is here." He patted his jacket pocket. "*No le falta.* It's our birthday gift to you—even if it ain't your birthday."

"But—I told you I can't smoke."

"But I told *you* we were going to work on it. Matt—the alto player—works with Bernard in the hospital, and he's borrowed a certain piece of new equipment."

"What?"

"Nosy bugger, ain'tcha?" He gave Gregor an affectionate jab in the snout. "Have faith. It ain't a needle. Just be patient a few minutes."

The band finished loading the van, and the other five, with waves and winks, hitched rides home with other cars going up the hill.

"C'mon, get in," Rudi said. "It's just you and me. And the reefer."

Gregor climbed into the passenger seat of a '36 Dodge van. Rudi gunned the engine and cranked up the heat.

"We're gonna need to stay warm. But there's an almost full tank of gas. Your tax dollars at work."

They drove off—north into the night.

"Where are we going?" asked the neophyte.

"Oh, I thought we'd head up towards the holy mountain for our spiritual journey."

"The Black Mesa?"

"Yeah. Why not? No one will be up there now. We can park, stay warm, and play with the little smoke."

"I don't know if I really want to do this."

"What are you, some kind of American? With that accent?"

"Why do you ask that? What's wrong with American?"

"Hey, we're violent, and booze makes it worse. Reefer would be good for us, more mellow. We all got a God-given right to get high. But no, it's too—I don't know—weird or something for Americans. Hey, George Washington smoked reefer. It's a certified fact."

"Well, I'm just not sure I'm emotion ready. It's been an overrich day."

"It's already tomorrow, man. Twelve-oh-six. Rich day, rich night, how can you complain?"

Gregor was silent, taking in the starry sky, and the huge shape looming up in front of him.


The Black Mesa, which the Indians call Tunyo, is a 2.7-million-year-old geological formation, sacred to the Pueblos, a stark, isolated volcanic butte rising abruptly from the desert, strange, dark, and huge, and even more evocative on a fierce moonlit night. In daylight, its color contrasts sharply with the buff, red, and gold rocks of the area; in the dark, the imagination can go wild.

"You know the story of this mesa? Tunyo?" Gregor asked.

"No. Do you?"

"Tilano told me. There was once a huge giant who lived on top, who ate little children in the pueblo. Name of I think Tsabiyo."

"Don't tell me that, man. You'll scare the shit out of me."

"It's okay. He's dead now," the roach reassured his friend. "Some War Gods killed him by getting eaten and then cutting their way out of his stomach."

"That's disgusting, man." Gregor was enjoying upsetting him. "So there's no more giant?"

"Well, I don't know. Maybe his son is still around. When Pueblo kids are bad, the mothers say, 'If you don't do what I tell you, I'll feed you to the giant for supper.' It works—so there must be something to it."

"So someone could still be up there?"

"I've never been there, but Tilano says there's a ceremonial stone circle, and right in the middle there's a huge boulder in the exact shape of a skull."

"The giant's skull?"

"Who knows?"

"Man, cut it out."

Rudi took the paper bag from his jacket pocket, pulled a packet of rolling papers from his shirt, expertly rolled a cigarette with one hand, and then three more. Gregor watched with the fascination he always had for someone doing things superbly.

"So how am I going to smoke those?"

"Just a minute, I ain't finished yet."

Rudi took a small dropper bottle from his pants pocket and ran a thin stream of greenish liquid along the seam of each cigarette.

"Is that to keep them rolled?" asked an ingenuous Gregor.

"Nah. Spit'll do that. This is some high-powered medicine from our GI medicine-man-witch-doctor lab. You'll like it. Okay, Kilroy, follow me."

"I thought we were staying in the van."

"We are, but we're going in back."

Rudi and Gregor each got out.

"Around the back, roach."

He held the left back door open.

"Inside."

Gregor crawled in and found the dark closeness quite pleasant. The band instruments and PA system had been packed and tied in tightly along the right side of the van, leaving a long narrow space of free floor on the left.

"On your back, kook. Oh, wait. I guess you can just crouch down there if it's more comfortable."

"What are you going to do?"

"Speaking of George Washington, you are of course familiar with the famous George Washington Crile, and his contributions to the study of surgical shock?"

"I can't say . . ."

"That's all right. I never heard of him either. Bernard gave Matt a report he wrote called 'The Resuscitation of the Apparently Dead.'"

"Now wait one moment . . ."

"Don't get upset, it's just about his G-pants, which, in case you're interested, ain't no relation to G-strings."

Gregor didn't know what G-strings were.

"The G-pants—G is for gravity—were his dying gift to the Air Force last year. Or so I'm told. The G-pants"—he pulled them out of a wooden Red Cross box in the van—"go tight around your legs and abdomen, in your case, we'll just snuggie them around up to these middle legs, like so, and we'll tighten up the strap up here, like so, and we'll tighten these around your ankles or whatever you call them. Comfy?"

"Yes. I think I see what you are doing."

"Elementary, my dear Samson."

"You know I breathe through the holes in my sides."

"Hey, what do you think I am, a dummy? I suffocated plenty of insects in my time."

Rudi inserted the pump into one of the ankle seals and pulled out a reefer and his Zippo.

"Now, I light up one of these little stickies." And he blew the smoke into the intake hole at the bottom of the pump.

"That'll hold the smoke and still give you some space to breathe."

He worked rhythmically for a few minutes.

"Feeling anything yet?"

"Just a little dizzy."

"Okay, I'm gonna push on your back between pumps, all right?"

It looked like an exotic version of CPR, perhaps something you might see in a field hospital.

"Oh, that's much better, much deeper," the patient said.

The doctor himself was not exactly unaffected by being smoke-mediator to the pump. His boisterous laughter got Gregor going, too, and a duet, giggly and uproarious, echoed faintly in the cold desert night.

"It is tonight," Gregor announced, "that we must die laughing." And at this solemn pronouncement they both almost did.


"Got the munchies yet?"

Gregor found Rudi's chocolate almost unbearably intense. The human bodily envelope, with its awe-inspiring endurance for pain, has surprisingly little capacity for pleasure at too high a pressure. Imagine, then, the levels that could be built up inside a hard, chitinous shell. Gregor's heightened sensitivity embraced the cosmos to the farthest, and innermost, firmament. Even in the echoing confines of a metal van ringing with laughter, he was able to hear the slightest rustlings outside: the scurry of a lizard, the whistle of wind, the howl of a coyote ten miles away. The tympanic membranes at his knees were in a state of high alert; his whole nervous system seemed hugely enhanced, his giant neurons pulsing rivers, his inward eye enlarged. His thoughts themselves became stimulants, not product. The simplest words, the most trivial ideas, assumed new and strange guises; the word "egg," for instance, had him initially in stitches, until he stumbled into the profundities of eggness, and was astonished at ever having found it so simple.

At one point, Rudi got out his trumpet, put in the mute, and began to evoke a quiet, snaky path—or so it seemed to Gregor—an arteriole knotting together the earth and spirit worlds. The roach observed in amazement how the musical notes turned into numbers and imaginary numbers, how the melody, still sensuous, transformed into a huge arithmetical process in which numbers begot numbers in a net that enveloped the universe. His silly euphoria was gone now, replaced by a state close to anxiety, but somehow numbed and nonthreatening.

Rudi put down his trumpet.

"You know what's funny?"

"What?"

"Next week is the birthday of my brother's graduation. Yeah, he was a January graduate."

"From where?"

"From life. Commencement into the other world."

"What do you mean?"

"Hey, this is a righteous war, no? Good versus evil? Everyone's behind it, cheery about it as possible. But you know something?"

"What?"

"God, we have such a phony picture."

"Who?"

"Americans. Americans over here—not over there. The real war will never get in the books or the papers."

"Right," said Gregor, also somewhat ignorant. After a pause, Rudi continued.

"You know those dead bodies in *Life* magazine? They all look like people. I mean they're dead, but they're all . . . intact, sprawled out maybe, but they look like people, you know? Wanna hear about my brother?"

Gregor was too humane—and too high—to refuse.

"You'd think that soldiers on the front line—like the Marines at Guadalcanal, right?—you'd think they'd be hit by bullets and shrapnel and all that, you'd expect it, right? But you know what split open my brother's skull? His buddy Frank's detached head. Frank's detached head."

Gregor didn't know if he wanted to hear the rest of the story.

"It's true," Rudi continued. "Artie Giannini came over to tell us about Karl—that's my brother. He got hurt by the same guy. Frank's legs kicked Artie in the neck and crushed his airpipe. Got him a discharge, though. And a Purple Heart. Got Karl graduated, good old Frank. Wanna know what happened to Frank?"

"Not really."

"Okay, I'll tell you what Artie told me. They were cleaning up the Japs, right?, going on a sweep, and all of a sudden there was this blinding flash a few yards in front of them, and this head comes flying back and whacks into my brother's face, and these legs go another way and kick Artie in the throat. See Frank was up front with a mine strapped to his belt, and he picked up some friendly fire from behind. Hit the mine and blew him into three pieces."

"Oh."

"I don't know what happened to his chest."

Rudi began to laugh. Gregor saw laughing fangs and animal spittle, and nausea came on him, distantly. He tried to get up, but found he could barely summon the will to move. It was as if the bonds of matter and spirit had been severed.

"Frank's guts were all over the hillside. Karl wound up wrapped up in 'em. Sorta like a poncho. That's what Artie said."

Gregor had raised his body enough to grab the handle and open the rear doors out to the starlit night. As he inched his way out of the van, Rudi waxed philosophical:

"Some guys complain about being out here with this ridiculous project whatever it is, but that's because they don't know what's really going on out there. I'll take the domestic bugle corps anytime." He shut the doors that Gregor had left open. "Gotta conserve heat," he yelled after his friend.

Gregor could no longer feel his body; he moved by sheer willpower in an unresisting medium. In spite of the Ruditalk behind him, perhaps *because* of it, he now felt benevolence, a flaccid, dumb benevolence, a total softening of the nerves. Things seemed to glow around the edges, their contours standing out sharply against their backgrounds. Everywhere he focused his gaze seemed real and clear, but everything on the periphery seemed infinitely far away.

Perhaps it was the piercing quality of the high desert air, but he could swear he felt rhythmic pulses of cold in his gullet, the way a human might on inhalation. A sharp gust of wind whipped his antennae from back to front, and as Gregor tried to smooth them back in place he felt them detach from his headpiece. He reached out, panicked at the thought of their blowing away into the dark desert, but he found that his middle pair of legs would simply not move: he was hemiplegic, a biped. He dropped to all fours. There! A quadruped. Better than nothing.

An unwonted tingling in his front claws made him pull them off the ground and sit back up against a boulder, and stare at them intensely. He held up his right claw the better to focus on it, and found that in making the arc around to eye level, two of his hooks seemed to turn flittingly into—fingers? He couldn't believe his mosaic eyes. He played with the phenomenon. He seemed to be surrounded by some invisible, egg-shaped membrane. When he thrust his arm past the border, the distal part turned into tingling fingers, tingling fingers on a tingling hand, a hand with wrist, a hand with wrist and forearm. As he pulled his arm back in again, it would turn again into familiar, comfortable chitin. He tried his left arm: same amazing transformation. Same with both, simultaneously. He thought—now with horror—of a sixteenty-century woodcut he knew, a man poking his head out of the sublunar, terrestrial sphere into the un- limited, star-streaked cosmos. He was terrified of what might happen should his head poke through, but even now he could feel unaccustomed tastes in his mouth, and unaccustomed thoughts of power.

"Help!" he screamed—and screamed and screamed, until he heard the van door open and the staggering steps of Rudi Schildknapp, approaching.

"What's up, buddy? Oh, you got it bad."

Rudi reached right through the barrier, grabbed a forearm, pulled Gregor up to unsteady hind legs, and walked him to the cab of the truck.


On the way back up the hill, Gregor was unfazed by his barely present driver, zonked out of reason and reaction-time, offering up their lives to hairpin turns. He was focused on the offer he had been made: to step back into the human world, to go back to the way things were so long be- fore, to bid goodbye to exile and loneliness, to re-embrace the ordinary. "I wipe my face," he thought, "and chitin drips off, melting. I can turn into whatever I want. Transformation. No body. Beyond body. Beyond thought." Rudi leaned over to yell in the side of his head:

"Hey, George. Hey, Bugger!"

Gregor just stared out at the winding road coming up fast in front of him.

"Hey, anybody home? I got a question for ya."

With no answer, and probably none forthcoming, Rudi continued.

"Which came first, the reefer or the roach? I mean, why do they call this little thingy here a roach? Were there roaches when reefer was in- vented? I used to go the museum and look at the dinosaur exhibits, you know, behind glass, and they paint the background and you can't tell where the real stuff ends and the fake stuff begins, and I swear, I re- member it really clear, there were huge marijuana plants growing all over. I mean, they were probably stuffed, but it looked like some significant shit!"

"No," said Gregor. Said or thought. "It's a gift, a poisonous gift." By which he meant that he was more valuable in his present form.

"What kinda gift?"

"From the insect god. An insect god gift. A cross-pollination."

Rudi thought about that for a while, and then said,

"George, you sure are one fubar'd cat."

Gregor looked bewildered.

"That's army for 'fucked up beyond all recognition.'"

Plutonium: pee-yew!

Plutonium, like Gregor, was something new on planet Earth: the crossing of their world lines was probably inevitable. Once neutrons had been harnessed, once atom smashers were conceived, once the labile nature of heavy metal nuclei had been demonstrated, it was only a matter of time. It fell to Glenn Seaborg, a tall, lanky, Michigan Swede, to stick in his thumb and pull out—Element 94.

On August 20, 1942, Seaborg's group had successfully precipitated a microscopic particle of plutonium, less than 1 μgm, from a large mass of neutron-bombarded uranium in an experimental Oak Ridge pile. One microgram is very little. One U.S. dime weighs 2.5 grams—2,500,000 micrograms. But good—and bad—things come in very small packages, and the step from zero to 1 μgm was a huge one: a theoretical beast had been born into the material world, and snared in Seaborg's elaborate net.

Conservative Swede that he was, he named element 94 after the planet Pluto, discovered twelve years earlier. In this, he was echoing Martin Kaproth's logic when, in the fateful year of 1789, he named the newly discovered "uranium" after the newly discovered Uranus. And droll Swede that he was, Seaborg chose Pu, rather than Pl, as the chemical symbol for the new element. He thought the metal would be rambunctious and stinky to deal with, and he thought "P.U." would best capture its unpleasantness. It was a thoughtful gesture: $Pu_{239}$ was one of the nastiest characters ever to materialize on the world stage. But who cared then, in summer 1942, with only a microgram in existence?

Transmuting $U_{238}$ to plutonium in a chain-reacting pile was one thing, but extracting the baby from the mother quite another. The new element was present at a concentration 250 parts per million—a tiny amount, uniformly dispersed through two tons of uranium mixed with highly active fission products. It was like looking for a needle in a haystack, except the needle was dispersed in tiny pieces, and the hay was horrendously radioactive.

The discipline of ultramicrochemistry was young, but already there; Seaborg took a crash course. He learned to manage manipulations on the mechanical stage of a binocular microscope, using fine glass capillaries as beakers, and small syringes mounted on micromanipulators to inject and remove reagents. Tiny centrifuges separated precipitated solids from their mother liquids. His first balance consisted of an almost invisible platinum pan attached to a single quartz fiber fixed at one end. He would micro-load the micro-pan and observe how far the fiber bent. It looked, he said, "like invisible material being weighed on an invisible scale."

Oh for Lilliputian chemists here. Seaborg was six-foot-three and one of his graduate students, Lou Werner, six-foot-seven. It was a comical sight. But techniques improved, reactors and cyclotrons churned tortoise-like away, and a year and a half later, in February 1944, the first plutonium delivery was made to Los Alamos, a small, experimental quantity, less than 1 mg. A three-hundredth of a dime. For the experimental physicists who had been marking time watching the theoreticians' song and dance, it was as if the Holy Ghost had arrived, trailing clouds of glory. From Gregor's point of view, however, the clouds contained more than a whiff of sulfur: the arrival of macroscopic plutonium radically multiplied community risk.

The dangers had been somewhat foreseen: in the spring of 1943, design and construction of D-Building had begun—to house the CM Division (Chemistry and Metallurgy)—in the new era of plutonium. A host awaiting the guest, a bridegroom awaiting the bride, completed and occupied in December. D-Building, home of the Plutonic. Typically, it was designed to protect the plutonium more than its handlers.

"Groves is a riot," Feynman confided to Gregor at one more impromptu orientation. "A dangerous riot. And quite a hurdle for you, Herr Doktor Risk Assessor. Before you came, he gave us his big three principles."

For all his Brooklyn accent, Feynman did a pretty good Groves imitation:

"'All project design here at the site is governed by three rules: One: safety first against all hazards—known and unknown.' A good one, that, especially the unknown part. 'Two: certainty of operation—every possible chance of failure will be guarded against.' It's obvious the general don't know beans about science.

"'And three . . .'" Oppie chimed in. Feynman joined him for a recitation of the Third Principle:

"'. . . the utmost saving of time in achieving full production.'"

Feynman: "'Project Safety,' he calls it!"

Oppie: "'A utopian program of universal health care for all who live and labor behind these fences.'"

Feynman: "'A health plan including prevention, family care, and hospitalization.'"

Oppie: "It's so complete I have to defend it on the Hill against charges of 'socialized medicine.'" Fingers together at the heart, he nodded his head in Hindu prayer: *"Namaste."*

Gregor laughed at the performance, but apprehensively.

"For Groves, the indisputable first priority," Oppie observed, "is speedy production; the second, prevention of information leakage, liability, or bad publicity; and absolutely last, the health and safety of workers and unsuspecting neighbors."

"This puts you and him on a collision course, Samsa," Feynman observed, "in a pretty unequal battle. David does not always slay Goliath."

It wasn't an encouraging briefing.


Gregor began his job naively by applying the systems of risk analysis he had invented, and which by now were considered standard, even classical. His projected program included worker training, safe design, vigilant quality control, and effective regulation. To begin, he would need accurate estimates of every risk, its probability and potential destructiveness. But this was a new world of dangers.

He knew what had happened to the pioneers of radioactivity: not many of them had lived long. And here his charges were now, likely to work with materials millions of times more active than those of the early experimenters. What was it they could expect? He personally remembered the New Jersey scandal in the twenties: all the workers at United States Radium, young women licking their brushes to a fine point while painting luminous watch dials, suffering a wide variety of bizarre illnesses—rotting jawbones and bone marrow, acute long-term anemias, weakness, infections, cancers of all sorts.

Gregor, naturally, was not the only one aware of radioactive issues. The National Bureau of Standards had published a secret 1941 handbook detailing the dangers of radiation exposure: handling of radioactive materials; bombardment by proximity; breathing of radioactive dusts and gases; intake of elements by mouth or skin contact. It even raised the question of cancers emerging years after exposure. With such authoritative history and material, Gregor was sure he could forge ahead with his Herculean task. But it turned out to be more a story of Samson than of Hercules.

Safety depended on the prewar, and somewhat questionable, concept of tolerance, the amount of radiation living systems can absorb without permanent damage. But how valid were the standards? It was Gregor's job to ask. Were all the risks, toxicological and radiological, fully perceived? Would these new and strange substances pose unknown safety problems—such as container failure under constant particle bombardment? Were there better ways to detect radiation? Could radiation damage be treated if not prevented? These were Gregor's questions for a wide-ranging program of research.

Without clearing it first with Groves or Oppenheimer, he put out a memo to the community describing his dual mission: "Protection of the health of the workers on the Project," and "Protection of the public from any hazards arising from the operation of the Project." He spoke of "trying to establish tolerance doses, to predict more accurately future health problems, to devise means of detecting ill effects to personnel, and to discover methods of treating any person who might be injured."

The bureaucratese had been tweaked by Charlotte Serber, reference librarian. The Project, they wrote, had a "moral obligation to the personnel and the community," and this moral obligation was "to make certain that the weapons being developed would be a force for good, and that workers and citizens would not end up unwitting victims of the State, even in wartime." (One might have thought that after living in the White House for eleven years, he would have understood "going through channels." But channels were soft under FDR.)

The day after his memo, he was escorted by military police to General Groves's office. It was not a pleasant scene.

. . .

"Sit down, Mr. Samson."

"Thank you, sir."

"Samson, just who gave you permission to put out that memo?"

"No, one, sir. I thought it would be helpful to make clear our work."

"Samson, look, we've all got to get used to working together, the military and the crackpots. I'm on one side. Which side are you on?"

Gregor recognized this as an old Leninist phrase.

"I suppose I'm on the crackpot side, sir. But it is in everyone's interest to—"

"It's in everyone's interest," the general roared unexpectedly, "for us to drop our bomb on Hitler before he drops his on us." Then, more calmly: "And that will require certain priorities in our work. I am the one who sets those priorities. Who is the one that sets those priorities? Say it."

"You are the one to set the priorities." Gregor was not liking this discussion.

"Now I understand, Mr. Samson, that you are not a soldier, and therefore do not have to simply take orders from me. Therefore I will explain certain things to you—for the first and last time, I may add—so that we will both agree on our plan. Are you ready to listen?"

Gregor thought of his father.

"Yes." He looked at the general's belt.

"Would you like to take notes, since I hear you're a literary type?"

"No, sir." But aggressively sullen.

"I will take up the points as they appear in your memo." He took a copy from his desk. "The line between safe and dangerous radiation dosages does define everything—millions of dollars in construction, many months' difference in production time. There are already accepted industrial standards for safe dosages."

"But there are no agreed standards in the medical community," Gregor responded. "The 'tolerance dosages' are by little or no evidence. And we don't understand about fast neutrons, we know almost nothing about slow neutrons, and nothing at all, I am told, about alpha or beta emission. These radiations are all here now, and will get worse when plutonium really comes. We don't even know how thick working gloves should be."

"It doesn't matter how thick the gloves are if people won't wear them because they can't do their jobs wearing them. And they *won't* wear them. The machinists won't wear them because it's impossible to run a machine tool wearing gloves."

"But of course they're forbidden to know why they must wear gloves," Gregor injected.

"You think everyone is as concerned as you?"

"If not, they should be—or District will pay lawsuits until the end of the nineteen hundreds."

"Ah, lawsuits. There will be no lawsuits, Mr. Samson, if we define our health and safety responsibilities accurately, and with appropriate limitations. May I remind you that this is war, war with a totalitarian maniac. War is not about health and safety: it's about survival. Our boys in Italy and the Pacific have no right to stop work because of safety considerations. What makes us different? Do you want every worker here at the site worried about every little thing we don't know, spreading panic, calling for production boycotts until we are one hundred percent sure of the last jot and tittle? You health people better keep things in perspective. You let your humanitarian concerns get in the way of duty, and you may wind up sacrificing humanity."

"The least we can do is change around workers through heavy radiation jobs."

"Rotate them?"

Gregor nodded.

"I see. You don't think rotation will invite suspicion and have people wondering about their work? And have you asked the men about rotation? They get good pay for risky work. You take a civilian off a high-paying job, and he'll quit, leave the Project. And what if he comes down with something and goes for medical attention? You think we won't get asked what's going on here? Are you prepared to tell the national medical community what we're doing? That's where the suits will come from. And the scandals. We've got to keep our people happy—and keep them here. We've got to inspire confidence among the troops, even if it means fudging. You eggheads with your damn abstractions! You think we need some kind of ethical debate over means and ends? We need the right kind of health people here who can see the larger picture and not worry the community about measly issues. And you're not going to stand in my way, understand? Dismissed."

Gregor had dismissed himself long before. There was one point General Goliath had made with which he agreed: research did seem something of a luxury when he could not even keep informed of, much less regularly inspect, all the technical operations at Site Y. He would begin hazard studies immediately. Gregor Samsa would be everywhere. He would get Feynman to borrow records, exposure logs, accident reports, from locked files. He didn't need much sleep. He would work quietly: no more memos. He was getting the picture of how to work here.

So was Groves. The very next day, he appointed Dr. Stafford Warren as head of the Medical Section of the Manhattan Engineering District, commissioned him colonel, and designated him as his official medical advisor. Warren had the kind of credentials Groves was interested in: he had worked extensively as a consultant for the Eastman Company in Rochester, was supportive of the ethos of industrial production, and had the endorsement of Eastman's corporate policymakers. But his outstanding quality was that he was absolutely loyal to General Leslie R. Groves.

Dr. Warren's first act was to put out his own memo to contravene Gregor's. Rather than investigating possible hazards and determining limits to be set for their possible elimination, the Medical Section's mission would be henceforth to determine "what protective measures should be taken to eliminate or protect against any specific health hazard of a serious nature." The word "specific" gutted Gregor's interest in low-level radiation: "a fishing expedition," Warren called it. And the statement obviated the need to study long-term effects, since it required the problems to already be "serious." The very health hazards most characteristic of radiation were neatly avoided. In addition, all site inspections would be "advisory only," with no power of enforcement or authority to halt dangerous practices or order changes in procedure. This power would lie exclusively with Groves.

"Dr. Samson, I know you are concerned about low-level emission and long-term-effect studies."

"That is what I understand concerns safety, Dr. Warren."

"But Dr. Samson, we have to be practical. We have to get this job done. We have to apply a workable cost-benefit analysis, don't you think?

The only way to do this is by concentrating on clear, usable information about any acute illness."

"I think this is purposeful ignorance," said Gregor.


Groves was nothing if not consistent. His issue was control. That is how he had built the Pentagon; that is how he would build the atomic bomb. Militarize health care and you control information. Doctors under military control can be forbidden to report hazards. They can be ordered to refer patients to on-site medical experts, and to assure them that their injuries are not job-related.

Concerned with limitation of liability, Groves made no mention of radioactive contamination. The District and its three major sites became a vast, unofficial medical experiment with radiation exposure, plutonium and uranium inhalation and ingestion, phosgene gas poisoning, and beryllium overexposure. There were no controls, no scientific supervision, and no access to details that might aid treatment. There were consequential accidents and real injuries. There were corresponding calls for loyalty in a climate of secrecy, censorship, dissimulation, and threat. The priorities were clear: no human danger could be allowed to slow the production and employment of plutonium.

Gregor did what he could. He worked with electrical engineers to develop a portable counter for alpha emissions. He brainstormed with mechanical engineers on safe design for plutonium-handling equipment. He tried to promote his "unofficial" rules for working with radioactive substances.

In August, the inevitable happened: a vial of plutonium exploded in the face of Spencer Lusk, an SED chemist, who spontaneously gasped and swallowed, taking the material into his stomach and lungs. Gregor, one of the first on the scene, was confronted by the obvious and unanswerable questions: How to determine how much he has taken in? What were his risks, what were his chances for recovery? What to do to save him? Policy or not, answers had to be found.

How can plutonium in the lungs be measured? To solve this problem, Gregor came up with a rough method, but one that for many years provided the only approximation for inhaled Pu. The workers called it the

"Hot Snot" test, in which the inside of each nostril was swabbed with one square inch of filter paper. Readings higher than 100 counts per minute were arbitrarily seen as problematical, but all Warren would allow was a warning to improve technique. Better than nothing.

By June of 1944, batches containing gram quantities of plutonium began arriving at Los Alamos, and were quickly used and reused in extensive chemical and metallurgical experiments—more than two thousand separate experiments were logged by the end of the summer. Gregor needed all six legs.

All great enterprises have their crises. The Manhattan Project's came that July, as plutonium data began to emerge. Oppie called a special lunch-time meeting.

"Some of you may have heard about Segrè's results in the last few days of work. We suspected, and now we know, that what's coming from Hanford is a mix of isotopes. Pu-240, like its sister, is also an $\alpha$-emitter, and while there's not a lot there, it's far more jittery. Its emission rate is well over a thousand times that of enriched uranium—a million and a half spontaneous fissions per hour. When 240's $\alpha$-particles collide with an impurity nucleus, especially that of a light element, neutrons are created in $\alpha$-n reactions. Unless impurities are kept to an impossible level, the resulting neutron background will increase the chance of a fast fission chain reaction well before maximum supercriticality is attained . . ."

"And we'll get a fizzle," several in the audience rang out.

"A fizzle is what we'll get. The entire assembly will blow itself out without a significant explosion."

Thick gloom in Theater Two.

"I'm sure you get the picture. Our gun design, our beautiful, simple, guaranteed-to-work gun design will fail with the plutonium we have. Fizzling predetonation."

"And I take it we don't, we won't, have enough uranium for more than one bomb—at least in the next two years?" asked Ed Hammel.

"Correct. At least at current separation levels."

"And we can't get the plutonium any purer?" McKibben wanted to know.

"You know the difficulties."

Long silence. Then:

"What about Neddermeyer's implosion stuff?" It was Feynman, who had last pronounced it worthless. It seemed to smell better to him now.


Implosion design was far trickier than the familiar ballistics of cannons. A ball of subcritical plutonium would have to be compressed almost instantaneously, absolutely symmetrically, in order not to fizzle. Explosive lenses would have to be developed, shaped charges of various materials that would focus the otherwise unpredictable shock waves. A tamping container would be needed to reflect escaping neutrons back into the fission. A timing circuit and detonating system had to be invented that could trigger the jacket of lenses with fantastic accuracy so that pressure waves from all directions would converge in step toward their target. An internal initiator would be needed at the center of the plutonium core to provide an exquisitely timed burst of neutrons to initiate the process. And finally, diagnostics would have to be developed, ways of measuring all these processes—wave profiles, neutron flux, materials stress: super-high speed cameras, new X-ray devices, magnetic sensors, radiation detectors—all this without being able to test the crucial materials in full scale assembly. There was much doubt that such an intricate scheme could succeed; there had been far more confidence in the uranium gun design. Oppie was devastated, and considered resigning as lab director.


With the crisis, Gregor's demoted star went into a kind of complex retrograde. Disband the plutonium project? Gregor was associated with such opinion. Focus the work uniquely on plutonium implosion? Gregor's thigmotactic hijinks with Neddermeyer were well known. July of 1944 was Gregor's month for being whispered about, consulted, praised, and damned. Even Dr. Warren was moved to mend some fences. When the District Engineer recommended that maximum permissible dosages be increased, Warren invited Gregor into his office to put the following question:

"What dose of gamma radiation do you feel a superintendent can order one of his men to be exposed to with reasonable assurance that the chance of permanent damage would be slight?"

Gregor, honest as ever, confirmed Warren's attitude toward him. "A superintendent should never order anyone to expose to more than lowest tolerance. Before you ask overexposure, there should be determination of real dangers by a real radiologist."

"Don't you think wartime demands greater risk?" asked the senior radiologist of the risk assessor.

"Only if the men are informed complete about the danger, and only if they volunteer."

"I see. Well, if any cases of acute or chronic exposure come to our attention, we will notify you." Needless to say, Gregor was never notified.

His month ended in a blue, Sisyphian funk, with a sense of tenuous connection between his being and his world. In spite of all the recent attention, he felt more symbol than substance, ripe for evaporation, ripe, as Camus had noted two years earlier, for suicide, a common response to the absurd. Oppie worried about him enough to insist, perhaps inanely, that Bob Serber accompany him to the evening of Disney films scheduled for August 1. He was surprised to hear that Gregor already intended to go, and was looking forward to seeing Walt Disney's *Fantasia,* about which he had heard much, but had never seen.

It was the first time the film was to be shown on the mesa, and Theater Number One (the one with the cushions) was packed with couples, children, and dogs in spite of the fact that it was a Tuesday night with crisis-hectic work in the morning. It was a hot stuffy spell for August, and Gregor hung his jacket on a peg at the door as they entered.

Gregor, strangely and not so strangely, seemed to focus in on one of the lesser musical events, Paul Dukas's symphonic scherzo, *The Sorcerer's Apprentice.* Surely there were echoes of his Spengler studies in the teens and twenties, and the theme of man losing control of his tools was ever present on the mesa. He told Serber afterward that he had had to mem-

orize the original Goethe poem, *Der Zauberlehrling,* in grade school in
Prague:

*Stehe! stehe!*
*Denn wir haben*
*Deiner Gaben*
*Vollgemessen!—*
*Ach, ich merk es! Wehe! wehe!*
*Hab ich doch das Wort vergessen!*

*Stop! Enough!*
*For we have had*
*Quite enough of your bad gifts.*
*I see it now, oh dear, stop mop!*
*I've forgotten the word to make you stop!*

he recited, along with the gestures that went with it. Remarkable, what
we remember! Still, the multiplication of uncontrollable brooms and the
subsequent flooding was not what most moved him. He was struck most
by the short dream sequence in which Mickey stands on a rock conducting the planets and the comets and the sea, the surprisingly benign aspiration of a little man given complete control of the earth and its elements,
a diminutive Everyman sharing Tom and Huck's dream of "having a spectacular lot of fun without being malicious." Why could the scientists not
understand this? So much fun they were having!

Gregor chortled at one of the least-appreciated sight gags in the film:
Mickey is awash in a whirlpool, hanging onto, and frantically searching, a
book of magic for the missing words, trying to find the formula to make
the water stop—and he licks his finger to turn the page. Gregor found this
both hilarious and profound.

But the hilarity, even the profundity, vanished quickly when, on
exiting the theater, Gregor put on his jacket in the newly chilly night.
Thrusting his claws into its pockets, he came up with a folded piece
of paper he had previously been unaware of. He and Serber stopped at
a street lamp outside Fuller Lodge to read it. It had been pasted up,

letter by letter cut from glossy weeklies in mangy heterogeneity, and it read:

```
MISTER INSPECTOR

YOU THINK YOUR SO SMART
YOU THINK THAT THEN US
YOU KNOW MORE.
WELL I'M HERE TO TELL YOU
YOU OLD FUCKING FART
YOU WON'T KEEP US
FROM WINNING THE WAR.

ABOUT OTHERS YOU WORRY
THAT THEY WILL GET SICK
BUT ITS "U.S." THAT
YOUR MAKING FLOUNDER
WELL GO SNIFF AT YOURSELF THEN
YOU COWARDLY PRICK
STICK YOURSELF IN THE OLD
GEIGER COUNTER.
```

"Feynman?" he asked. Bob Serber looked more worried than usual.

"Doesn't sound like Feynman. He's not that patriotic."

"And he wouldn't rhyme 'flounder' with 'counter.' Think I should find a Geiger counter?"

"Definitely."

Shades of Roentgen!

They headed for the Tech Area, Building Q, headquarters for the Health Group. No one was working, and Gregor opened up with his key. He grabbed a Geiger counter from the lab office: Nothing.

"Must be just a joke," Serber muttered, "a pretty awful joke."

"Let me try one more thing."

Gregor returned from Hempelmann's office with one of the new alpha counters and turned it on. Two beings both jumped at the burst of clicking. A quick sweep located the source at his head: his beret and his antennae were both hot.

"You think it's plutonium?" he asked.

"What other alpha-emitters are we working with?"

"None I know."

"Let's check your head more carefully."

The beret was hottest at its center, and must have been the depository for the poison. Because of the way his antennae were curled up, the chemoreceptors at the base were uncontaminated, though when he focused attention on them, he was aware of slight tingling. Only the distal third of each antenna was active, and Gregor almost nonchalantly broke them off.

"Don't worry, they'll grow back. My version of a crews cut. I just won't be as attractive to women." Bob Serber didn't know whether that was funny ha ha, or funny peculiar.

Gregor recorded the incident in detail, delivered the note to security, and the beret and antenna ends to the Decontamination Unit the following day. After being carefully examined, he received operational radiological clearance.

The culprit was never identified. Gregor was strangely calm.

People close to him became concerned with Gregor's mental and spiritual health. Oppie noticed it, too, and invited him in for a talk. Genuine care here—in addition to security concerns.

"Gregor, have a seat."

"George."

"I won't tell. How are things going? Still healthy? That incident was—still is—very worrisome."

"I'm feeling fine," Gregor assured him. "It's well known who will inherit the earth."

"Insects."

"Naturally."

"Sounds like a line from a Nazi marching song. Today Germany, tomorrow the world."

Oppie puffed on his pipe.

"Smoke bother you?"

"It actually does. I'm sorry."

"No, no, it's fine." He put out his pipe in an ashtray.

"Yes. I'm good with radiation, but terrible with tobacco smoke."

"Well, we can avoid at least one of them." He dumped the ashtray into the trash. "So I just wanted to see how you were—and I have a little job for you, if you want it, something you may enjoy."

"What's that?"

"G2 tells me the rumors about us down in Santa Fe are getting a bit close for comfort. It was one thing for folks to be talking about a home for pregnant WACs, or our submarine windshield-wiper plant, but now folks are talking about the explosions."

"They can hear them."

"Yep. And we need to put something out that seems reasonable—and will cut off any more speculation."

"Disinformation?"

"Does that bother you?"

"Like what Dr. Warren is doing with health and safety."

"I know. There's nothing I can do. I'm overruled by Groves. But this is not going to hurt anyone. I'd appreciate it if you could help us."

"With what?"

"We need to spread a story that will account for all the civilian scientists, for the secrecy, and for the explosions. Any ideas?"

Gregor brooded awhile.

"How about an 'electric rocket'?" he offered. "We're making an 'electric rocket'?"

"Terrific! I like it. An electric rocket. Very good. We can call it the G2."

"Like the V2. I don't want to do it. I cannot tell a lie—what George Washington said."

"Okay, Boy Scout. Just hear me out. I'd like you to head down to the La Fonda and talk it up. Talk loudly, talk too much. Talk as if you've had a tequila too many. Get people to eavesdrop. Say things about us, like how the place is growing, and somehow slip in the electric rocket business. No one will know about this except us. You'll be spied on by our boys in G2, of course. You may be reported by other Los Alamos folks. But I'll step in if you get into trouble. Sound like fun?"

"Why me?"

"Can you think of anyone more able to attract attention—in a low-key way, of course?"

"I . . . I don't know. Wouldn't we need a woman? To talk to other women?"

"In the American West, it's men that talk to women."

"Like you say a pickup?"

Oppie nodded and puffed his pipe.

"I don't . . . I'm too bashful," said Gregor, flashing back on another hotel lobby with a woman in purple and white.

"Well, you're right. Good thinking. This would be more effective with a woman. Let me ask Charlotte Serber. Would you be comfortable with that? And Bob. You like him."

"Why them?"

"Bob can be Mr. Unassuming, Charlotte can be Mrs. Fierce and Believable, and you—you just have that . . . *je ne sais quoi* . . . don't you think?"

"Who will be married to whom?"

"Let the patrons guess. A triangle is always mysterious. It will attract the attention you need. Will you do it? You'll get extra brownie points."

Gregor had not expected such Feynman-like mischief from the celebrated leader of Site Y. Was Oppie scheming revenge for the Sanskrit mole? (A security episode in which a certain hand was all too obvious. Case discussed, fingers rapped, Groves appeased, case dismissed. But had Feynman ratted on Gregor?)

Every person ever thus accosted has testified to Oppie's charming persuasiveness.

"I can't do it. I'm sorry."

"It may help cheer you up."

"You don't think I'm cheery?"

"Well, if someone had tried to shampoo me with plutonium, I'd be . . . a little glum."

"That's because you're not going to inherit the earth."

They both laughed.

"All right. No hard feelings. Maybe Bob and Charlotte will do a duet." Gregor turned to leave.

"Oh, Samsa, I saved something for you to read. Let me know what you think. The Arendt piece."

He handed Gregor the *Partisan Review* that had been lying on his desk. Gregor eyed the contents on the cover.

"Franz Kafka, a Re-evaluation on the Occasion of the Twentieth Anniversary of his Death," Hannah Arendt. Gregor had heard that name before. He didn't know her work. But if Oppie wanted to discuss it . . . He turned to the first page:

Twenty years ago, in the summer of 1924, Franz Kafka died at the age of forty. His reputation grew steadily in Austria and Germany during the twenties and in France, England, and America during the thirties. His admirers in these countries, though strongly disagreeing about the inherent meaning of his work, agree, oddly enough, on one essential point: All of them are struck by something new in his art of storytelling, a quality of modernity which appears nowhere else with the same intensity and unequivocalness.

"Looks quite of interest. Thank you. I'll let you know what I think."
"And keep me informed about your health, will you?"
"Yes, sir. Among other things, this is my job."


That night, Gregor curled up in his straw with the *Partisan Review*—a singular apotheosis of the midcentury intellectual. But what he read so infuriated him, he pulled out his typewriter to write a response.


```
P.O. Box 1663
Santa Fe, New Mexico
30 August 1944


Dear Doktor Arendt,
   You may find this amusing or vile, but two months
ago, I bought a copy of The Trial and set it on fire.
That is, I tried to set it on fire. I stuffed a bucket
with kindling, got a nice blaze going, perfect for an
auto-da-fé, and dropped the book into the flames. It
quickly snuffed them out, my room filled with smoke, the
fire men came, and I had a hard time to explain my ac-
tions.
   To you, however, I will explain. I have just read
your "Re-evaluation" in the Partisan Review, and I feel
that while you make certain points against the grain of
most opinion, you surely join the mob of critics to wor-
ship an idol who walks the world with poisoning steps.
   For you, Herr Kafka is a Jewish outsider using his
only weapon—thought—against a "misconstructed world."
You see his characters as "facing society with an atti-
tude of constructively defiant, outspoken aggression,"
as ready to act against such a world "for the sake of
human values."
   But surely this is false. Most false. This writer's
heroes are far from fighters. His is an atmosfere of
fascist terror, and his characters are products of such
```

gruesome world. What kind of models are they for the
general reader? They react to the most horrifying events
as if they were perfect normal; they carry out their duties, without to understand them, in blind, slave obedience, where following rules is more important than the
rules themselves, more important than the morality of
the rulers. This is a world of unfreedom, not emancipation, and any transformation Herr Kafka offers leads not
to liberation but to damnation.

I agree with you that Herr Kafka rings an alarm bell,
and describes the world the way it is and should not be.
But is it making emancipation to depict the world's insanity? Rather Herr Kafka evokes a destructive, uncon-
solable picture of the way things simply ARE. He offers
no political or social vision, no encouragement for human beings as members of human community, only nihilism
that calls alienation and dehumanization. His characters
are so powerless in their fear and chaos that they seem
victims of inexplicable forces; they are not capable of
reflecting on their submission. They can only sit "outside the Law," remain silent, and obey.

Herr Kafka's stories may help intellectuals with
their feelings of helplessness and self-contempt, but in
the final, they justify the ways of a banal, bureaucratic, and incomprehensible fascist system. Readers become Herr Kafka's <u>victims</u>, unfit for life, allied with
death, tangled in the endless labyrinth of his obses-
sions and konfusions. His work suggests no solutions to
the problems he explores, and will never, ever, in
Kleist's lovely words, "help humanity to cultivate a
field, to plant a tree, to beget a child."

Surely you and I share the same goal: the liberation
of the human spirit from the dictatorial institutions
and machinelike administration of a modern world. But
the unrestricted pessimism of this Prague insurance
agent convinced of the impossibility of all guarantees--

```
this does not serve our needs. In short, Herr Kafka is
bad for the world. I hope you will come to agree and,
against the current of current opinion, truly "re-
evaluate" this overvalued writer.
    Sincerely yours,
    George Samson
```

It took him four drafts—retyping each—so that it was one exhausted blattid who, at the seven-thirty morning whistle, turned out the lights and nestled into his bedding. And it was one exhausted blattid that Bob awoke by banging on his door, Charlotte's *New York Times* in hand.

"Sorry to wake you. But you should see this."

"What?"

"Here. This." He pointed to two column inches on page one: NAZI MASS KILLING LAID BARE IN CAMP. "Someplace named Majdanek, near Lublin. Mass graves, death chambers with some kind of asphyxiation system—carbon monoxide and Prussic acid, furnaces for burning bodies, warehouses crammed with clothing and shoes from the dead—they estimate a hundred thousand killed. Look at this. Jars for ashes for selling to relatives, bodies numbered on their chests before burning—all gold teeth extracted. Do you believe this? The Russians found it, end of July." The paper shook in Gregor's claw.

"I've got to go to sleep," he said, and crawled back deep into the straw. Bob stood there for a minute, then left, closing the door gently behind him. Something strange was up with Gregor, something stranger with the world.

On hearing news of the first concentration camp found and freed, Gregor went to sleep. But then, he had been up all night. The world also went to sleep—with less excuse.

Although the Soviets gave it lots of play, the few stories and pictures published in the States had little impact on public opinion. People remained skeptical—except for those who already knew. The one British report on the camp was widely seen as "a Russian propaganda stunt." Hitler dismissed the news as an Allied attempt to defame Germany.

In that same summer of '44 the Russians overran three other Eastern camps: Belzec, Sobibor, and Treblinka. In doing so they actually freed few prisoners since the retreating Germans, fearful of being discovered, were evacuating and destroying the camps as best they could. Perhaps the low numbers explain the low interest. Almost none of the prisoners left behind were Jewish—most Jews had long since been disposed of. These early Russian liberations were mostly of common criminals, communists, gypsies, homosexuals, Seventh-Day Adventists, and political prisoners— none of them groups to evoke widespread cries of protest from a war-weary West. Perhaps another reason for the small response.

But the view of most of the group sitting around at Oppie's one evening was that the primary reason behind the lethargy was Western reluctance to give the Soviets credit for an accomplishment the Allies had evaded. The camps' existence had been known in Administration circles for almost two years—there had been no lack of reports. Liberating them, bombing the rail lines that fed them, Gregor observed, from his understanding of the White House, had not been considered militarily important.

Throughout the discussion, Gregor had been leafing through *The Story of Western Art,* one of the many nontechnical books on Oppie and Kitty's coffee table. Shortly after he had made the point above, he checked out of the discussion, so engaged was he in what he had found. He was staring at a reproduction of Holbein the Younger's *Body of the Dead Christ in the Tomb,* the strangely shaped painting—five feet wide and ten inches high in the original—Dostoevski had obsessed about in *The Idiot.* Even in miniature it was fiercely appalling.

It shows the Saviour, in a box, freshly dead: the blood not yet pooled, the thin skin of the face suggesting that hypoxic blueness that will shortly engulf the corpse. Rigor mortis and gangrene have not yet set in. One can almost feel the warmth departing. There is no hint of beauty, of transcendence, no spirituality, no supernatural aura, as was commonly represented by painters of the time. This was simply the remnant of a man who had undergone unbearable torment, had been wounded, beaten, tortured, had carried his cross and suffered the agony of crucifixion. According to tradition, it had been modeled after a Jewish corpse fished from the Rhine. The blank eyes are rolled up into the head, the mouth hangs limply open, and one fingernail catches in the soiled and rumpled sheet, bunched up at its ends, too large for the already cracking coffin.

Gregor held the book up to the others in the room, like some woeful child offering a wordless, unrequested show-and-tell. The discussion petered out as the participants noticed the odd, out-of-context behavior of their companion.

"Schrödinger's Christ!" exclaimed Fermi.

"No cyanide," observed Teller.

"Looks like an indeterminate state to me," Fermi maintained. "Wave function of a superpositioning of death-resurrection events. Equal parts living and dead Christ at this point. Could go either way. Pass that here, will you?" The book made its way slowly around the room.

"Why do you show us this, Gregor?" asked Philip Morrison. "What's it mean for you?"

"An extreme work, I think. So shut in . . ."

"Thigmotactical," Neddermeyer called out from the bar. "But he doesn't look as happy as Gregor."

"Holbein surely shows his deepness faith," Gregor went on, ignoring him "—that from this repulseful condition, Christ could rise in glory. But for Dostoevski, I remember, this painting was a biggest challenge to belief—how could anyone seeing a such corpse possibly believe Resurrection? Alone, heartsickly holiness meat. How can the laws of nature be mastered if even Christ could not conquer them?"

"Which is it for you?" Oppie probed. "Holbein or Dostoevski?"

"Perhaps I am Schrödinger's roach here. I am of both feelings. Maybe more the second."

Kitty pulled her *Idiot* off the shelf and flipped through the pages. "Here's what the old man thought." She read:

"Looking at that picture, you get the impression of nature as some immense, merciless, and dumb beast, or to put it more correctly, much more correctly, though it may seem strange, as some huge machine of the most modern construction which, dull and insensible, has clutched, crushed and swallowed up a great, priceless Being worth all nature and its laws, worth the whole earth, which was perhaps created solely for the coming of that Being! The picture seems to give expression to the idea of a dark, insolent, and senselessly eternal power, to which everything is subordinated . . ."

The room was silent until Teller broke the spell:
"Nah, the Heisenberg Uncertainty Religion."

The discussion turned from the newly discovered camps to speculation about Heisenberg and the status of the German bomb project. Hitler and Goebbels kept hinting about some "secret weapon" soon to be completed that would quickly decide the war. What else could this be but the same baby all in the room were nursing?

Yet many, Teller especially, felt such statements to be only the brashness of despair. The Germans were on the run. The Allies had retaken Paris at the end of August, he said. Verdun, Dieppe, Artois, Rouen, Abbeville, Antwerp, and Brussels in the first week of September. This group at Oppie's knew Belgium was the major bank for uranium ores mined from the Belgian Congo—those very ores about which Einstein wrote the Queen. The Alsos project was busy tracking down all ores known to have been captured by the Germans.

"Remember the scare last year of large amounts of thorium which were moved to Germany?" asked Fermi. No one in the room did.

"Did this mean the Nazis were developing a thorium bomb," Morrison asked, "or using thorium to potentiate uranium?"

"*Eccolo*–the shipment was part of a plot–to corner the postwar market on a toothpaste adding to whiten the smile. Brush your teeth with Thoriia–the scientific toothpaste! Sounds like a Leo idea." Laughter, but respectful.

The group could come to no conclusions. Real evidence concerning the reputed Nazi bomb was maddeningly elusive. It looked as though no large program was under way for using uranium products in the near future, but Groves wanted every last lead nailed down before drawing conclusions–every ounce of uranium ore recovered, every German lab searched for hints about nuclear piles and possible plutonium production. Epistemological snafu noted by all: negative findings were no findings: it was always possible something was missed.

The evening broke up at eleven. They had to be early at work. Christ lay on the coffee table, endlessly dying, while all were abed.

In late October 1944, word began to leak out that the Alsos spy project had completed its work: It had accounted for all known uranium, had captured and debriefed most of the key German scientists. In short, it seemed there was no German bomb project; there had likely never been a German bomb project. Perhaps it was Hitler's need to believe in imminent victory without one. Perhaps Heisenberg had sabotaged the research. All that had been found were the makings for a tiny proto-pile, far smaller than Fermi's initial attempt in Chicago two long, work-filled years ago. There was much joy in Mudville.

When Gregor first heard the news, he joined in the general–if tentative–optimism. It was hard to pin Groves down. Something bad might still turn up. Still, alone in his little room that night, he was filled with exultation, almost rapture. He knew it was true, he had always known it. There had never been a bomb project. He would have had disturbing dreams if there were.

Gregor couldn't contain himself. Now there would be no need to continue this dangerous, satanic work. Now the best and the brightest could turn to human progress, away from dreams of vast destruction. Without even thinking about it, he roached the roof. There he was, upside down, six and a half feet over the floor of a converted chicken coop, giving out the cockroach version of a crow.

And yet the next day was not a holiday. The next week was not declared off. In mid-November Groves commented, "Without the Alsos report, I would have probably worked you all to death racing to be first." But he didn't stop racing them to death. Racing toward Death.

Here was the horror for Gregor: In April of 1943, Fermi, the project god, had researched using radioactive isotopes to poison the German food supply, a preemptive strike against a similar possible German attack. Such might be an alternative in case a fission bomb proved impossible. Oppie swore Fermi to secrecy—a secrecy within the overall secrecy of the Manhattan Project—and the Italian went quietly to work. Oppenheimer, the man who Gregor had *really* worshiped, the man dedicated to *ahimsa*—doing no harm—wrote to Fermi, "I think that we should not attempt a plan unless we can poison food sufficient to kill a half a million men, since there is no doubt that the actual number affected will, because of nonuniform distribution, be much smaller than this." As risk consultant he had to bite on this, an apple from a most forbidden tree.

This was far worse than FDR's political cowardice. Gregor was trying to protect an enterprise where the best and worst of men had been caught up in the whirlwind of technique, and had been brutalized in their flight. The pace continued to be frenetic, the energy high, the collegiality blinding and inspiring. No German bomb? The work would go on. It would fall then to the Japanese to be targets for the Gadget. Gregor's mind was made up.

Kafka once said, "From a certain point onward there is no longer any turning back. That is the point that must be reached." The spirit of Kafka hovered over the land.

. . .

At the very end of the year, Gregor found a surprise in his mailbox. He had almost forgotten he had written.

```
365 W. 95th St.
New York 25, N.Y.
20 December 1944


Dear Mr. Samson,
    Thank you for your provocative letter. I hope you
will have patience with the extended answer I believe
such a letter demands.
    I must admit I found your auto-da-fé amusing, though
not for its slapstick quality. Rather it demonstrates an
unfortunately typical misdirection of goodwill: destroy-
ing the messenger does not invalidate bad tidings.
    We agree, I think, on the message Kafka brings to a
misconstructed world: the ancient admonition to "Know
Thyself." The truth of our time must be disclosed or un-
covered from within its all-pervasive and seductive
trappings. It requires a scalpel as sharp as Kafka's to
do such deep surgery. Modern man stands amidst the con-
fusion of the time and seeks guidance, and Kafka pro-
vides not only guidance, but the intellectual momentum
for constructive escape.
    Let us look together at two of Kafka's little para-
bles, in some ways contrasting, even contradictory, and
in some ways additive. Here is the first:

"He is a citizen of the world, secure and free--since he
is anchored by a chain long enough to allow him to roam
the earth, but not so long as to let him fall off. But
at the same time, he is also a free and secure citizen
of heaven, held there by a similar, heavenly chain. If
```

he wants to head to earth, he is strangled by his heavenly chain, and if he heads for heaven, by his earthly one. Nevertheless, he feels all possibilities are his, and even refuses to blame the situation on any error in the original chaining."

Kafka tells us that earthly freedom—the freedom granted by "the world"—is not enough. For there is a dimension of other-than-earthly activity which also belongs to any citizen of the world: he is bound also to this transcendent realm, and gives up his citizenship at his peril. That is Kafka's first great message: not one of limitation, but one of transcendent connection, a connection which also protects from too great immersion in the ordinary. True, there is conflict, tension, even paralysis in this situation, and you, Mr. Samson, may see the protagonist as defeated by his sadistic author. But the protagonist is not defeated. He is actually aware of the possibility that there is no error in the structure, that if deeply perceived and adroitly handled he may be able to operate bountifully within these strictures, as a poet does within the limitations of strict forms. It is not stubbornness or stupidity behind his analysis. It is the smell of real freedom.

The second story is this:

"He has two opponents: the first pushes him from behind, from the source. The second blocks him from the front. He fights with both. Actually, the first supports him in his fight with the second, pushing him ahead. And similarly, the second supports him in his fight with the first, forcing him back. But this is only in theory—because it is not only the two opponents who are there, but also himself, and who really knows his intentions? It remains his dream that once, in some unguarded moment—which would indeed require a night as dark as

```
any that ever was--he might jump out of the line of bat-
tle and, because of his fighting experience, be promoted
to referee the fight between the two."

   This tale pictures a crushing, suffocating thought-
world miraculously evaded. However you choose to inter-
pret the it, Mr. Samson, it again urges corrective
action. True, the night will have to be at its darkest--
to provoke, to inspire, and to hide--but such a condition
is already a regular occurrence in our dark times. And
the man who can dream such a jump, such a discontinuity,
such a transformation, that man is more than halfway
toward its realization. Let Kafka whisper in your ear and
things may evolve which have never appeared before.
   Forgive my presumption in suggesting that you concen-
trate not on the fetters, or the darkness of the night,
but rather on the taut potential for situational meta-
morphosis. Kafka discloses what our blinded eyes have
ceased to see, and such revelation has the power to
trigger the springs of action.
   I remain yours sincerely,
   Hannah Arendt
```

A thoughtful letter.

At the 5:30 go-home-for-supper siren, letter in pocket, Gregor trudged out of D-Building, the center of plutonium work. Since West Mess was serving steak that night, he thought he'd eat at North Mess—as it would be a lot less crowded—and head home to hit the straw. He was just raising potatoed fork to mouthparts when the fire siren shrieked and the loudspeaker cried, "FIRE IN THE TECH AREA! FIRE IN THE TECH AREA!"

The North Mess crowd went ashen. It was everyone's greatest nightmare, an event so potentially catastrophic that all except Gregor—whose job it was—had relegated it to the remotest parts of their minds. There was a rush to the coatracks; people bundled up and ran toward C-Shop, where the flames were raging, just inside the Tech Area fence. Frantic MPs were struggling to keep the area clear, while children ran under their linked arms. The administration building with all its records was right next to the fire. Would it catch? The firefighters seemed to be making little headway. Had there been a wind, the whole town might have gone up in flames. The roof of C-Shop collapsed.

Gregor found himself huddling next to Genia and Gaby Peierls.

"Thank God there's no wind tonight," he said.

"Perhaps sabotage, you think? *Bozhe moy*, thank God is not D-Building."

Though his relationship to the Deity was unclear, Gregor found himself in silent but fervent Amen.

After more than two hours, the flames flickered and died, and the freezing populace, reeking of smoke, went back to their homes, those with highest clearance chastened by the thought of what might have happened had the nearby plutonium burned, melted, and scattered itself on ashes to be breathed.

When Gregor got home, he found a Western Union envelope tacked to his door. The Day of Surprising Envelopes. It was good the censors had already gotten to it, as he might have been too tired to tear it open. The telegram read WARNER CHOCOLATE CAKE RECOMMENDED STOP LEO. He fell asleep with his overcoat on, pondering its meaning.

## 39.  A  PIECE  of  CAKE

He half-awoke to the smell of smoke, in the vagueness of alpha-state, confused with that of the White House kitchen cabinet, Mrs. Nesbitt burning feather dusters . . . and then, no, it was his chicken coop, his own chicken coop in Los Alamos, and, located with scanning antennae, his own blanketing overcoat setting off his neural smoke alarm. The seven-twenty-five siren framed up his still ragged reality, and he noticed the telegram, yellow against the creosote floor.

Conundrum: WARNER CHOCOLATE CAKE RECOMMENDED STOP LEO. Well, that was easy, even at seven in the morning. Go down to Edith Warner's for some of her chocolate cake. Not a bad idea: the cake had already become a tradition among the group she called her "hungry scientists." But *why* go for chocolate cake? Was this just another Szilard joke? There was only one way to find out.

At noon he took an extended lunch break from his task of checking C-shop cleanup for hazards, and drove down the mountain to arrange a place for dinner. When he arrived, Edith had his chocolate cake all ready. How did she know he wanted it? In fact, he hadn't come for cake, but only to make a reservation. Gentle, but as firm as usual, she asked him to wait in the small bed- and sitting room that faced out to the east, the room she saved for talks with friends. Gregor was honored to be thus ushered into her personal life, but like most of her guests, he was mildly intimidated by her quiet strength, her efficiency, her determined neatness.

Edith's rooms were as faultlessly opaque as her being: low ceilings with hand-hewn *vigas*, whitewashed adobe walls, tables under each window, and, on the north wall, a desk between two bookshelves. Except for the Bible and the few art books, Gregor recognized none of the titles. On the top shelves, Indian pottery, two orange and blue basket plaques from Hopi country (Tilano had pointed some out at the feast day), a Navajo doll, and a pair of candlesticks. On the desk, a tiny white stone carving.

Gregor got up to examine it more closely. It seemed some kind of insect, a scarab or beetle. Gregor sat back down again, feeling furtive, embarrassed by this glimpse of what he took to be a private, mysterious icon, and waited quietly, sitting on the bed, staring out the long, sliding windows toward the Sangre de Cristos, studying the play of light and shadow on their snowy walls.

Edith returned with a cup of tea garnished with a thin lemon slice and a spicy clove—and a plate with the largest slice of her chocolate loaf cake he had ever seen served. Like a true modern Puritan, she denied herself while indulging others—but in moderation: her cake was usually served in half-inch slices. This portion was fully three inches thick.

"This is an awfully large piece," Gregor observed, as politely as he could, not wanting to reject her kindness.

"You look hungry. Your coat smells of smoke. Did something happen?"

Gregor began to describe last night's fire.

"Better drink your tea while it's hot," Miss Warner suggested.

The visitor sipped his tea, and after a while found himself describing another fire he had witnessed as a child in Prague, a synagogue burning in Josefov, the Jewish ghetto, the grand playfulness of arson. Miss Warner listened quietly, asking occasional questions. When Gregor put his teacup down and picked up his fork for the cake, she said she had to help Tilano, and left the room.

What a strange woman, Gregor thought. So polite and friendly, yet so hidden. He sucked on the luscious cake, cold from its storage in the snow, let it fill his mouth space, then sipped the hot tea to melt and dissolve it, and wash it deliciously down his gullet. Roaches do love chocolate cake. The third time his fork cut the surface, it was stopped by some hard object inside. Was it a nut, a large, unbroken piece of chocolate? Gregor felt around its periphery, then exhumed a film can from its cakely vehicle. Leo! Meshuggener!

Even more surprising was the obvious inference that Edith Warner, Edith Warner of the trim shirtwaist dresses and upswept gray hair, the quiet, unflappable, apolitical Edith Warner, was in cahoots with Leo Szilard on this—what?—trick?—communication tactic?—espionage? He didn't know what to call it because he had no idea what was in the can. It sounded packed when ticked by claw.

Gregor wiped off the container, stuck it in his pocket, and finished the tea and cake. Not a balanced lunch, but it would surely do for today. When Edith did not reappear, he assumed she was being discreet, and decided to repay her in kind. He walked out into the dining room and peered into the kitchen, where she and Tilano were arranging canning jars on a pantry shelf.

"Thank you for the cake," he called in.

"You're very welcome," she said. "Thank you for the news and the story."

"You're welcome. I hope to see you soon," he said, and walked out to the car.

He was conflicted about whether to report right back to C-shop, or to stop at his room to inspect the contents of the can. High curiosity won out over Responsibility: he drove right to his house and locked the door behind him.

The film can was densely packed with three onion-skin sheets of single-spaced typing, extractable only with the help of cuticle scissors, which left puncture wounds in the paper. He unfolded the papers, smoothed them out, and settled down to read.

Leo Szilard was the man General Groves was born to hate—though Szilard had dreamed up the whole concept on which Groves's operation was based. For his part, one of Szilard's deepest instincts was to question authority—and stupid military authority in particular. The conjunction of these two had all the makings of opera bouffa.

One way an unstoppable force defeats an unmovable object is to go around it—and Szilard continually went over, under, and to the side of Groves's head—several times, via Einstein, to the President.

Generals do not like this.

In a 1946 interview, Groves would comment that "Only a man of Szilard's brass would have pushed through to the President. Take Wigner or Fermi—they're not Jewish—they're quiet, shy, modest, just interested in learning. Of course most of Szilard's ideas are bad, but he has so many. And I'm not prejudiced. I don't like certain Jews and I don't like certain well-known characteristics of theirs, but I'm not prejudiced." Punch the Jude. Step right up.

Gregor was about to get involved in a dynamic of more moment than a single blattid, sitting alone at his table, might have realized.

Szilard's papers read as follows:

27 January 1945

Dear Samsa,

Your letter of 20 December received through Trude and much appreciated. Alsos evidence sounds compelling. One might have expected the housepainter to harness German Wissenschaft more aggressively, but I also imagine him saying Nein! to any project that might take longer than the ever receding "two more weeks" he thinks it will take to win the war. Self-limiting megalomania.

With your news in hand, I have drafted a petition to Roosevelt to be signed by scientists here in Chicago, and chez vous at Site Y. I will gather signatures at the former, if you will take care of the latter.

However small the chance might be that our petition may influence the course of events, I personally feel it would be a matter of importance if a large number of scientists who have worked in this field went clearly and unmistakably on record as to their opposition on moral grounds to the use of these bombs.

Please read carefully and return a copy with comments via the same channels. I will then send a final draft. I hope you are doing well at 2,400 meters. How are your red cells? Do you have red cells?

Best,

LS

The draft petition followed—two pages of dense, Szilardian argument. It ended with the following appeal:

In view of the foregoing, we, the undersigned, respectfully petition: first, that you exercise your power as

Commander-in-Chief to rule that the United States shall
not resort to the use of atomic bombs in this war unless
the terms imposed upon Japan have been made public in
detail and Japan, knowing these terms, has refused to
surrender; second, that in such an event the question
whether or not to use atomic bombs be decided by you in
the light of the considerations presented in this petition as well as all other moral responsibilities which
are involved.

Gregor checked the clock, placed the papers under his bedstraw, and returned for the afternoon to inspect the nooks and crannies of what was once C-shop for radioactive contamination. But as the cleanup crew seemed protectively dressed, according to his morning's instructions, and the meter readings were quite low, as hoped, his mind began to drift back to the task Leo had assigned him: how to get the signatures.

It seemed the fastest and most powerful route might be to start at the top. Oppie's signature on the first line would do more to induce others than hours of his own begging one-to-one. True, he had only a draft version, but it seemed fine to him as is, and perhaps Oppie might have some suggestions he could forward to Leo. From all he knew of Oppenheimer—his ascetic yet caring life, the depth of his thought, his wide-ranging culture, his fundamentally religious and poetic worldview—Gregor was certain of a sympathetic response. Which only goes to show that blattids may have a simplified view of human *Dasein*.

"Samsa, do you think the President doesn't know all this—plus far more about the military and political dynamics than you do?" he said after perusing the draft. Gregor stood there, taken aback, as Oppie raised his voice. "What makes you think scientists—and you're not even a scientist!—should influence politics? Do we have special, relevant knowledge here? No fiddling with politics is going to save our consciences or our souls." He knocked his pipe fiercely out into an ashtray and took his feet down from the desk. "You want to know something? I think it would be best to drop the damn gadget as soon as possible to give the public a real picture of what they're dealing with—I mean, assuming it works." He sat there, his eyes closed, leaning his head on his hands.

Who was this long-fanged Oppie in executive disguise? Gregor, bewildered, backed out of the office with his papers and an ambiguous nodding of the head.

He thought of all the things he might have said. He thought of quitting the Project. He thought of becoming a spy, of giving information to the international community, or at least to the Allies; he thought of a direct appeal to the American people. Yet on reflection, he realized that Oppie had not, even in ostensible fury, prohibited circulating the petition. Groves would have torn up the paper and warned him about spilling one word of it. He could hear his voice: "I'll have you executed for treason!"

But not Oppie. A more nuanced relationship to power.

At the end of the day, Gregor found the following note in his mailbox:

```
Samsa, Sorry I lectured at you today, but I still be-
lieve I'm right with regard to policy. Want to know why?
I would suggest you check the Bhagavad Gita, esp. XI:12.
JRO, the Sanskrit Mole.
```

Gregor did not recognize the reference. But a second note arrived the next day.

```
Excuse me. I should not assume even your knowledge of BG
chapter and verse. In XI:12, Krishna the god counsels
Arjuna, the reluctant warrior--to renounce desire and
relinquish any fruit of action. Then, and only then,
will authentic death emerge--a part of XI:12's cosmic
effulgence:

    If the radiance of a thousand suns
    were to burst into the sky,
    it would be like the light of the Great Spirit
    in the true majesty of his form.

How's that for a Stabat Pater? JRO
```

It was called "the Little Green Schoolhouse." Some with finer color sense called it "the Bilious Green Schoolhouse." The school had been conceived by a University of Minnesota education professor who had fantasized a radical high school for brilliant children of brilliant scientists, and if a school building alone could be summa cum laude, this would be it. But a school is not a school building. In the real world of Site Y, the students were too young, and the teachers too few. The average age of Los Alamos parents was twenty-seven. Only the most senior scientists had middle-school-aged children, and these were few. And even the tiny upper division failed its utopian plan since the great majority of high schoolers came from laborers' homes with little or no academic tradition.

While there were major academics from all over the world on campus, they were far too busy to become elementary or high school teachers. Their educated, academic wives were an obvious pool, but in Groves's mania to minimize housing and maximize security, any wife who could work was recruited for the urgently needed pool of secretaries and calculators. In short, there were only three full-time teachers involved in Central School—and not one physicist.

Nella Fermi and her friends Jane Flanders and Gaby Peierls were the stars of the small but savvy preadolescent crowd. They were not used to being with children of nonacademic parents and so had formed a tight, defensive circle that outsiders condemned as snobbish. And the outsiders were right. Nella was the thirteen-year-old daughter of Nobel prize winner Enrico Fermi; Jane, one of the daughters of mathematician Moll Flanders; and Gaby, the twelve-year-old intellectually precocious daughter of Rudolf—but more significantly of Genia—Peierls, the terrifying Russian whirlwind. There were no boys their age who were socially or intellectually acceptable, so they spent their romantic time flirting and occasionally necking with GIs and junior scientists they could not bring home. A proto-dangerous crew.

Gregor was shocked and flattered to find in his mailbox one early spring day, a calligraphied letter of invitation:

*The Mademoiselles Fermi, Flanders, and Peierls*
*cordially request the presence*
*of*
*Mr. George Samson,*
*also known as*
*Herr Gregor Samsa,*
*to their presentation of*
*"Images of Change in a Fable of La Fontaine"*
*at the*
*Alliance Française*
*Central School Classroom Eight*
*Monday, March 19, 1945, at 16:45*
*RSVP*

Gregor wrote back immediately to all three, gratefully accepting. Although he spoke adequate French, his acquaintance with classical French literature was filled with gaps, and La Fontaine was one of them.

The "Alliance Française"—Nella, Jane, and Gaby—met irregularly after school with Peg Bainbridge, who had taught French at Radcliffe, and Françoise Ulam, a native speaker, both of whom were too busy for full-time teaching. Most grown-ups thought that if any language should be learned by Los Alamos children, it should be Spanish. Nevertheless, the three girls assigned themselves topics and presentations in French, and assigned Peg and Françoise to supervise them. Gregor was the only other adult in the room, and he was eager to learn.

The girls entered from the hallway at precisely four forty-five, as if for a performance of "Three Little Maids from School." They began with a choral reading of the La Fontaine poem *"La Chatte Métamorphosée en Femme,"* with vocal solos, duets, and trios charmingly arranged throughout the text. Gregor could follow well the sense, though their French pronunciation ranged from Northern Italian to German British to Amherst, Massachusetts. He was quite intrigued by the choice of text.

It seems a man had fallen madly in love with his cat, with an affection so deep and prayers so fervent that Fate granted him his dearest wish, that she metamorphose into a woman and become his bride. And a loving bride she was: never was man so completely adored. The enchanted groom looked forward to the wedding night with his beloved wife, the cat-no-longer. But in the midst of marital bliss, a group of mice began gnawing away at a mat in their bedroom, and the good wife sprang out of bed and pounced upon them. What must the poor husband have thought?

La Fontaine's moral: once things have set in their natural forms, Nature scoffs at any attempt to change them.

*Jamais vous n'en serez les maîtres.*
*Qu'on lui ferme la porte au nez,*
*Il reviendra par les fenêtres.*

You'll never be Nature's master. If you push it out the door, it will climb back through the windows. A delightful image, Gregor thought, and probably true. He resolved to read all of La Fontaine.

But now the scenario abruptly changed as the maidens called "Exhibit A, Mr. George Samson, aka Herr Gregor Samsa, to the stand!" Nella set out a stool for him at the front of the room, next to the teacher's desk. The adults looked at one another, surprised and wary. The three girls pulled classroom chairs up to surround him.

"Mr. Samson, *comment vous appelez-vous*?" asked Nella.

"My friends call me Gregor. You may call me Gregor. My French is not so good. Can we speak English? Or German?"

"We can speak German," Gaby said.

"I can't speak German, and you know it, Gaby," Jane objected. "We all speak English. Why not speak English? Madame Ulam, Madame Bainbridge, will it be all right to speak English for the questioning?"

"Seminar, not questioning," Nella corrected.

"Okay. For the seminar. English for the seminar."

Madame Ulam interposed: "But does Mr. Samson *want* to be questioned?"

"Oh yes," insisted Nella. "He was invited. He said he wanted to come."

"For?"

"For a seminar on *La Chatte*," Gaby maintained.

"It's all right," Gregor assured the teachers. "Though I don't know much about *La Chatte*."

"Ah, but you *do* know much about *les insectes, n'est-ce pas?*" Nella asked. "And metamorphoses?"

There was a moment of embarrassed silence. Where was this going? Even in the tight, smart community of Los Alamos, Gregor's class affiliations (Insectiva) were rarely openly discussed. Still, he felt, there was really nothing to be embarrassed about. He belonged here. He even had a white pass and could enter the Tech Area.

Nevertheless, Peg Bainbridge tried to protect him: "Mr. Samson, are you sure you want to—"

"I'm fine. Yes, Nella, I have certain insights into insects and metamorphoses."

"So do you think it is really possible for a human to fall in love with an animal?" Gaby wanted to know. "Not love an animal the way I love Shard . . ."

Jane being helpful: "Her poodle."

"Yes, I know Shard."

" . . .but 'in love'—moony, swoony, loony, smooch, smooch, smooch . . . ?"

The girls giggled. Gaby had fallen in latest love last week with a mounted MP guarding the Tech Area perimeter. Peg and Françoise settled back for some pre-teenage silliness.

"We want to know," said Jane, "if you think that love and sex between species is possible, and whether you would approve of such an affair, even if they were consenting adults and were married. I mean how would he . . . you know . . ."

More giggling, even from the faculty. Gregor felt a wash of sweet, piercing back pain as his heart melted in a flood of Alice. It was too much to speak of to children. Besides, his experience was probably not generalizable. He chose to skirt the issue.

But Nella was ever serious: "And how does one metamorphose? All at once? Little by little? A slight mustache, then whiskers?"

"She might just wake up one morning changed," Gregor said. "Isn't that what your father does—change things?—pouf!—from one thing to another?"

"I don't know what my father does. Did she just pounce on the mice, or did she eat them?"

"I don't know. La Fontaine doesn't say."

"Well what would *you* do?" asked Gaby.

"I don't eat mice. Just like you."

Gaby, undeterred: "And if animals can turn into people, can people turn into animals?"

"We already know that," said Nella, gesturing at Gregor.

"We don't," said Gaby, asserting her acknowledged higher IQ scores. "There may be more to Exhibit A than appears. If La Fontaine is correct that inner nature will always assert itself . . . Mr. Samsa, how long have you . . . you know . . . been this way?"

After quick calculation: "Almost thirty years now."

"That's a long time. How old were you before?"

"Twenty-four."

Nella was catching on: "So you have been this way longer than you were that way."

"Yes, I suppose so."

Jane, the mathematician's daughter: "Do you think it's possible then that this is your real self, your real inner self?"

"And that the other way, the first way, was only a temporary metamorphosis from this?" added Gaby.

Nella cut to the chase: "And that once again, as in La Fontaine, we have a beast temporarily changing into a human being, and not the other way round? You see we—I think I can speak for the other members of the Alliance—we're concerned about the opposite—humans possibly turning into beasts, and we thought you . . ."

Gaby: "If you are actually the other way, then *this* is the real person . . ."

Gregor now understood what was going on. Here were three beautiful preadolescents, each with budding breasts (ummm, they thought) and budding acne (eeeww, they thought), very smart and sensitive, completely naive, and oh so vulnerable to a community of fenced-in young and not-so-young men with whom they spent much time being in love. Suppose they were to take some GIs, some junior scientists, under their young wings, allow them into their civilizing plumage? Would beasts climb in the windows?

Gregor turned emptily avuncular: "We all grow and change . . ."

Peg and Françoise, sensing the impropriety of possible girl-talk in such a setting, decided to bring the seminar to a close. *"Allons-y, allons-y, mesdemoiselles. Il fait tard. On peut continuer la discussion. Merci beaucoup, Gregor.* Thank you, Gregor. *Il faut souper. On va s'inquiéter. A presto, Nella, Wiedersehen, Gaby,* we continue next Monday, just the Alliance." Gregor off the hook.

Walking slowly home, he rethought what must be going on. The girls were as confused and scared about the world as—was he. They understood that the explosions in the canyons were not lovingly meant. More than this, Nella must have known the reality of Mussolini and the Black Shirts and Gaby surely knew the terrors of an evacuated child, separated at seven from her parents. They had all seen the site's posters about Hun and Jap beasts. And they were savvy enough to know there must be similar posters over there about Americans.

The global dimension of their questioning came crashing down on Gregor two days later when, on March 21, Genia Peierls, Gaby's mother, produced and presented a community dance to the music of Stravinsky's *Rite of Spring.* There was, as noted, much artistic talent on the mesa, and even among nonperformers, great enthusiasm for concerts, shows, cabarets, reviews, satires, and general letting-down-of-the-laboratory-and-military-hair. Thus there had been excellent attendance at Genia's rehearsals over the last three weeks, and on Wednesday night, the first night of Gregor's last spring, performers of all ages far outnumbered the audience. Gregor had known about the rehearsals of course, but because of his dislike or even dread of Stravinsky's masterwork, had chosen not to participate. Perhaps he only feared what the piece might do to him should he become trapped in its powerful jaws. Once devolved, twice shy. Still, given his history of performance epiphanies, he acceded to the three little maids' request to be scribe to their debut performance. No rehearsals required. Since he was going anyway.

. . .

*The Rite* was born in 1913, the same year Gregor was conceived. And though it was part of a generalized artistic reaction against effete bourgeois culture, with its abrupt, harsh rhythms and remarkable instrumental sounds, it seemed to evoke more than any other work the threat of barbarity lurking just under the surface of civilization. An aggressive, chaotic invocation of human savagery and uncontrolled primeval force, its opening night sparked a riot at the *Théâtre Champs-Elysées*. It was banned in Stalin's Russia and in Hitler's Germany, where it would not do to acknowledge the barbarism already in practice.

The plot concerns a pagan ritual of pre-Christian Russia, a ceremony to put winter behind and call forth spring: a virgin is sacrificed by stern elders and a primitive, uncivilized mob, a community that propitiates its gods with orgiastic liturgies of cruelty and murder—so that the cycle of birth, growth, and death may proceed. If such distant, prehistoric activity seemed menacing in a civilized European theater, how much closer it might appear here, where the civilized society on the hill was preparing to embrace gods of such power as had yet to be encountered.

Genia Peirels's goal was seditious—a withering comment from an unheeded Casssandra. For Gregor, perched over the event on a high judge's seat borrowed from the tennis court, the message was clear enough—and devastating.


The dance was held in Theater Number Two, the larger of the two recreation halls, the one used for school phys-ed, Tuesday night colloquia, and pickup basketball. Tonight, the backboards had been covered with camouflage cloth. This may have been history's first presentation in full-surround sound, for although the recordings were monophonic 78 RPMs, Genia had borrowed twelve speakers from various homes and offices, set them up along the walls, and had the electronics boys wire them up to Rad Lab's biggest amplifier and Moll Flanders's best-on-campus Victrola with mechanical changer. A stickler for details, she had even installed a new needle.

At the 7:30 starting time, there were few in the audience, a cause for some tsk-tsking by those who had arrived promptly. But it turned out that the small audience was the only audience left, a population remnant from the enormous cast of players milling about the doors, waiting for their entrances. A small audience was a good thing, too, since most of the benches had been commandeered for stage use by the imperious producer-designer-director.

The house lights went out, and the room was plunged into the darkness of March 21—the first evening of spring. Genia's shadow, projected by the amplifier's tiny red light, seemed accidentally but appropriately monstrous on the south wall. She flicked the lever, the first record dropped, and the eerie sound of a bassoon playing high above its natural register snaked its way into the room, sounding something like music must have sounded before the beginning of time.

The first of many flashlights came on, its operator dark behind it, and began slowly to explore the room. As more instruments joined, erupting arpeggios from the womb of darkness, more flashlights were added, playing out their spidery crisscrossing of sounds and beams and clearings, building to a short riot of calls in unstable light, tune fragments from the depths of centuries, all of which stopped short, the lights coming abruptly together at the centerline. Behind them the audience sensed humanity, invisible, embedded in nature, predating the creation of a personal God. The solo bassoon began its song again, and the pool of light split in two and slowly edged its halves upward to reveal the now-bare giant God-faces mounted on the backboards: to the east was Oppie; to the west was Groves.

This scenic revelation occasioned the audience's first and last laugh, which Gregor punctuated with the scratching of his scribal pen. He wrote on like some manic, unstoppable soloist, accompanied by the gears of the record changer. Although he was merely a "mysterious" scenic prop, he had taken it upon himself to record his own feelings, and those audience reactions he could fathom, as well as the inadvertent behavior of the cast as they went through their appointed rounds. He had heard the piece often enough to dislike it thoroughly—but he had never really imagined it with human bodies as flotsam and infusoria to the sound.

At the opening of the second dance, "The Augurs of Spring," Genia's plan began to reveal itself. Enter Enrico Fermi in chinos and black leather jacket who, with a snap of his fingers, caused a spot of light to fall directly downward in the center of the floor from the one mid-court bulb Genia had left screwed in. The orchestra began to pulse with accented string chords, mechanical in obsessive meter, but wildly unpredictable in accent, and the first of the *raboti* entered, carrying one of the missing benches. As the worker left, another appeared with another bench, and another with another, and so on, until it became clear that, under Fermi's direction, they were erecting a structure built from benches, a structure similar to the pile he had conceived and created at Stagg Field. A group of eight children, gloved in yellow, entered from the south door and proceeded to blow up green balloons and insert them into the matrix of benches, just as Fermi's uranium spheres had been cradled among its graphite bricks. This activity went on through this and the following six dances, utilizing all the benches from Theater Number Two and Theater Number One, a few from North Mess, and a large load of lumber from various construction sites—so that by the end of the first half, "Adoration of the Earth," a ziggurat reaching halfway to the ceiling had been created by the mechanical work of robotlike men.

Revealed by exposed bulbs of the south door exit light, the audience saw a group of young men in GI uniforms, on hands and knees, being taught by a masked old hag. From the chicken feet she held in both hands, one could gather that this was Baba Yaga, the nightmare witch of every frightened Russian child. The group moved jerkily to the orchestral pulse, as the wise woman instructed them in divinations—until all was brought to a halt by a sudden percussion crash.

Then Gaby, Nella, and Jane emerged in street clothes from the north door, and the GIs took leave of their cackling teacher to approach them slowly, a Russian chorale tune sounding on four trumpets behind them. At the sight of them, the girls began a dance that grew to bacchanalian frenzy, as the boys lunged and pulled them from their small group into their own larger one.

Under a succession of string chords and syncopated drumbeats, the young men grasped the girls—then froze, as the Victrola arm retracted and side three dropped, a classical Brechtian alienation effect.

With an extended four-flute trill calling up a primeval melody on clarinets, the "Round Dances of Spring" began, slow and grave incantations connecting the dancers to the huge earth beneath them, while the male group added performers with lab coats and flashlights, and split into two: scientists and soldiers.

Three circles spun around themselves while revolving, planetlike, around the rising ziggurat—then leaped up on the first three tiers of the structure, women above, military next, and scientists on the lowest level, like electrons quantum-kicked to higher orbit. The slow dance continued until, the orchestra quieting, the men returned to earth, while the three girls watched them from above.

Gregor wrote that the massive rootedness of this section reminded him of trying to pick up a small cube of uranium for the first time, a shockingly heavy mass that resisted any attempt to free it from the earth. Above the girls, the *raboti* kept slowly building as the next record dropped.

And then there ensued, to urgent rhythmic beating, "The Ritual of the Two Rival Tribes"—competitive dances, rough skirmishes, and flashlight-beam duels of blue and white light. Military vs. Science. The tymps beat out the rhythm, and eight horns cried out war. There was no stopping the barbaric tubas and loosed testosterone until, in the "Procession of the Oldest and Wisest One," Niels Bohr was pushed in, descending a high, rolling stepladder. As the orchestra held a quiet, long chord, and the others trembled, he spreadeagled out at center court and kissed the floor. Niels Bohr—prostrate—the earth responding with a long, harmonic, triple piano "yes."

With Bohr's kiss came "The Dancing Out of the Earth," a frenzied celebration, drunk with spring, finally freed from its wintry bondage. There was a wild drumming pulse, and the whirlpool became a boiling cauldron as, to syncopated shrieks on brass and woodwind, the dancers in separate, asymmetrical, electrified clumps leaped and fell convulsively out the exit doors, as the breathless scene ended.

The room was dark and silent, the basketball court now empty except for the ever watching eyes of Oppie and Groves, which now in darkness, with no other distractions, glowed clearly from their luminescent sclera. The house lights came abruptly on, and Genia walked onstage dressed as a cigarette girl, hawking "Stravinsky popcorn," "Diaghilev yablaki," and

"Nijinsky limonad." The audience laughed, and was left to gather in customary groups to discuss the show.

"Something is coming," Gregor wrote. Usually transparent, he could become annoyingly cryptic when disturbed.

The lights flickered, the audience took its seats again, and Gregor reluctantly climbed back on the judges' stand for "The Great Sacrifice," the dreaded second half. After initial darkness and a repeat of Genia's unintended monster show in red, the room was illuminated in the murky light of the single bulb directly above the twelve-foot, balloon-stuffed ziggurat. The record dropped like a pellet of potassium cyanide into sulfuric acid.

In the dim light, in tensely watchful silence, the youths milled around, melancholy, desolate, to the strange color of muted trumpets and horn calls. An old Russian tune suggested a human world, but clearly evoked was an area of feeling where the palpable and tangible disappear and where humans, in a gloomy, shadowed world devoid of objects, moved timidly, with the caution of uncertainty and fear. The gloomy coloration seemed like some mood of the unfree—a quiet bleakness of imprisoned creaturehood.

The three girls entered again, trembling, to dance their circle in the mystery and panic of nature's night. They moved around the ziggurat, which now seemed a sacrificial pyre in the garish light. They danced to a languid legato melody on six solo violas, against a background of pizzicato cellos. They rose and fell from tiptoe, dropping their right hands and jerking their heads. Then eleven huge chords—one of the most threatening moments in all music—and they sprang up to the first level of the pile. It was time for "The Naming and Honoring of the Chosen One." To ecstatic woodwind shrieks Gaby, Nella, and Jane leaped convulsively up and down the sides of the ziggurat with chugging, fragmented rhythm. In the chaotic changing of levels, Gaby seemed left above, almost randomly chosen. Gaby, daughter of Genia, would be sacrificed. Elders entered, and soldiers, scientists, workers, and children gathered round the pyre to praise and glorify her.

Next came priests to evoke the ancestors, a group of eight masked figures who emerged from tunnels in the ziggurat to surround the scene.

One looked like Einstein, one like Beethoven, one something like Hitler. Then, the real-world fathers: Moll Flanders climbed the ziggurat steps to kiss Gaby, and in returning to ground, carried an exhausted Jane to safety. Enrico Fermi likewise claimed his Nella, and carried her away as a bass clarinet dipped down and back from the underworld, and as all faced the pyre and focused their gaze on the platform twelve feet above.

Gaby, aloft, seemed to be in a trance, seated alone, eyes closed, on an eight-by-eight platform, a light directly above her head. "The Sacrificial Dance of the Chosen One" called out of a universe of time to a world so rhythmically shattered as to be beyond any countable measure. Her eyes opened slowly, and as she tilted her head sideward, Gregor saw her dawning sense of mystery, then her horror, and then her panic in the face of the unknown just ahead of her.

The orchestra began to bubble with blood-curdling ejaculations—threats and laughter from the erupting forces of nature over which she fatally presided. She was galvanized into twitches and leaps of increasing frenzy, her attention withdrawn from the group below and ejected out beyond self to the cosmos. Hysterical turns on the violins and piccolos ascended in a nightmarish way, and she began to spin, to spin more and more dizzily on the unrailed platform. "Where is her mother?" wrote Gregor. "Where is her father to catch her?" And time became ever more complex and unbalanced, in a mounting, centrifugal confluence of exaltation, ecstasy, sexual climax, sacrifice, and death. It was a mad dance, non-dancerly, naive, the dance of an insect or a factory blowing up. At last she fell, exhausted, her being dispersed like windblown seed. She tried to rise, but in vain. Her last breath, a tiny gurgle, a little upward run on the flutes. There was a short silence, and then a final convulsive chord, sharp as the blade of a guillotine.

*Consummatum est*. But no one dared applaud. In the stunned silence the Godfaces were raised off the backboards, floated to the center of the room, and tented quietly over the dead young girl, Oppie and Groves, in rare but necrophiliac caress.

*Consummatum est*. On a budget of less than ten dollars, Genia Peierls had evoked the barbarism of human life, of our life, the violence of the soul;

she had proclaimed the cruelty of nature, the community as a hovering sword, the instinctive savagery of a tribe wedded to Eros and Death, and Fate, powerful, primordial, random as the ruler of a godless universe. She had unveiled a sacrifice antihumanistic to the core, the final stage of a power struggle between nature and humanity.

The lights came on. The huge cast assembled to belated, embarrassed applause, with slight increase as Gaby got up and descended the ziggurat. Moll Flanders presented the three girls with bouquets of spring flowers sent up from Santa Fe. As if rehearsed, the three of them walked over to Gregor and presented their bouquets to him. He was dizzy with vigilance and uncertain longing.

Outside, the radiation of an equinoctial moon.

# 41. *The* UNCERTAIN GLORY *of* APRIL

On Good Friday, March 30, 1945, a shrunken Franklin Roosevelt limped zombielike toward his Warm Springs, Georgia, spa, too exhausted to acknowledge greetings from fellow patients and friends. Three weeks earlier, he had been propped up on the world stage at Yalta, a sagging husk, victim to Stalin's fierce, portentous depredations and Churchill's wry, observing eye:

> I am sorry to say that I was rather shocked at the President. He did not look well and was rather shaky. I know he's never a master of detail, but I got the impression that most of the time he really didn't know what it was all about. And whenever he was called upon to preside over any meeting, he failed to make any attempt to grip it or guide it, and sat generally speechless, or, if he made any intervention, it was generally completely irrelevant. It really was rather disturbing.

During the first week of April he seemed somewhat to recover his appearance, appetite, humor, and sense of well-being. He began to work on his Jefferson Day speech, to look over new stamps and play with his little Scottie, Fala. News from the fronts was good: British and American troops had crossed the Rhine, the Russians were fighting in Berlin, and in the Pacific, American forces had landed on Okinawa, closest yet to the Japanese mainland. He could push war worries to the rear and concentrate on the founding UN conference scheduled in San Francisco later in the month—his largest legacy to the world. And he looked forward, too, to Lucy's arrival on the ninth, Lucy Rutherford, his mistress and love, the woman for whom he had given up his marriage bed.

On Thursday, April 12, Lucy's friend Elizabeth Shoumatoff was painting a portrait of the President. It was she who reported FDR's last words at a quarter to one: "We've got just fifteen minutes more."

Cerebral arteriosclerosis does not get better. At one, he slumped in his chair, never to regain consciousness. He had been scheduled to attend a minstrel show that afternoon.


Children were the first to hear it, the flash breaking into their radio programs, the shortest in history: FDR DEAD. Mommies and daddies were next to learn, and the nation quickly gathered in a net of intensity. People remembered where they were when they heard the news.

In Berlin, just past midnight, Goebbels ordered the best champagne from Chancellery cellars and telephoned Hitler, sixty feet deep in the Bunker. "My Führer, I congratulate you! Roosevelt is dead! It is written in the stars that the second half of April will be the turning point for us. This is Friday, April the thirteenth. It is the turning point!" Even in his drugged stupor, the Führer was in ecstasy. His enemy was dead—Roosevelt the "sick, crippled, criminal Jew." Surely this was a sign that the Almighty would rescue the Third Reich at the eleventh hour. There was joy in a joyless place. Goebbels's secretary wrote, "This was the Angel of History! We felt its wings flutter through the room. Was that not the turn of fortune we awaited so anxiously?" It was "a divine judgement, a gift from God."

In this lunatic atmosphere, national leaders grasped at the stars and, amidst the flames of Valhalla, rejoiced in the death of the American President.

It was Eleanor who broke the news to Truman. For a moment a stunned vice-president could not bring himself to speak; then, "Is there anything I can do for you?" he asked. "Is there anything we can do for *you?*" ER countered. "You are the one in trouble now." She left for Warm Springs, breaking an appointment for later that afternoon, an appointment long awaited by Leo Szilard. He had something for her—a memo for her to bring to her husband's attention, a long memo on avoiding a nuclear-arms race with Russia.

When the news reached Los Alamos, Oppie came out onto the steps of the administration building to be with the men and women who had gathered. Unanimously pro-Roosevelt, they were devastated at the loss. In addition, they were concerned about the Project, which Truman, ap-

parently, knew almost nothing about. Would it continue? Oppie scheduled a Sunday morning memorial service for the entire community.

Another Rite of Spring. The mesa was deep in snow, blue shadows in
soft whiteness, silent, cold, but consoling. In Theater Number Two, Oppie
spoke quietly for three minutes to the whole community:

> When, three days ago, the world had word of the death of President Roo-
> sevelt, many wept who are unaccustomed to tears, many were reminded
> of how precious a thing human greatness is.
>
> We have been living through years of great evil, and of great terror.
> Roosevelt has been, in an old, unperverted sense, our leader. All over the
> world men have looked to him for guidance, and have seen symbolized
> in him their hope that the terrible sacrifices which have been made, and
> those that are still to be made, would lead to a world more fit for human
> habitation.
>
> In the Hindu scripture, in the Bhagavad-Gita, it says, "Man is a crea-
> ture whose substance is faith. What his faith is, he is." The faith of Roo-
> sevelt is one that is shared by millions of men and women in every
> country of the world. For this reason it is possible to maintain the hope,
> for this reason it is right that we should dedicate ourselves to the hope,
> that his good works will not have ended with his death.

That sacrifices still to be made in American souls and Japanese flesh
would lead to a world more fit for human habitation—such was Oppenheimer's faith that defined and sustained him through the terrible days
ahead.

The community was somber; people spoke of their experiences in
FDR's America. The Europeans spoke of contrasting experiences in Europe. Laura Fermi told a cryptic story of answering Mussolini's call for all
Italian women to contribute their wedding bands to Italy, of the com-
munal emotion of the women in the room as they exchanged gold for
government-issued steel.

Gregor had trouble concentrating. The room seemed to spin; he
leaned hard against the standing-room wall and gripped the doorjamb.
Was it emotion over his lost friend? Friend-enemy? Friend-enemy-father?
How he had betrayed his father in thought and deed! My son the roach—

a boast not made by one Jewish merchant in Prague. Failure. He had betrayed his father, Mr. Ives, and seen hog-mind risk run rampant. He had betrayed his father the Sanskrit mole, now in trouble with security. Perhaps it was he himself who had fingered him. Clawed him. He couldn't remember.

His legs felt twitchy. His arms all trembled. His antennae were flexing wildly under his cap. And suddenly he became aware of a long-standing pain, becoming ever more acute, in the indurated rim of the wound pressed hotly, oozingly, against the wall. He fell forward, grazing the shoulders of two GIs standing in front of him, then flat, prostrate, onto the wooden floor, tock, like some thin board come thwacking down.

He awoke strapped into a bed, if "awake" can describe his swirling semi-consciousness billowing through the infirmary isolation room. Lieutenant Jim Nolan, pediatrician, gynecologist, and surgeon, and Captain Rudolph Bernard, pediatrician, were at his bedside. For medical and security reasons they had decided against sending him to Bruns Hospital in Santa Fe, fifty miles of rough road from the site. For other, less clear, reasons, they had decided to treat him themselves, and not turn the case over to Lieutenant Thomsett, the head veterinarian.

Intermittent spiking fever, with wide diurnal variation. Increased muscular twitching. Chills. Purpuric sub-chitinous blisters. Arrhythmia suggesting pericardial infection, perhaps endocarditis, general abdominal tenderness (exquisite) suggesting peritonitis, inflammation of the large joints. Diastolic pressure falling, potential for shock. Hemocytopenia, cellular debris in the hemolymph, coagulaocytosis, increased uric acid in the anal Malpighian tubules. Pustular infection and abscess (probably staph) in preexisting cuticular wound. The diagnosis was clear: septicemia—generalized infection in the circulating hemolymph, probably metastasized from back wound, threatening all organs, potentially grave, requiring vigorous therapy.

Dr. Nolan had drilled a route through Gregor's thoracic cuticle and inserted two central lines in the softer abdominal area. IV penicillin was delivered at 20 million units per day, supplemented with both parenteral and topical streptomycin. In those early days of antibiotics, one could usually get by with such a combination. In Gregor's interior, grapelike clusters of staphylococci sported their last, at FDR's great wake in the hemolymphatic Bunker. The doctors had incised the abscess, drained and cleaned the wound, cauterized it as best they could, then dressed it and hoped for the best.

Gregor's room had "a view of the lake"—actually just Ashley Pond, but one of the few round bodies of water in that part of New Mexico. At the steps to the door just outside his window lay Timoshenko, the huge Great Dane–Russian Wolfhound mix whom Gregor confused with Aage Bohr–Genia Peierls, and with Cerberus, barker for the Great Tent of Hell, intent on Gregor's attendance.

". . . unhealing wound of Amfortas, king over the Waste Land." It was Bernard, doctor of medicine and *littérateur,* expounding while changing the dressing.

Echoing in chitinous shell: *Remember thy Creator while the evil days come not. "Deinen Schöpfer,"* Gregor moaned, *"die bösen Tage."*

"Is he talking Yiddish?" asked a nurse.

From his bed he saw mosaic mountains, o most unfocused Blood of Christs.

. . . *while the sun or the light or the moon or the stars be not darkened.* ". . . *nicht finster werden,"* he breathed. And Death eyed the chime on Master Hanus's clock.

Oppie—elegant, intelligent—said: "No, Ann, German—his childhood Bible."

"Ah."

"The land becomes sterile," Bernard continued, "on account of the sexual wound, a curse which can be removed only by a knight who will question the . . ."

"DA, DA, Da, Da, da, da, da, da, da . . ." Gregor erupted.

"He wants his daddy," Ann said.

"Daaaatta. Dayaaaaadhvam. Damyaaaata,"

"Do we have his parents' . . . ?"

DA DA DA

Siss Boom Bah

YES YES YES

Those are pearls that were his eyes.

"Give, sympathize, control," Oppie corrected, translating, *"Datta dayadhvam*—that's for Gregor. *Damyata*—that's for the rest of us." He pulled on his empty pipe. "After such knowledge," then to himself, "what forgiveness?"

"DA DA DA DA DA DA DA DA DA DA DA DA—" Gregor's shriek cut off sharply.

"Give him a liter of saline, nurse. . . ."

"Admonitions of the thunder," Oppie observed, "the thunderword to a hundred-lettered world.

"A liter bolus of saline."

The lab director leaned down to the bed and uncovered Gregor's knee.

"Gregor, tomorrow I will read you a sutra of thunder, the meaning of thunder, the link between the universe and the silence beyond. . . . Da. Da. Da, my friend."

*The hallway of the wind.*

"Thunder is the honey of all beings, the immortal spirit of vibrating sound—this the Brahman, this the universe."

*A thunder which brings no rain . . .*

The nurse shook her head, and headed for the stockroom.

"Thirst for the waters of faith and healing."

". . . the waters that would fertilize the Waste Land."

"Just so."

*Left no address . . .*


The smell of pipe-smoke filled the room. Oppie's clothes? Or was it sulfur? *C-shop is burning! I can't move.*

"Burning burning burning burning," Gregor said. "Sitio."

*All things, O Priests, are on fire.*

*The eye, O Priests, is on fire. The ear . . .*

Porkpie hat on bedstand.

"Nurse, can you get Dr. Nolan?"

*Ach, wer bringt die schönen Tage, wer jene holde Zeit zurück!* Who will bring back those beautiful, pure days?

"Easy, easy. Brahman is the lightning too, for freeing one from darkness."

*Fire. The ear is on fire. What is that sound? Hoards, swarming the cracked earth. The locusts shall be a burden and man's desires shall fail....* "*Heuschrecke!*" Gregor shrieked.

"He's in the Chapel Perilous," said Bernard, placing his hand on his patient's brow, finger stroking antenna's base.

Healing touch.

Calming.

If unknowing.

Fires of hatred, of passion, of despair burnt lower. Dust goeth to dust, and man to his long home.

"Yes, Dr. Bernard," Ann said. "I'll get him."

*I AM THE ROACH OF GOD CARBONIFEROUS, A LIVING RUMOR OF ETERNITY.*

"A little prick."

Nembutal. Numinous. Nirvana. Nothing.

Porkpie hat off bedstand. A thin man went back to his office in the ramshackle world of suffering.

*Watchman, tell us of the night,*
*What the signs of promise are . . .*

The two physicians sat talking in the dark while Gregor slept. Bernard explained to Nolan the nature of the plot:

"Parsifal's spear is a true *pharmakon*, at once poison and cure."

"Only the weapon which made the wound can cure it, eh?"

Gregor heard them far away. But their buzzing was mere background to the Ommmm in his head, the Om that spelled b . . . o . . . m . . . b . . .

At his desk in T-building, Oppie opened his *Gita* and read:

```
Into darkness fall those who follow action. Into
deeper darkness fall those who follow knowledge. Thus we
```

`have heard from the ancient sages who explained this`
`truth to us.`

Sanskrit has ninety-six words for love.

". . . the infinite melodies of desire," Bernard said, "the void between Eros and pity."

Nolan tapped his knee with a reflex hammer.

". . . a process of aging which ends in corruption of faith, frustration of will, and perversion of action . . ."

"The decline of the West," said Nolan.

Gregor from far away said "bomb apple spear bomb apple spear."

In the deep night, Alice came to lick his wound.

By April, Berlin was defended only by an army of motley volunteers—the Hitler Youth, boys from twelve to sixteen, and the Home Guard—men who were divided into two categories: those with and without weapons. Morale was low to nonexistent. Party members and police cadets set up roadblocks to prevent people fleeing, and scoured cellars for deserters. Lampposts were festooned with corpses labeled "I hang here because I am a defeatist," or "I hang here because I criticized the Führer," or more plaintively, "I am a deserter and thus will not see the change in destiny."

Hitler, as everyone knows, was in his Bunker. But this Bunker was not the secure space capsule of common myth. It was a small air-raid shelter, built quickly to hold an emergency few from the Chancellery, a completely deficient communications center, its few phone lines running through the central Berlin exchange, a claustrophobic den with inadequate water, sewerage, ventilation, or power, badly planned, badly built, a ridiculous place to choose as a command center, its only virtue being, as a sarcastic Soviet colonel was later to remark, that it was "near to the shops."

No spiffy SS habitat this, with shiny boots crisply clicking down hallways. It housed—or rather hid—a commander-in-chief who in person could have commanded neither the respect nor the obedience of his troops. Hitler had been stricken by some rapidly progressive, debilitating,

Parkinsonian-like disease, whose symptoms were consistently described in the diaries of those closest to him. Prematurely aged, grossly weakened, stooped, partially paralyzed, and uncontrollably shaking, he had become a food-stained, urine-soiled caricature, incapable of writing his own signature, barely capable of reading a wall map even with his glasses. A man often melancholic, an impotent insomniac, barely able to mutter his wishes, he was still capable of vindictive raging against his hatreds and phobias from earlier years. Allowed to lie in torpor for days, like some mud-caked crocodile, isolated from outside circumstances, he was cynically manipulated by opportunistic sycophants who, on the one hand, consolidated their power, and on the other remained slaves to their slavering master. Here were the cream of the German military indulging a corporal from another era, listening to his irrelevant rants and obvious inaccuracies, all against a backdrop of impending disaster. They knew Hitler was incapable of carrying out the simplest of military operations; they held him in utmost contempt. Yet out of habitual subservience and a sense of patriotic duty, they continued to help him destroy the fatherland, carrying out his orders, putting into practice ideas that all acknowledged to be military madness, all in an atmosphere of general filth and squalor.

By choosing to remain in the Bunker, Hitler had deliberately abdicated responsibility for the conduct of the war. Overwhelmingly afraid of retribution from his own people, fearful of a revolt, or of being handed over to the Soviets humiliatingly alive, on April 30, the housepainter Adolf Hitler, né Schickelgruber, either took his life or was murdered by his Bunker associates. Evidence and testimony is conflicting as to details. His new bride, Eva Braun, and his large Alsatian, Blondi, shared his fate.

The uncertain glory of April: Gregor delirious; FDR and AH, archenemies of the century, both stricken, both dead.

## 42. PRINCIPIUM INDIVIDUATIONIS

Gregor sprang back more quickly than anyone expected. Such is the elasticity of chitin.

Though outwardly involved in his continually frustrated safety work, it was clear that he had made his final decision. He seemed simultaneously pregnant and more opaque, as if he were growing, inside the chrysalis of self, another organism, with other goals, which would molt and hatch in a final metamorphosis.

His friendship afforded no special privileges: he conversed just as often with his colleagues, but there was a veil between Gregor and them, a withdrawal of candor on his part that would brook no inquiry.

"Are you all right?" several had asked.

"Yes, of course," he would answer.

"Is there anything bothering you?"

"No, nothing."

And here he may have been disclosing a subjective truth: from his point of view, pregnant with death, he *was* all right; nothing was bothering him.

Yet he did keep mentioning, inscrutably, his "trials"—likely not "trials" as in "trials and tribulations," and not the trying of colleagues at his private tribunal, but rather "trials" as in testing—testing the icy waters of death with trial suicides, using a slow but enlightening method.


On the morning after an intense, late-night session with Teller, Gregor found a note in his mailbox:

Samsa,

    First of all let me say that I have no hope of clearing my conscience. The things we are working on are so terrible that no amount of protesting or fiddling with politics will save our souls. But I am not really con-

```
vinced of your objections. I do not feel that there is
any chance to outlaw any one weapon. If we have a slim
chance of survival, it lies in the possibility to get
rid of wars. The more decisive the weapon, the more
surely it will be used in any real conflicts and no ar-
guments will help. Our only hope is in getting the facts
of our results before the people. This might help con-
vince everybody that the next war would be fatal. For
this purpose actual combat-use might even be the best
thing. I feel I should do the wrong thing if I tried to
say how to tie the little toe of the ghost to the bottle
from which we help it to escape.
     ET
```

Unfortunately, the Hungarian, for whatever reason—perhaps to win some sort of security points—had sent a copy of this out-of-context communication to the boss, who summoned Gregor to his office that same day. He looked ghostly. Like a sick eagle.

"How goes it with your meeting?" asked the boss.

"Which meeting?"

"'The Impact of the Gadget on Civilization' meeting. The one you've been postering for."

"Oh, that hasn't happened yet. It's this Friday." Oppie—who knew every detail of every activity on-site—was playing dumb. "Will you be able to come?"

"Samsa, I think there's something you don't understand. I'll explain it to you in five words. The atomic bomb is shit. You understand? This is a weapon which has absolutely no military significance. It will make a big bang—a very big bang—but it's not a weapon that is useful in war."

"You mean it's too terrible? Like poison gas?"

"Too terrible. Too difficult to make. Too expensive."

"So why go ahead?"

"The politicians want it. They don't spend two billion dollars every day. Your colleagues want it—in case you haven't found out. You don't put in seven days a week of pregnancy, eighteen hours a day for two years without wanting to see your baby born. A great discovery is a thing of beauty, don't you agree? Our binding faith here is that knowledge is good—good in itself—an instrument for our successors, who'll use it to probe elsewhere, more deeply. It's an instrument for technology, for human affairs."

He puffed on his pipe. Gregor waited for a quote from the Gita—in Sanskrit, of course. But the quote never came. After a long silence, Oppie simply dismissed him and went off "to a meeting." He had been in many meetings in the last month—mostly in Washington, along with Fermi, Lawrence, and Compton, as part of the Interim Committee—the group designated by Secretary of War Stimson to determine whether, how, and where to use the bomb. Pushed by Oppenheimer, over Fermi's taciturn objections, decisions had been made: withholding the bomb was never seriously discussed; a "demonstration blast" was dismissed as being too iffy. It should be dropped without warning on a real military/civilian target—and as soon as possible, before the Soviets became involved in the Pacific. As Secretary of State designate Jimmy Burns had instructed the new President, "the bomb might well put us in a position to dictate our own terms at the end of the war." Gregor knew nothing of these meetings—perhaps a good thing.

It was shortly after this most recent encounter with Oppie that Gregor began his little notepad, the record, it would seem, of his "trials." He labeled it "DEATH BY A THOUSAND CUTS SPIRAL NOTEBOOK." It contained quotes from the people he had asked to sign Szilard's petition, and from those engaged in wider discussion of the bomb.

DEATH BY A THOUSAND CUTS SPIRAL NOTEBOOK

1 June. A demonstration is not worth serious analysis. Why give away the element of surprise? It would be empty fireworks. Only the destruction of a town would be incontrovertible. IIR (Theoretical)

1 June. If God hadn't loved bombs, He wouldn't have created Japanese. PT (Theoretical)

1 June. It doesn't keep me awake at night. JRR (Gadget)

"June Is Bustin' Out All Over!" *Carousel* was the musical hit of 1945: "If I Loved You" had made the top ten, and when the calendar came round, the June song made a two-week excursion into the charts. At Los

Alamos, it is true there were gorgeous desert flowers. But the burst that brought joy to all educated hearts was—finally!—a large and ongoing shipment of explosive lenses, the lack of which had delayed testing dangerously close to deadline. Plutonium was arriving in good supply now, Alvarez seemed to have solved the detonator problem, the initiator design looked good in Bethe's calculations, and only adequate firing circuits remained a problem—one that seemed lightweight compared to those already solved. The Faustian spirit was high come June.

> 2 June. Extra people might die as a result of the delay in making arrangements for a demonstration—even if it was only two weeks. You don't want to have extra people die to make yourself feel good, do you? NFR (Delivery)
>
> 3 June. Why are people so scared of atomic weapons? I'm making an important contribution to national and international security. I want to make the weapons safe. I don't trust others to do it. Mostly what I work on is making things safe. AG (Ordnance)
>
> 4 June. You want a warning? You're not flying the airplane! SSR (Delivery)

Laboring away at the most deadly work of the Project, at Omega site deep in Pajarito Canyon, as far as possible from labs and town, Louis Slotin was manipulating deadly materials with a screwdriver, playing with assemblies—how much material, in what shape, would go critical? He had used uranium all year, designing constructs named Jezebel, Godiva, Honeycomb, Scripts, Little Eva, Pot, and Topsy. Now he was working with plutonium.

> 8 June. I'm interested in the physics. This is the ultimate toy shop. And I love being a Peeping Tom on Mother Nature. BM (Research)
>
> 9 June. My ethics is my own business, just between me and my God. If I didn't do it, someone else would. JF (SED)
>
> 11 June. Hey, the United States is the good guy. This is a demonstrable fact. We are good guys. It's self-evidently appropriate to do this work. JJG (SED)

A year later Slotin would be dead, the Project's second nuclear accident victim. But on June 12, just in time for that week's colloquium, he tested two full-scale plutonium hemispheres for the first time, and nailed down their optimal configuration.

> 12 June. I'm not responsible for the decisions about what to do with this. Is the automobile manufacturer responsible for people killed by drunk drivers? CL (Exterior Ballistics)
>
> 12 June. Why is it worse to drop an atom bomb than to firebomb Tokyo or Dresden? AAB (Theoretical)
>
> 12 June. It's a matter of posturing. Peace comes by being too tough to tackle. It's okay to be an idealist, but you also have to be a realist. There's no such thing as an ideal world. RTL (Fermi Group)

Ah, so. Gregor knew his time at Los Alamos was over, and the moment had come to travel down to the Trinity test site, Ken Bainbridge's project, 160 miles south.

> 13 June. When I can't look in the mirror when I shave in the morning, I'll quit. RW (Explosives)

Trinity! What a name! Name upon name! An Oppenheimer product, of course, though there are two different stories as to its origin. The most quoted story is that when queried about a code name for site and test, his mind flashed back to a John Donne poem he had been reading the previous night:

*Batter my heart, three-person'd God; for, you*
*As yet but knock, breathe, shine, and seek to mend.*
*That I may rise, and stand, o'erthrow me, and bend*
*Your force, to break, blow, burn, and make me new.*

Plausible, though hardly what ensued, as the three-personed God o'erthrew him a bit too hard.

There is another extant explanation more related to his fierce interest in Hinduism: for Oppie, Trinity would surely resonate with Sanskrit *trimurti*, the three forms of god—Brahma, the creator of life on earth; Vishnu, the preserver of life on earth; and Shiva, the destroyer of life on earth. It was likely no accident that his famous comment on the Trinity explosion was "Now I am become Death, the Shatterer of Worlds." It was the metamorphosis from Vishnu to Shiva to which he might have been referring. In any case, "Trinity."

> 14 June. I like working on problems that are more than truth and beauty, on problems that have an impact on society and its future. For the first time ever I worry about whether my answers are right or wrong. IF (SED)
>
> 14 June. If you say "Get rid of atomic bombs," you say, "Let's make the world safe for conventional war." PT (SED)

Name upon name. In August 1944, Groves had approved a test site in the Jornada del Muerto Valley, so named for its lack of water—which left early travelers' skeletons bleaching in the unforgiving sun. Part of the Air Force's Alamogordo Bombing Range, it had the best attributes of any site inspected: isolated, yet within commuting distance to the Hill, flat for ease of sighting and instrumentation, walled by mountain ranges east and west, thus shielding larger towns from blast effects, and so uninhabitable that evacuation of indigenous population, if necessary, would be minimal.

> June 15. I make a bomb. The fact that I make a bomb doesn't mean it's going to be used. I make a bomb, and it has the potential for evil as well as the potential for good. There is sin in the world. A human being can't touch anything without the potential for sinfulness to be attached to it. MN (Gadget)
>
> June 15. So what kind of a weapon *would* you like? LLR (Water Boiler Group)

Gregor had watched the mesa population dwindle as electronics experts were shunted down to wire up the testing devices, and all available soldiers were pulled off the Hill to do the early grunt work. With risk protocols as safe as they would ever get under General Groves, and with lab inspections up to date, Gregor received permission to temporarily relocate to Trinity as part of the radiation assessment team.

16 June. It's the President and Congress who's responsible, and the people that elect them. It makes me uneasy, but I assume our national leaders know their business and will act in the public interest. ZR (Teller Group)

16 June. If you want to engage in self-flagellation, you can concoct a scenario where what you're doing is pivotal and humanity goes down the drain and all that. TF (Gadget)

16 June. Someday the Russians will build bombs, so we better have them now and stay ahead. DE (Ordnance)

It was already somewhat late. On May 7, the day the Germans surrendered, the group already in the wasteland had carried out a trial explosion using 100 tons of TNT, backbreakingly stacked on a platform, the largest intentional explosion in history. For verisimilitude they had buried a slug of Hanford plutonium in the midst of the pile, like a poor wife doomed to *suttee* on her husband's pyre. The blast sent smoke and debris up to 12,000 feet, and was contained there under an inversion layer.

17 June. I don't experience any moral dimension. I just do what I know how to do. If you try to think rationally about this stuff, you can go crazy. EEH (Research)

Scientists found measurable radioactivity only within a radius of thirty feet from the platform. But they noticed that the cloud was carried right over the towns of Carrizozo and Roswell by a 30-mile-per-hour wind. Gregor was most upset by this and by the unpredictable conditions for the vastly larger real test in July. He felt that if the bomb went off, the physicists might rejoice—and then leave the consequences to the physicians. On arrival Gregor continued his notebook, and personally plunged into many experiments with Ground Zero sand.

18 June. I'm a bombhead. It's the thrill of the chase. KK (Gadget)

The setups were primitive, but the results disturbing. If the cloud were to rise only 12,000 feet, and radioactive particles were to condense at the same ratio as the 100-ton shot, a large and dangerous amount of radioactive debris might be blown into nearby towns.

> 19 June. As long as sinful men control this earth, there will be need to take up the sword. We're just helping to fulfill prophecy. REY (Water Delivery)
>
> 19 June. I was in Tokyo. I seen that laid flat, I mean with other conventional-type bombs, fire bombs, stuff like that. War is not pretty, any way you look at it. BH (Administration)
>
> 20 June. Hey. We all die. We're not permanent fixtures here. GJL (SED)
>
> 20 June. Let's quit killing each other. Let's find the utopia. But until Christ runs out of patience and comes back, we'll never find it. AR (Ordnance)

Gregor made enough of a stink to have several instruments added to the array buried directly under the bomb tower—enough to study blast, earth shock, and neutron and gamma radiation that might be dispersed in a wind-borne cloud, instruments sensitive and fast enough to relay their information in the instant before they were incinerated.

> 22 June. If you don't work on these weapons, think of all the people you may be endangering by leaving them undefended. HHL (Research)

Armies of construction men were moving into the Trinity site to erect the hundred-foot tower for the Gadget, the jungle of wires to measure its effects, the communication lines and roadways necessary for construction and transport vehicles.

> 23 June. I was a career military man. I would have pursued the military with or without atomic weapons. It doesn't make any difference to me—atomic weapons or not. TU (Theoretical)
>
> 24 June. Anyone who pays taxes is buying this stuff. Am I more involved just because I use my expertise to build it? LKN (Theoretical)

All personnel rose at five to take advantage of the cooler part of the day. They broke for lunch at noon, for some crude air-conditioning in the cafeteria, or a swim in the McDonald ranch house cistern.

25 June. We need even-tempered people handling this. Better me than some nut. VH (Gadget)

Temperatures were over 100 degrees in the afternoon; Gregor was not as affected as some. He felt, in fact, more energetic. But like his colleagues, he was tortured by the alkali grit that covered his exposed parts and ate into his chitin. It was inescapable: the cold showers laved him in water so hard as to leave a thorough crust of magnesium oxide, incompletely removable by towel.

26 June. I don't ever lose any sleep, and I don't want to dwell on this stuff. BB (Water Boiler Group)
26 June. I'm only a small cog in a complex machine, but I try to do my job competently and earn my pay. EEW (Gadget)
26 June. Safe scientists drink in silence. WL (Theoretical)

There were dangers aplenty. Gregor had placed himself on the crew excavating and laying instrumentation for the Ground Zero pit he would know so profoundly. In one day, the workers had to deal with two tarantula bites, one scorpion sting, and a rattler who had taken underground refuge during lunch break. The next day, a march of furious fire ants whose tunnels had been disturbed, a poisonous black and orange Gila monster, come to see what all the fuss was about, and of course, ubiquitous and venomous centipedes. Gregor thought it interesting to be cast among the anti-Insectiva crowd. He found himself swept along by human group-think, a kind of species-chauvinism that, mutatis mutandis, could lead to war. His evening showers were as much to cleanse his soul as his body. And equally futile.

27 June. I'm a human being and I don't like weapons any more than anyone else, but this is the closest you get to playing God. SSH (Explosives)

Nightlife was wretched at Trinity. Poker was the big sport. Some GIs figured out that by driving off-road with lights out, they could escape the ever more restrictive security regs and have a night on the town in Carrizozo or Socorro—not exactly the big time, but still enough to use their beer money and condoms. The only problem was that, driving back blind drunk and blind, in the darkest hours of the early morning, they would invariably slice through carefully laid electrical connections or low-slung telephone wires—which then might be discovered and repaired the following day. A special detachment was assigned to make such daily rounds. "Antelopes" were blamed.

29 June. To some extent I believe in the inherent goodness of our country. RY (SED)

29 June. I'm doing what I can to make waging unlimited war dangerous and expensive. It's like holding up a caution flag to humanity and demanding we make peace. BVC (SED)

If he hadn't before, Gregor came to mistrust the military, which did not always protect and serve. Not once, but twice, "dummy" bombs carrying five pounds of high explosives had landed on base camp at night, dropped by ignorant crews from the Air Base on their training runs. Lights in the desert at night? Get those varmints! The first time, the carpentry shop went up in flames, the next time, the stables. One could stay in at night, but even daytime was unsafe. One afternoon a B-29 flew lazily over the test site, its tail gunner hunting antelope with a .50-caliber machine gun. A dozen scientists and technicians in his blind spot directly under the plane were almost ripped to shreds. The fruits of secrecy.

30 June. Mother Nature is a mean bastard. She always collects. The only question is who pays and when. She always collects. HD (Theoretical)

The Waste Land. What better place to read Schopenhauer? And read him Gregor did, in a war-time edition of *Die Welt als Wille und Vorstellung*. It was almost inevitable. "On Death and Its Relation to the Indestructibility of Our Inner Nature"—he had referred to it during his sideshow seminar on animal consciousness. Surely this was a philosophy to die by, and dying correctly was Gregor's larger task, not just for himself, but for helping heal the world.

But what *was* the world? One had best know the patient to cure the disease. The world, says Schopenhauer, is a manifestation of the Will. Whose will? *The* will. Simply Want, without subject or object. The will to existence. The ultimate, irreducible, primeval principle of being, the source of all phenomena. But Will is blind, and needs eyes and intelligence to see. Thus the *principium individuationis*, the principle of individuation, Will creating things in its wake: people, insects, nations, atomic bombs, bringing forth intellect to achieve its goals. Intellect—even Oppenheimer's or Fermi's—serves the Will, and not vice versa.

Here was a paradigm shift to which Gregor could assent, for it seemed to absolve these men he so loved and respected from the horrendous crime they were intending, exonerating their fallenness in a larger momentum so forcefully conceived. *And with much power, always, always much more love.*

Gregor relaxed, gratefully, into Schopenhauer's indictment of the state of things, the struggle of all against all, the turbulent division of Will against itself, *homo homini lupus* bringing forth jealousy, envy, hatred, fear, ambition, avarice, and so on without end, the utter misery of the world. The pages brought forth a strange satisfaction—that mere letters on paper could express such deep human indignation, such spiritual rebellion against what is, the revenge of the heroic Word.

But Gregor would not settle for such peace as death had to offer, freedom from the impossible role he had been dealt at the beginning of the First Great War. No. Rather, he would demand redemption of the mindless whole by the mindful part. "REDEMPTION, NOT FREEDOM, IS THE GOAL!" he wrote, in the largest of capital letters, then, mysteriously, "CARBON TO SILICON."

Perhaps that was it: carbon to silicon, a carbon-based life-form handing over an age to another element, silicon, the next analogue down in the Periodic Table, a chemically similar colleague that would so fulfill its crystalline connections as to thwart entirely the Will and its misguided *principium individuationis*. Gregor! Two full years before the discovery of semiconductors, Gregor choosing to unite himself with the silicon sands of the southwest desert, priest and sacrifice at once.

On the evening of July 6, Bob Serber found a note from Gregor in his box, delivered by some commuter from the south. It was marked "INDE-PENDENCE DAY!", the dateline ostentatiously decorated with crude American flags and red, white, and blue Jolly Rogers, a type of humor he associated more with Feynman than with Gregor.

```
Dear Bob, next time down, please bring the Tellers'
Victrola and their album of Also sprach Zarathustra.
Already permission from Edward and Mici. We are planning
a science party. You are invited.
    G
```

Well. *Très gai,* he thought. His impression was that they were *already* having a science party down there.

They arrived at the Trinity site "for the duration" on the tenth—Serber, Fermi, and Sam Allison in Sam's old jalopy. Sam had been chosen to do the countdown for the test, so they stopped in Santa Fe to try to get his old Bulova fixed on the spot, like having a heel repaired. The jeweler couldn't do it immediately, and Sam, frustrated by not being able to pull either rank or historical inevitability, threw an embarrassing tantrum, which only trapped him into having to buy a new watch. Fermi played Chico Marx to Sam's Groucho, while Bob filled Harpo's silent role—without his talent. They did hear the owner complain to his wife in the back room, "Goddam longhairs!"

"Guess we aren't as incognito as we think," Sam remarked.

A trip with Fermi-Unleashed is a memorable experience. Normally taciturn, perhaps even shy except when making invariably correct pronouncements on physics, that day he was positively manic. But his wit had a sardonic edge, one that would become sharper and quite destructive over the next few days. He made crack after crack about radioactive fallout, and about the bomb being far more powerful than anyone had imagined. After experiencing a huge pothole-without-springs just south of Socorro, he remarked to Sam, "I guess if we make it down okay in this heap, we'll come out of Trinity alive," and was silent for the rest of the trip.

If his jokes were unnerving it was because "The Pope" was rarely wrong about physics—in fact, never—in anyone's experience. Over the past two years, within the physics community, legitimate questions had arisen from legitimate fears, especially concerning the inadvertent ignition of atmospheric nitrogen. Worst-case scenario: the entire atmosphere going up in flames, destroying all life on earth. The possibility of catastrophe was taken most seriously—by serious people. At the time of Trinity, all the best minds—Oppie, Szilard, Bethe, Teller, Wigner, Compton, and others—were working on it. The horrifying fact was that no one was truly sure.

Approaching the Trinity site, the open car followed the practice path of the B-29 that would parachute measuring instruments in the final minute of countdown, then photograph the blast from the air, and try to get away. It was truly a heroic (some would say insane) assignment, since no one knew how large the explosion would be, how quickly it would expand, or to what dimensions. All this information was necessary for the safety of the Nagasaki plane, but what about the survival of this one? The three watched the pilot approach what they assumed was the tower, bank sharply, then attempt to get high and far as fast as possible. By the time they arrived at the gate, they had admired three different versions of this feat. Fermi remarked dryly that Alvarez and Parsons would be on that plane to register the speed and pressure of the fireball, operating and monitoring radio receivers, oscilloscopes, cameras, Geiger counters, microphones, and transmitters. This the others had not known. Funny how feelings change when family is involved.

Keeping speculations going, and fertile ground for Fermi's scare tactics, was a scientists' betting pool, both on the mesa and at the site. You entered for a buck, and the pot would go to the person who most closely guessed the measured yield in tons of TNT equivalent. Teller, ever the enthusiast, had made the most expansive bet: 45 thousand tons. Level-headed Hans Bethe had guessed 8,000, and cynical Kistiakowsky, the explosives king, 1,400. He felt he was being optimistic. Norman Ramsey, a Harvard physicist, made what he thought to be the cleverest bet in the pool: zero.

But it was Oppie's bet—300 tons—that was most disturbing. That the project leader, the commander determined to encourage the troops, the man with every detail of the entire project in his head, should guess so low was a slap at all the calculations, all the work, all the hopes that had fueled so many hearts for the last two years. Three hundred tons? At ten million dollars per ton? Why bother? It was discouraging. People didn't talk about it.

Except for General Groves. His spies relayed the betting news, Groves consulted with staff psychiatrists, and with his hardheaded practicality, immediately worked out an alternative chain-of-command, should Oppie break down completely. To minimize the chance, he flew Oppie's old friend I. I. Rabi out from the East Coast, though he had no role at the test but to play "companion." Rabi's arrival in the sweltering desert in a dark suit, homburg, galoshes, and carrying an umbrella was comically reassuring that there was another world still out there.

Gregor scheduled his "science party" off the cuff, the very night the phonograph arrived. There were no competing attractions. Klaus Fuchs, Edward Teller, Otto Frisch, and Rudolph Bernard were invited to appear at eleven forty-five P.M. (sharp!) at the little blockhouse fifty yards from the W. 10,000 shelter, a building housing one of the three searchlights that were to illuminate the test and its aftermath. A quarter-moon lit the sign on the door: COME IN, SET UP VICTROLA WITH STRAUSS SIDE 3, TAKE YOUR SEATS, TURN ON MUSIC. THANK YOU. GS. Had he gone off his rocker?

Cautiously opening the door, the four of them filed into the small room. Collective IQs approaching 800. At the eastern end was the big searchlight, staring blankly through a bullet-proof window out into the darkness of the bomb tower. At the western end was a light brown, regulation army desk, and on it a dark brown Gregor, Hunger-Artist thin, lying naked on his back, lit only, *à la Rite of Spring,* by a flashlight hanging from the ceiling, three feet above his abdomen. Between the dark light and the light dark were four folding chairs.

There was something acutely embarrassing about this. People rarely think of animals as naked. It's not just the hair. Is a butterfly naked? An elephant? One would think Gregor's dark, chitinous cuticle would serve admirably for dress. Not so. There were no exposed genitals or private orifices. Nevertheless. Perhaps it was just his position: supine, legs undulating slightly in the air above him—so ultimately vulnerable. A little unnerved, the physicists took their seats and waited for something, not knowing whether they had come to the right place, for the right thing. But what other place was there? What other thing?

Eventually, Teller remembered the box on his lap. He got up, searched in the dark for an electrical outlet, found one on the north wall, and plugged in the Victrola. Serber took the record out of its album and handed it over to him after making sure side three was topside. Teller put the record on the turntable and said, partly to Gregor, and partly to the attendant God of Oddness, "Do you want the music now?" It sounded so peculiar, a simple human question, subject, verb, object, so out of place in this dark cubicle, out in the midst of this martian, colonized wasteland, with that odd object lying on the table. There was no answer; the legs simply kept waving. What could he do but put the arm on the platter?

The room filled with hiss as the needle traversed the empty grooves around the rim. There followed then a sound that seemed as native to the odd occasion as Teller's voice had sounded foreign, a barely perceptible rumble that seemed to come from the rocks under the sand, from the slow magma under the rocks, a long vibration whispering guttural resonance—perhaps a hymn to the bomb soon to be assembled.

Side three of *Also sprach Zarathustra* consists of two sections, *Von der Wissenschaft (sehr langsam)*, and *Der Genesende (energisch)*. "On Science" (very slow) and "The Convalescent" (energetic). Science. This was a "Science Party." Science here was a slowly growing fugue, the most "intellectual" of musical constructs, the epitome of Learning, a fugue arising, pianissimo, from the depths of the orchestra, reaching out in a long arch toward ever greater, ear-shattering, triple forte wildness. "Science" here was an all-inclusive structure, a fugue subject containing every chromatic pitch in the octave, in common time, triplets and triplet augmentation—all in four grave measures. It lumbered from the simple C major of Nature, to the gnarled B major of Man, a half-tone below, like some underground creature afraid to breathe pure air, a grim Alberich, slit-eyed and clench-jawed, forswearing love and plotting revenge. Science.

The Europeans knew well the Nietzsche passage Strauss was addressing, a struggle Teller, at least, had found urgently compelling in his undergraduate years. A "conscientious man" asserts that fear is the original and basic feeling-state of mankind, the source of all its virtues, the fount of Science. Fear of wild animals, including the wild animal in oneself. Such old fear—refined, spiritualized—is Science.

Nonsense! cries Zarathustra. Fear is the exception. Courage and adventure, and pleasure in the uncertain—*that* is mankind's gift. Stealing the virtues of the wildest, most courageous animals: *that*—refined, spiritualized—is Science.

As Zarathustra's energy overcomes that of the conscientious man, the music quickens. Beginning in the same supination he must have awakened to on that horrifying morning during the First War, Gregor, here toward the end of the Second, began to wave his legs in startling, unpredicted patterns, almost as if he were spelling mysterious messages in semaphore, finally generating such torque as to flip him off the desk and onto the floor. So Nietzsche's Convalescent:

> One morning Zarathustra jumped up from his resting place like a mad-man, roared in a terrible voice, and acted as if somebody else were still lying on his resting place who refused to get up. Up, abysmal thought, out of my depth! I am your cock and dawn, sleepy worm. Up! Up! My voice shall yet crow you awake!

German-speaking roosters do not say "Cock-a-doodle-do." Through some strange linguistic contortion, they tend to cry out "Riki-riki-riki." And that is exactly what Gregor did, screeching and bounding nervously around the room, roaching the roof, climbing over the walls and ceiling, over the large searchlight, a hair-raising display to dark-adapted eyes. The music leaped into completely unexpected flights of fancy, a fantastic dance high in the upper winds, rushing and trilling, while the "Disgust" motif began its feverish appearance until the music, and Zarathustra, and Gregor, all fell down as if dead.

After a long pause, seven days in the poem, seven seconds in the score, a rebirth begins, sketching out an understanding of the human mission on earth—accompanied by one of the most remarkable passages in the orchestral repertoire, astoundingly light, humorous, Till Eulenspiegel once more, and not Death.

Swish-click, swish-click, swish-click. The automatic changer tried to drop the next side, but none was there; side three was all Gregor had requested. He lay, supine again, diagonally disposed on the floor behind us. Bernard took the needle off the record. The audience sat there in the grotesque light of a hanging, gently swinging flashlight and waited, again unsure what to do. After a pause of perhaps half a minute Gregor, from the floor, recited *"O Mensch, gib Acht!,"* the tremendous eleven-line poem that occurs next in Nietzsche, though not in Strauss:

> *One!*
> *Mankind, listen well –*
> *Two!*
> *Listen to the words of black midnight:*
> *Three!*
> *"I was asleep, asleep*
> *Four!*
> *"And then from dream's abyss awoke.*
> *Five!*
> *"Deep is the world*
> *Six!*
> *"Deeper than daylight can imagine.*
> *Seven!*
> *"Its pain is deep*
> *Eight!*
> *"But its joy is deeper still.*
> *Nine!*
> *"Pain says: 'Be gone!'*
> *Ten!*
> *"But Joy desires eternity,*
> *Eleven!*
> *"The most profound eternity!"*
> *Twelve!*

A "madman" keying out humanity.

For the twelve strokes of midnight, a skeletal Gregor, still on his back, reached out with his leg toward a contraption previously unnoticed—a hammer hanging upside down from a cord slipped over a ceiling beam. By pulling the rope with his toe claws, the hammer was made to strike the metal casing—which emitted not the expected clack, but a surprisingly full, bell-like tone. In this desert where no clocks chimed, it rang out the apotheosis of midnight.

The final bell having struck, Gregor paused a moment, then leaped up, came around to the front of the chairs, and addressed his audience directly:

*If we shadows have offended,*
*Think but this, and all is mended,*
*That you have but slumber'd here*
*While these visions did appear.*
*Man—a bridge, and not a goal,*
*A rope stretched o'er the giant hole.*
*Good night, good night,*
*Now comes the light.*
*Parting is such sweet sorrow.*

And he reached up behind him and switched off the flashlight, leaving the group in darkness. After several minutes of sitting in silence, Teller decided Gregor was serious about having said good night, and got up to leave. The rest followed. As Bernard, the last to leave, was about to close the door behind him, Gregor said in a low voice, as if to him alone, "With all its eyes the creature world beholds the open. Report me and my cause aright to the unsatisfied."

Some science party! The partyers drove back to base camp stunned and silent after only twenty minutes. Though Gregor must have been quite pleased, his audience dispersed with bare good nights to its own disturbing dreams. They seemed to avoid one another over the next few days, as if they had shared common witness to some shameful event that would not stand acknowledgment or discussion. They also found themselves avoiding Gregor in those, his last days. He seemed too distant, too strange. Besides, he was spending much time off-campus with Nolan, Bernard, and Hempelmann, working on fallout issues, consulting discreetly with the Governor's office, and with the mayors of Socorro, Carrizozo, and Roswell concerning possible evacuations.

Oppenheimer arrived at the site on Wednesday, the eleventh, having said goodbye to Kitty and arranged a code message for a successful test. But like many other Los Alamos leave-takings that week, there was an unspoken whiff of "I may never see you again." Embraces were poignant.

That night, in Omega Canyon, at the foot of the mesa, plutonium ingots were checked and arranged in the vault, and were loaded the next day into Bob Bacher's sedan for their destined trip south. Philip Morrison sat in the backseat with two suitcases full of subcritical pieces, arms draped over each to "protect" them in case of an accident. With a security car in front and trailed by the nuclear assembly team, the portentous load began its five-hour trip to Trinity.

About eight in the evening, the motorcade turned off a dirt road a mile east of the tower and pulled up in front of the McDonald ranch house. Its sixteen-by-eighteen living room had been converted by the Army into an assembly site, vacuumed thoroughly of dust, its windows covered with plastic and sealed with tape. Morrison placed the suitcases on a table covered with brown wrapping paper, and removed two hemispheres of plutonium, warm to the touch. Taped to each box were the following instructions:

PICK UP *GENTLY* WITH HOOK.

PLUG HOLE IS COVERED WITH A *CLEAN* CLOTH.

PLACE HYPODERMIC NEEDLE *IN RIGHT PLACE*. CHECK THIS CAREFULLY. [This, to monitor the neutron count.]

BE SURE SHOEHORN IS ON HAND.

SPHERE WILL BE LEFT OVERNIGHT, CAP UP, IN A SMALL DISH PAN.

At one minute past midnight, up at Los Alamos, a second caravan began to move south for a far more dangerous journey. George Kistiakowsky, head of X-Division, had wanted to transport the high-explosive lens assembly on Friday the Thirteenth. Although not "atomic," this cargo could do far more damage to its carriers should any accident—or even untoward jolt—occur. The men drew straws to see who would ride with it. "Death Wish Movers," they called their operation. "We Move Anything." The cargo was one of two identical assemblies, both zealously supervised by Kisty, who had personally drilled out all minute cast holes with dental equipment, filled them in with molten explosive slurry, and passed on every one of hundreds of X-ray images. An implosion dress rehearsal was to be carried out on one of them by Ed Creutz at Los Alamos, and the results called down for any last-minute adjustments to its identical twin at Trinity.

The truck with its huge, steel suspension crate crept carefully down the hairpin turns, off the mesa, heading toward Santa Fe. With it were Kisty in a lead car, three jeeps of armed MPs, two sedans of security agents, and a second truck loaded with spare parts: an impressive—and lethal—caravan. Lights flashed and sirens screamed as it drove through the occasional small town in the wee hours of the morning, a tactic to scare off drunken drivers who might be weaving home late. While there were no accidents en route, the transport did turn out a lot of puzzled sleepers staring out bedroom windows at the supposedly secret transport. By noon on the thirteenth, it had reached the tower after a grueling, twelve-hour ordeal.

By then, the final plutonium assembly at the ranch house had been under way for three hours. An eight-man team in white surgical coats hovered over the hemispheres, searching for holes that might leak neutrons, smoothing down blisters, and rubbing gold foil into any remaining depressions. Four jeeps stood parked, facing away from the ranch house, engines running, getaway cars against the possibility of a slight slip, a moment's criticality. Oppie paced the room until he was asked to leave.

At 3:18 P.M., Kisty called from the tower: the explosive sphere was ready for the insertion of the core. The size of a small orange, the eighty-pound ball, a whisker away from criticality, was lifted on a litter and carried to Bacher's waiting sedan. Under green canvas shading hung from the base of the tower, the core was attached to a manual hoist, lifted above the explosive assembly, and carefully lowered in toward the center.

Wind flapped the tent—the only sound in the breath-holding silence. Never before had so much nuclear material been handled, so close to criticality. One jar, one knock, could start a chain reaction. A violent thunderstorm was seen approaching; there was fear a lightning strike might somehow detonate the bomb.

Suddenly, crisis. The core was stuck, unable to reach the center. Someone said "Shit!" and Oppenheimer froze to attention. Bob Bacher quickly figured out the problem: the tube, being cooler than the core, was slightly too narrow. They were left in contact to come to equilibrium, and the whole assembly slid precisely into place, as planned. Bacher had earned his K-rations for the day. After the nuclear crew left, Kisty and his men moved in to replace the charges over the core, occasionally using duct tape to snug up the fit. The reassembly went off smoothly, the bomb was put to bed at ten, and the exhausted crew went back to camp to sleep or drink off the day.

At eight the next morning, Saturday, the fourteenth, the assembled bomb began its trip to the top of the tower, one hundred feet above the desert floor. The crew didn't want to think about the cable snapping, but a few self-styled "realists" imposed "Operation Mattress," looting three dozen GI bunks and building a crisscrossed, twelve-foot mattress pile under the bomb, a pea without a princess, swaying slightly, three feet higher. Most observers found it amusing. Some found it pathetic or frightening. A motor-driven hoist slowly wound the five-ton sphere up the final ninety feet at a foot a minute, several engineers climbing the tower ahead of it, removing platforms so the cargo could pass through. Who knows what would have happened were the wind to have whipped up and knocked the assembly against the tower sides?

At the very top, Leo Jercinovic lifted the trap that opened into the three-sided shed that would house the bomb, steadied it on through the hole, rebuilt the flooring, and strapped the baby in its cage, a mighty infant, laughably contained. But there was no celebration for a job completed: a team of weathermen under Colonel Jack Hubbard were now predicting thunderstorms throughout the area for the next two days.

That was not the worst. That evening, Oppie received a call from Creutz at Los Alamos. The tests on the northern explosive shell had failed terribly. A nuclear explosion of its Trinity twin was highly unlikely. Oppie got visibly ill; he called an emergency meeting on whether to go ahead. He and Bacher were furious with Kistiakowsky for shoddy work on the explosive assembly, but Kisty was imperturbable. "Have Bethe check Creutz's results," he said. "I'm right. The test results are wrong. I'll bet you my month's salary against ten bucks it'll work." Oppie looked despairing as he shook on the bet.

By late afternoon the final work on the bomb had been done in an electrical storm so violent that Oppie debated lowering the assembly again to the ground. The Gadget was now crawling with wires and switches and cables and looked for all the world like a Gorgon head poised to turn a victim to stone.

He slept poorly that Saturday night, but a phone call early Sunday filled his gauntness with energy. It was Bethe from Los Alamos: the Creutz experiments had been incorrectly done. There was no reason the explosion should not go off according to Kisty's calculations.

Hallelujah.

It was the Christian Sabbath, but there was no rest for the weary. The overcast morning was dedicated to checking the hundreds of instruments focused on Ground Zero: seismographs, geophones, ionization chambers—boxes, meters, dials, transmitters, wires, cameras, microphones, sprinkled all over the desert, many with names out of *Winnie-the-Pooh*. Electricians checked Eeyore; physicists checked Tigger; radiochemists checked Kanga; engineers checked Roo—while Death waited above.

Stafford Warren assembled his minuscule fallout team—including Gregor and the weathermen—for a noontime briefing. Their main concern was that a radioactive cloud might be caught up in a thunderhead and pour out swift and widespread consequences. But at this point what could one do other than monitor, and be prepared to evacuate with inadequate forces. All Trinity workers received gas masks, coveralls, and booties.

At four o'clock, Oppie climbed the swaying tower in a high wind to be alone with his creation. Did he pronounce it good? Thunder rumbled in the distance as he went over every connection and switch.

Groves, Conant, and Bush arrived from up north at five, and Groves immediately began to pester the weathermen for accurate predictions. The rain's potential for radioactive fallout did not bother him so much as its capacity to short-out firing circuits.

The weather was deteriorating rapidly. The test was only eleven hours away, and needed to be done in darkness—to best be photographed, and to be out of sight and earshot of sleeping New Mexicans. Teletypes clicked in Meteorology, planes flew with weather balloons, smoke pots were lit and photographed. Fermi circulated with his own betting pool on whether the explosion would wipe out the world or merely destroy the state.

At dusk, Don Hornig was dispatched to arm the bomb. Alone in the tower, he replaced all the connections from the dummy firing unit with wires from the real one. Leaving the tower, he made sure that the firing switch was open, and its covering box locked. A counterpart switch at the S. 10,000 control center was similarly checked. The Gadget hung over the desert, awaiting its command.

The wind was building, the rain was coming, a Mississippi flood. But postponement would be calamitous. All energy had been aimed at four A.M. on the morrow. People had been days without sleep, preparing, people who would need to be razor sharp. Still, because of weather, Oppie and Bainbridge were besieged with requests to postpone. Groves would have none of it—Truman was waiting at Potsdam for word of results. His comportment vis-à-vis Stalin, perhaps the whole future of postwar relations hung in the balance. For Groves, this test must go, and go tomorrow, as close to schedule as possible. He and Oppie agreed to meet at midnight to review the situation. "Get some rest," the fat man advised the skinny one, and Groves trundled off to a sound few hours' sleep.

Oppie was not the sleeping type. With frayed nerves fueled by caffeine, he sat alone in his room trying to concentrate on the Gita. It was close to ten. Gregor knocked quietly at his door.

As lonely as he had ever been, Oppie received his guest warmly, if with exhaustion. He asked permission to smoke. Gregor nodded. Referring to the book already in Oppie's hand: he was ready, he said, to dissolve the Veil of Maya, to encompass the All in his one small Part, to move in person from Atman to Brahman. Oppie smoked, and nodded. Such metaphysics needed no background. Gregor quoted Schopenhauer, another Oppenheimer familiar, on the inconsequence of individual life or death.

"Death," Gregor said, "is the great opportunity to no longer be I."

He expatiated on what he called "the wound of I" and for the first time showed the lab director his injury.

"How did you get that?" Oppie asked.

"My father. An apple."

Oppie nodded, construing the words incorrectly as part of the myth of the Fall. Gregor spoke of the insect in a cocoon, a being who must cease being what he is in order to be born into his true nature. Oppie rolled another cigarette. Gregor noted the calm with which such an insect dies, having given birth to new life, new ideas, new spectacle. Oppie had been previously unaware of the calm.

"So what can I do for you?" he asked.

Gregor reminded him of their previous discussion about Krishna and Arjuna, how he had played the part of the death-aversive prince, and Oppie the part of the Shatterer of Worlds. Now Gregor was asking for the roles to be somewhat reversed, for Oppenheimer to accept Gregor's embrace of death, and to aid him in his goal.

"Go on," said the Thin Man.

There was a long pause.

"I want you," Gregor said, "to smuggle me to Ground Zero, right now. I have prepared a space under the tower where I can lie a moleperson among the instruments. I want to greet your child and embrace her."

Outside the silent room the rain could be heard, pelting the tin roof of the messhall. Oppie searched Gregor's eyes with his. Never had human gaze so deeply penetrated the mosaic eye. The director felt his own eyes moist over, and Gregor turned, embarrassed, away from too-great intimacy.

"Let's go," Oppie said, got up briskly, grabbed his hat and slicker, led Gregor to his white jeep, and drove out toward Ground Zero in the torrential rain. The MPs waved the familiar figure through the two-mile checkpoint, and in another five minutes they pulled up at the base of the tower. Above, the beast slept quietly while lightning cracked and thunder roared—*King Lear* and *The Bride of Frankenstein.*

Gregor appeared calm as they made their way through the canvas wrap around the tower base. Though his emotions were unspeakably complex, Oppie wanted to be cognizant of every detail. Where exactly would Gregor lie in the instrument pit? In what position? Would he be comfortable while waiting? Was there any danger of his drowning if the storm were to continue? Would his presence interrupt any of the instruments or affect the measurements? These last questions were offered not in the spirit of officious administration but as balm to Gregor—so he would know his plan could be carried out without harming the Project.

When Gregor was snugly packed in among the boxes and wires, Oppie wished him well, and said goodbye.

"The joy of the worm?" Gregor asked.

"The joy of the worm," Oppie repeated, his eyes moisting over. "I don't know what else to say."

He reached down and touched Gregor's claw, then closed the trapdoor. Time capsule. He stood leaning on the leg of the tower for several minutes, the rain leaking down his too-large collar. Then he drove back to camp. The MPs waved him deferentially through, without asking where his passenger had gone.

At punctual midnight, Groves pounded on Oppie's door, ready to consult—or rather to be consulted. He had decided, en route to the meeting, that the tower was inadequately defended against last-minute sabotage, and had just dispatched an armed party out into the rain. Two jeeps and a sedan were riding off to the tower—carrying Bainbridge, McKibben, Hubbard, Lieutenant Howard Bush, head of the MP detachment, in the jeeps, and fiercest of all, George Kistiakowsky, with machine gun, muttering about Groves's paranoid stupidity. Gregor heard them settle in for the vigil.

Throughout the camp, in the long night, anxious soldiers drank beer, played quiet poker, wrote letters to sweethearts and wives. A few scientists were compulsively checking their instruments, should the shot be a go. In the blockhouse at W. 10,000, Private John Fuqua checked his searchlight and was puzzled by the Victrola, and the hammer hanging from the beam. Victrola spelled party, not spies, and since all was well with the light, he decided not to report an incident. He shone his beam over the crisscross of tower girders and the whipping snakes of wires hanging from monster to ground; those guarding the base covered their eyes with their forearms.

Groves complained to Oppie about the doltish weathermen who had predicted clearing in time for the test. Since the men were so upset by the failure of their long- and even medium-range predictions, it would be wisest for him to make his own. Weather forecasting was a field in which Groves had no special competence. Still, someone had to make decisions. Oppie sensed a hidden agenda. Why was the chief meteorologist out there guarding the tower?

Chief Meteorologist Jack Hubbard, in consultation with every group leader, had early on drawn up a list of the best and worst conditions for the test. But instead of tailoring the operation around desired weather, Hubbard was faced with a fait accompli—Truman was in Potsdam, and weather be damned. July sixteenth was it. "Right in the middle of a period of thunderstorms," he wrote, "what son of a bitch could have done this?" Everything unwanted was present: rain, high humidity, inversion layer, and unstable wind. None of the optimum requirements had been met. Rain could scrub the clouds and bring down high levels of radioactivity in a small area. Unstable conditions and high humidity increased the chances that the blast could induce a thunderstorm. Still, Truman was in Potsdam, and Groves had become weatherman.

At two-fifteen Hubbard's men were projecting a lull in the storm, a small possible window between five A.M. and dawn at six. Groves seized on the news to announce a definite go for five-thirty. The decision made, however faulty, eased the tension, and Oppie seemed to relax with his coffee and cigarettes—until Fermi rushed screaming into the mess hall, fearful of the camp's vulnerability to radioactive rain, and pleading for a postponement. Evacuation routes were inadequate for the population, he said, and were in any case unusable in the downpour. The Pope warned of a catastrophe.

Groves, sensing Oppie's agitation, sent Fermi away and suggested that the director accompany him from the madhouse of base camp to the relative sanity of the Control Center at S. 10,000. In the face of opposition from those who balked at the possible cremation of their leader, Oppie followed Groves to his car.

At two-thirty A.M. the storm hit the tower directly, shorting out a searchlight and plunging it into darkness. The photographer Julian Mack sent out a frantic call for soonest possible repair so he could set and focus his cameras. Kistiakowsky grabbed the most powerful flashlight he could find and, in the midst of torrential rain, climbed the slippery, lightning-attractive metal ladder to mid-tower, where he hung on for the next two hours beaming his light toward Mack's cameras. This, from an acrophobe.

At four A.M., the rain stopped, and the tower guards ended their frightful vigil. Joe McKibben had fallen asleep at the foot of the north pier. Bainbridge leaned over him, shook him gently by the shoulder. "Come on, Joe, it's time now." At 4:45, Bainbridge received news of shortly breaking weather. Within fifty minutes, the overcast would be scattered, and wind conditions would hold for the next two hours. He called John Williams at S. 10,000. "Prepare to fire at five-thirty."

The final arming sequence began. Bainbridge, McKibben, and Kisty would now close all the switches that connected the bomb to firing and timing circuits at central control. The three drove out to a pit 900 yards from the tower, lifted the lid of a half-buried box, and, as Kisty read off the sequence, McKibben engaged the switches that would send automatic timing signals to all experiments. At 4:55 they returned to the tower, where Bainbridge lit the aiming lights for the B-29 pass. Then, both McKibben and Kisty carefully checked Bainbridge as he unlocked the box Don Hornig had checked, and closed the switch, connecting the bomb end of the firing circuit. Not twenty feet away, Gregor listened with fascination to the read-off of instructions.

There was one last step: at the S. 10,000 Control Center, Bainbridge visited the sister box and threw the switch. Both ends were connected. The Gadget was fully armed, ready for detonation.

.   .   .

5:10 A.M., July 16, 1945. "It is now zero minus twenty minutes." Sam Allison's voice rang out from loudspeakers strung out across the wasteland. No sooner had he spoken than the second phrase of "The Star-Spangled Banner," "By the dawn's early light . . ." blared out, unbidden and unexpected. KCBA, from Delano, California, had crossed wavelengths with the Trinity frequency and was opening its morning Voice of America broadcast. By "the bombs bursting in air . . ." the anthem had faded and was making its way to other etheric climes. The only sound that could be heard was the croaking of toads and, if one listened carefully, the beating of hearts. One soldier went round back of a trench at base camp and returned muttering, "Too damn scared to piss."

The five-minute siren sounded, the five-minute flare started up, and fizzled. Many had the same thought: an omen? At zero minus two minutes, Oppie turned to General Farrell, said, "Lord, these affairs are hard on the heart," and gripped a post to steady himself. On Compania Hill, twenty miles away, hundreds of scientists lay on the ground, facing north, away from the site, equipped with blue welder's goggles for protection. Teller wore heavy gloves and an extra pair of dark glasses under his goggles. Bethe was sharing his sunburn oil. Feynman, ever disobedient, was watching directly through the window of a truck, sure that the windshield would protect his eyes from any UV rays. He would be struck temporarily blind.

Base camp seemed an isle of the dead, with motionless bodies scattered in shallow graves, listening to the hypnotic "Minus fifty-five seconds . . . minus fifty seconds . . . At minus forty-five seconds, McKibben closed the switch initiating the automatic timing sequence.

At twenty-five seconds, the music returned—unbelievable!—the "Dance of the Sugar Plum Fairy" from *The Nutcracker Suite*. Breathing lightly, entwined in wires, a blattid grinned. Was there ever subtler accompaniment: the delicate chromaticism of a celeste as prelude to the nuclear age? Surely a curious nut being cracked.

At ten seconds a gong sounded—in just the right key. Ken Greisen turned to Isidor Rabi and whispered, "I'm excited now." At five seconds, cameras began shooting from the north, south, and west, and Sam Allison, distinguished physicist, was seized by fear that the explosion might somehow feed back into the microphone he held in his hand. He dropped it on the desk and screamed as loud as he could, "Now!"

Desert sand melts at 2,700 degrees Fahrenheit. The temperature at the center of the blast was four times that at the center of the sun, and more than ten times that at its surface. The pressure on the ground below the tower was more than 100 billion atmospheres.

As the fireball prodigiously grew, a four-star general drew in his breath and said, half to his neighbor, half to himself, "Oh, my God! The longhairs have let it get away from them!"

Kisty, blown down by the subsequent shock wave, scrambled to his feet and, covered with mud, grabbed Oppie from behind. "Oppie, Oppie," he screamed, jumping with joy, "I won the bet, I won the bet! You owe me ten smackers!" Oppie, with a blank stare, reached mechanically for his wallet with shaky hand. "I haven't got it, George. You'll have to wait."

The two men embraced.

# AFTERWORD:
## SOME REFLECTIONS *on the*
## FINAL METAMORPHOSIS

Rudolph Bernard, M.D.
*Hospital Director, Manhattan Project at Los Alamos*
*Founding Chairman and Professor of Occupational Medicine,*
*Mount Sinai School of Medicine of the City University of New York*
*Senior Member, Institute of Medicine, National Academy of Science*
*Medical Director Emeritus, Occupational Safety and Health*
*Administration, New York City*

Gregor's was the most expensive assisted suicide in history. Expensive, and also rich in strands, in complexity, in resonance. After fifty-six years, I am still far from a clear gestalt.

Defending his role in the Japanese bombings, Oppie once remarked that "the decision was implicit in the project." The long line of Gregor's path seems to demonstrate the same thing. For as all life bears death within it, Gregor's unique existence brought forth an extraordinary consummation.

At one time we understood "the good death" and "the bad death" as the possibility of dying authentically, on intimate terms with Death—and the possibility of dying almost inadvertently, a death inessential and false. Rainer Maria Rilke, Gregor's favorite poet, prayed for faithful dying:

*Dear Lord, bestow on each man his own death,*
*A dying grown from teeming life and deed,*
*His unique path of love, and thought, and need.*

Nietzsche, too, wished to die his own death: not a "detestable, grimacing death, which advances on its belly like a thief," but a death self-chosen.

On the one hand it would seem that Gregor had captured the uttermost prize, a truly owned, passionate, infinite death, with clear mind, and almost sound body untouched by madness or deep disease. Like Rilke's nun, he would appear to have "plunged into God like a stone into the sea."

On the other hand, can there really be an art of dying a "good death" in this century, in the context of tens of millions of lives intentionally extinguished, and the gaping possibility of planetary annihilation? Can there really be a good death via a weapon of mass destruction? The authenticity paradigm seems desperately inadequate here.

But then one might ask more subtly: just when *did* Gregor die? Was his not a death in parts, expertly accomplished along the way, the bomb being only the final, dramatic punctuation? An intimate courtship was here, an elegant, graceful dance, with Death disrobing, becoming transparent, and Gregor finally assenting to Death's only word: "Yes." This was not mass-death, extermination, annihilation, but an I-Thou pact of the most intense kind. No inattention or betrayal here, but an expert leading a gifted partner. Fred and Ginger. Death and the maiden, Gregor.

Perhaps his assent had been tempted by experience, by double death. After all, had he not died once before? The first was already a beautiful, clean death, immaculate extinction: the fabric salesman who left no remnant. But then, what did Gregor remember of this, what did he understand?

Did I say double death? Perhaps it was triple, quadruple, nay, most multiple. For was not Gregor's extreme otherness a spirit connection to the electrocuted Italians? Or the abandoned Jews, the Japanese in camps, and those soon to be incinerated, indeed to the clockmaker and all those "others" lynched and burned by hooded mobs—were Gregor and they not intimately bound?

Speaking of himself in the third person, Rilke wrote, "If something prevented his dying, perhaps it was only this: that he had overlooked it once, somewhere, and that he didn't have, like others, to go on ahead in order to reach it, but on the contrary, to go back the other way." Perchance, like Rilke, Gregor needed to turn back, to revisit his singular moment in an equally singular manner.

If the true painter spends his life seeking Painting, and the true poet, Poetry, then surely—even in the age of mass death—Gregor could be seen as an artist of Life and Death, a journeyman who never betrayed these high powers, his masters.

I am now eighty-eight years old. I am a retired physician, now a medical administrator. I, too, am dying—of cancer.

Mine is lung cancer in a nonsmoker. Why? Who knows? Perhaps from low-level plutonium contamination. Five years ago I had a six-month cough. I thought nothing of it—winters in the East are cold and wet. Then it became hard to breathe. I thought it was just my payback for longevity—until I started spitting blood. My chest X-rays were negative but bronchoscopy showed a friable bronchial mass. My surgery was "successful," but Death's knock-at-the-door prompted me to think again about Gregor Samsa, my friend. Last year, during a routine physical, my doctors picked up abnormal liver functions, and subsequently, a positive biopsy. Now I am developing bone pain, and last month had a positive bone scan: metastasis. They give me another year; three at most with radiation and chemotherapy. But I have decided not to bother—fourscore and nine will be a more than adequate allotment.

As Gregor asserted his Jewish privilege to define a Jew, I now want to assert the increasingly maligned privilege of the aged—especially aged physicians—to ruminate unmercifully on Life, Death, and History. The surely fatigued reader may skip to the end, though I can assure him that he will not find out who did it.

This world now seems to me a Kingdom of Death, a Plague-World without antecedent. What is unprecedented is not simply the scale of mass destruction, but that it is the product of systematic rational calculation. The efficiency of it all, the celerity! Gregor's second war, the Manhattan Project's war, took approximately five years. Our last war—some would call it "massacre"—took all of five days. Five days to slaughter hundreds of thousands of human creatures who happened to live on top of oil reserves that took seven hundred million years to form, and will take less than two centuries to use up.

In my lifetime, I have seen the crucial change from wars fought between armies—bad enough—to wars declared on civilians. Vast numbers of faceless persons are now simply marked for annihilation. Adversaries are no longer considered human, no longer even those humans of whom it is written *homo homini lupus*. The struggles are between complex bureaucratic structures that serve the ideological needs of civilization's death machine. Deplorable.

Death has extended its domain even to the living. Auschwitz and its brethren, not to mention Democracy and its embargoes, encourage a new social form, a death-world of the living dead embedded in a larger society. As we look at the automata running the world, and the subsidiary automata taking their direction, we can't help but notice the next transition: from the death of body to the even broader death of spirit.

It may be that we are truly undone: there is too much competition for the Meanest Show on Earth. The mathematician J. Carson Mark once suggested that all heads of state be forced to witness an atmospheric nuclear explosion once a year. Would he still propose such a tactic? Fallout aside, would such a demonstration not just produce euphoria and even greater weapons sales? Perhaps I'm being cynical, but cynicism is the prerogative of age, and mine is well earned.

In the face of cynicism, though, I am sure of this: the really "new frontier" of our age will not be defined politically. It will be delineated only by a revolution in our instinctual lives comparable to the Industrial Revolution. That is why Gregor's life, his example, held such great promise. Even though the trajectory of human history seems to be toward complacency, decadence, and coldness of heart, we may still be saved by obscure efforts of heroic individuals whose passion it is to redeem the world, they who live a faithful life, and will rest in unmarked graves. The Lamed-Vovniks, if you will. The second half of the last century did not produce another Gregor, but I have not yet given up hope. One must believe the future into existence.


Kafka, in a note from his Diaries, makes a remark that bears reflection:

> . . . the best material I've written is based in my ability to be able to die content. In all the really good and convincing parts someone is dying,

finds it difficult, unjust perhaps, cruel at the very least—and in my opinion, the reader finds this moving. But for me, who can likely be content on his deathbed, such depictions are a secret game: I actually enjoy dying in the character I'm writing about.

I find this intriguing, I who will soon have to submit myself to the same test—Kafka's art as a playful relation with death. Wherein lies the capacity to die content? Is great fatigue or absence of pain the *sine qua non*?

> *. . . for many a time*
> *I have been half in love with easeful Death,*
> *Call'd him soft names in many a mused rhyme,*
> *To take into the air my quiet breath . . .*

I think not. In Kafka's case, in Gregor's, and I hope my own, a contented death means being able to find satisfaction even in supreme dissatisfaction. Kafka's heroes carry out their lives in death's space. His achievement has been to snatch his every sentence joyfully from that zone of insanity into which common sense has wandered in our time.

In the inbox on Gregor's reading desk, under a pile of work-related papers, I found the following note, with its envelope, clipped to a musical score.

```
Cambridge, 13-04-45

Dear boy,
    Please accept a little present I couldn't help filch-
ing and sending. R. S. has been a friend of the family
since before the (First) War. This is his latest--just
finished, as yet unperformed. Looks meisterwerkisch to
me. I persuaded him to let me make a copy to send.
Thought you'd appreciate it.
    These last years have been a dark time. I once wrote,
```

```
perhaps rightly: "The earlier culture will become a heap
of rubble and finally a heap of ashes, but spirits will
hover over the ashes." Yours likely will be chief among
them. What more is there to say?
    Come see me in Cambridge if you get the chance.
    LW
```

Who else could it be but Wittgenstein? Who else so commitedly unpolitical as not to mention the death of FDR the previous day? Under the signature, in answer to the question, Gregor had scrawled: 7. WHAT WE CANNOT SPEAK ABOUT WE MUST PASS OVER IN SILENCE.

The score? Richard Strauss's late masterpiece, *Metamorphosen,* an elegiac streaming for twenty-three solo strings, a threnody for the death of the West. The master's long career had always seemed to me to be unconsciously, mysteriously, dedicated to Gregor. Fools were his subject, holy and not-so-holy: *Don Quixote, Till Eulenspiegel, Don Juan.* Philosophy was his subject in *Zarathustra,* and transcendence. *A Hero's Life, Death and Transfiguration.* One of his very last songs summed up my impression of Gregor:

> *. . . the unattended soul*
> *wants to hover, flying freely,*
> *in night's magic circle*
> *to live deeply—thousandfold.*

*Tief und tausendfach zu leben.* That was my friend, Gregor Samsa. I shall follow him soon. And *après moi? Le déluge?* Let us hope not.

What will there be to say, when all is done? Only this perhaps, along with Emily Dickinson—dearest Emily, next to my beloved Donna, the great love in this healer's life:

> *I reason, Earth is short—*
> *And Anguish—absolute—*
> *And many hurt,*
> *But, what of that?*

*I reason, we could die—*
*The best Vitality*
*Cannot excel Decay,*
*But, what of that?*

*I reason, that in Heaven—*
*Somehow, it will be even—*
*Some new Equation, given—*
*But, what of that?*

Shantih shantih, Gregor, shantih.

NEW YORK CITY, *April 2001*

# WORKS *in the* MIX:
# A BIBLIOGRAPHY

VIENNA

ALLEN, FREDRICK LEWIS. *Only Yesterday: An Informal History of the 1920's.* New York: Perennial Library, 1964.

BANGERTER, LOWELL A. *Robert Musil.* New York: Continuum, 1989.

DAVIES, NORMAN. *Europe, A History.* New York: Oxford University Press, 1996.

GORDON, DAVID GEORGE. *The Compleat Cockroach: A Comprehensive Guide to the Most Despised (and Least Understood) Creature on Earth.* Berkeley, CA: Ten Speed Press, 1996.

HUGHES, H. STUART. *Oswald Spengler.* New York: Scribner, 1962.

JANIK, ALLAN, AND STEPHEN TOULMIN. *Wittgenstein's Vienna.* New York: Touchstone, 1973.

KAFKA, FRANZ. *The Complete Stories and Parables.* New York: Quality Paperback Book Club, 1983.

MONK, RAY. *Ludwig Wittgenstein: The Duty of Genius.* New York: Free Press, 1990.

MUSIL, ROBERT. *Precision and Soul: Essays and Addresses.* Chicago: University of Chicago Press, 1990.

NITSKE, W. ROBERT. *The Life of Wilhelm Conrad Roentgen, Discoverer of the X-Ray.* Tucson: University of Arizona Press, 1971.

PETERS, FREDERICK G. *Robert Musil: Master of the Hovering Life.* New York: Columbia University Press, 1978.

RILKE, RAINER MARIA. *Duino Elegies,* trans. J. B. Leishman and Stephen Spender. New York: Norton, 1963.

SPENGLER, OSWALD. *The Decline of the West,* trans. Charles Francis Atkinson. New York: Knopf, 1926.

WITTGENSTEIN, LUDWIG. *Culture and Value,* trans. Peter Winch. Chicago: University of Chicago Press, 1980.

WITTGENSTEIN, LUDWIG. *Tractatus Logico-Philosophicus,* trans. D. F. Pears and B. F. McGuinness. London: Routledge & Kegan Paul, 1961.


NEW YORK

ALLEN, LESLIE H., ed. *Bryan and Darrow at Dayton: The Record and Documents of the "Bible-Evolution Trial."* New York: A. Lee & Co., 1925.

BRUMBAUGH, ROBERT, ed. *Six Trials.* New York: Crowell, 1969. (Scopes; Sacco and Vanzetti)

BURKHOLDER, J. PETER. *All Made of Tunes: Charles Ives and the Uses of Musical Borrowing.* New Haven, CT: Yale University Press, 1995.

COWELL, HENRY, AND SIDNEY COWELL. *Charles Ives and His Music.* New York: Oxford University Press, 1969.

DAVIDOFF, NICHOLAS. *The Catcher Was a Spy.* New York: Pantheon, 1994. theelectricchair.com

FAST, HOWARD. *The Passion of Sacco and Vanzetti: A New England Legend.* New York: Blue Heron, 1953.

FRANKFURTER, FELIX. "The Case of Sacco and Vanzetti," *The Atlantic Monthly,* March 1927 (on atlantic.com).

HOFFMAN, FREDERICK J. *The 20's.* New York: Free Press, 1965.

IRWIN, INEZ HAYES. *The Story of Alice Paul and the National Woman's Party.* Fairvax, VA: Denlinger's, 1977.

IVES, CHARLES. *Essays Before a Sonata, The Majority, and Other Writings.* New York: Norton, 1962.

JIRÁSEK, ALOIS. "The Legend of the Old Town Clock," in Paul Wilson, ed. *Prague: A Traveller's Literary Companion.* San Francisco: Whereabouts Press, 1995. (Source of Gregor's story of Master Hanus's Clock)

LANOUETTE, WILLIAM. *Genius in the Shadows: A Biography of Leo Szilard, the Man Behind the Bomb.* Chicago: University of Chicago Press, 1992.

OVID. *The Metamorphoses of Ovid, translated into English by Henry T. Riley, M.A.* London: George Bell and Sons, 1898.

PERLIS, VIVIAN. *Charles Ives Remembered: An Oral History.* New Haven, CT: Yale University Press, 1974.

SINCLAIR, UPTON. *Boston, a Novel.* New York: Boni, 1928. (Sacco & Vanzetti)

SMITH, PAGE. *Redeeming the Time: A People's History of the 1920's and the New Deal.* New York: Penguin, 1987.

SWAFFORD, JAN. *Charles Ives: A Life with Music.* New York: Norton, 1996.

W A S H I N G T O N ,   D . C .

BURNS, JAMES MACGREGOR. *Roosevelt: The Lion and the Fox.* New York: Harcourt, Brace & World, 1956.

EVANS, HOWARD ENSIGN. *Life on a Little-known Planet,* illus. Arnold Clapman. New York: Dutton, 1968. (Gregor's lab work taken from the experiments of Peg Ellis, as here reported)

FRIEDEL, FRANK, ed. *The New Deal and the American People.* New York: Prentice Hall, 1964.

GRAHAM, OTIS L., AND MEGHAN R. WANDER, eds. *Franklin D. Roosevelt: His Life and Times, An Encyclopedic View.* New York: Da Capo, 1985.

HOBSBAWM, ERIC. *The Age of Extremes: A History of the World, 1914–1991.* New York: Vintage, 1994.

LASH, JOSEPH P. *Eleanor and Franklin,* New York: Norton, 1971.

MILLER, NATHAN. *FDR: An Intimate History.* New York: New American Library, 1983.

SMITH, PAGE. *Democracy on Trial: The Japanese American Evacuation and Relocation in World War Two.* New York: Simon & Schuster, 1995.


LOS ALAMOS

BRODE, BERNICE. *Tales of Los Alamos: Life on the Mesa 1943–1945.* Los Alamos, NM: Los Alamos Historical Society, 1997.

CHURCH, PEGGY POND. *The House at Otowi Bridge: The Story of Edith Warner and Los Alamos.* Albuquerque: University of New Mexico Press, 1960.

COLES, ROBERT. *The Old Ones of New Mexico.* Albuquerque: University of New Mexico Press, 1973.

ERDOES, RICHARD, AND ALFONSO ORTIZ, eds. *American Indian Trickster Tales.* New York: Viking, 1998.

FEYNMAN, RICHARD P. *Surely You're Joking, Mr. Feynman: Adventures of a Curious Character.* New York: Norton, 1985.

FEYNMAN, RICHARD P. *What do YOU Care What Other People Think? Further Adventures of a Curious Character.* New York: Norton, 1988.

GLEICK, JAMES. *Genius: The Life and Science of Richard Feynman.* New York: Vintage, 1992.

GOODCHILD, PETER. *Oppenheimer, Shatter of Worlds.* New York: Fromm, 1985.

GOUDSMIT, SAMUEL. *Alsos.* New York: H. Schuman, 1947.

GROVES, LESLIE M. *Now It Can Be Told: The Story of the Manhattan Project.* New York: Da Capo, 1983.

HALES, PETER BACON. *Atomic Spaces: Living on the Manhattan Project.* Urbana: University of Illinois Press, 1997.

JETTE, ELEANOR. *Inside Box 1663.* Los Alamos, NM: Los Alamos Historical Society, 1977.

JUNGK, ROBERT. *Brighter Than a Thousand Suns.* New York: Harcourt, Brace & World, 1958.

LAMONT, LANSING. *Day of Trinity.* New York: Atheneum, 1985

Los Alamos Historical Society, *Behind Tall Fences: Stories and Experiences About Los Alamos at Its Beginning.* Los Alamos, NM: Los Alamos Historical Society, 1996.

POWERS, THOMAS. *Heisenberg's War: The Secret History of the German Bomb.* Boston: Little, Brown, 1993.

RHODES, RICHARD. *The Making of the Atomic Bomb.* New York: Simon & Schuster, 1986.

TRUSLOW, EDITH C. *Manhattan District History: Nonscientific Aspects of Los Alamos*

*Project Y 1942 through 1946.* Los Alamos, NM: Los Alamos Historical Society, 1997.

WILSON, JANE S., AND CHARLOTTE SERBER. *Standing By and Making Do: Women of Wartime Los Alamos.* Los Alamos, NM: Los Alamos Historical Society, 1997.

WYDEN, PETER. *Day One: Before Hiroshima and After.* New York: Simon & Schuster, 1984.

# *The* AUTHOR THANKS

The many friends and family who plowed through a Brobdingnagian manuscript with constancy, courage, and comments.

His agent, Dorian Karchmar of Lowenstein Associates, so good-humoredly nurturing of life forms crawling in her slush; so courageous in her edits, tender in their applications, and persistent in her advocacy.

His editor, Fred Ramey, untiring, unflappable, ever-enthusiastic and sharp of wit and pen.

Birgitte and Josh, who found out Rumpelstiltskin's name.

The immortal Franz K. for his generous visit to Burlington, Vermont.

The authors and historians who were his guides on Gregor's mountain path.